The Curio
Bc

MW00944196

Agents, spies, and tinkerers conspire in this
collection of romantic steampunk tales

AVA MORGAN

Other Books by Ava Morgan

Steampunk Titles:

The Lady Machinist (Curiosity Chronicles, #1)
The Armored Doctor (Curiosity Chronicles, #2)
The Industrial Spy (Curiosity Chronicles, #3)
Lydia's Decision (A Curiosity Chronicles Short)
Abigail's Discovery (A Curiosity Chronicles Short)
The Aether Alchemist (Curiosity Chronicles, #4)

YA Fantasy Titles

Uprooted (The Grafters, Book One)
Transplanted (The Grafters, Book Two) –Coming Soon
Grafted (The Grafters, Book Three) –Coming Soon

Table of Contents

Preface

The Curiosity Chronicles series is set in a fictional world, similar to what our own past looked like in the 1830s-40s. Amid this age of rival empires and steam-driven industry, however, you are sure to notice a few differences. This series follows the agents of the Cabinet of Intellectual Curiosities (COIC), a group of brave men and women from very different walks of life who discover scientific feats, engineering marvels, and that most rewarding of findings, love. Pour yourself a cup of tea, sit back, and enjoy.

The Lady Machinist

A romantic steampunk tale of clockwork soldiers, persistent pirates, and political intrigue

Curiosity Chronicles, Book One

In memory of my dear friend Ginger, who, during her lifetime, always loved a curious tale.

Chapter 1

"Turn your ship around and go back where you came from."

Despite her nervousness, Lydia Dimosthenis held her ground and stood on the beach, addressing the six foot four captain and his crew of four armed British sailors. Five, counting the hasty brute who stormed into the Machinists' Guild—pin-trigger blunderbuss at the ready—while they were in the middle of the weekly meeting.

Thank goodness her assistant, a clockwork soldier, was guarding the door that afternoon. The automaton's iron alloy armor held up nicely against the blunderbuss' smattering of grapeshot as she and her fellow machinists dove for cover.

"And take your spy with you."

The seven-foot automaton bore the captured sailor in its brass-coated arms. Lydia raised her voice to her assistant and issued a command in her mother tongue of Greek. Upon hearing her order, it lifted the blond sailor and dumped him in the white sand approximately five paces from the captain's polished black boots.

The captain didn't so much as blink. He appraised Lydia with a confident stare, though the anger in his expression was clear. "My dear woman, call off your automaton and the ten standing behind you. Then perhaps we could sort out this misunderstanding." His English carried a musical lilt, not at all like the coarse-sounding pirates from New Britannia who invaded the island weeks before.

But the British couldn't be trusted. Not after that invasion. Those pirates ran from Lydia's small army of mechanical and clockwork soldiers. She intended to send this giant of a man and his crew back on their way in similar fashion.

The crew trained their pistols on her. Although the captain's gloved hands rested at his sides, sans weapons, he appeared unafraid. Sending him running away might be a more difficult objective to accomplish than she first thought.

She reverted to English, the common language of diplomacy and commerce throughout Europe and along the Mediterranean. "From where I stand, you've made your intentions clear. Your scout fired at me and three men with this." She balanced the sailor's blunderbuss under her arm. Her muscles compensated to support the heavy firearm. "You're lucky no one was harmed."

"The wench is wrong. I didn't fire at anyone." The sailor crawled nearer to his captain and pulled himself to his feet. "I shot at that automaton beside her. It raised an arm cannon at me." He shook sand from his sweat-stained shirt.

Lydia defended her creation. "The automaton was guarding the entrance. You triggered it to attack when you blundered in with your blunderbuss."

The captain's baritone cut in before the blond sailor could counter. "Speaking of which, you can lower that weapon. My hands are empty."

"Your crew's hands aren't." Lydia kept her sights on them and drew more breath into her lungs. She and the automatons outnumbered the sailors two to one.

But their captain gave no sign of retreating.

"You have my word that my crew won't harm you. Weapons down, men."

The crew obeyed.

The brass buttons on the captain's coat winked at her. "And what about your automatons?"

"They won't fire unless I give the order." Lydia hoped she could hold the sailors until King Sabba and his guards came from the palace. One of the machinists ran from the Guild to warn His Majesty.

"Did you fashion those automatons?" the captain asked. His rich, dark brown eyes lent warmth to a face with strong angles and commanding features. Not the face of a hard, harsh pirate, but not one of a man to be trifled with, either.

"I did." She expected him to scoff and make some disparaging remark about female inventors.

Surprise did cross his face, but he moved to doff his hat. "You are the person I came to see. Rhys Cartret, ambassador of New Britannia and agent of the Cabinet of Intellectual Curiosities, at your service."

"Ambassador?"

Rhys lifted his head. The sun gleamed upon his ink-black hair. "I'm here on official diplomatic business."

That still didn't explain why his crewman opened fire or why he sailed his ship to the remote side of the island instead of the port. Something wasn't right.

"Why was there no official word preceding your arrival?" Lydia read his face for rapid blinking, flared nostrils, a nervous tic—any sign of falsehood.

His deep-set eyes, straight nose, and chiseled mouth belied none of those things, though a look of impatience flashed in his eyes. "I'll be more than willing to explain the circumstances surrounding my arrival, but if you don't mind, I'd prefer to do so without a blunderbuss pointed at me."

Lydia cradled the firearm, despite her muscles cramping. "I do mind. The last British sailors to intrude upon our shores were pirates."

"Lady Dimosthenis is correct." Lydia heard the king's booming voice behind her. Judging from the wary, widened eyes of the crew, she guessed that he brought the entire host of his guard with him.

Good.

King Sabba strode to her side, flanked by his adviser Nikolaos Abeiron and guards armed with muskets and sabers.

***

Rhys assessed the unusual predicament set before him. When he learned that his ship would be too large to make port at Aspasia's tiny dock, he sent his navigator Finley to alert the local gentry of their presence.

And alert them he did.

Outnumbered and outgunned, Rhys faced a displeased monarch, a scowling official in red robes, twenty guardsmen armed to the teeth with double-barreled muskets and sharp sabers, and eleven automatons. Little good the pistol Rhys kept in his coat lining would do against this brood, even if the bullets inside the gun were metal-piercing.

Then there was the new wielder of Finley's blunderbuss. Rhys's gaze returned to the lone Aspasian woman the king referred to as Lady Dimosthenis.

She held that gun steady on Rhys, balancing it against her tall, lithe form. The hot island breeze blew sand on her clothing, which consisted of black trousers, white shirt, knee-length boots, engraved metal gauntlets on her forearms and a leather vest that was studded with an array of brass chains and toggles that cinched her waist. The corseted effect of it provided the only ladylike touch to an otherwise masculine wardrobe.

The monarch and his official dressed in the traditional clothing that Rhys had seen on the Greek mainland. The official's bright red robe and striped trousers distracted from his small build. The king's white *fustanella*, pleated trousers, contrasted with the vibrant green of his wide-sleeved shirt and silk mantle. The mantle snapped in the wind.

"I am Sabba, King of Aspasia." His English was thickly accented. He wore no crown, but a very simple and very solid band of gold that circled his head. "Why have you trespassed and fired weapons upon my subjects?"

Lady Dimosthenis tilted her head, awaiting an answer. The hue of her hazel-gold eyes intensified as the sun hovered above the beach. If it weren't for the fact that she brandished a destructive firearm at his person, Rhys could appreciate the striking color against her brown olive skin. In this instance, however, her eyes reminded him of a great cat poised to claw if he wasn't careful.

He descended into a diplomatic bow before the king. "Your Majesty, my name is Rhys Cartret, ambassador for New Britannia. Please forgive the actions of my crewman. The blame rests on me. I sent him to alert the dockworkers to our presence. Our ship was too large to make port." He thumbed back at the three-masted ship *The Enlightened* languishing off the coast.

"A ship with steel and iron trimmings. That looks like a war vessel to me." The red-robed official declared his observation in a quiet tenor. The tassel hanging from the golden cord of his hat fanned in the breeze.

"All ships need protection these days, but I assure you, it's a merchant craft." Rhys deflected from the fact that *The Enlightened* was outfitted to defend itself. The starboard side held eight automatic swivel cannons cleverly concealed by retracting iron screens, all powered by the onboard engine, the first steam-powered mechanism of its kind.

King Sabba spoke. "Ambassador Cartret, understand my adviser's wariness. Thirty-one days ago, pirates invaded Aspasia. "

"Word reached New Britannia of the invasion. Reports told of pirates thwarted by iron soldiers. No one has been able to create automatons strong enough for warfare until now."

The king glanced at Lady Dimosthenis. "Aspasia owes Lydia a debt of gratitude for her inventions." His eyes turned cold once they settled again on Rhys. "Which is why I will not simply give them to you."

Rhys saw Lady Dimosthenis'—Lydia's—small, triumphant smile in his peripheral vision. He didn't come all this way to give up his mission that easily.

"I know why you British are here," King Sabba continued. "You want the automatons as weapons in your rivalry against France. We Aspasians are not so far removed that we are unaware of what takes place on the Continent. France will do anything to build an empire larger than yours."

The king's understanding of the current political climate left Rhys momentarily at a loss for words. That was the primary reason the COIC sent him to Aspasia posthaste. If not for the speed of *The Enlightened*'s engine, he was certain that the French would have already beaten him to it. "King Sabba, may I discuss this in a more private setting with you, your adviser, and Lady Dimosthenis?"

Lydia shook her head. Sable strands were pulled in a neat topknot pinned at the crown. "His Majesty just said he wouldn't give you the automatons."

"I will handle this," the king reprimanded her.

Her dark lashes swept down in apology. "Yes, Your Majesty."

Rhys studied her gesture. It seemed second nature, as though she had to apologize frequently for speaking out of turn. Part of him admired her boldness while the other became annoyed with her shooting down his objectives before he could even voice them. "King Sabba, I'm not asking you to give me the automatons. I want to buy them from you."

The king, Lydia, and the adviser all looked at him. Even a few guardsmen cleared their throats. At last, he gained control of the conversation.

Sabba made a sound of disapproval. "Those automatons are our defense structure. They are not to be sold like cheap wares."

"Certainly not. New Britannia has a proposal that I think you'll find suitable."

"I'll be the judge of that. Bring your proposal to the palace. We will discuss it over supper."

"Thank you, Your Majesty." Rhys caught Lydia's surprised expression. Her full lips parted with an unspoken protest.

The king signaled for his guards. "Lord Abeiron will show you to a guest room in the palace. We dine in two hours."

Ten guards escorted Sabba off the beach while the others remained with his adviser. Lydia's eyes followed the king.

"Lady Dimosthenis."

She didn't speak a word as she turned to Rhys. Her eyes did the talking, and what they had to say wasn't pleasant.

"I'm sorry for the disturbance at your Guild. My crewman will be disciplined."

Finley hiccupped behind Rhys, but he pretended not to hear. "I'll take his weapon off your hands."

Lydia kept the blunderbuss.

Lord Abeiron leaned her way. "I can hand him the weapon if you prefer."

Lydia carried the gun past him and the guards. She reached Rhys in four paces. The gun stood between them, but at least this time she had the courtesy to point the barrel off to the side.

Rhys took it from her. "I'll see you tonight, then." He put on a smile.

A tight line formed around her lips. "Soldiers, to me."

Rhys translated her Greek communication to the automatons. The eleven iron soldiers did an about face and followed her up the path from the beach.

Chapter 2

Lord Abeiron folded his arms within the sleeves of his robe and waited for Lydia and the automatons to depart. "Pardon Lady Dimosthenis for her conduct, Ambassador. Our previous encounter with foreigners did not bode well."

Rhys hefted the blunderbuss over his shoulder. "I understand her suspicion. Pirates still flourish, despite the navy's eradication efforts."

"They landed here twice before the automatons were operational. Our neighbors reported seeing pirates in waters near France, Italy, and northern Africa. The pirates hail from many nations."

Rhys recognized the adviser's tact, how he blamed everyone and no one for the world's piracy problem. "Credit that to the times. More production of goods, more things to steal."

"Undoubtedly." Lord Abeiron rubbed his black beard. "I will wait while you gather your belongings."

"I need to return to the ship for them." Rhys dug his heel in the sand and pivoted towards the shallow. His crew remained behind. Finley followed.

"Captain, I didn't intend to shoot anyone in that guild hall."

"I told you to leave your firearm strapped on your back *in case* you needed it, Finley. Why didn't you follow orders?"

"The building—temple, or another—was in the woods." Finley eyed his gun being carted away on Rhys's shoulder. "I couldn't chance someone jumping out at me."

"I briefed you on the protocol."

"I beg your pardon, sir, but I was following my navy training." The tone of his apology sounded anything but repentant. "It's kept me out of danger thus far."

"But not out of discipline."

Finley was a sailor tried and true, but his days as a naval officer were over when the COIC chose him to sail with Rhys's crew. Too bad he often had to be reminded of that the hard way.

Rhys doled out a punishment. "You'll stay onboard the ship and perform all chores the bosun sets out for you."

"But Captain—"

"Do not interrupt me."

"Yes, sir." Finley conceded to his temporary lot with a poor show of acceptance. His fingers curled in partial fists.

Upon reaching a longboat situated on shore, Rhys laid the blunderbuss on the boat floor and pushed the small craft out to the water. "You'd best hope the Aspasians don't remain put off by your intrusion. What else did you see in that Guild?"

"Just the wench and the machinists."

Rhys climbed in the longboat and grabbed the oars. "She is Lady Dimosthenis, not 'the wench'. Remember that."

"Aye." Finley grudgingly stepped out of the knee-deep shallows into the boat.

"Malcolm likely will want you to scrub the decks first." Rhys referred to the bosun, his business partner and trusted friend. As strict as a schoolmaster and just as fussy as one, Malcolm was sure to find a slew of unenviable chores to keep Finley busy.

But time was fleeting for them all. With France a short sail away and pirates patrolling the waters, Rhys needed to get what he came for and sail back to New Britannia as soon as possible.

Rhys rowed to the ship, where Malcolm stood alone on deck. The bosun tossed a rope and ladder over the side. Finley went up first. After securing the boat, Rhys clambered up the ship's side and over the rail with the blunderbuss strapped to his back.

"Ahoy, captain," the broad-shouldered Scot rumbled in his terse brogue. "What news on shore?"

After Rhys told of what transpired, Malcolm sent Finley off to fetch a swab and water bucket. "Arrogant navy whelp." The bosun shook his head. "He thinks serving with this crew is beneath him. A stay in the brig would remind him who his superiors are."

Rhys propped the blunderbuss against the rail. "I'll reserve that for the next time he disobeys orders. Did you see how that automaton pitched him in the sand?"

"Aye. The sight was one to behold." Malcolm didn't hide his amusement. "But I thought I'd have to let the cannons loose on that metal army led by that wee boy."

"That 'wee boy' is a woman. Lady Lydia Dimosthenis designed the automatons that ran the pirates off."

Malcolm raised a bushy gray eyebrow. "A female machinist? From this distance, I saw a pair of knickers. Is that how women dress on this humid isle? Ach, I'm ready to return to Scotland."

Rhys wiped sweat from his face. The wind blowing off the Mediterranean did little to fan the mugginess that hung over the island heavier than a wet canvas tarp. "I'm to dine with her and King Sabba tonight to discuss the automatons."

"He's willing to sell?"

"He's willing to hear the proposal. That's more than I can say for Lady Dimosthenis. If it were up to her, we'd be sailing home now empty-handed."

Malcolm cast his gaze towards the island. "What of that red-robed fellow?"

"Lord Abeiron seems agreeable, but that's not for certain. I have to get those documents." Rhys strode from the forward hull to the door leading below deck. The ship's engine hissed softly as its steam valves cooled beneath the metal casing housed within the center of the top deck.

He descended the steps into the cool darkness. In his cabin, he gathered his suitcase and the envelope containing the proposal. He hauled them back to the topside door, where Malcolm rested his stocky form against the frame.

"I canna picture a woman tinkerin' with machinery." His brogue deepened the more perplexed he became.

"Lydia is a peculiar sort," Rhys agreed. Ye her peculiarity made her all the more interesting. He'd seen many things in his voyages in the Mediterranean and East Asia, but never a woman so unorthodox, as evidenced in her clothing and bold approach when confronting men. Rhys certainly was not used to being challenged by a female. The experience was aggravating and yet oddly intriguing.

Malcolm griped again. "Eve's daughters should swaddle babes, not blunderbusses."

"If you feel that strongly about it, quit sailing and become headmaster of a finishing school," Rhys gibed.

Malcolm scoffed. "No headmaster could sail upon *The Neptune* and live to tell about it."

"Keep that to yourself." Rhys's humor waned at the mention of the horrific experience. He scanned the deck to determine if Finley overheard. The navigator was occupied wringing water from the swab.

Malcolm pushed off the doorframe. "Be at ease, Rhys." He lowered his voice to a murmur. "Our unwitting stint as pirates is long past. You talk as though it were only this morn when we walked away from it all."

"You mean led away in cuffs." Rhys spoke low as well. Guilt hit him heavy and cold as the iron shackles that were placed on his wrists when he and Malcolm were tossed into prison two years ago. "Eleven months, Malcolm. We served less than a year in Coldbath Fields for piracy and destruction of the *Donna Dulce* merchant ship. I can't decide what more to be ashamed of, the charges or the light sentence."

The bosun puffed his jowls. "*The Neptune*'s captain seemed a legitimate importer to do business with. I didn't know he was a scalawag when I came aboard. Neither did you."

"And that alone keeps you from feeling guilty?"

"When I feel guilt, I count my blessings. We were pardoned in exchange for service with the COIC. You were given this ship and crew. Isn't that enough?"

Rhys knew it could never be enough, or that easy for him to put aside the reality of being unable to stop a senseless tragedy. It haunted him ever since that ill-fated day.

When he didn't respond, Malcolm changed the subject. "What of this lady machinist you're to dine with? She should know that you mean to get what you want."

"Given my introduction to Lady Dimosthenis earlier, I suspect she's not one to be easily scared into cooperation."

"There are other ways to charm the fairer sex." Malcolm wagged his brows.

Rhys wondered if Lydia would be susceptible to any charm he could muster, given her earlier imperviousness. Still, it was worth another try. "I'll send the crew back to the ship. Keep an eye on them until I return tomorrow. And don't let Finley ashore."

"Aye, Captain."

Before Rhys climbed down the rope ladder to the longboat, he noticed Malcolm was more watchful of the king's chief adviser on shore than he was of Finley or the ship.

***

Lydia hurried after the king. Her clockwork assistant's gears clicked steadily as it followed at her heels. "King Sabba, I entreat you to reconsider inviting the ambassador to the palace. We know nothing about him."

The king slowed his progression, as did the guards flanking him. He waited until she reached his side. "You should not have sought to engage the British sailors in combat, Lydia," he scolded her in the Aspasian dialect. "You could have been killed."

Lydia stared at the sand on the toe of her boot. "I thought to hold them off before they could reach the inhabited part of the island."

"You should have waited for help. You are not a guard, but a machinist, and the only woman in Aspasia able to call herself such."

Lydia inclined her head as he reminded her yet again of her privileged place in the Guild.

"You disobeyed me." Sabba's stern eyes glared a hole through her skin. He commanded his guards to continue without him. Once the men outdistanced him by ten paces, he resumed speaking in the presence of Lydia and the automatons that moved along behind her. "State your case, before I consider taking your title and position in the Guild away."

Lydia's blood stilled. "Your Majesty, I meant no disrespect. I only wanted to drive the sailors away."

"There is another reason. Your deceased husband."

A tiny ache pricked her heart. Lydia spoke in a soft voice. "Yes."

King Sabba's countenance softened. "Lydia, there was no proof that pirates were involved in Galen's accident. The ship my nephew was on sank due to a gunpowder explosion."

She heard that report so many times in the past two years, but still retained her doubts. "There was no proof that pirates were not involved, either."

"Your resolve to eradicate piracy has made you suspicious of every visitor to Aspasia. I demand you be present tonight to hear Ambassador Cartret's proposal." Sabba resumed walking to the palace.

Lydia picked up step beside him. "But Your Majesty, you told the ambassador that you wouldn't give him the automatons. Why hear the proposal?"

"I said I would not give away the automatons. I never said I would not sell them. Aspasia is struggling. Only a few officials know, but the coffers will be depleted in less than a year."

Shock turned Lydia's muscles to ice. She knew about the country's economic troubles, but not the extent of their severity.

"My attempts to develop modern commerce with the Guild proved insufficient to compete with the industry of larger nations." The king's plight made his shoulders hang heavy beneath his mantle. "And with pirates in the region, merchants do not come as they used to. Your father can attest to slowing sales of his clocks."

Lydia heard her father speak often of his trade's recent lack of progress. Most shopkeepers were short on business. "If the problem is with pirates, how will New Britannia help us?"

"We need a powerful ally. Their funds can help us create more automatons to defend ourselves, even if Ambassador Cartret purchases the ones you have now."

Lydia looked out to sea, where the ambassador's ship lay anchored in the shallows. "What if New Britannia seeks to lord over us? Their young Queen Victoria has an empire extending from the Caribbean isles to India."

"Her empire is vast, but she has extended a peaceful invitation to participate in commerce. If I do nothing, Aspasia will be subject to the next ship that comes, be it from New Britannia, France, or even pirate lords." Sabba's expression was dismal.

A flutter of anxiety rose in Lydia's chest. The clashes between New Britannia and France, as well as the opportunistic rogues that sought to profit from their skirmishes, were forcing all countries to take sides whether they wanted to or not. "Is there no other way to retain our independence and neutrality?"

"Independence, perhaps, but there is no such thing as neutrality in these times. I will do what is best for Aspasia." Sabba continued on to the palace.

Lydia took her automatons down another path towards the Guild. She bit down on her lip as her apprehension rose. King Sabba had no guarantee that the automatons would be enough to save Aspasia from financial ruin. Why should Rhys Cartret be trusted?

Chapter 3

Lydia left the Guild, cut through the marketplace, and went to her family's residence close to the palace. Her mother Iris and father Hector were at the door.

Hector hurried to her. "We just heard about the Guild intrusion. The guards ordered everyone to leave the marketplace and return home. Have you been harmed?"

"No, *baba*, and neither were the other machinists. The automaton stopped the sailor in time."

Iris drew her into the house. "I was afraid something like this would happen after that last raid. Are these sailors also pirates?"

"No, but they've come to bargain for the automatons. Their captain is a diplomat from New Britannia." Lydia explained the encounter to her parents once her father closed the door to the house. "King Sabba will negotiate with him tonight at dinner, but the last thing Aspasia needs is to get in that conflict between New Britannia and France."

Hector agreed. "I remember when we helped Greece break away from the Turks years ago. I thought that would be the last of our involvement in war for a long time, but it seems to be coming to us again."

"It sounds terribly complicated," said Iris. "Perhaps you should let Lord Abeiron handle this for you, Lydia."

"I created those soldiers, *mana*. Nikolaos does not know enough about them to negotiate on his own."

"He is also given to following wherever the coin leads," Hector provided. "I never understood why Sabba thought him to be a sufficient adviser. So greedy a man is Nikolaos."

"Listen to you both." Iris placed her hands on her full hips. "All doom and gloom about Lord Abeiron. I think he is a practical, level-headed man, one who would be able to care for you, Lydia, after your father and I are no longer here."

Lydia knew her mother would branch into that territory. She did so every time the subject of Nikolaos was brought up. Lydia voiced her oft-repeated stance. "Nikolaos shows interest in me only because the line to the throne extends to me through my marriage to Galen. If not for the king and queen being unable to produce an heir, he wouldn't look at me." She walked down the small hallway from the communal room to her own chamber. "I have to get ready for dinner. It starts in less than an hour."

Iris followed. "I'll help you."

After Lydia quickly bathed, her mother helped her into a dress reserved for ceremonial occasions. The blue silk skirt reached Lydia's ankles. A white blouse, green jacket, and gold waist sash completed the ensemble, each trimmed in the elaborate embroidery that her mother was famous for throughout the region.

"I know you work with machines, but I do wish you would style your hair. You have such thick, lustrous curls." Her mother remarked as Lydia sat down at the vanity table. "Tell me, what kind of man is the ambassador?"

Handsome. Lydia blinked as she picked up a comb and handed it to her mother. Why was that the first thought that came to mind when she considered Ambassador Cartret? "Most diplomats are old men, but Ambassador Cartret can't be too far past the age of thirty. He's very self-assured."

Iris smoothed Lydia's curls into elegant waves. "A diplomat must act the part."

"Something about him seems out of place. I don't know what it is." Lydia's mind formed the picture of his face, recalling an unspoken intensity within his dark eyes.

"You said that the ambassador apologized for the sailor who fired upon the Guild. Perhaps his intentions are not for ill."

"Or he realized that he and his men were outnumbered on the beach."

"Where do you and your father get such cheer and goodwill?" Iris shook her head with a smile. "There. You look beautiful." She took a hand mirror from the vanity table and held it before Lydia's face.

Lydia gave a cursory glance at her reflection. She took after her father in strong features as well as opinions. She didn't consider herself to be beautiful with her prominent cheekbones, slightly long nose and full lips, but the hairstyle her mother configured lent softness to her appearance. "Thank you, *mana*. I should hurry."

A knock sounded from outside the chamber. "Lord Abeiron is here to escort you to dinner, Lydia," her father announced.

Lydia put the mirror down. "Nikolaos does not relent."

"Persistence is a good trait in a suitor," Iris defended him, inciting a groan from her daughter. "I just want you to be happy again, Lydia. You've been so focused on perfecting those automatons ever since Galen's accident."

"We collaborated on the automatons before he left for Italy to attend that lecture. I would see them finished. And I don't wish to hand them off to Ambassador Cartret."

"Are you certain it is the automatons you struggle to let go?"

Lydia sighed. "I know Galen is in a better place. Though I still miss him sometimes, I don't mourn heavily as I used to."

"No, but you don't take interest in life as other ladies do." Iris went to get Lydia's head covering from the garment trunk. The small hat bore a golden cord with the russet tassel of the Machinist Guild. "Despite wars and talk of wars, the world still has its charms. And men and women still enter into marriage."

Lydia bent so her mother could place the hat on her head. "Can we discuss this when I return?"

Iris swatted the silk tassel across her daughter's nose. "You're still young. I don't want to see you become a grumpy old widow."

"*Mitera*," Lydia gasped, addressing her mother in the formal. "Please. I have to go."

"Yes, and take your *tambouras*. Lord Abeiron should hear the new song you learned."

Lydia glanced at the stringed instrument that sat at the foot of her bed. She had no intention of playing it for Nikolaos, but if taking it to the dinner would quiet her mother's well-meaning criticisms, so be it.

She grabbed the *tambouras* before leaving her chamber. Her father walked her to the entrance of the house, where Nikolaos sat in a cushioned chair.

He did not wait for her approach. He advanced towards her and bowed with a flourish, apparently not to be outdone by Ambassador Cartret's earlier gesture on the beach. His robe dusted the floor rug in a wash of crimson. Rising slowly to full effect, he offered Lydia his arm. "May I compliment you on how you look this evening?" The words rolled off his tongue as easily as the fabric swirled about his feet.

"Greetings, Lord Abeiron." Lydia rested her hand atop his sinewy arm.

Lydia's father held open the door for them. "I trust you will escort my daughter home promptly once the dinner is over, Lord Abeiron."

"Yes, Hector." Nikolaos didn't bother to address her father by his surname Korba. "Lydia will be safe with me."

Hector leaned in and kissed Lydia's cheek. "His robe is silk. Food stains do not wash out," he whispered in her ear.

Lydia suppressed a grin. Sometimes her father could be filled with absolute mischief. "I will pass your greetings on to the king, *baba*."

Nikolaos' mouth twitched as he no doubt strained to hear their exchange.

Once he and Lydia left her residence, they walked the pebble-lined path to the palace and through the king's garden. Lydia often enjoyed the view of the gardens from her house. The palace, though much smaller than the royal dwellings on the Continent, shone resplendent against the evening sun with its Classical architecture. Designed to pay homage to the ancient Athenian palaces, its pillars and steps were limestone.

As Lydia inhaled the fragrance of flowers, her sensory pleasure was cut short. The heavy scent of Nikolaos' perfumed beard burned her nostrils as he leaned in to speak. "I see you brought your *tambouras*. Music lightens a tense atmosphere. Perhaps the ambassador will enjoy an Aspasian folk tune while he dines."

"It was my mother's idea." Lydia breathed through her mouth so as not to take in the scent of his cologne. All that did was substitute the urge to sneeze for the inclination to cough.

"Iris is an astute woman."

They passed among the marble statues that lined the garden walkway.

"I took the ambassador on a short tour of the palace grounds an hour ago," Nikolaos said. "I wanted to see if he would reveal more details for his visit."

Lydia's ears perked. "What did he say?"

"He talked about the hot weather and remained silent as to his true interests. No matter. I will find out soon enough at dinner."

"I'm anxious to hear his proposal, too."

"And have you given any thought to *my* proposal?"

Nikolaos and her mother were forging a united front against her. She was sure of it. Lydia held her skirt as she climbed the palace stairs. "I declined your previous marriage offers, Nikolaos."

He persisted yet again. "But should we wed, you needn't worry about preserving the wealth young Lord Dimosthenis bequeathed you."

Lydia stared at the double doors of the dining hall at the end of the corridor. King Sabba appointed ceremonial guards for the occasion. "My work with the Guild proves I can take care of myself."

"One needs more than a scientific mind to prosper." He paused, placing his free hand over hers as though he were a courting lover. "Many wellborn women would not hesitate to accept my offer."

Lydia caught the hidden barb. She was born a commoner, holding royal title only by marriage. She would have never met Galen or become a Guild member had he not visited her father's shop and seen one of her clockwork designs. Even so, she refused to allow Nikolaos to bleed his blue blood all over her pride. "If you're intent on providing security for someone, help us all by donating your wealth to Aspasia and my uncle." She read his reaction to her newly acquired knowledge of the country's financial state.

Nikolaos wore a pleasant expression for the servants that passed them in the corridor. "Your late husband's uncle, you mean. Sabba tires of keeping a ward unrelated by blood or profitable ties."

He succeeded in stirring her indignation. "My value doesn't depend upon profit. If not for my inventions, Aspasia would have fallen to pirates."

"There is more to maintaining a noble title than building engines and arranging cogwheels. Instead of marrying me to solidify your place for the throne, you tinker with steam boilers at your leisure, using His Majesty's funds to do it. Do not think he will tolerate that or your outspoken candor for much longer. "

Lydia glimpsed the lavishly-displayed food on the table as the dining hall doors opened and closed behind the servants. She lost what little appetite she had for dinner. Surely Sabba would not force her to marry Nikolaos against her will? "You seek my hand only to get to the throne, Nikolaos. You have no affection or love for anyone but yourself."

She moved to take her arm away from him, but he held on, pulling her into the dining hall. He spoke under the melodious strains of a lyre being played by a musician. "Even with your title and wealth, you fail to catch the interest of any man in Aspasia. You are not a beauteous woman. You are twenty-eight years old and engage in a man's profession, further diminishing what minor charms you do possess. You cannot spurn me forever, Lydia."

If he thought to hurt her pride with his harsh appraisal, she would not give him the satisfaction. "I would be *ilithios* to marry a scheming, uncaring man like you."

Lydia gathered her strength and used enough force to yank herself free. The momentum sent her arm behind her body. She heard a soft grunt and looked over her shoulder.

To her horror, Ambassador Cartret doubled over in pain.

Chapter 4

Still holding her *tambouras*, Lydia put her free hand on Rhys's broad shoulder, prepared to steady him in case he lost balance. His tanned face grew ruddy. He muttered unfamiliar words in English. The forcefulness behind them made her guess that he was swearing.

The musician stopped playing the lyre and stared aghast at what transpired. The servants halted their traffic in and out of the kitchen door. Nikolaos made his thin eyebrows into a long black worm that stretched across his forehead in a frown.

Embarrassed, Lydia spoke English to the ambassador, but could not form sentences smoothly. "Ambassador Cartret, I—I beg your pardon. Standing there, I didn't...I didn't see you standing there."

"Not to worry." He ground the words out through his teeth, doing a poor job of concealing his pain. "After all, how could you see me standing behind you?"

"Forgive her, Ambassador." Nikolaos's tone became syrupy. "As Lady Dimosthenis works amongst her machines almost daily, she is unused to being in such close quarters with those not made of metal."

Lydia wished her elbow had gone into Nikolaos's ribs rather than the ambassador's stomach. "Shall I find a physician?"

She could tell Rhys still ached as he put up a resilient front. He stood tall again. "No need. I took worse blows when I worked on the Swansea docks in Wales as a youth. I can stomach this. Although, your strength is impressive, even without a blunderbuss." His eyes twinkled with humor.

The back of Lydia's neck warmed.

Nikolaos cleared his throat. He indicated for Lydia to look at her hand. She still held the ambassador by the shoulder. She dropped her arm to her side.

"I was following too closely." Rhys straightened his black tail coat. The color matched his hair, which was combed neatly and gave a blue-black sheen under the chandelier. He certainly was young for a diplomat. And a dapper one at that. "I approached to tell you that we're seated next to each other at the table. I hope that won't be too much of an inconvenience."

"Yes. I mean, no. I shouldn't think it will be. " Lydia regained her composure. At this rate, he would think her a dullard as well as an oaf.

He offered his white-gloved hand. "I'll escort you to your chair, if Lord Abeiron doesn't mind, of course."

Lydia knew that Nikolaos did indeed mind, but he inclined his head politely to the ambassador and went to stand by the door.

Being seated next to Rhys would be a welcome respite from Nikolaos, even if he did hail from New Britannia. She allowed him to take her to the table, his hand sure and warm through the glove. Why he chose to wear such things in warm weather was beyond her understanding. She wanted to ask whether his countrymen always dressed for the cold, but she dare not say anything more to make herself sound uncouth. She needed to appear competent to negotiate.

"You look lovely this evening," he conversed while they stood waiting for the king to arrive. "And I see you brought an instrument. It looks much better in your hands than a firearm." He smirked.

"You should have stopped after the first compliment, Ambassador Cartret. Perhaps then I would have believed you."

His smirk deepened. A dimple appeared in his left jaw. "I spoke true to both compliments. And call me Rhys. After tonight, we'll be seeing more of each other."

Lydia set the *tambouras* against her chair. "You're very confident of your success when we have yet to hear the proposal, Ambassa-*Reez*. Is that how you pronounce your name?"

"Close enough."

"You may call me Lydia, though not here. It would be inappropriate before the king." The heat of the cooked food and the hall's warm temperature prompted her to remove her jacket.

Rhys's gaze settled on her arms, bare from where her blouse's sleeves capped at her shoulders. "So you do admit that we will meet again after tonight?"

She was taken aback by his joviality. "Are you attempting to poke fun at me?"

"Considering how you prodded me with your elbow, fair is fair, my lady."

A peculiar man. Lydia heard that New Britannia was a land of eccentrics. With Rhys, she began to believe it.

The guards announced the king's arrival. Sabba took his place at the head of the table, apologized for his queen's absence due to headache, and the meal began. Lydia ate quickly, hoping the others would do the same.

An hour later, after the dishes were cleared and the servants and musician departed, King Sabba finally broached the subject of Rhys's proposal. "Ambassador, you may speak before us. But first tell me, what exactly is this COIC agency you hail from?"

Rhys removed an envelope from his inside coat pocket. "The Cabinet of Intellectual Curiosities is an agency that promotes and funds the development of scientific innovations. We've partnered with The Crown to find these breakthroughs. Our agents are stationed all over the world."

King Sabba listened and nodded. "And your offer to purchase these innovations, is this what your agency normally does?"

"No, Your Majesty. We usually invite inventors to submit their work to us for consideration. But these automatons—Lady Dimosthenis's automatons—are most impressive." He stole a glance at Lydia.

She crossed her ankles under the table. Was he using flattery to cajole her?

Rhys held up the envelope. "This is the agreement to purchase the automatons. New Britannia will pay Aspasia eight thousand pounds."

One glance at the king and Nikolaos and Lydia knew they already converted the currency. The amount was substantial by any nation's estimate, more than enough to replenish Aspasia's coffers.

"Eight thousand pounds is very generous," Sabba voiced when he appeared to have survived the initial shock of hearing the sum. "In addition to restoring the coffers, Aspasia would be able to expand the port and build new ships to carry goods to the Continent and North Africa."

"And you would receive all the protections and privileges that an alliance with New Britannia affords," Rhys added.

"We would insist that several of the automatons remain in Aspasia so that we may continue to defend the island."

"Understandable."

Nikolaos entered the talks. "A grand offer, but all things carry prices. What else does the agreement entail?"

"The timeframe for the acquisition and the rights of ownership." Rhys removed his gloves at the start of dinner. Lydia watched his long, tapered fingers move as he took his time breaking the envelope's seal and withdrew a document. "I'll explain more once I see the soldiers in action."

"Lady Dimosthenis will provide a demonstration at ten o' clock tomorrow morning," the king promised. His gaze dared Lydia to object.

She peeked over Rhys's shoulder and squinted at the tiny print of the document. "You mentioned rights of ownership, Ambassador Cartret. Does it pertain to the automatons or their design schematics?"

"Both."

She bit the inside of her jaw. To sell the automatons was one thing. To give New Britannia access to the mechanics behind their productions was quite another. "May I see that agreement?"

Nikolaos reached across the table and intercepted before her fingers made contact with the parchment. "His Majesty will need to study this first."

"I have a duplicate, but I'll need it again before we leave." Rhys removed a second set of documents from the envelope and gave them to Lydia. Nikolaos stared at the ambassador for a long moment.

Sabba pushed his chair back. "Lord Abeiron and I will deliberate the agreement amongst ourselves." He stepped to the end of the long table. Nikolaos drifted after him.

While they distanced themselves, Lydia perused the document's ten pages. She was no solicitor, but the language of the agreement was free of discrepancies at first glance. "What will happen if Aspasia refuses the offer?"

Rhys raised a black eyebrow. "Eight thousand pounds is a very large sum of money to refuse."

He didn't appear anxious and flustered at her challenging question. Instead, he studied her while toying with the edge of the tablecloth, running it between his fingers slowly. "My lady, you seem threatened by me. I'm here to purchase your invention and seek your friendship. Unless…you think I'm not suited to have either?"

Lydia didn't know what to do with his intimate tone or the peculiar way he looked at her. It didn't help that she could feel the body heat rising from him due to their shared proximity. "I'll tell you what I think," she said in a hushed voice. "I don't want the automatons' power being misused. I designed them to defend, not go to war and build empires."

Rhys looked to her as if the fate of New Britannia's empire rested solely on her shoulders. "France poses a danger to everyone, including Aspasia. There are agents abroad who operated in the old Napoleon regime. They're forming new allegiances as we speak. If surrounding nations don't ally to defend against this threat, then we'll all be faced with war."

"Why should Aspasia favor your country over France? They've not harmed us."

Light settled into the angles of his jaw. "There is a French industrialist by the name of Emile Broussard. COIC reports show that he's resorting to robber baron tactics, buying lands in foreign countries for thrift and then plundering their resources. He's also been known to steal inventions before they're patented, and he has pirates in his employ of smugglers and thieves."

Lydia felt the muscles around her mouth lift. "You tacked pirates on at the end as though that would make me latch onto your argument."

Rhys showed no humor. "I don't make light of this man or his supporters. Your automatons are formidable, but it will take scores of them to combat the forces Broussard is capable of putting together. You wouldn't be able to match his resources without the ability to manufacture on a large scale. New Britannia has that capability."

Lydia frowned, perplexed and apprehensive at his words. She sensed there was truth behind this tale of a French criminal mastermind, but how much was relative to Aspasia's affairs and how much was simply Rhys's attempts to persuade her of the merits of a signed agreement with New Britannia?

The king rustled the pages of the agreement as he put them in order. "I will finish reading this tonight. After tomorrow's demonstration, we will reconvene to sign, if all is satisfactory."

Rhys seemed pleased enough. "Of course, Your Majesty."

Lydia handed the duplicate agreement back to Rhys. What was going through his mind? Triumph? Satisfaction?

Sabba returned to his original seat at the table. "Before we adjourn, we should hear a song from Lydia. Have you heard the *tambouras* played, Ambassador?"

"I don't think I've had the pleasure."

The king indicated for Lydia to pick up her instrument. "If you would honor us. Something light and of good cheer."

The exact opposite of how the talks seemed to be going, at least from her perspective. Lydia reached for the *tambouras* propped against her chair. As she did, her arm brushed against Rhys's trousers. She tensed. Sitting beside him may not have been a good idea after all.

She took the stringed instrument and settled it in her lap. The men watched as she tested a few notes to see if the instrument was in tune. She began to play the new music she composed, a simple song about a young woman who stood on the beach, watching the sunrise. She sang of the woman's curiosity of what lay over the horizon.

By the second verse, Lydia began to relax, letting the melody flow from the chords beneath her fingers and carry in harmony with her voice. Rhys's eyes never left her once. He watched as though he were attempting to learn the song himself, his eyes venturing from her fingers as they played the notes to her lips as she phrased the words. He continued to linger his gaze on her mouth after the song came to an end.

Rhys applauded her. "Well done."

Nikolaos and King Sabba also clapped. Nikolaos remarked, "Lady Dimosthenis's talents go beyond forging automatons. She could be a musician if she wanted to."

"How fortunate for all of us that she excels in both crafts." Rhys's statement made Lydia embarrassed. She got the sense that he wasn't saying those things merely to flatter her.

King Sabba rose. "I believe we will adjourn on that good note."

Lydia lingered as the king and Nikolaos started for the door. She knew Nikolaos would wait to escort her home.

Rhys pushed his chair in. "Is something wrong?"

An idea came to her, one that bore quite a risk. "Tomorrow morning, meet me on the island's remote side at eight."

"But the king said the demonstration was to be at ten."

"He did, but I'll need time to ready the automatons." She wanted to speak with Rhys about the agreement terms without Sabba and Nikolaos present. "You wish to know how that process works, too, do you not?"

Curiosity made that mischievous expression return to Rhys's face, along with the dimple. "Eight, it is. Good evening, Lydia."

"Good evening, *Reez*." She gathered her jacket and *tambouras* and left the hall, hope lightening her steps even as she resigned herself to being escorted back to her family's residence by Nikolaos.

Chapter 5

Rhys watched Lydia practically float from the hall, a far cry from her angry march off the beach earlier. She had something up those little capped sleeves, and she'd make sure he'd see it first thing in the morning. As though his job weren't already challenging enough.

The agreement still went unsigned, regardless of the positive impression he left on King Sabba. And he still needed to convince Lydia to work with him. How was he going to do so if she was skeptical of his every word?

The servants came to clean the dining hall, a signal for Rhys to clear out. As he left, he saw Lydia at the end of the hallway walking alongside Nikolaos. The chief adviser kept lowering his head to view the *tambouras* taking residence so inconveniently on Lydia's arm that he intended to grasp.

Rhys leveled his sights on him. The chief adviser's too-studied demeanor made him wary. And angry. He noticed how Lydia worked to distance herself from Nikolaos when they first entered the dining hall together. Rhys wanted to grab him by his robe collar and demand to know what that was all about.

Rhys retired to his accommodations in the palace's east wing. Perhaps he shouldn't intervene in that matter. It was Lydia and Nikolaos's business, not his. But when he saw Lydia that night, with her long brown curls framing her shoulders, his impression of her changed. And when she played those dulcet tones and sang in that warm, pleasing alto, he temporarily forgot the purpose of the dinner.

So much for him being the charmer of the evening.

Rhys pulled off his jacket and tossed it over a chair, grateful to have one less layer of clothing on. Maybe charm wasn't what Lydia needed to see from him. Her actions showed just how much she appreciated diplomatic niceties. What could he do to combat that?

He fell asleep wondering.

***

The next morning Rhys found Lydia waiting for him on the beach. Dressed in a work shirt of roughspun cloth and brown pants, she sat cross-legged in the sand. A cap shielded her face from the sun.

"I see you wisely dispensed with the coat this morning. It didn't suit you." She adjusted the brim of her cap. Her shirtsleeve retreated up her arm as she did so, revealing a leather wristband with a metal dial.

Rhys gave it a passing glance, amused by her preference for old breeches and odd jewelry. "I could say the same for what you're wearing. The ensemble you wore last night was much more becoming."

She averted her eyes, hiding them beneath her lashes. "I cannot work in a dress." She rose and dusted her pant legs of sand. "Were you seen by any guards upon leaving the palace?"

"A few, but they didn't stop me when I left."

"They may have alerted the king. We shouldn't be out in the open. Come."

Rhys followed her as she headed north. The coastal shoreline soon gave way to the forested hillside, where Rhys initially sent Finley to find the quickest way around the island.

Lydia took him to an area of dense green vegetation, treading onward to a copse of tall cypress that lined the perimeter of a columned building that matched Finley's description of a temple. She climbed the well-trodden steps. "This is the Machinists Guild, formerly an ancient shrine to Hephaestus." A crumbling statue of the Greek god stood at the entrance.

"How fitting. A place that once housed an ancient god of forgers now serves as a meeting place for modern craftsmen. And women," he added quickly. "Are there other female guild members?"

"I'm the sole woman currently. One of the former Guild members bought a miniature clockwork piece from me when I worked in my father's shop. He admired my work and invited me to study here." Unspoken thoughts settled upon Lydia's face as she pushed the cap from her forehead.

Delicate was not a word to describe her features, but they possessed a character that Rhys found appealing.

"And what of you, Rhys?" She pronounced his name accurately. "You know your Greek mythology and language. Who taught you?"

"My mother. She was a governess before she married my father, a merchant sailor. She made sure I was schooled in the Classics." Rhys came to the Guild entrance.

"Was that why your country and its curio cabinet agency—"

"Cabinet of Intellectual Curiosities." Rhys corrected her, but couldn't resist chuckling at her abbreviated reference to the COIC.

"Why were you chosen to come to Aspasia?"

She was determining his credibility. If she knew of his past association with pirates, he'd never acquire those automatons. "I used to sail the Mediterranean with a shipping company. Queen Victoria thought that qualified me to represent her in the region."

That explanation was true, for the most part, and seemed to suffice with Lydia. She said no more as she approached the sealed entrance of the Guild building. She removed the metal dial from her wrist, placed it in a round setting in the door, and turned the dial twice.

A loud grinding occurred as stone grated upon stone. The first panel slid into a wall. The door behind it groaned as it opened.

Lydia went through first, taking the dial mechanism with her. Rhys ducked in, running his hand along the cool, rough surface of the limestone wall.

"Our meeting was taking place in that room on the left when your crewman entered." Lydia pointed to it. "Since the door can only be opened from the outside, we left an automaton to stand guard by the wall."

"You should think about putting up a gate to keep Guild members safe." It would increase the lifespan of bungling sailors, too, but Rhys didn't care to share that observation.

She walked ahead of him. Daylight provided dim illumination for their passage along the sparse halls. "Most people are afraid to visit while the automatons are still being perfected."

"Should I be worried about an ambush?" Rhys asked in half-jest, but he still patted his waistcoat for the revolver stored beneath.

"They've been shut off. I'm sure you've dealt with greater perils than dim hallways on your travels."

"Where I've gone, dim hallways are never a good sign."

Lydia paused before a tiny alcove, where candles and a box of matchsticks resided. She used a match to light two lamps suspended from wall sconces and took one for herself. "Better?"

Rhys took the other one. "We'll see."

After traversing yet another hallway, they reached a large work area. Tables, diagrams, and odd bits of machinery were categorized on shelves.

"This is the main room." Lydia's voice produced a soft echo throughout the interior.

"I see automaton parts, but not the models themselves. Where are they?"

"I'll take you to them, but first, I wish to discuss additional terms concerning their purchase."

Rhys set the lamp on the table. "I knew it."

She wrinkled her brow at his flippant statement. "In exchange for the automatons, you will permit their designs to remain with Aspasia."

The flame atop the lamp wick danced when Rhys gave a big sigh. She insisted upon challenging him at every turn. "Are you sure King Sabba won't mind you negotiating for him?"

Lydia remained undeterred. "Do you accept my terms?"

"Your terms are to prohibit New Britannia from mass producing your soldiers."

"They should remain Aspasia's property. Consider it a trade agreement."

Rhys noticed her breathing sped. Was the heat getting to her, or her nerves, due to inexperience at negotiating? If it was the latter, then he could still come out on top and win the dispute. "This isn't a trade agreement. This is a one-time exchange of money for goods."

"You'd pay us once while your nation profits continually from the automatons. How is that fair?"

She had a very good point. It wasn't fair, but it was in neither his authority nor ability to challenge an age-old practice nearly all countries resorted to. "Lydia, New Britannia is a powerful nation. It would not do to pass off an alliance when we can protect you from France."

"I do not fear France nor you, Rhys Cartret. How dare you try to intimidate me?" She folded her arms. "If King Sabba heard you now, even he would tell you to make better terms."

"I'm sure he'd also be pleased to hear how you tried to persuade me to rescind my offer without him knowing."

A smidgen of wind left her sails. "I meant *amend* your offer, not rescind."

Rhys's insides twisted at having to be so firm with her. She only wanted what was best for her country. But so did he, when it came to New Britannia. At least she didn't have an entire Cabinet of officials to hound her should a mission fail. "You want me to leave Aspasia, but I'm not going anywhere until that agreement is signed. Are we clear?"

"Typical diplomat's arrogance." Huffing, Lydia grabbed her lantern and marched into an adjoining chamber.

He used a firm approach and she still accused him of being diplomatic. Rhys grumbled before venturing after her.

In the next chamber, five rows of automatons stood in formation, their eyeless, featureless faces vague and uniform.

Rhys tapped the shoulder of one nearest him. "Are all of these models voice-responsive?"

"Yes." Lydia moved between the rows, still visibly irritated as she explained the components of her machines. "Their armor contains a copper alloy that registers sound. Sound travels to the central wiring at the base of their backs, where the wire forms an imprint of the controller's voice. You must speak into the wire first to control them. This method works well for the automatons with the steam propulsion engines, but on the hybrid windup models, sometimes the mainspring of their clockwork motor interferes. I'm still working on those."

None of that made much sense to Rhys. "Show me one of them."

"The hybrid model is along the back wall." Lydia went to the area where the largest automaton stood dormant. She slipped behind it and opened a panel on its back. Rhys heard her wind up something before taking a wire in her hand. "Give the engine time to warm."

After three minutes, she spoke into the wire. "On your guard," she said in Greek.

He stepped back as the automaton's gears whirred and it turned its head his way. "What is it doing?"

The automaton progressed towards him. Rhys moved out of its way. The floor vibrated with each heavy iron footfall. It kept advancing towards Rhys.

"Make it stand down."

"You have to be quiet and remain still or it will keep coming at you."

"Not likely." He reached for his revolver.

"No," Lydia shouted.

The automaton reacted to her elevated volume. Lumbering on two tree trunk-size pistons for legs, it came at Rhys. He aimed the revolver at the automaton's chest.

***

"Stop," Lydia cried.

She ran around the automaton and rushed to Rhys's side, shoving his arm down. "If you shoot it, you'll risk the engine combusting."

The automaton, registering her shout, increased its advance.

"Are you mad, woman? Your machine is on the attack." Rhys pushed her away and squeezed the trigger on the revolver before it could take another step.

The shot rang within the confined space, amplified as the bullet struck metal. The automaton came at Rhys again, unencumbered by the saucer-sized dent in its chest plate. Lydia saw the hydraulic fluid trickle down its torso.

"You're going to get us killed."

"And this monstrosity isn't?" Rhys fired a second shot, and a third.

The sharp tang of gunpowder mixed with smoke from the automaton's damaged parts. A high whirring issued from its engine as oil spewed from the wiring connecting the head to the torso.

A fourth bullet cracked the air.

"For goodness sakes, Rhys, stand down." Lydia reached for one of the leather engineer's aprons hanging on the wall and flung it over her head. She drew in close to the automaton.

Its movements slowed. Oil pooled at its feet. Hydraulic fluid pelted Lydia's apron, sizzling atop the thick grain of cowhide. She got behind the automaton and found the panel door dangling where the impact of Rhys's gunfire shook it open. Copper wires spilled out of the voice receptor box.

"Cease."

The order did no good with the box damaged. The automaton was locked onto her first command, still on its guard. Lydia extended a hand out from beneath the protective covering of the apron. Drops of hydraulic fluid hit her skin.

Burning pain seized upon every nerve in her hand. Lydia grabbed the wires and pulled them loose. The whirring inside the automaton stalled. The machine gave one final groan before it ceased altogether.

The room returned to its former quiet, save for the hiss of steam that poured out of the fissures of the assistant's broken engine. Lydia heaved a sigh just before Rhys appeared beside her.

"What did you do?" He kept the revolver aimed at the downed machine.

"Helped you nearly destroy four years of hard work, that's what." She whipped the apron from her head. The action sent her hand into flares of agony. "If you had listened to me instead of brandishing that firearm, none of this would have happened."

"You set that automaton on me. You told it to be on guard." His stare took on an accusing, hard gleam. Smoke trailed from the gun barrel in his hand. He did not move to lower it in front of her.

Lydia involuntarily trembled. "I say 'on your guard' to all of the automatons after their engines are powered. It's my order for them to await my next command."

"Why did it come towards me?" Rhys ground his words out between his teeth. His voice was deep and devoid of any consideration of what she just said.

"The wires in its voice receptor box are fine tuned to respond to changes in pitch and tone. When you took out your gun, it heard me shout and thought I was in distress."

"Machines can't think." He finally put the revolver away.

"You know what I mean." Lydia gazed in dismay at the jumble of wires sticking out from the automaton's back. Why were they moving?

"Look out." Rhys knocked her off her feet.

Lydia heard a crash just before the two of them landed on the floor. He sheltered her from the impact, holding her against his chest. The room came alive again with the sound of clanging metal.

Once the din settled, Lydia peered over her shoulder. The assistant was on its back, having brought two rows of automatons with it. Oil and hydraulic fluid mingled on the floor in an orange-brown pool of sludge.

"It was going to fall on you." Rhys spoke into her ear. His breath tickled the sensitive area.

Unnerved by such close contact, Lydia looked into his face. The brash, teasing manner that lightened his features before gave way to a darker, focused countenance. He hid much beneath the cloak of civility he chose to don. She wondered just whom New Britannia sent to deal with her, and for the first time, became uneasy with the thought of what he might do if he didn't get his way.

"You're a dangerous man, ambassador," she whispered.

"You're welcome." He lifted himself and her off the floor with little effort on her part. "I'll help you clean up."

"There's no time. The demonstration starts in half an hour. I need to ready the remaining soldiers. The ones that are still standing, that is." Lydia straightened her clothes, making an attempt to stop noticing the absence of his touch.

She approached the fallen automaton and winced at the scrap metal Rhys's armor-piercing bullets made of its torso plate. "That wasn't even an armed model."

"And yet it nobly defended you." Rhys found a stray bullet lodged in a piece of the armor plating that had broken off at the automaton's shoulder.

She took it from him and examined it under the light. "How did you come by such a vicious firearm?"

"Custom-made. You're hurt."

Lydia dropped the armor and covered the reddened skin of her hand. "A mild abrasion from when I shut the assistant down."

Rhys took her hand, inspecting the wound. "This is a burn."

"Nothing a bit of comfrey balm won't soothe." She drew back, sucking air through her teeth when Rhys touched the burn. "I'll tend to it after the demonstration."

"It's already blistering." He took a handkerchief and wound it gingerly around her hand. She bit the inside of her cheek to keep from vocalizing her pain.

He tied the handkerchief. "That should stay for a while."

Lydia studied the overhand knot. Only sailors made those. Maybe he was telling the truth about his profession. "Thank you." Embarrassed at being tended to by him in such an intimate manner, she changed the subject. "You should go back to the palace. The king will look for you soon. I'll show you the path back."

"I know the way."

She took him to the entrance and watched him take sure, confident strides along the hillside before she retreated into the Guild's warm, dim interior.

She tried to chase away the new sensations in her mind and body that occurred when Rhys put his arms around her, shielding her from harm. After that last encounter, she didn't know if she was doing anything right anymore.

Chapter 6

The clean lemon scent of Lydia's hair lingered in Rhys's nose as he took the longboat to *The Enlightened* and clamored up the rope ladder. He found Malcolm reclining at the ship's helm with a bowl of breakfast porridge.

"There's to be an automaton demonstration in twenty minutes. You'll need to see how many we can fit in the ship's cargo hold." Not waiting for a reply, Rhys went below to his cabin and shut the door behind him.

No time now to return to the palace. He'd have to meet King Sabba and Nikolaos on the way. At least this served as an excuse.

His writing instruments waited for him on the solid mahogany desk. Rhys attempted to push his close encounter with Lydia from his mind as he slid into the chair. He proceeded to draft additional terms to the purchase agreement. He scribbled the new terminology onto a sheet of parchment, hoping the COIC's solicitors would have little to find fault with. Lydia drove a hard bargain with her lofty demands for licensures and guarantees.

A gob of ink spurted from the tip of the pen, rendering his sentences lost in a black pool. Rhys crumbled the parchment and started again with a fresh sheet. A notion came to him at that moment, one that he wished he thought of in the Guild when he was too distracted protecting Lydia from her own mechanical creation. Too busy ministering to the wound upon her soft skin.

He finished the second draft without incident from the pen. After blotting and fanning the ink dry, Rhys stuffed the parchment into the envelope containing the original agreement and sprang for the door.

Lydia could insist upon her own way, but even she would not be able to refuse these new terms.

***

The demonstration began on time. Rhys stood on the beach with King Sabba, Nikolaos, Malcolm, and a handful of the palace guards. He watched through protective lenses as the automatons moved about, firing low-grade artillery at a distance.

Lydia's voice reached them through the brass speaking trumpet she used to command the automatons. She ordered the front line to send incendiaries out. Sand kicked up from the resulting blast to land unnervingly near.

Rhys felt a rough tug on his sleeve as Malcolm backed away several feet. "What is it?" he asked when he was sure they couldn't be heard over the din.

"I don't like the looks of this. You want to transport those volatile machines on the ship?"

"That was the whole point of saving room in the cargo hold."

Another round of incendiaries exploded. The blasts sent tremors through the ground.

Malcolm bared his teeth at the automatons. "Supposing a breaker shakes one of their gunpowder cartridges loose? Or one explodes and leaves a gaping maw in the hull?"

"*The Enlightened* faces risks every time it transports cargo. This is no different." Rhys said the words and knew them to be only half-true. Just that morning he came close to having an automaton's metal hands clamped around his throat. Should that happen on the ship, he couldn't very well fire a gun below deck to stop it.

Only Lydia's distinctive voice would have an effect.

Across the beach she stood behind the defensive line of automatons. The wind assaulted her hair until curls fell over her brow. She hardly noticed as she issued another command for the soldiers to open fire.

A mortar hit the ground seven yards from Rhys's feet. The device blasted sand and pebbles into the air. Rhys covered his head as debris pelted his arms and rolled into the opening of his shirt collar. "Well, I did ask for a demonstration."

Malcolm cursed. "The crazed lass did that on purpose."

Rhys could neither prove nor disprove him. "At least she gave us protective lenses." He brushed sand from the goggles strapped around his head.

Lydia came running to him after acknowledging King Sabba and Nikolaos, who stood far enough way to get no more than sand in their shoes. "I didn't expect that mortar round to land so close to you."

Rhys hid a smile. She must have read Malcolm's mind. "No harm done. Automatons can't always be perfectly controlled."

Her eyes flashed at his hinted reference to earlier in the Guild. "I'll tighten their trajectory. Are you sufficient as well, Mr. Clark?"

"He's fine," Rhys answered for Malcolm. "In fact, the bosun inquired about transporting your soldiers aboard the ship. I told him that you'll make sure to prevent any mishaps."

"Of course." Lydia clutched the speaking trumpet at her side. Sea breezes played with her clothing, molding it to her figure. As much as she preferred to dress as a London street urchin while she worked, she was unable to hide that beneath the coarse fabric rested the soft curves of a woman.

"Is there anything else you'd like to see, ambassador?" She rested the trumpet against her hip.

He realized she referred to the automaton demonstration. "I've seen enough."

"Enough to sign the agreement?" Nikolaos asked, but Sabba was the one who looked the most eager to hear an answer.

"Yes, but I have new terms."

Lydia narrowed her eyes. He supposed he'd have to get used to her frequent expressions of disapproval.

Sabba poured over his copy of the agreement in his hand. "What new terms? You said you were satisfied with the demonstration."

"The terms are not unduly burdensome, Your Majesty, but it's clear that no one knows the automatons' capabilities better than Lady Dimosthenis. I request that she journey to New Britannia with me to oversee their production."

Malcolm and Nikolaos spoke in unison. "What?"

Lydia jerked her head in Rhys's direction. Fine lines formed around the otherwise smooth skin of her brow.

"Why does she need to accompany you?" Sabba asked.

"Having Lady Dimosthenis present will ensure that no mistakes are made. She'll also have peace of mind knowing that no scientist or engineer can abuse her inventions." Rhys put the full truth of it before them all. "I've taken the liberty of drafting an amendment." He opened the envelope containing the addendum. "Never mind the handwriting."

Malcolm opened his mouth to blurt out something. Rhys shushed him with a glare before he gained the opportunity.

The king read the addendum before passing it onto Lydia. "Do you understand what Ambassador Cartret requires of you?"

She managed a stiff nod as she read the terms. She sighed heavily and looked to Rhys. "How long am I to be away?"

"Until the first production is complete," he answered. "You can return to Aspasia afterward, if you wish."

"I trust you to hold true to these terms, ambassador. Don't make me regret it." Lydia gave the addendum back to the king and walked away to return the automatons to the Guild. Her steps were noticeably heavier.

An urge to go after her took hold of Rhys, but he held firm. This was the simplest, most effective way to ensure Lydia's cooperation. It had to be done.

"We'll adjourn to the palace," announced Sabba. "Nikolaos will be witness to the signing."

"And I for New Britannia," Malcolm rejoined.

"We'll meet you there shortly," said Rhys.

Nikolaos and Sabba were escorted back to the palace by the guards. Malcolm turned to Rhys with a face of complete disbelief. "What was that?"

"What?"

"Don't play daft. Your new *terms*. The COIC will have your head for bringing that woman to New Britannia without express orders. "

"It was necessary. Lydia took repeated stance against me about maintaining control of her inventions."

"Is that why her dainty hand was bandaged with your handkerchief, because she struck you and bruised her fingers?" Malcolm smirked. "I'd not have known but for the overhand knot you commonly use for the sail rigging."

"She didn't strike me." Rhys found himself rushing to explain away the morning's dalliance in the Guild. "She suffered a minor mishap while handling an automaton. It was before the demonstration."

Malcolm's braying laugh startled the seagulls that pecked for snails scattered in the mortar blasts. "So you did have a private audience with her after all."

"And nearly lost my neck in the process."

"A feisty one, is she?"

"Get your head out of the bilge water. Lydia keeps the automatons in the Guild. She showed them to me and one happened to go on the attack." Rhys ran his hands through his hair, feeling grit and sand in his scalp. "She burned her hand while attempting to stop it. I'm to blame."

"How?"

"I shot the automaton at close range. A poor solution, given the machine's tendency to leak hydraulic fluid. Oh." Rhys blurted out the last thing Malcolm needed to hear.

The bosun wagged his head with force. "Those monstrosities cannot be put on the ship. We'll be sent to a watery grave or burnt to cinders."

"Pray that we don't, Malcolm. Our interests rest upon those inventions." Rhys's eyes followed Lydia before she disappeared over the hill. "Let's get this agreement signed before more amendments have to be made."

*****

The purchase agreement weighed heavily on Lydia's mind, although it rested light as sea foam in her hand when she added her name to the collection of signatures.

She brooded as Rhys took the agreement from her and handed the duplicate transcription to King Sabba. Rhys gave her exactly what she wanted. That, and so much more. She shook her head in a bemused state. She thought herself capable of playing for her country in the ambassador's game of high stakes when he so elegantly overturned her hand.

Rhys tucked the envelope under his arm and stood to leave the counsel room of the palace. "We set sail in six days. Have the automatons and your belongings ready to load onto the ship in five. Malcolm will give further instructions."

The burly bosun, witness to the signing, had a frown frozen in stone for Lydia.

She had yet to tell her parents of her impending journey. Her hands grew cold at the prospect. Worse still, she was to part from her family for an indefinite amount of time.

Lydia took the path to her residence once the signing ended. The windows were raised and the aroma of soup wafted outside. She concealed her bandaged hand in her pocket as she approached her mother inside.

Iris sat rigid in the chair before the door, a cup of tea on the table beside her. "Something has happened to you."

Lydia exhaled. She never could hide much from her mother. "The ambassador requires that I go to New Britannia to oversee the automaton production."

Her mother sat mute for several moments as the teacup beside her sent curlicues of steam through the still air. "You must do what he says," she said, finally.

Lydia didn't expect her mother be so acquiescent. "This sits well with you?"

"I do not wish for my daughter to journey over a thousand miles from me, but you have your duty to the king and to Aspasia. Was this part of the agreement?"

"I pressed the ambassador to let me retain control of the automatons. He gave me my wish, but this is his way of making sure I don't cheat New Britannia of its investment. He doesn't trust me."

"You would do the same if the roles were reversed."

"That's not true." Lydia raised her eyes and saw her mother's amused expression. "Well, I wouldn't be nearly so smug about it."

Iris sipped tea. Lydia noticed her hands trembled. "Well, let us be practical. You should think about what you will take with you. I hear New Britannia can get very cold in winter."

"It's the journey I worry about." Lydia pictured the great expanse of ocean she would traverse in order to sail north. There was much to prepare for and not enough time. "I'll write often, *mana*."

Her mother cast a glance out the window towards the sea. "I will settle for often enough. If the ambassador is as demanding as you describe him, your hands will be very full."

Beneath the secure binding of Rhys's handkerchief, Lydia's injured hand smarted.

Chapter 7

Within the end of the week, Lydia stood on the shore on the eve of her voyage to New Britannia. She observed as the automatons were hoisted onto Rhys's ship.

Rhys supervised his six-man crew on deck. In stark contrast to his calm was Malcolm, who roamed about the ship, giving orders for transporting the automatons to the cargo hold. Malcolm's shouts carried.

"One at a time. Those cable wenches canna support the weight of two automatons at once. Finley, Smythe, have care not to drag them. I swear, you'll send this ship up in flames before the anchor's raised."

Lydia shook her head. Before the crew began loading the cargo, she told Malcolm how a simple command would enable the automatons to walk to the cargo hold on their own.

He had flatly refused her suggestion. "There'll be no machines roaming freely about the vessel on my watch."

She continued to stand by as the crew loaded the remaining automatons on board. She sensed Rhys's stare wash over her.

Not too long after, he called to her. "Come see how the crew placed the automatons in the cargo hold. We don't want them falling over when we reach open waters."

A stout, grizzle-haired crewman by the name of Thomas rowed her to the ship. She climbed the rope ladder. Rhys took her hand and helped her as she swung over the rail. Her skin tingled where he touched the tender flesh of her still healing hand.

Three crewmen made way for her to walk across the deck, their faces wary. She passed Finley, the sailor who intruded upon the Guild a week ago. He steeled his jaw and strode to the navigation room on the quarterdeck.

"I thought most ships of this size need a full crew," Lydia remarked to Rhys.

"Because the engine handles most of the operations, a large crew is unnecessary." He led her down to the lower levels where it was dark, cool, and confined.

She appraised the ship's interior. The wooden floor was reinforced with metal rivets running along the sides and reinforcing the middle. The walls were lined with metal. She ran a finger down the section of the wall. Cannonry on the outside. Bessemer steel lining on the inside. Would the fate of the *Donna Dulce* been different if it was outfitted like this vessel?

Lydia abandoned her speculation as Rhys ushered her down to a third deck level and through a wide door to the cargo hold. Lydia ducked her head under the low ceiling beams, straightening again when they gave way to an arched middle. She crossed the floor, much of it piled with crates labeled as containing silks, china, and spices from Aspasia's marketplace. The sweet smell of licorice competed with earthy saffron.

"The automatons are against the wall to the right." Rhys directed to a row of canvas-covered objects. "Malcolm thought it best to store them where the extra weight would be evenly distributed."

"They should do well so long as they don't shift. One of my trunks is open." Lydia pointed to a small steamer case, where two texts and a notebook had fallen out. "I must not have latched it properly."

Rhys picked up the binder. "Who is G. Dimosthenis?"

Lydia paused in placing a text atop a pile of mechanical engineering tomes. "Galen Dimosthenis. My husband."

His gaze came to rest on the bare fourth finger of her left hand. "You never said you were married."

"He is deceased." She watched Rhys carefully as she divulged additional facts. "He helped me become a Guild member. We collaborated on the automatons initially."

A note of compassion shown in his eyes. He held the binder out to her. "I'm sorry."

"You didn't know." What would he think of her now that he knew she was a widow? Lydia closed the trunk and made sure the latch was secure. She then reached in her pocket and produced his handkerchief, washed and neatly folded into a square. "I need to return this to you."

He accepted it without a word.

"I should go home and finish packing." Why did it always sound as though she needed to make excuses to leave his presence?

"We leave at first light." Rhys moved the trunk into a corner where it couldn't tip over. "Get plenty of rest."

Knowing sleep would not come easily on her last night in Aspasia, she bent her head to exit the low door of the cargo hold.

***

Rhys remembered what Lydia told him of her deceased husband. How sad. She was too young to be a widow. What happened to Galen Dimosthenis? He wondered during the morning of departure as he rose before dawn to ready the ship to set sail.

By the time daylight came, Malcolm was already barking orders to the crew.

"Ready to go back to the cold Channel waters already?" Rhys quipped as he read over the ship's estimated travel coordinates that Finley prepared yesterday.

Malcolm harrumphed. "I couldna sleep last night. I kept thinking I heard those metal contraptions walking in the cargo hold."

"You should cease reading scary bedtime stories. Lydia disabled the automatons."

"I'm not fond of bringing her on board, either. You know what's said about women on ships."

"Surely you don't believe that old fishmonger's tale about women being bad luck."

Malcolm did his best to pretend otherwise. "It could be trouble keeping the men away from her."

Rhys had already thought about that. "Lydia will have my cabin. I'll stay in the crew's quarters."

"Where is the lass, anyway? Didn't you tell her to be here at first light?"

Rhys lifted his eyes as the sun began its ascent. What was keeping Lydia? Perhaps she was at the palace with the king and Nikolaos. They had yet to arrive to see the crew off.

Finley called down from the door of the navigation room. "Captain, shall we weigh anchor?"

"Shortly. We have to wait on Lady Dimosthenis."

"Look 'round to see if there's another pair of pants running about. She may already be on board." Malcolm's comment produced laughter from the crew.

"Enough jokes. Ready the engine," Rhys ordered.

No sooner had he uttered the phrase that Lydia came striding towards the shore's edge. A man walked with her, bearing one of her smaller travel trunks. She carried the other. Rhys took a longboat to meet them onshore.

Eschewing conventional ladies traveling clothes, she had on fitted dark trousers tucked into black boots. A utilitarian vest was cinched over her blouse with straps that crossed and buckled around her waist. At least no knives or cartridges were present this time.

"Are we ready to sail?" she asked.

Rhys did not let the distraction of her figure, clad within the corseted structuring of her vest and fitted pants, keep him from giving her a piece of his mind. "The crew and I have been ready for an hour."

"I was saying goodbye to my mother. She couldn't watch me sail away. This is my father Hector Korba." She indicated to the older gentleman standing beside her.

Rhys then noticed the resemblance between the two of them. "How do you do, Mr. Korba?"

"Ambassador, I am entrusting you with the safety of my only child. Promise me that she will be protected and receive the utmost respect from you and your men."

"*Baba*," Lydia muttered. "I will be alright."

"I will hear it from the ambassador." The man's eyes never left Rhys.

Rhys saw where Lydia got her boldness from. "Sir, I will personally see to Lady Dimosthenis's every need. No harm will come to her on my watch."

"Nor mine." Nikolaos strode down the embankment, flanked by four guards wheeling a cart piled high with luggage. Dressed for travel, he wore a shorter red robe and dark trousers. "King Sabba insists that Lydia not travel alone. I will accompany her."

Rhys heard Lydia's soft gasp. Her father squared off against Nikolaos.

"What agenda do you have, Lord Abeiron?"

"That of King Sabba's, Hector. I am her appointed guardian. If you don't believe me, ask His Majesty."

Rhys saw the king of Aspasia come down to shore, flanked by ten guards.

Nikolaos wore a satisfied smile as he motioned for the palace guards to bring his trunks forward. "Kindly direct them to my guest cabin, Ambassador Cartret. They will also need accommodations."

"There are no guest cabins." Rhys held his peace in front of Aspasia's king, although he wanted very much to protest Nikolaos's attendance on the journey. "Space is tight on a ship. Lydia has the only private quarters. You'll have to room with the crew."

Nikolaos kept his face expressionless. "I shall do what I must to ensure the lady's protection."

"I can't spare room for your guards."

Sabba scanned the top deck. "I see but a six-man crew, Ambassador."

"Your Majesty," Lydia said, "I saw the ship's lower decks. Most of the space houses the engine. There is a galley and cargo hold, but not spare rooms for passengers."

"I could show you, if you'd prefer," Rhys offered.

"I trust Lady Dimosthenis's observations," the king said. He embraced Lydia. "Godspeed. When you reach New Britannia, send word of your progress."

"I will, Your Majesty."

Sabba nodded to Rhys. "I leave you to set sail. Albeit brief, your visit has been both informing and favorable." With that, he left the beach, along with the palace guards that had deposited Nikolaos's trunks in the sand.

Rhys afforded Lydia and her father a moment to say their goodbyes while he signaled for his crew to cast another longboat to shore. Fifteen minutes later, he stood on deck with Nikolaos and Lydia.

Rhys called for the crew to weigh anchor. The sooner he left the Aspasian port, the sooner he'd be done with surprise changes to his plans. "Follow me, Lydia. I'll escort you to your cabin. Wait here, Lord Abeiron." He secretly enjoyed seeing Nikolaos's face twist as the man was forced to loiter about the deck.

Lydia's precise footsteps followed him. He increased his pace, moving past the surrounding steel walls that were welded to curve around the shape of the vessel. The engine's steady hum could be heard throughout the corridor.

"Rhys, please slow down."

He halted and pivoted on his feet. "Whatever business is between you and Nikolaos, I won't have it affecting this journey."

The ship lurched as it cast off. Lydia stopped herself from crashing into him, splaying her hand against the wall before she could pitch forward. "I didn't know he was coming with us."

"Why is Nikolaos really here?"

She looked behind her as though the chief adviser was hiding on the steps. "I stand to inherit the Aspasian throne if the king and queen don't produce an heir. My husband was Sabba's only next of kin."

"So Nikolaos wants to marry you for the lineage." Rhys's muscles tightened in a flash of hostility as he considered Nikolaos's ambition. "I witnessed his courtly display as he dragged you into the dining hall last week. I take it Sabba is unaware of how you're being treated by his most trusted adviser."

Lydia rubbed her arm as though recalling the event made it hurt. "I snubbed Nikolaos's advances that night."

"He should have heeded."

"It doesn't concern you."

"It does now. You're my responsibility until we reach New Britannia."

Rhys walked to the end of the corridor and unlocked his cabin door. "You'll stay here. Keep the key on you at all times." He gave it to her. "Malcolm will see to your meals."

She closed her fingers around the key. "Can I venture to top deck?"

"Only if I'm with you."

She hooded her eyelids. More sultry than intimidating, but Rhys decided not to bring that to her attention.

"And don't bother the crew. I need them focused on making the journey home."

Lydia pocketed the key. "For what it's worth, I don't like the idea of Nikolaos sailing with me, either."

"Then I suggest you keep your door locked." He left her to attend to his second passenger.

On deck, Nikolaos watched Aspasia grow smaller in the distance. His robe billowed in the breeze. Three days' exposure to saltwater and wind and it would be reduced to an expensive rag to mop the decks. "Has Lydia been seen to?"

"She's my charge now. You needn't worry about her."

"As her guardian, it's my duty to do so."

"She's within her accommodations. My crewmen are not to disturb her. The same applies to you."

"With all due respect, Lady Dimosthenis and I are subjects of Aspasia, not New Britannia." Nikolaos's mouth remained locked in a tight smile.

"You are passengers on my ship. You will abide by my rules. Is that clear?"

"Very well, Ambassador."

"Captain will suffice."

Nikolaos glided down the steps and waited at the base. "My quarters, if you would, Captain."

Rhys glared at him. It was going to be a long voyage.

Chapter 8

After depositing her small toiletry case on the bedside table, along with a pistol given to her by her father, Lydia assessed her new surroundings. There was no mistaking this was Rhys's cabin.

His effects were arranged neatly around the efficiently furnished room. On the polished surface of the mahogany desk, a heavy brass compass served as a paperweight to stationery engraved with Rhys's initials and ambassadorial title.

She proceeded to a narrow door nestled in the corner of the back wall. She opened it to find a water closet with facilities, a sink, and a curious glass cabinet with a copper nozzle protruding from the wall.

Lydia turned a knob. Cold water shot out of the nozzle. She drenched her sleeve as she turned the knob back into its original position. The water flow ceased. That which had fallen swirled on the tiled floor of the cabinet before going down a drain.

Marvelous. Indoor plumbing on a ship. Only the wealthier homes in Aspasia contained such.

Lydia blotted her sleeve with a towel before leaving the water closet. A knock at the cabin door shook her from her musings. "Your ladyship." Malcolm's gruff voice sounded from the other side.

He barged in as soon as she unlocked the door. He shook a wooden tea tray. The teapot clattered against a saucer holding two stacked biscuits. "Where do you want this?"

"The desk." Lydia scurried out of his way before he could run her over in his haste to deposit her breakfast. Tea leaked from the spout to drop on the desk. Muttering an oath, Malcolm used the hem of his shirt to wipe the surface dry.

"I'll come back tonight with supper."

"Thank you, Mr. Clark."

Her expressed gratitude made him slow his harried movement. "I see you discovered the ship's water pipes." Malcolm looked at her wet sleeve. "You'll be in here for the trip duration. I'll bring some sails in need of mending to keep you occupied."

"I…I don't sew, Mr. Clark."

"Don't sew?"

"Well, it's not that I don't. I can't, at least not very well."

"Women tinkerers." Malcolm ducked out of the room like a bull, his head and lumbering shoulders leading the rest of his body.

Lydia poured herself a cup of tea. She shuddered as the bitter liquid hit her tongue. If the British were exacting in their tea preparation, then Malcolm was the exception.

Teacup in hand, she circled the small room again, looking at the brass knobs of the desk and bookcase. Though she stifled the urge to nose around in Rhys's belongings, she couldn't help remain curious. Rhys was bundled with contradictions, the least of which were his assorted occupations of ambassador, COIC agent, and merchantman. Beneath that charm, there was another aspect of him, something not very refined at all. She saw glimpses of it in his dark eyes when he gazed at her for a little too long and in his touch when he shielded her in the Guild. Now she was traveling on a ship with him. Unless she confined herself to her cabin for the entire duration and refused to go up on deck for fresh air, she'd see him again. And often.

Lydia let another sip of bitter tea wash down her throat. Rhys intrigued her, and she didn't know what to do about it.

***

Mediterranean Sea, off the coast of Sardinia

"I should have given Lord Abeiron his own space upon the ship," Rhys remarked to Malcolm on the fourth morning of their voyage. "Then we'd all be able to sleep at night and breathe through our noses."

Nikolaos stood on the other side of the deck, shoulders and head over the rail. Well into a nasty bout of seasickness, he kept the men awake at night in the crew's quarters with the sounds and smells of his distress.

That morning, the crew took breakfast above deck instead of in the galley, where they would be forced to experience Nikolaos's illness in close quarters.

Rhys ate a bowl of porridge. "Have you taken a meal to Lydia yet?"

Malcolm nodded as he swallowed coffee. "Aye, but she didn't answer the door. Her dinner tray was outside, untouched. These Aspasians don't take well to sailing."

"Or she's already homesick." By Rhys's calculations, the ship would reach the open waters of the Atlantic in two days' time.

Malcolm let his mug clatter against the ship's rail. "Maybe self-starvation is the lass' way of not going to New Britannia."

Rhys mused on Lydia's circumstances. Since the agreement was signed, he pondered the merit of granting her a full production license after all. She made a compelling argument. But what would the COIC say? "She wouldn't starve herself to prove a point. She's faithful to stand by her work."

"You think so?"

"I know so. She's proved honest."

Malcolm took another swig of coffee. "But Rhys, she has that look on her face, the kind all women get when they start to meddling around. I hope you hid anything important in your cabin."

Rhys thought about his COIC correspondence locked away in the bookcase. They detailed his prior missions. Unless Lydia broke a glass panel, she wouldn't gain access to them. Still…

"I'll see about her." He set his empty breakfast bowl on the damp floor of the deck and went to his cabin.

Lydia's breakfast tray rested outside the door. Steam rose from the bowl of porridge and condensed along a portion of the wall. He rapped his knuckles on the door. "Lydia?"

He heard her feet pad across the floor before she opened the door. Rhys escorted her on deck yesterday afternoon, but overnight her face had lost its vibrancy, replaced by a sickly, slightly greenish pallor. A fine sheen of perspiration covered her brow. Her eyes were listless as she looked up at him.

"You look terrible."

"And a fine morning to you, too." She started to shut the door.

He stuck his foot in the frame. "You should eat. It'll help with the seasickness."

Lydia stared at the gray porridge as though it were a bowl of worms.

"Tea, then?"

"The brew was a bit strong for me last time."

"Malcolm's experience with brewing only goes so far as the local tavern." When she failed to laugh, Rhys let the matter of eating and drinking rest. "At least come on deck for air."

She closed the door behind her and staggered forward. She had changed into a long tunic and pants. Her hair was brushed back in loose curls that rested between her shoulder blades. "One would think a ship with an engine wouldn't pitch so often."

"Blame the water currents. We're coming upon the Atlantic."

But Rhys felt a change in the air as they went topside. Though accustomed to the motion of sailing, he noticed that the ship did cut a choppy path through the water. The Mediterranean wasn't usually so rough. Perhaps the ship got off course. He intended to have Finley brief him on their coordinates.

The navigator found him first. He carried a spyglass in his hand. "Captain, a word."

Lydia wandered off to the railing on the starboard side, leaving Rhys to converse with the crewmember.

"Where are we, Finley?"

"Twenty knots out from Sardinia. Look." Finley jabbed his finger toward the eastern sky before giving him the spyglass. "The storm approaches over the horizon. It just appeared when you went below deck. Red sky at morning..."

He didn't need to finish the rest of that well-known verse. Rhys gritted his teeth as he viewed the crimson heavens above the rising sun. Dark clouds moved in. "That will reach us before noon."

The ship reached a small breaker and dipped. That was enough for Lydia to leave her post at the railing. "I think I've had enough fresh air for the time being." She passed Rhys and walked on unsteady feet down to the second level.

He remembered Nikolaos situated on the other side of the ship. The man's head disappeared over the rails again. "Someone take Lord Abeiron to quarters before he falls overboard."

The engineer O'Neil accepted the task.

"Captain." Two of the deckhands, Duncan and Thomas, ran towards Rhys.

Duncan was the first to catch his breath. "Ship sighted east at three o' clock."

Rhys aimed the spyglass in the appropriate direction. Through the lens, he saw the sails and three masts of a frigate. The vessel was coming upon them. He adjusted the spyglass lens to focus on the flag flying from the highest mast. A crimson *jolie rouge*.

"What is it?" Malcolm came with porridge bowl in hand.

"Pirates," Rhys ground out. "French."

He marched to the row of flip switches on the forecastle deck. He pulled down three, shutting off reserve valves for the water pipes, galley stove, and boilers. He flipped two in the upward position before returning to the main deck and shouting, "All hands."

Within seconds, five crewmen assembled from all sides of the top deck, exchanging worried glances as they awaited his orders.

"I've deviated all power to the engine and side cannons. Smythe, find O'Neil and both of you go monitor the engine room. Malcolm, steer us northwest of that ship. We can't rely on the ship's self-configuration mechanism. Finley, stand by him with navigation. Duncan, Thomas, I need you both to man the cannons in case they need reloading."

"Are we gonna make a stand against the pirates?" Duncan asked.

"If need be, but our ship is fast. I intend to outdistance them."

Finley raised his eyes skyward. "I don't know how fast we can outdistance a storm and pirates with all that weight in the cargo hold."

Rhys saw Finley's point. The extra weight of the automatons did slow them down, but not enough to make the ship a sitting duck in the water. "We'll make it."

He thought about Lydia, but he didn't have time to warn her of the pirates. The best thing she could do was stay in the cabin and pray for better weather, a speedy engine, and quick cannons.

As the crew moved to carry out his orders, Rhys went to gather rope to secure the supplies stationed on deck. The pirate frigate was getting closer. All the while, the storm gathered overhead.

***

Thunder jarred Lydia awake.

She sat up in bed where she dozed off, despite her queasiness. The thrum of the engine grew louder until the sound resonated in the walls and through the furniture. It sounded like it was clogged.

She donned her boots before standing, and promptly fell back onto the bed as the room tilted. The glass panel of the bookcase opened and spilled tens of volumes on the floor, along with her books and papers she placed on the outside mantle.

Lydia threw all of her belongings back into her trunk and shut the lid. She picked up the encyclopedias. A set of folded papers lay at the foot of the bookcase.

She unfolded them to see if they belonged to her.

The letterhead read *Cabinet of International Curiosities*. Correspondence from Rhys's organization. No, it wasn't correspondence, but orders of some kind. Lydia thumbed through the documents and saw references to coastal towns and trade routes along the Mediterranean. She spotted the words *mission* and *reconnaissance* on the pages.

The hairs on the back of her neck stood on end. Since when did a merchant need to partake in reconnaissance?

Rhys lied to her about the details of his line of work. Or rather, withheld information. He came to Aspasia to purchase the automatons, but what else did he collect? Lydia opened the tenth volume encyclopedia. A third of its text had been carved out, allowing for the stashing of documents. She shoved the papers into it and stuck the volume back into the case. Just as she closed the glass panel, something hit the ship.

Everything that wasn't nailed to the floor came crashing down.

Lydia sprinted from the cabin into the dim corridor and dashed up the stairs. Water seeped through the door leading topside, splashing the front of her legs in cold brine. The ship rocked, tossing her against the wall. Lydia regained balance and pushed the door open.

Rain poured on the deck. Rhys stood in the center shouting orders as the crew scrambled to furl the rigging. The men moved in an organized chaos, ropes and tethers flying everywhere.

Lydia hit the deck as a cable flew past her head. Thunder partially drowned out her cry of surprise.

Rhys heard her and turned. His hair was plastered to his head as rain drenched his shirt. "Get below deck. We're under pirate attack."

Chapter 9

A sudden coldness ran through her. Lydia raised her neck and looked starboard side at a ship that rivaled the size of *The Enlightened*. Though it was not close enough for its crew to board, she saw the men dressed in motley tatters scrambling to light cannons and ready their boarding axes. The rain and rough winds diminished their efforts, but by no means halted them.

"Fire," a shout came from the starboard side as one of Rhys's crewmen flipped a switch. The sound that Lydia heard before was magnified eightfold as all of *The Enlightened's* cannonry let loose their iron rounds.

The blast sent tremors through the deck as the cannons pounded the other ship. *The Enlightened's* timbers creaked as waves bucked against the hull. Lydia grabbed a railing for support. One of the crewmen scurried past.

"Captain, the ship's taking in water. The pirates breached the hull at the waterline."

"Patch it best you can." Rhys twisted to look at the engine's air vents as they sputtered water and seaweed on deck. "Smythe and O'Neil have to get that engine unclogged. Lydia, I told you to get below deck," he growled.

"I can get the automatons to help you."

"And let the pirates know we have them in our possession? Why do you think they're after us?"

The ship bucked again as a giant wave approached. Water rose above the rails and over Lydia's head, slamming her with frigid fists. The force shook her hold off the rails and sent her feet careening out from under her.

She slammed shoulder first onto the deck. The shock of the fall knocked the wind from her. Lydia opened her mouth only to receive an onslaught of water. Coughing, she got back on her feet before a second smaller wave washed over the deck.

A pair of strong arms seized upon her waist and hauled her backwards. "If you don't get back below, I'll toss you down myself." Rhys dragged her in the direction of the door, kicked it open, and did exactly that.

Lydia caught herself from landing on her face. She looked back just in time to see him bang the door closed. The bolt slammed home on the other side.

The sounds of the storm and battle produced an eerie symphony within the interior of the ship. The floorboards moaned beneath Lydia's feet while the wall facing the exterior of the ship seemed barely able to contain the roaring water that battered the heavy wooden frame. With each pitch and sway of the vessel, the sound of glass breaking and objects falling was not far behind.

Lydia clutched her stomach as her own fear produced a new bout of nausea. She groaned as the bile rose in her chest and burned the back of her throat.

"Lydia?" Nikolaos's voice sounded from down the corridor.

She turned as he rounded the bend, stumbling as the ship rocked hard to the left. The hem of his trousers was wet and soiled in the water at his feet. "Have we hit a squall?" His wan pallor had grown paler since the voyage commenced.

"Yes." Lydia braced her feet in a wide stance as she put one hand on each wall. From her perspective, the floor tilted and dipped as though she were in a flour sifter. "And we're being attacked by pirates."

A splintering noise resounded from above. Surely that wasn't the ship breaking apart. Not when she and Nikolaos were locked down below. "Rhys locked the topside door."

Nikolaos tottered forward, choking back what had to be his breakfast. "Does he intend for us to go down with the ship?"

Lydia strained to hear voices above deck. All she heard was the roar of the ocean and the clamber of boots pounding from stern to prow. Were they pirates or Rhys's crew?

Another cannon fired. The groan of a wooden structure followed, ending with a heavy crash. Lydia felt the impact's reverberations in her chest. The din above ceased. Only the straining engine sounded.

Were Rhys and the crew still onboard? She climbed to the topside door and pounded on it, calling out. No one answered.

"The ship is taking in more water." Nikolaos pointed to the topside door, where water sloshed, rushing in through the foot of the entrance. Two of the light fixtures floated, knocked loose from their wall mounts.

Lydia drew several gulps of air and willed herself to keep calm. She jumped down to the floor. "We need to split the door and get to the longboats."

"You mean to the other ship."

She stared aghast at Nikolaos, but his face remained very serious.

"Whoever these pirates are, we must cooperate with them. There is no other way off this vessel alive. We will give them money, the contents of the cargo hold, whatever they want."

She curled her lips in disgust at his craven behavior. "We can't give up. We made an agreement."

"This is no time for holding steadfast to the agreement with the ambassador." Nikolaos shadowed her. "He and his crew abandoned ship."

"We don't know that," Lydia said as she fought her fear that Rhys and the crew had all been swept away by the waves.

Above, a large object rolled across the deck before it came to a halt midway. Lydia heard the timbers creak against its weight. Thunder rattled the walls. The metal structures of the ship caught the vibration and issued a discordant, tinny response. A clanging issued from a different part of the ship. "Did you hear that?"

Nikolaos's shoulders sagged as he worked to move his ill body. "Hear what?"

"A voice. I can just make it out." Over the rain that steadily bulleted the ship, Lydia detected the distressed calls of a man. "It's coming from the engine room below us." She fled for the stairs leading to the third deck.

Nikolaos straggled behind her. "The water is rising. We must leave."

The calls grew louder as they neared the stairs. Water rushed down the steps. Lydia plunged one foot after the other down into the swirling water, hoping she'd find a foothold on the slippery metal grating. "Anyone here?" she shouted.

Both doors to the engine room and cargo hold were vaulted closed.

The male voice sounded from behind the entrance of the engine room. "The door is jammed."

Water pooled over Lydia's boots and soaked her feet. She pulled on the door's spindle wheel handle. The water formed a seal around the door, preventing her from getting it to open. "Nikolaos, help me."

He still stood on the stairs, looking disparagingly at the steady swell of water flooding the base.

"Nikolaos, please."

He trudged down.

The man on the inside of the engine room door began to beat upon the frame. "The water pump's broken. You've got to get us out."

She spoke in a calm voice, even though her own distress was growing. "I'm going to try to pull the door open, but I need you to push as well. Are you ready?"

"Ready."

Nikolaos grabbed the handle with Lydia.

"Now."

The three of them worked against the force of the water. A sliver of space appeared between the frame, widening until the seal broke. Both Lydia and Nikolaos were hit with a blast of warm air and steam.

The man heaved a sigh of relief as he was once again free. Lydia recognized him as the young, ginger-haired crewmember Smythe. Over his shirt and soaked trousers, he wore a leather engineer's apron with a toolbelt around his waist. "I've been calling for I don't know how long. O'Neil and me went down to see about the engine when it started to take in water."

Lydia saw a second man slumped against the left wall below the engine, water creeping up to his chest. A thin trickle of blood ran from a gash at his temple. She navigated through the jungle of pumps and drainage pipes and uptake valves to get to him. He was unresponsive, eyes closed. "What happened to him?"

Smythe straightened O'Neil into a seated position. He shouted over the metal drum that made up the engine's lower half. "Engine valve struck him. The pressure got too high. We were changing it to draw water to the pump."

Water shot out from where the valve separated from the drain pipes. Steam combined with it, heating the room an additional twenty degrees. Near the back wall, the water pump gurgled uselessly as the pipe that connected it to the engine hung loose and scraped against the floor.

Lydia assessed the clogged engine and drainage system. "Can you reattach the valve?"

"Aye." Smythe swiped a thick-gloved hand across his freckled brow. "But I need someone to hold the main line steady."

Lydia felt Nikolaos's cold, wet hand clamp down on her shoulder. "We've no time."

She edged out of his grip. "There's still a chance to drain the water. And even if the ship can't be saved, we can't leave these men."

His eyes became hard. "Do you want to die like your husband, Lydia? Come with me now."

"The door's closing." Smythe raced to the stairs.

With an agility Lydia had never thought Nikolaos possessed, he sprang past Smythe and clambered up. Before either man could get his hands on the door, it swung shut on its frame. The water pressure behind it forced a vacuum seal.

Smythe drew air in through his teeth and cursed. "None are us leaving the ship now."

Nikolaos beat upon the door, failing to make so much as a dent. Lydia shut her ears to the noise as she attempted to quell panic rising in her own mind.

"Enough," she said aloud.

Nikolaos and Smythe looked at her. Lydia stood up and girded her arms around the unconscious O'Neil's chest. The water made it easier for her to drag him to the stairs. "Nikolaos, keep his head above water. Smythe and I will reattach the valve and divert the water to the pump."

Smythe removed O'Neil's gloves and gave them to her before handing the man off to Nikolaos's care. "You'll need these. I have the valve and connecting pipe." He fished them from the foot of the stairs, tucking the pipe in his apron pocket.

The water line climbed to Lydia's knees. She waded to the engine and ducked under the steam torrent where the valve broke off.

"Careful," Smythe warned.

She closed her hands around the pipe, feeling water pressure and heat course beneath the copper.

Smythe angled the valve and pushed it through the steam. The pipe shook in Lydia's grasp as he worked quickly to tighten the valve with a wrench. Hot water sprayed his apron as it was now able to flow from two connectors. He turned the valve to divert the flow. Then he retrieved the connecting pipe and attached it to the valve body. "I need to secure it to the pump."

While he carried the pipe along the wall, Lydia glanced at Nikolaos. He had dragged O'Neil to the top of the stairs and stood over him. Nikolaos faced the door, waiting for the slightest indication that the water seal would break.

Smythe called for Lydia to let the pipe go. She moved over to the valve and waited as he maneuvered the pipe to the water pump attachment.

"Is it fixed?" Nikolaos turned around and took notice of their effort.

"We'll see." Smythe slogged through the water to get to the manual control levers on the wall. He cranked until the bellows of the pump contracted and expanded. He nodded for Lydia to reverse the valve.

Once she did, water flowed into the pump. They listened for several minutes as the bellows sent it through a hose and out of the ship.

"It's working. The water line's beginning to recede." Excitement built in Smythe's voice.

Lydia saw the mark on the wall as the water level dropped an inch. A small start, but it was enough to give her hope. "*The Enlightened* won't sink today."

Nikolaos pushed against the door. "It will if that breach isn't found."

"We'll look for it when the water drops." Smythe continued to work on the manual levers. "See to O'Neil and find the crew."

"Can you not see that this ship is not operational? The crew is gone. I'll see to myself and Lydia." Nikolaos put his shoulder against the door and prepared to give it a shove. The water seal gave way and the door opened before he had a chance.

Rhys stood before him. "Care to repeat yourself, Lord Abeiron? I'm afraid my men and I only heard that last part."

Chapter 10

Rhys entered the engine room, flanked by Finley and a muscled crewmember whose name Lydia did not know. Rhys's clothes were soaked from the storm. His shirt was torn at the shoulder, and he bore a haggard, worn face. Still, his authoritative stance broke through. "We made the pirates turn back. The storm should keep them from returning. "

At the sight of the captain very much alive, though somewhat weathered, the tension ebbed from Lydia's body, replaced by relief and an urge to rush and put her arms around him. She curbed the swell of emotion and clung to the network of pipes on the wall instead.

"What happened to O'Neil?" Rhys inspected the still unconscious engineer.

"Hit by a flying valve," Smythe spoke.

"Finley, Duncan, take him to the infirmary table and have Malcolm look at him. Was this an accident?" Rhys's probing stare fell on Nikolaos.

Nikolaos proceeded to save face. "Lydia and I found him that way when we entered this room."

Rhys continued his descent as the crewmen tended to O'Neil. "I told Lady Dimosthenis to stay in the cabin where it was safe." He turned to Lydia. His mouth reduced to a firm line of disapproval.

Surely he wasn't going to scold her like a child before everyone. She lifted her chin and stared him down.

Water covered Rhys's boots when he walked out to her. He spoke below his breath, his voice filled with a sarcasm that was only a little more saturated than the floor he stood on. "You'll pardon me for inconveniencing you with orders, my lady, but they are meant to keep you in one piece."

Her breathing quickened. "I thought the ship was no longer in one piece. I heard a loud explosion. How could I stay put after that?" She matched his stare until Smythe's strident voice broke through in her ears.

"Captain, the hull breach needs patching up."

Rhys nodded to the apprentice engineer. "Thomas will see to it once we get O'Neil on deck. I'll aid you as well, after I see to our passengers' safety." He referred to both Lydia and Nikolaos, but he didn't shift his eyes from her as she edged by him.

Lydia left the engine room and stepped back into the ship's corridor. Nikolaos and Rhys came behind.

"You must not blame us for employing our own means of escape, Captain," Nikolaos further placated Rhys when they ascended to the second level.

"Since you refused to aid O'Neil and Smythe, you can do their share of the work on top deck. See to it." He gave Nikolaos a look that dared him to object.

Nikolaos spared a few choice words for the ship's captain. Lydia heard his Greek mutterings when he sidled past her to go upstairs.

"He forgets I can understand every word." Rhys walked beside Lydia. In the narrow confines of the ship, his arm brushed against hers.

Heat ran along her skin at the contact. "I don't think he's learned how to swear in English yet."

"He'll have ample opportunity before this voyage is through. The ship needs multiple repairs, not to mention extensive bailing. I've yet to inspect the hold for damage."

Lydia thought of the automatons and the rest of her personal belongings stored in the cargo hold. However, the welfare of the crew and the ship were of more importance at the moment. "Where did those pirates come from?"

"France. Broussard's gaggle of sea thieves spotted *The Enlightened* and thought to take the ship for their own."

Lydia shook her shoulders free of tension. All of them came too close to being at the mercy of pirates.

The door to the cabin hung wide open as Lydia left it when she dashed out. The water had drained, but the bedcovers lay ruined at the foot of the bed. Her trunk didn't tip over, thankfully, but papers from Rhys's desk had spilled from the drawers and formed a pulpy mass on the floor.

Water squelched and bubbled from the rug as Rhys walked upon it. He surveyed the open bookcase. Lydia tensed as he set the volumes in order one after the other.

He shut the glass panel. "Gather your remaining dry clothing and blankets. You'll have to make do with our company on deck until this room is dry again."

Lydia set to her task, grateful that he decided not to leaf through the encyclopedias. "How did Mr. Clark and the others fare?"

"Most are injured but all are accounted for."

His succinct manner made her uneasy. Since the voyage began, Rhys's polished veneer chipped bit by bit until today's violent storm and pirate attack scraped it away completely. What remained was raw, determined, and would not tolerate defiance from anyone. The similar demeanor of the pirates that she fought off from Aspasia's shores came to mind. Perhaps the perils of sailing gave all seafaring men a coarse edge.

She threw items into her toiletry case. "You have things to tend to. I'll make it up to topside shortly. You needn't wait for me."

"I can't have you traipsing around alone. The men are ill at ease. Half of them think having you onboard brought on the dual misfortune."

She clutched a stack of shirts and a set of linens in her arms. "When you speak like that, I believe you think as they do."

"I'm not one for superstitions, but I do expect obedience from anyone that sails under my flag."

Lydia's weary sigh was muffled by the linens as she shifted them to one arm. She reached for the toiletry case with the other. "All I heard was the storm battering the ship. I thought you were gone. Fallen overboard or—or swept away." She stopped, ashamed of herself when she realized her voice had grown high and distraught. The last thing Rhys needed to think was that he brought a fretful, histrionic woman aboard.

He came forward and took the linens from her arms. He lingered in front, his body separated from hers by a few articles of folded fabric. "I would not leave you."

He waited for her to come before he closed the door to the cabin.

***

Rhys knew he locked the glass panel of the bookcase well before Lydia came to occupy his cabin. The pitching of the ship must have knocked the tumbler loose during the storm. He meant to return and see if the COIC mission papers were in their rightful place. Hopefully, he wouldn't find them in the mass of pulp that sat by the desk, sponging more water from the carpet.

The pile of linens caressed Rhys's jawline when he shifted them in order to open the topside door. Their soft texture and clean juniper scent tantalized as though they were Lydia herself. Either the passing storm managed to lay waste to his senses, or Malcolm was right. It was fast becoming perilous to bring Lydia onboard. Even her bed sheets were getting the better of him.

She moved through the door ahead of him, having no inkling of the thoughts she stirred within him as she went past. Her hair hung wet down her back, producing a line of moisture that snaked down her shirt to well at the curve that was the small of her back.

Her hips undulated as she walked ahead of him on deck and jolted to a halt an instant later. "There was an explosion." She assessed the fallen mainmast as it laid split in two upon the deck. Both pieces partially obstructed access to the quarterdeck. All that remained of the cables was scattered among broken crates and frayed rigging lines.

"Pirate cannon struck the mast." Rhys kicked a piece of glass from a broken bottle over the rails. "It made short work of just about everything else."

Lydia surveyed the four crewman and Nikolaos as they labored to clear the deck of debris. She drew a ragged breath when she saw their injuries. O'Neil's head injury was now bandaged. Thomas's leg was bloodied from where a timber split off the prow and pierced the muscle of his calf. Malcolm's hands and arms bore the angry purple and red abrasions from grabbing a cable when it broke loose from the mast. The rest of the crew suffered varying degrees of gashes and scrapes.

Rhys headed to the quarterdeck "I'll see you to the navigation room." A rumble of distant thunder made him look heavenward. The gunmetal skies were ready to release another onslaught of damage.

Rhys seethed at their predicament. How easily a sea squall and French pirates endangered the lives of his men and nearly destroyed the ship. Their chances of getting to New Britannia safely, let alone on schedule, were sorely diminished. It would cost them precious days, if not weeks, to regroup. No telling how long it would take to patch the hull, hammer new boards, and get the engine unclogged.

As expected, Lydia uttered a protest before he could light the lanterns and set her belongings down on the chart table in the navigation room. "I can't sit idle while your crew salvages the ship. Allow me to help with something."

Rhys found a swab left by the ship's rails. Next to it was a tin pail. He set it at Lydia's feet with a clatter. "You do know how to swab a deck, don't you?"

"It's no different from cleaning a workroom floor." She bent to pick up a blue-finned fish that somehow washed upon the deck and flopped into the navigation room. "Except at home, these don't make it past the beach." She tossed the wiggling creature back into the ocean.

Rhys admired her resilience, if not her knack for discovering every nook and cranny of the ship. The navigation room held only a chart table with an etched depiction of the known world and map collections of sailing routes and ports of call, so he had no reason to be concerned.

Seeing her squared away for the time being, he returned down to the engine room to check on Smythe. The apprentice had the water drainage system working at normal speed again. The pump drained half of the room's water volume.

"Captain?" Smythe scratched the back of his neck, as was his nervous habit. "I didn't say anything before, but the lady helped me repair the water valve."

"She did?"

"Yes, sir. I didn't put her to work on purpose. Her travel companion, the Aspasian lord, refused to do anything. It was every man for himself, by his reckoning."

"Nikolaos is learning fast that his methods don't work on this ship. But, Smythe, why didn't you speak up about Lady Dimosthenis?"

The young man spoke with care. "You were stern with her. I didn't want to appear as though I was challenging your authority."

Was he so harsh with Lydia that even the crew noticed? To think, he reprimanded her for leaving her quarters. If she had done as he instructed, none of them would have kept their heads above water. Rhys uttered, "I have a number of things to remedy on this ship."

Smythe scratched his neck again. "I meant no disrespect, Captain."

"Not you, Smythe. You've done well. There are other matters I need to address." Rhys went to check on the crewmen at work patching up the hull.

***

After Lydia moved her belongings to the corner of the navigation room, she did her best to mop water from the interior without disturbing the sensitive instruments and collections of maps and charts along the walls. As she finished tossing out the last bucketful of water, the rains returned, sending a cold, gusty downpour through the room's interior. Swab in hand, she scurried to shut the door.

Seconds later, Malcolm burst in, ruining her efforts to keep the room dry by tracking in wet, grimy footprints. Finley followed, adding more work for her to do.

"Confound this rain, Finley. We need to set a new course away from the line of storms and pirate bays." Malcolm reached for the nearest chart from a slot in the wall and threw it upon the table. He didn't see Lydia behind the door.

Nor did Finley. "I told you, it's no good if we make our heading now. The hull's being patched. Besides, the winds blew us off course." He removed the chart and flipped open a case built into the bottom right corner of the tabletop. A compass appeared off the southern tip of Africa. "Look. This storm's interfered with all the navigational instruments."

Lydia swallowed. "So we're lost?"

Both men looked to her for the first time. Finley's eyes narrowed. He cleared his throat. "I wouldn't say that. Once the storm passes, the instruments should work again."

The ambiguity of his statement left her unsettled. Malcolm rotated his column of a neck Finley's way. Even from her vantage point, Lydia could see the blue vein pulse on the side. "And what are we supposed to do until then? Let the ship keep runnin' adrift?"

"There's little else we can do. The mast is down, the lower levels are flooded, and the engine is clogged."

"For all the rarefied and newfangled contraptions on this 'modern vessel', I'd sooner swim to the nearest shore." Malcolm banged a fist on the

67

table, sending the compass back into the Atlantic. "Mayhap I'll reach another island. Only instead of automatons, someone will have engineered a better navigator."

Finley clenched his lower jaw. "I cannot be to blame for a sudden squall."

Malcolm pressed on in his mockery. "I think I'll commission her ladyship to build an iron navigator this very moment."

Lydia grimaced at his inclusion of her in the argument.

Finley ended the conversation with a bit more refinement. "I'll find our direction as soon as the equipment is operational. Until then, the captain has given me other work to do. If you'll excuse me." The nails in his boot soles struck the floor as he ventured back into the wind and rain on deck.

"Close that door," Malcolm ordered Lydia.

She wondered if risking pneumonia from the chilling rain would be a better alternative to being in closed confines with Malcolm. The bosun appeared ready to lay waste to the little room. She kept the deck swab with her as she shut the door and came to stand across from him at the table.

He brooded over the Americas on the map, although she guessed his mind was not fixated on the Florida peninsula. "Worthless navy whelp. I have more years at sea than he. I don't know why the COIC saw fit to have him as part of the crew. On their 'state of the art sailcraft' at that. Devil take him and this industrial nonsense." Malcolm opened the compass case again and studied the needle as it moved in an endless circle. "Why are you in here?"

Lydia realized he was talking to her instead of at her. "The cabin is flooded."

He grunted as he watched the compass needle twist its way around the eight directions. "Can your machines' motors get the ship going again?"

"None of them are big enough."

"Sails it is, then. I'll get us back on course by the morrow if Finley won't." Malcolm stampeded his way from the navigation room.

Rain coated the floor again before Lydia got to the door. She left it open by a crack and watched the crewmen labor on deck. Behind them, the night sky merged with the black ocean on the horizon.

Another sight stole her attention. A lantern light floated across the deck and up the quarterdeck as though it were being carried by a specter. It came to a stop at the door. The light illuminated half of Rhys's face and left the other in shadow. "Are you going to let me in?"

Lydia moved for him to enter. "I didn't know who you were."

"I left a cask of freshwater for you by the door." He set the lantern on the table, along with a flask, a pewter cup, and a small platter of hardtack, an apple, and some Aspasian dried figs. "It's all that's available from the galley until the flooding subsides."

Her stomach growled at the sight of the simple fare. It occurred to her that she hadn't eaten all day. She closed the door on herself and the captain. "How are the men this evening?"

"Cold. Wet. Alive. No man on this ship will let himself be done in by a squall or pirates. Not one from the crew, at least." His tone darkened as he referred to Nikolaos. He opened the flask and poured a dark liquid into the cup. "Every crewman gets a reward ration of rum tonight." He held the cup out to her.

"I didn't do anything."

"Don't insult me, Lydia. You helped Smythe fix the water pump, thereby saving the ship."

She took the cup. "Thank you. If you don't mind, I would eat something first."

Rhys closed the flask. "Of course."

"Aren't you having a drink?"

"I will when I rejoin the crew."

Lydia admired him for valuing his crew and rewarding them for their hard work. Of the men she had seen in high positions, most looked down on their subordinates, refusing to regard them as fellow human beings. Rhys commanded respect, but also gave it to his men in kind. He saw them as his equals, and from what she witnessed in Malcolm, Smythe, and a few others of his crew, they were all the more loyal to him for it.

She set the cup down and began to eat. The hardtack was flavorless, but it felt good to put solid food in her stomach again after days of being ill.

Rhys nibbled on a fig. "The storm cured your seasickness."

"Only to replace it with a fear of drowning."

"You had that well before the storm."

"Oh?"

"I've watched you cast a wary eye at the waves and brace yourself every time the ship pitched more than usual."

"I'm not accustomed to sailing long distances. Those French pirates didn't help, either." It didn't seem appropriate to tell Rhys that Galen's fate also affected her views of sailing, so she remained silent on the matter. She didn't want to leave herself any more vulnerable and exposed before him. "Do you always watch me so closely, Rhys?"

His dark, molten gaze was inescapable. "I find myself doing so without intention. You're an attractive woman, Lydia."

Warmth curled up her neck. He noticed her in a way that no man had in a long time. His direct and heated stare was ripe with desire as it traveled from her face to the bare skin peeking out from her collar before coming to settle again on her mouth. Lydia moistened her dry lips. What else did he notice? Could he somehow sense the way she was drawn to him as well?

She shouldn't feel this way about a man so soon. Not when there were important things to accomplish, and certainly not after learning that Rhys operated as a spy for New Britannia.

"It's cold." Lydia followed the abrupt randomness of her words with an equally awkward move to get away from the table and find a jacket from her clothing bundle.

She didn't get far. Rhys's warm hand came to cover her fingers. He touched her shirt cuff. "No wonder you're cold. Your clothes are damp." He moved his fingertips beneath the cuff and gently rubbed the sensitive skin under her wrist.

Lydia's senses awakened at once. Her nerves tingled beneath his touch, sending the sensation traveling throughout her body. She peered at him through her lashes.

"And you're getting gooseflesh. You should change into something warmer."

She knew that her reaction had very little to do with the room's temperature. Rhys's heated expression told her that he knew it, too. She put her hand on his, not allowing him to go further, but not pushing him away, either. Rough calluses lined his thumb and palm, the strong hand of a man accustomed to vigorous work. "I will change clothes when you leave. I don't require assistance."

"I wasn't offering any." He drew her to him, closing his arm around her waist before she could stop him.

Lydia's palms flattened against his chest. She felt his heartbeat pulse a strong, steady rhythm. Before she could utter a word, he lowered his mouth to hers and kissed her hard.

Chapter 11

Mediterranean Sea, coordinates unknown

Lydia closed her eyes as Rhys's kiss produced a dizzying effect of surprise and longing. Feelings that had lain dormant now rushed to awaken. Her blood raced as her heart pumped a fierce beat to match his, drowning out the patter of rain and wind that battered against the ship outside. She wrapped her arms around his neck, yielding to his strength as he held her in a tight embrace.

He coaxed her lips apart with the tip of his tongue. A wave of pleasure raced to her core as she tasted him, an intoxicating, masculine mix of passion, vitality, and the salt sea. She felt the soft tug of his fingers through her hair as he tilted her head back.

"You do not kiss like a gentleman." Her voice was a throaty whisper when he took his lips away from her mouth and pressed them against her neck.

Rhys pushed a tangle of curls behind her ear. "You don't sound too disappointed." He spoke low in her ear, his words carried by that sensual, musical Welsh lilt that lulled her into helplessness.

"I don't know how I feel." She closed her eyes again as he nibbled her earlobe. She heard the breathlessness of her own voice. "One moment you make me so—" He interrupted her with another kiss. "Disagreeable and the next—I—stop that. You're distracting me on purpose."

"You think you don't distract me, Lydia?" His voice deepened with a yearning that both startled and excited her. "You've been my focus for this entire mission, despite my efforts to maintain priority."

"Yes, priority. To our countries." She broke away from him and backed away. Her body protested with an ache that left her mortified by its reaction. "We're breaching protocol. You hardly know me."

"A circumstance that I've been in the process of amending."

"I certainly don't know much about you."

"You knew enough to return a kiss." His eyes followed her towards the back of the room.

Ashamed of herself, she used her arms as a shield, crossing them in front of her chest. "I wasn't thinking clearly."

"I beg to differ. Your actions showed perfect agreement with the desires of your mind." His dimple appeared in the glimmer of a knowing smile. "The language of the body rarely can be hidden. One of the first lessons COIC agents are taught before being sent into the field."

"Stop trying to impress me with your agency's tactics." She rubbed her forehead as a headache started to form. "My lapse in judgment is due to the day's events. They've tried me."

"No, facing danger has done away with your pretense. It took such to bring out the passion you've kept secret."

His words peeled her layers of defense apart, exposing the tender core. In Aspasia she had been orderly and exacting, but Rhys brought out another aspect in her. He coaxed a daring spirit within her that sought the company of a man and the possibility of falling in love again, notions that were getting the better of her every day that she spent in close proximity to him. Her life and work had no place for such volatility, but with Rhys, those passions found their home.

She scrambled to deflect his observations. "Don't speak to me of secrets. Today's events revealed things about you, too. "

He lifted his eyebrows. The rest of his chiseled features remained immobile. "Was that why my bookcase was open?"

Lydia stood at the precipice of the hole she just dug for herself. She couldn't walk away from the edge now. "I found your COIC mission papers," she confessed.

"You've been spying." He availed himself of his ardor before her eyes, though some of it lingered in the tenseness of which he held his body and in his measured stare.

"They fell out of the bookcase when the ship took cannon fire. I wasn't spying, but according to those documents, you were. In the Mediterranean and in East Asia, to be specific."

"By Order of Her Royal Majesty, I'm an importer of international goods as well as secrets."

It stunned Lydia that he didn't make any denials. She remained at the wall. "You lied to me. You did come to Aspasia to spy."

"My mission was to procure those automatons. Nothing else." He reached the door of the room in two long strides. The breadth of his shoulders left little space between him and the doorframe. "I operate in affairs of state. You saw diplomacy during our negotiations, but my COIC duties can involve far more. Sometimes reconnaissance, and, as today's skirmish illustrated, the use of force."

She took a deep breath of tension-riddled air. "Would you have resorted to force if King Sabba refused to sell the automatons?"

"I would have made a different offer."

"I'm hardly comforted by that admission."

Firm resolve settled on his face, closing off the remaining traces of warmth that he'd shown her just minutes before. "You'll have to accept that there are things about me you can never know."

She raised her chin in defiance. "Even if I had chosen to remain in your arms?"

No qualifying answer came from Rhys. "As you said, we breached protocol. It won't happen again."

"Never," she affirmed. It hurt to hear his declaration, but despite her mixed emotions, she had no choice but to agree. It was the right thing to do, even if it felt wrong. She bit down on her lower lip, which was already starting to bruise. "And I don't say that just because of duty. I can't embrace a man who abides in secrets."

"You just did." He pointed out the obvious with sharp alacrity.

"Don't jest. You know what I mean. Despite my lapse in letting you hold me and put your lips on mine, I could never allow it to go farther. I may be widowed, but I haven't divorced my principles."

"Principles, I understand. But is that what you consider what we shared? A lapse?" His anger brimmed as he latched on to the one word that demoted the emotions they just experienced. Lydia realized then that she used the wrong term, but it was too late. Rhys smoldered.

"In that case, I am even more motivated to find our coordinates speedily. I won't have you suffer these lapses for much longer." He closed the door with a quiet but affirmative click.

Lydia locked it after him and stood listening to his receding footsteps in the rain. His words had a right to sting her. She rejected him. Disappointment crept into every fiber of her body. She just saved herself from committing a big mistake. So why did she feel as though something were lost?

***

Rhys forgot his lamp. He left it on the chart table of the navigation room, but decided not to go back for it. Lydia made it very clear that she had no desire for him to come near her again tonight, and never in the fashion that took place.

Cold rain knifed through his shirt as he navigated past the tarp covers lining the quarterdeck. The downpour was ill effective at cooling his anger or the racing fire in his blood that one taste of Lydia's lips stoked.

He broke nearly all boundaries with her. Everything he preached to the crew about holding fast to the mission fell in the face of one heated moment. No, he couldn't lie to himself. There were many moments when the sight of Lydia tempted him.

His body still warmed at the remembrance of her feminine softness beneath the damp fabric of her clothes, her arms about his neck, every smooth curve pressed against the length of him. She was shaken by the storm and from being far from home. No matter how capable and quick-witted she was, her intelligent attributes did not conceal her vulnerability. His reaction to that vacillated from wanting to protect her to an even greater, primal urge to comfort her. Not just with assuring words, either.

Rhys shook his head free of the notions. He hated that the very drive to do those things would be the same force that would wreak havoc on both of their causes if he had acted upon them. More importantly, there was Lydia's honor to consider. Perhaps it was a blessing in disguise that her will prevailed over his. If she wanted him to remain in that navigation room for much longer…

"How fares the lass?" Malcolm cut in on Rhys's thoughts as he reached the deck.

He wondered if Malcolm or any of the crewmen kept track of his time in the navigation room. If so, they would realize that the duration was a bit longer than it normally took to deliver a tray of food. "Better than any of us." Rhys kept his reply simple.

"Aye, at least she has a roof over her head." The bosun swilled rum as he surveyed activity on deck. The crew started to settle for the night, with each man seeking rudimentary shelter from the elements under makeshift tarpaulin awnings and inside the longboats.

Rhys wiped rain off his face. "I'm surprised you ask about her."

The bosun stiffened his lip. "I asked because that whelp Finley will need the use of the navigation room on the morrow. Where will you put her, then?"

"The cabin will be dry if we can continue to draw water out from the manual pump. Have a crewman switch shifts in the engine room every hour." He stopped when he heard a smug voice sound nearby.

"I am an Aspasian noble. I will not be forced to sleep out in the rain."

Rhys peered in the direction where Nikolaos's voice hailed and saw him arguing with O'Neil. The engineer sat under a makeshift tarp awning and shot back a retort.

"I don't care who you are. I'll not give up my tarp. There're canvas coverings stored in the sail room. Get one and make your own shelter."

Nikolaos's beard dripped water from the rain when he raised his head and took notice of the navigation room on the quarterdeck. "Never mind. I will sleep there for the night."

Rhys stepped up to him. "That area is off limits to you."

Nikolaos took stock of him and sneered. "But not to you. Is that why you took your time delivering Lady Dimosthenis her evening rations?"

"If you ever make an insinuation about Lady Dimosthenis and me again, I will tie you to the hull and have you dragged from bow to stern."

Nikolaos remained insolent. "You'll have to speak Greek to me, Captain. I'm afraid I'm not well-versed in nautical terms."

Rhys seized him by the collar and yanked him up and over the side rail of the ship. "Shall we start with 'man overboard'?"

Nikolaos attempted to gain footing on the rails, but Rhys held him out too far. "You wouldn't drown me for wanting to sleep out of the rain."

"No." Rhys moved closer to the rails, so Nikolaos's legs danced a jig in mid-air above the rolling ocean. "But I should for you attempting to oust an injured man from his shelter, as well as refusing to lend aid earlier when he and Smythe needed your help. Why should my men see to your comfort when you have no regard for their lives?"

The crew formed a semicircle near Rhys and observed as he meted out justice. Rhys gave the Aspasian lord a shake. "Answer the question."

Nikolaos clawed for a hold on the rails. "There was no time to save anyone but myself and Lydia."

"You didn't even bother to help her open the engine room door for Smythe until she begged you."

"I am on diplomatic business. I am not required to give aid to workers."

Rhys bared his teeth in disgust at the man's arrogance. "Let's see how well your diplomatic immunity can repel sharks." He let his hold on Nikolaos's collar slacken.

"No. Pull me up." Nikolaos's murmur could barely be heard over the ocean's roar. "I will not make any more demands of the crew. I will sleep in the rain."

"You're a coward. Unfit to scrape barnacles, much less be of use to anyone." Rhys hauled him up and tossed him on deck like a fish.

He landed sprawling. The crew jeered him as he rose on all fours. He peered at Rhys with indignation and the will to preserve what remained of his dignity.

"You want shelter from the rain? I'll give you one. Finley, Thomas, lock him up in the brig," Rhys commanded.

The crewmen stepped forward to remove Nikolaos. As they took him below deck, the remaining men returned to their nesting spots for the night.

Malcolm remained where he stood. Something was on his mind.

"What?" Rhys asked.

"Do you think a man of his ilk can withstand a night in the brig?"

"He'll be in there longer than a night. Noble or not, his behavior won't be tolerated."

"You didn't confine him for insubordination. You sentenced him because you didn't want him going near the lass."

Rhys's anger maintained its high point, even though Nikolaos was well away. "Nikolaos has every intention but the right one when it comes to Lydia. I promised her father that I'd protect her. I mean to stand by my word."

"Is that the only reason?"

Now his irritation turned on Malcolm. "Are you questioning my orders?"

The bosun parried the accusation. "I just thought to caution you. Best not overcomplicate the mission."

Rhys hated to admit it, but Malcolm's logic was sound. He sighed, frustrated with himself and the endless mishaps that struck *The Enlightened* in one day. Now he lashed out at his long-standing friend. "Your advice has been noted."

"Fair enough." Malcolm sounded, in his normal gruff tone. He went to his pallet. "I'll see to the morning's rations in a few hours."

When Rhys was the only man left walking on deck, he went down below to see how Nikolaos fared in his new accommodations.

His lungs worked harder as the air thickened in the ship's lower depths. The space would be unbearably hot and stuffy with the smells of mildew and rotting bilge by noonday tomorrow. He didn't care to pay Nikolaos a visit for too long.

Rhys entered the brig. Nikolaos's neck drooped as Finley and Thomas finished securing him behind the bars of a small holding cell that hung suspended from the rafters by heavy chains. Barely big enough to stand upright in, it hovered several inches from the ground.

"I'll speak to him," Rhys said.

The crewmen made no complaints of taking their leave early. The water's motion was felt in every part of the ship, but the brig was the worst. Even the hardiest of salty dogs had been known to lose the contents of his supper after watching the ribs of the ship lurch to and fro.

Rhys stepped lightly along the crisscross wooden framework that made up the base of the ship.

"How long do you intend to keep me in here?" Nikolaos asked.

"Until we reach New Britannia. You'd better hope Finley can set our course soon."

Nikolaos spat in the brown sludge water that covered his ankles. "Wait until Sabba hears of what you have done."

"Before or after he learns that you took advantage of my hospitality? That constitutes a breach of agreement."

"Was taking liberties with the king's niece also a violation?"

Rhys planted his feet as the ship swayed. "You don't know what you speak of."

Nikolaos's dark eyes probed him. "Lydia has been a longsuffering widow. Who knows what sweet whisperings and careful ministrations you may have used to make her comply with you?"

A low growl issued from Rhys's throat. "Hold your tongue if you wish to keep it."

"You have a temper. I will give you that. That volatile nature may have Lydia momentarily fascinated, but it will not last. Did she tell you of Galen?"

"What of her late husband?"

"When the young Lord Dimosthenis perished at sea, she took what remained of herself and threw it into her work."

No wonder Lydia feared the ocean. Many of her actions made sense to Rhys now. His heart stirred with affection and equal parts sympathy for her. "In that case, it seems your efforts to make her your wife were doomed to fail, Nikolaos."

"Mock me as you wish. This journey is not over yet. But why are you here, Captain? Judging by your impassioned responses to my words, it is obvious Lydia has done something to send you across this ship of fools looking for answers concerning her." Nikolaos laughed. "I thought you looked perturbed this evening."

"Don't let those iron bars give you a false sense of security. They only prevent you from escaping. And on a ship, you only have so far to go."

Rhys locked the door to the brig behind him. He walked alone through the two lower decks, the scarce wall lanterns casting dark shadows upon the floor. All the while, he thought of what Nikolaos said about Lydia, her husband's death, and the fierce way she kept everything about herself so carefully guarded. It burned him that Nikolaos knew such intimate details, and incensed him even more that the man had no reservations about using them for his own purposes.

Rhys made it to the second level and entered his cabin, stepping past Lydia's trunk to reach the bookcase. He pulled out the COIC mission papers and shoved the documents in his pocket, wondering what went through Lydia's mind as she learned about the authorities granted him by the Crown. Espionage and battling pirates were hardly the tasks of a typical diplomat. Now what was he supposed to do, just when he managed to build a working trust with her?

When he reached topside, Rhys stole a glance at the navigation room. No light shone through the crack at the bottom of the door. Lydia must have gone to bed.

He made his own pallet between the quarterdeck and longboats. The rain finally stopped. He laid awake, soaking in the damp chill of the night air and watching the sky, searching for a hint of true north. The expanse was muted and devoid of stars.

Rhys closed his eyes, letting go of any hope of finding clear direction for the ship or his association with Lydia. Tonight was truly a night for the lost.

Chapter 12

Lydia woke up the next morning with a stiff back and sore neck from sleeping on the floor of the navigation room. She brought a hand to her mouth, where her lips remained tender from Rhys's kiss. She thought of him for a long time last night before sleep finally overcame her.

Lydia didn't know what made her more unsettled, the way Rhys so easily took command of her emotions and body, or the fact that she could not experience that closeness again with him so long as he remained secretive.

She turned on her side, drawing the blanket around her shoulders. Daylight grew stronger, coloring the navigation room in dusty grays and blues. Finley would soon be in to check the instruments. She needed to be up and out of his way.

Lydia went outside and found the cask of water Rhys left by the door. She retreated into the room to wash and dress. Finley arrived just as she carted her belongings outside. He barely made eye contact with her before he shut himself inside the room.

Lydia saw the sun peeking behind a filmy veil of clouds. At least there would be little chance of storms today.

"There you are."

She stopped contemplating the heavens and stared at Malcolm as he lumbered around the fallen mast, dragging bolts of white cloth behind him. "Good morning. Are you making more repairs?"

He heaved the cloth bolts her way. They rolled to a stop at her feet.

"I'm giving you a sewing lesson. We'll start by mending these sails." He tossed a small leather pouch onto the cloth.

Lydia opened it to find needles and a spool of thread. "I don't know about this."

"How is it that you were never taught to sew?"

"My mother tried to teach me. I just never learned properly. I was better at making clocks in my father's shop."

Her answer gained a scoff from Malcolm. "Can you at least thread a needle?" He made use of a crate as a chair.

Lydia found similar seating and gathered her new set of tools in her lap. After four attempts, she had the thread through the eye of the needle.

"Good." Malcolm's tone was unconvincing. "Here's what we'll do. The first sail has a tear near the bottom row of seams. You'll need to make a diagonal stitch to reinforce it. See?" He showed her the work he already started.

She gazed at the cross pattern of stitches until she lost their beginning and endpoints. "Are you sure you want to entrust me with this?"

"Can't say I do, but the crew has other work. It leaves just you and me."

Lydia plunged into her task, remembering to knot the thread first. Once the first seam was done and Malcolm issued no objections, she made progress on the sail's tear, pulling the thread tight with each stitch.

"No. What are ye doing, lass?" Malcolm's sudden cry made her prick her thumb on the needle.

"Mending the hole in the sail?"

"You'll pucker the canvas that way. Make smaller stitches, like so." He showed her his handiwork on a different sail. "Maybe I should wait for Rhys to finish work in the engine room. He could do this."

Despite the captain's absence on deck, there was still no avoiding him. Lydia broke from mending to scour the deck and noticed another man was missing. "Where's Nikolaos?"

Malcolm's vision was fastened to the needle and thread that he weaved expertly through the tough canvas. "You'll have to ask the captain."

"Is Nikolaos seasick again?"

"I said, ask the captain." Malcolm's voice sharpened.

She sat, bewildered by the quick return of Malcolm's bad temper. All she did was inquire of her unwelcome travel companion.

Malcolm resumed his work. The deck was quiet save for the sounds of boards being hammered. Lydia got the ill sense that something unscrupulous transpired after she went to bed last night. Some crewmembers considered her presence onboard to be bad luck. Maybe they thought the same of Nikolaos, since he was her associate. What did the crew do to him?

***

Rhys had been up since dawn. After checking on O'Neil and visiting the cargo hold to confirm nothing was damaged, he went to aid Smythe with the unclogging of the engine.

"I have most of it done." The engineer apprentice brought his attention to a tangle of kelp, dead fish, and ocean debris heaped in a putrid-smelling mass on the floor. Smythe stood in front of a disassembled lower half of the engine, parts gathered in tidy piles along the wall.

To Rhys, that sight was worse than seeing the rubbish. "How much time did you spend taking apart that engine?"

"Three hours, but it won't take as long to get it back together," Smythe promised with the buoyancy and chipper spirit of his twenty-three years.

"Let's be sure of it. O'Neil is still recovering from that head injury."

That snuffed some of the flame of confidence from the apprentice's youthful fire. "I'll get the engine back." He hit the structure, and sand fell to the floor in wet clumps. "A good bit of that gumming up the rotors. Must have picked it up when the ship anchored in Aspasia."

Rhys and Smythe spent the next two hours digging into and hurling insults at the engine. The machine refused to relinquish its store of kelp, hanging onto stringy bits of it that broke off when they attempted to pull it from between the rotors. Every time they brushed sand from it, more got caught between the crevices. Rhys planned to suggest that the COIC's engineers design a better filtration system on their next line of ships.

Rhys wiped his brow on his sleeve. "I'll finish up. Come back to reassemble the engine after midday rations." He wished he could tell Smythe to rest the full day, since his work proved to be the most exhaustive within the past twenty-four hours. However, every hand was needed if *The Enlightened* was going to make the journey home.

Smythe reached the top of the stairs. "Should I tell one of the men to come help you?"

Rhys flicked sand from his fingers. "Lady Dimosthenis would be the better choice. Women's hands are smaller. She'd have this engine cleaned before any of us could. She'll also help you put it back together."

"Should I knock on the navigation room door?"

"I'll see if she's indisposed." After last night, Rhys intended to give Lydia her distance, but necessity called for them to be together in order to get the engine repaired. Once they reached New Britannia, she'd have all the space she needed away from him. The notion left a sour feeling in the pit of his stomach as he followed Smythe to the top deck.

The late morning sun heated the deck and the backs of the men as they repaired the splintered boards. Smythe ran off to find a shaded corner to rest. Rhys filled a cup with water from a standing cask and drank his fill of the lukewarm liquid. His empty stomach gnawed in protest.

Finley crossed Rhys's path before he reached the quarterdeck. "The navigational equipment is working again."

"Good. Did you find our heading?"

The navigator hesitated to answer. "We veered off course."

"How far?"

"Some thirty knots from the Balearic Islands. You can thank the storm winds for that."

"Then we're still a good week's journey from our destination if the weather and machinery agree with us."

Finley nodded. "How is the engine?"

"Still getting it operational. Was Lady Dimosthenis in the navigation room with you?"

"No, she and Malcolm are repairing the sails." Finley directed Rhys to the flurry of white canvas partially obscured by the broken mast. "I don't think it'll do much good. The wind isn't strong today."

Rhys knew his navigator and bosun didn't get along. Finley's remark indicated they had another tiff. "Until we get the engine working again, it's worth the attempt. None of us want to be caught in the doldrums."

Rhys left Finley and found Lydia outside the navigation room, swathed in a mountain of sails. Malcolm sat across from her, equally shrouded. Rhys watched Lydia as she jerked her right hand in the air, carrying with it a slender thread. The thread drew taut and snapped.

Malcolm groaned. "You broke it again."

She huffed. "I told you I've no business sewing."

"You pulled the thread with too much force. You're using a needle, not driving a nail," he clucked at her. Rhys bit his tongue to keep from laughing.

Malcolm removed his gully knife from his belt and gave it to Lydia. "Break the seam and start again."

Rhys intervened before Lydia could do more harm to herself. "If your pupil can tear herself away from her mending, there's another task we need her for."

Lydia stopped removing the thread and glanced upward. Her eyes were bright in the sunlight, the irises rimmed in deep gold. "Does it involve needlework?"

"No, but it requires a woman's touch. The engine needs unclogging and none of us have fingers small enough to complete the task."

She looked at Malcolm.

"Go." He waved her off, grimacing at her crooked stitches.

She politely thanked him for the sewing lesson and returned his knife. In the midst of removing the sails from her lap, she stuck her finger with the needle. "Ouch."

Rhys chuckled again. She heard him and shot a scathing look as she applied pressure to her index finger.

He addressed her when they went below deck. "I checked the cargo hold this morning. The automatons seemed to have weathered the storm, but you'll need to determine any damage."

Lydia nodded, her face neutral. Did she forget about last evening already?

They stopped at the cargo hold and Lydia inspected the automatons with great care, checking their metal plating for rust and their wires for corrosion. "You're right. They don't seem damaged. But the windup model needs to be repositioned."

Rhys glanced at the automaton, where it leaned a little too far to the left. "I'll fix it later. We need to get the engine running as soon as possible."

She threw the canvas back over the automatons. "To the engine room, then."

"Yes." His voice turned stilted and mechanical. Was this the way it was going to be between them for the next week or more? The awkwardness was stifling.

Lydia picked up a brush when they got to the engine room and proceeded to scrub sand from the engine cylinder. "I was told to ask you of Nikolaos's whereabouts."

"I separated him from the crew."

She stopped scrubbing. "Where is he?"

"He's still alive and on the ship."

"No, that won't do. Something took place last night after you and I ki—after you left. I would like to know where Nikolaos is, and what transpired to put him there."

Rhys really should have known that offering a veiled answer would do little to deter Lydia. "He's detained in the brig for refusal to aid a distressed crewman. He'll remain there until we reach New Britannia."

Her eyes challenged him. "His actions were deplorable, but you can't jail him for that."

"I won't let Nikolaos run roughshod over my crew because he has diplomatic immunity. He also tried to go sleep in the navigation room, knowing you were in there."

Disgust crossed her face, which pleased him. "But what if he tells the COIC what you've done?"

"I'll deal with it. I have a crew to look after."

Footsteps pounded. Duncan's voice boomed as he reached the bottom stairs. "Captain, the sails need raising."

"Malcolm's finished mending them?"

"Aye, he says we need to jury rig the bowsprit to replace the broken mast."

A dangerous task, but one Rhys suspected they would have to do if the engine wasn't operational in time. "Wait until I get there."

Duncan grunted an assent and turned to go topside.

Rhys stretched his sore back in preparation for the rigorous activity of climbing the bowsprit. "I'll send Smythe down to help you put the engine together."

"But—"

"I've said all I will about Nikolaos. He stays locked up."

Lydia brushed sand from the engine with force. "He's supposed to act as my guardian. This will only worsen things diplomatically."

"Don't defend him. I've kept you safe, as I promised your father. When has Nikolaos done anything to protect you? " Rhys stopped as he registered how jealous he sounded. He couldn't explain the need to guard Lydia from Nikolaos's influence, but it ran deeper than he could contemplate or dare say to her.

He left her staring after him as he exited for the top deck. Rhys passed through the sublevels, barely glancing at the rooms and corridors still littered with fallen items. He leapt over an empty water cask at the foot of the door leading topside.

On deck, the men waited. He strode towards the toolbox chained next to the longboats and lifted an axe from its contents. "Four of you hold the ropes of the bowsprit once I take it down. Two on each side."

Thomas did not run to the prow like the other men. He made his way to Rhys instead, still limping slightly on his injured calf. "Captain, is this ill turn of fortune the woman's fault? The men say it's magic she wields."

Being a sailor all his life, Rhys knew all of the superstitions. He even entertained a few of his own upon occasion, but Thomas's frank question was a surprise. "Magic?"

The deck hand bobbed his head in all seriousness. "*The Enlightened* sailed fine and true all the way to Aspasia. Then a week after we leave, things start to happening. Bad things."

Rhys played devil's advocate with the weak-minded Thomas. "If you truly think Lady Dimosthenis a conjurer of sorts, why would she risk her own life by causing the ship to nearly go under?"

Thomas tilted his head left and right as though he were earnestly giving thought to the logic.

Rhys marched to the bowsprit. "Enough with these superstitions. That goes for all of you. These old fishwives' tales are unbecoming for a crew commissioned by the COIC."

Duncan's voice rose above the murmurs of the crew. "Not all of us got training in diplomacy."

Malcolm sniffed. "That's got nothing to do with keeping a ship afloat. Get to work or you'll see diplomacy."

Was Malcolm defending Lydia's reputation? Rhys wondered. Perhaps she softened up the old crusty sea dog. Why couldn't she be equally as charming around him instead of arguing at every opportunity?

The amusement that swept over Rhys was replaced by soberness again. "We will complete our mission. There will be no more time wasted with idle talk of bad luck. Is that understood?"

"Aye," the crew uttered. Duncan and Thomas had the least enthusiasm.

Rhys grabbed a part of the rigging that extended out to the bowsprit. It held taut. He climbed over the guardrail of the prow and gingerly set his feet down on the narrow base on the other side. The ocean churned up a white froth. If he fell, he'd be swept under the ship.

Behind him, half of the crew kept murmuring about omens and witches. He made one coarse shout at them. They desisted and fell back into order.

Rhys held his axe above the heel of the bowsprit. Perhaps the greater danger did not lie in falling into the sea.

Chapter 13

Mediterranean Sea, near Balearic Islands

Though Rhys had gone topside half an hour ago, the tension from his last words stayed in the engine room with Lydia. Rhys's ship, Rhys's rules. There wasn't a thing she could do about it.

"Mmph," she grunted, hefting a large engine rotor off the floor.

"Midday rations." Malcolm came into the room, delivering her lunch. The steam rising from the bowl smelled almost as bad as the components that clogged the engine.

"What's the fare for this afternoon?" Lydia asked while attempting to quell a rising in her stomach.

"Salmagundi with salted beef tongue. Best to use the perishable ingredients left over in the pantry before they rot."

Lydia suspected it was too late for the beef tongue. "I'll eat as soon as I finish cleaning this engine component."

"Good thing the sails are being raised since the engine lies scattered. Smythe told us that it could be reassembled in a few hours."

Lydia found a wrench in the toolkit near the stairs. "It will take longer than that."

"Well, he is an apprentice. Speak of the devil, here he comes."

Smythe came from the top of the stairs, sidestepping the salmagundi. "I haven't been called that since I left the orphanage years ago."

"You'll be called worse if you don't put that engine back in working order," Malcolm snapped.

Unbothered, Smythe waltzed up and plucked the wrench from Lydia's grasp. "I can take over from here, ma'am."

Lydia plucked it right back from him. "The two of us can assemble this engine faster than one alone."

"I agree with her," said Malcolm. "See that you're on your best behavior in front of the lass. I'll be helping to get that bowsprit raised." He ambled up the stairs.

Smythe looked at Lydia's plate of salmagundi. "Are you going to eat that?"

Lydia shook her head. "Take it."

He flashed a childish grin. If not for his height, he could say he was seventeen and none would be the wiser.

By evening, she and Smythe had the engine assembly close to completion. Malcolm brought them a late supper of bean mash and pickled herring and another cask of water. "Still working?"

Lydia wiped her face on her damp shirt sleeve before helping herself to the water. "It won't be much longer."

"You need to eat. Captain's orders."

Lydia tipped the water container to her mouth. How typical of Rhys to express his concern in the form of a command. She paused. Was she that familiar with his quirks already? Why shouldn't she be? She gained familiarity with him in other areas.

While trying to assuage her guilt, Lydia closed her mouth too soon as she kept the container tilted. Water splashed her chin and dribbled down her shirt.

Malcolm and Smythe observed her child-like drinking habits without a word, though their faces said enough. She employed the use of her sleeve again to dry her face. "Mr. Clark, please inform your captain that I appreciate his concern, but I have a job to do."

"I'm too old to play messenger boy so's the two of you can quarrel. Eat." Malcolm walked out with the empty lunch tray.

Lydia and Smythe worked into the night. The inlet valve of the cylinder gave them trouble, refusing to open. Close to ten, they had a fully assembled engine.

"Would you care to throw the switch?" Lydia asked Smythe.

He plodded over to the wall. Exhaustion settled upon him, leaving his back with a droop. He extended an arm and pulled the switch. The engine kicked on with a gurgle. He issued a relieved sigh. "It's Thomas's task now to keep the engine fed during the second shift."

The sound of boots running down the hall came to a halt when Rhys burst in. "The engine turbine's moving on deck."

"I revived the engine." Smythe beamed. "I mean, Lady D did a good share of the work, too, of course."

Rhys gave the apprentice a vacant stare. "Lady D?"

"It's quite acceptable," Lydia said as she wiped the tools clean. "Dimosthenis is a difficult name to pronounce, especially for those unaccustomed to the Greek tongue."

"I can pronounce it just fine."

Rhys just had to speak his mind about everything. She hated to admit it, but she was beginning to see how tiresome the habit could be when someone else did the talking. "Yes, well, not all men profess to have such a gifted tongue."

He inclined his head in mock deference. His simmering look sent heat up her spine. "Thank you, my lady. How kind of you to notice."

Lydia had the most distinct sense that he wasn't referring to the pronunciation of her surname anymore.

Rhys appeared to be enjoying this bit of mischief. His lips drew into a wicked little smile as he flicked a charm switch behind that handsome face.

She wouldn't allow him any more satisfaction. She straightened her spine and gave him the most confident, authoritative look she could muster as she switched topics. "All of the ship's engine-driven facilities should be in operation."

"We'll have hot water again. Good."

Lydia agreed. The past two days left a certain degree of grime upon her skin that a washbowl was little effective in eradicating.

She became self-conscious of her appearance before Rhys. It did no good to hide her grease-stained hands behind her sweaty clothing. "Where did Smythe run off to?" She searched the room for the ginger-haired apprentice, but he was nowhere to be seen.

Rhys remained with her. "He's relieved for the night. You'd have seen him leave if you didn't have that faraway look in your eyes."

"I was thinking of weighty matters."

His droll expression said he didn't believe her. "You'll have plenty of time to contemplate. I moved your belongings back to the cabin. Most of the floor is dry."

Lydia skirted past Rhys and set her feet to ascend the stairs. "Just when I was beginning to enjoy my freedom to roam the ship."

"So I noticed." Rhys advanced on the step behind her. He stood so near to Lydia that her body responded just thinking about being in his embrace once more. "Don't worry. I won't express my appreciation by kissing you again."

She gripped the stair rail. "You shouldn't tease me then, either."

"You made your point clear the first time."

Was that hurt she heard in his voice? Lydia thought Rhys's anger trumped all such emotion within him after last night. She peered at him over her shoulder, fighting an urge to remain with him.

But that was foolish.

Hurt or not, Rhys wasn't going to change anything about himself or reveal his past to her. She needed that in order to even consider letting him get close to her, although the temptation to do so was not afar. She retreated up the stairs.

"Sleep well, Lydia."

She didn't look back to see if Rhys followed. She kept straight for the cabin and shut the door, locking it before she could talk herself out of it.

Lydia took a look around. With the exception of a faint water evaporation line on the baseboards, the cabin barely revealed that a storm had struck. The books on the bookshelf had all been repositioned. Rhys must have moved them. And the COIC mission papers.

She paused as a cold sliver of shame moved along her back. She invaded his privacy and yet accused him of breaching her trust by withholding information. They were both guilty of compromising each other's trust in different ways.

She left the bookshelf alone and plopped in the chair to unlace her boots. How did it happen? One day she was spending her time perfecting small engine boilers. The next she was matching wits with a mysterious foreigner whose stubbornness gave her indigestion and whose kisses and strong arms turned her insides to jelly.

Her heart was turning, moving towards something that she would not allow herself to feel since her husband passed. Was this what her mother meant by being alive to the world and open to its charms? To Rhys's charms? How could she trust in such circumstances when they—Rhys—

caught her unawares and left her confused and conflicted?

Besides, after her arrival to New Britannia, would she even see Rhys at the COIC headquarters? Or would he merely deposit her on shore and sail off on his next mission, giving her nary a second thought?

She winced at the idea of him charming her just to get the automatons and get her to his country with minimal interference. Then Rhys would be no different from Nikolaos, only using her for his own greedy purpose. The possibility that everything about him could be a ruse left her raw inside.

***

A night and day went by. Whenever a knock sounded on the cabin door, Lydia briefly entertained the notion that it was Rhys. Instead it was always Malcolm and his rations of hardtack, strong tea, and salmagundi. At least she was becoming an expert on the many ways to make salmagundi, which was not bad once she started eating the dishes that didn't contain salted beef tongue.

"Five days," Malcolm said as he delivered her supper the next night. "We'll soon reach the Channel."

Reality set in once more for Lydia as she contemplated the distance from the north Atlantic and the Mediterranean. She never thought she would be so far from home or loved ones. So alone.

She dozed off at half past ten, too tired to change out of her clothes. Deep sleep began to overtake her just as something scraped the outside of the door.

Lydia opened her eyes wide in the darkness. She squinted over the bedcovers, trying to see past the shadowy shapes of the desk and bookshelf.

The sound came again, this time softer and closer. A shuffle. From the inside. A chill crept under her skin. Whatever was responsible for that sound was in the room with her.

Lydia reached over to the nightstand for her pistol. As her hand closed around the barrel, she heard the hammer of a gun lock into position behind her ear. She gasped before a large, rough hand clamped over her mouth.

"No need to act rash now, ma'am. I won't hurt you, so long as you keep mum and don't try to run."

Chapter 14

Atlantic Ocean, south of Spain

Avoiding temptation was harder work than Rhys imagined.

He avoided Lydia's path since she repaired the ship's engine. Knowing contact with her would make things more awkward, he focused all his energies on keeping *The Enlightened* on a steady course to New Britannia.

After bouts with pirates, stormy gales, busted engines, breached hulls, and one insolent, pampered king's adviser, he was thankful for the mundane drudgery that his responsibilities as captain presented. That is, even if they did start to make him a little drowsy.

Rhys yawned as he finished the final inventory of the cargo hold. While Malcolm previously made sure to catalogue the rum stores, he overlooked two rows of boxes along the back wall. Rhys pried the lids open and looked for broken items. He gathered that the bosun conveniently forgot about the boxes because of their near proximity to the automatons.

But Malcolm wasn't the only cautious crewmen aboard. Duncan and Thomas acted as though the automatons would come alive at any moment.

Rhys saw that the seven-foot clockwork model was tilted again, even after he straightened it that morning. He dug his heels into the floor and put his back into moving the automaton.

It budged the space of three fingers, its armor plates creaking at the hinges. Rhys shoved again to align it beside the smaller, six-foot soldiers. Iron clanged against iron before a steel rod clattered to the floor.

There went his goal of keeping the automatons in one piece.

Rhys picked up the rod. From where did it fall? He inspected the automaton's limbs and torso. All plates were intact on the front. He looked behind it and saw an open panel on the center of its back.

"There we are," he said aloud as he reached between the automaton and the wall. The steel rod served as its key to wind up. Tucking the wire back inside the panel, Rhys then flipped the panel closed and returned the rod to its place. He wound it until it clicked. "That should do it."

The automaton produced a soft ticking sound that gradually faded.

Rhys admired his handiwork. A simple fix it may be, but it probably just saved New Britannia's investment.

He finished crossing items off the inventory list, picked up his lantern, and started for the cargo hold door. A vague wariness settled upon his shoulders as he ventured into the hallway. How quiet it was.

He listened for the engine, gritting his teeth when he heard no steady whir. The machinery must have cut out. Splendid. Just when the ship was finally back on course.

He rapped on the engine room door. "The engine's stopped. What's happened?"

He waited for someone to reply. Thomas had the first shift tonight. Was he even inside? Rhys tried the door again. Instead of knocking, he pulled it open.

Steam flew in his face. Coughing, he waved his hand in front of him and waited for most of it to dissipate before entering.

Sweat beaded on his forehead as the heat met him. His fingers came away slick with moisture as condensation collected on the stair rails. He took a bird's eye view of the room and found no one on the floor. The lanterns flickered through their protective cage structures on the wall.

He treaded down the slippery steps and cut a path between the maze of pipes and valves. "Who's down here?"

He arrived at the engine. The mouth of it hung open, wide and black, with wisps of residual steam emitting from it. Rhys groaned. What would possess anyone to abandon a working engine?

Unless there was something else more pressing to attend to.

Rhys went back up the stairs and turned left down the hall. The entrance to the ship's third level was left ajar. His crewmen knew that one of the main rules on his ship was that it be locked at nightfall. He descended to the lowest part of the vessel.

The corridor was narrow and pitch-black. Rhys held his lantern in front of him as his feet remembered the pattern of the uneven path. As he got closer to the brig, he saw the door to that area was also open.

He reached for his revolver and moved forward. As he got closer to the brig, his lantern cast a dim glow towards the back of the interior. The light shone on an empty cell. Rhys went straight for it and searched the surrounding dark corners.

Nikolaos was gone.

A noise. Something landed in the bilge water. The resulting splash was too big to be a rat. It sounded like a footstep.

Rhys swung the lamp around just in time to catch sight of a meaty fist before it slammed into the side of his head.

***

The tang of copper and salt mixed in Rhys's mouth. He felt cold all over. His head pounded as something warm slid down his ear. Voices sounded nearby, though he was unable to make them out.

Gradually, a dim light filtered through his closed eyelids. He opened his eyes to find two figures standing over him. One held his lantern.

"Finley," Rhys grated out.

"How was your nap?" The navigator made conversation as though they were sitting for afternoon tea. "I thought you'd be out longer, but your head is thick."

Rhys touched his temple, coming away with dirt and blood on his fingers. "You struck me."

"No. Thomas struck you. He also put you in that cell, but it was all my idea."

Rhys shifted his focus and saw for the first time the black bars that separated him from the two crewmen. Instinct made him reach for the keys at his belt. They were gone. He attempted to raise himself up from his prostrate position. His clothes were drenched in bilge. "Why?"

Finley sighed. "Do I have to explain? It would take longer than I'd care to devote time to."

"This is treason."

"Don't talk to me of treason." Finley replaced his flippant tone with a sharp order. "I spent years defending New Britannia from seafaring criminals like you. I was on the ship that apprehended *The Neptune*."

Rhys stared in shock at the physical manifestation of his past come back to haunt him.

"You don't remember seeing me. I had orders to remain in the chart room while the admiral stormed *The Neptune*, but my navigations led us to you. And how does the Crown reward me for my work?" Finley's eyes glinted with hatred as he grabbed the cell bars. "Her Majesty appoints you, the very scourge of the sea, as an ambassador and COIC agent while ordering me to navigate your ship like a common cabin boy. There lies the real treason."

The former naval officer shook with jealousy, so much that he rattled the bars of the cell. Thomas remained silent next to him, a mask of repugnance upon his face as he returned Rhys's glare.

Of course. How did he not see it before? The two of them had days, weeks even, to stage this. Finley worked in close proximity to Thomas. That allowed him to fan the man's already highly superstitious and suspicious nature.

The makings of a neat little mutiny.

This was the last time he let the COIC pick his crewmen. "If you didn't want to sail under my flag, Finley, you could have refused the position."

"Spoken like the ignorant pirate that you are. No one refuses a royal appointment to the COIC, even if the outfit is organized with felons."

Rhys spat blood. "Then you should feel right at home. You're a traitor. You and Thomas conspired to detain me and usurp my authority. Do you honestly think the rest of the crew will follow you?"

"They will if they want to live."

"Where is the crew?"

"Thomas, show him."

The deck hand raised the lamp overhead. As light covered more of the room, Rhys saw the remnants of his crew. Malcolm was slumped in the far left corner. Smythe and O'Neil were positioned to the right.

Finley prodded Malcolm in the rib with his foot. "I know these three are doggedly loyal to you and would refuse to join me. They've had a dousing of chloroform from the infirmary table. Perhaps they'll see reason once they wake."

Finley and Thomas must have administered the chloroform while the crew was asleep and while he was residing unconscious in the brig. Did they do the same to Lydia? Rhys prayed they didn't get to her, that she was still safe in the locked cabin until he could come for her. "Am I to assume you've also rallied Duncan to your cause?"

Finley gave a thin smile. He nudged Malcolm over, so that all but the bosun's nose and mouth were covered in the filthy water.

"What happened to this cell's last occupant?" Rhys asked.

"Nikolaos is waiting in the galley. I told him of this in advance."

Rhys muttered, "Nikolaos doesn't waste an opportunity, especially if he thought you would gain the upper hand."

"He was correct."

"That remains to be seen." Rhys turned and addressed the deck hand. "What made you take part in this, Thomas?"

Thomas spit between the bars of the cell. "Captain Finley told me about your pirating days. I won't sail under no jolly roger. And no true captain lets a woman run his ship."

Finley released a little chuckle. "Thomas, get the engine operational again. I'll guard the prisoners until you return."

"Aye, Captain."

Once the deck hand left, Finley circled Rhys's cell, smug in his victory. "Your talent for observation lapsed since going to Aspasia. That woman must have done more tinkering with you than with the engine."

Rhys's blood stirred at the mention of Lydia. "Where is she?"

"I haven't done away with her, if that's what you mean."

"If you've harmed her—"

"You see, that's why you came to be in that cell. You lost your wits by falling in love with that cow." For one moment, Finley was close enough for Rhys to grab him. He stepped back with a small laugh.

Rhys growled, ready to smash his smug face through the bars. "If you've harmed Lydia in any way, it will be better for you to throw yourself overboard before I get out of this cell."

"You are in love with her. Amazing what some men will give up for a woman's fleeting affection." Finley wiped the sarcasm from his face, replacing it with a hard and resolute determination. "Your position and *The Enlightened* both should have been mine. I will remedy that."

The ship jostled as the engine kicked into gear. Thomas came back to the brig. Finley started for the exit.

Rhys rose up and called after him. "Even if you kill me, Finley, you can never go back to New Britannia. You'll get the gallows for this."

Finley hovered in the doorway. "Who said anything about returning to New Britannia?"

Chapter 15

"Drop the pistol, your ladyship."

Lydia did as she was told as Duncan pressed the cold barrel of his gun hard against her scalp. Her firearm clattered to the floor beside the bed.

The room fell silent again, except for Duncan's heavy breathing. His palm was clammy against her mouth and stank of sour sweat. "When I move my hand, you'd better not scream, or I'll shoot you. Got it?"

She nodded.

Duncan took his hand from her face, but kept the gun positioned behind her head. "Get up."

Lydia considered diving for her pistol, but not knowing where it landed on the floor in the dark, she wouldn't have time to find it before he pulled the trigger of his gun. She chose to comply with his demand.

Her back brushed against his arm when she sat up. Lydia felt a sharp tug on her shirt as he yanked her from the bed and thrust her against the wall. She put out her hands to keep her face from smashing against a rivet.

"Not one word." Duncan dragged her from the wall and set her ahead of him. "Walk to the door."

He remained close behind as she traced her steps in the dark. The toe of her sock caught the edge of her trunk. She doubled over and tripped. Duncan cursed before hauling her to her feet, keeping her shirt in his fist as he deposited her in the corridor. "Keep moving."

Lydia immediately assessed her surroundings in hopes of a chance to escape. The guide lights in the hall were out, save for one flickering lantern at the far end past the galley. At Duncan's direction, she stumbled through the hall towards it.

They passed the crew's quarters, where the door hung wide open. Where were the other men? Dread swept through Lydia as she stopped and craned her neck to peer into the blackness.

Duncan jerked her. "I told you to keep moving, I did. Do I need to knock some sense into you?"

Pain exploded in her head as he smacked the butt of his gun against her temple. The corridor became a blur as she staggered. Air rushed past her ears like the sound of rolling waves as she experienced the sensation of being lifted off her feet.

Lydia blinked several times before her vision cleared. Her head bounced with every lumbering step as Duncan carried her down the hall over his shoulder, murmuring something about wanting to use chloroform. She closed her eyes as the jarring motion caused bile to rise in her throat.

Minutes later he deposited her on a cold, hard surface. Lydia's eyes popped open to see the wooden benches and stove of the galley. One large lantern illuminated it all, residing on the table closest to her. She pushed herself into a seated position on the floor.

Duncan kept the gun pointed at her as he backed into the doorway. He remained there, watching her and blocking the entrance.

"Lydia."

She turned. Nikolaos sat on the floor beside her, his hands restrained in his lap with a rope. He looked distressed, but certainly not confused. "What's happening to us?" she whispered in Greek.

Nikolaos's eyes shifted to Duncan. When he saw that the deck hand wasn't moving from the entrance, he addressed her. "A mutiny has taken place. Cartret is no longer captain of the ship."

Sweat broke out on the back of Lydia's neck.

"The deck hands removed me from the brig. They restrained me when I refused to take part in the mutiny. I watched them take the crewmen's bodies past this room."

"No." Lydia inhaled, but air would not go into her lungs.

Nikolaos studied his bound wrists. "Before they took me upstairs, I saw...Lydia, I saw Thomas drag the captain's body into the brig."

A wrenching ache fell over her. Her heart squeezed in her chest as her blood ran cold. Nikolaos called her name again, but she couldn't respond.

Her lips went numb. Her entire face had no feeling except for the hot tears that began to spill down her cheeks.

"Lydia, you must remain coherent. I think the remaining crewmembers intend to spare us—" Nikolaos didn't finish his sentence as Duncan came forward and delivered a kick to his stomach.

"Enough with that island gibberish. Shut up before I gag you both."

"Duncan, that's no way to treat our foreign dignitaries." Finley strode through the door with Rhys's revolver in hand.

Through her tears, Lydia watched Duncan straighten. "Apologies, Captain Finley. I didn't know if the two o' 'em were plotting an escape in that guttural."

"Where would they go? We're in the middle of the ocean." Finley snapped his fingers at Lydia and Nikolaos. "Get on your feet."

Lydia's legs were stone. Her head pounded from Duncan's assault.

"You must stand." Nikolaos used the wall to push himself to his feet.

"I'll get her to stand." Duncan plodded forward.

Finley stopped him. "No. I'll assist her."

Lydia froze when she saw him deposit Rhys's revolver in his belt. Chills ran down her arms when Finley's hands touched her and pulled her up. The hands that took Rhys's life.

"Are you sufficient now?" he questioned without the slightest bit of concern.

She looked up at him. His face was locked in an unreadable expression, though hardness shone in his eyes. "Did you kill Rhys?"

"You don't need to know how I assumed control of the ship."

She lowered her chin to keep it from trembling. "What do you have in mind for us?"

"A proposal. You'll find it better than anything that pirate Rhys Cartret ever offered you."

Pirate? Lydia parted her lips to speak, but Finley moved on.

"Unlike Cartret, I respect you."

She balked at the boldfaced lie. "Rhys would have never held me at gunpoint."

"Aren't you the hypocrite? Not that you greeted me amicably when we first met. But all that is past." Finley fabricated a forgiving smile. "Duncan brought you here this way because I had to ensure you'd come without a struggle. Not that it worked, from what I see of that knot on your head.

Was she too much for you, Duncan?"

Duncan snorted. "Hardly. It wouldn't have hurt to use some of that chloroform on her, though."

"Come stand over her with that gun while she sits at the table."

Once Lydia and Nikolaos were seated, Finley pushed his hands in his pockets. "There are two ways we can go about this. Let's try the diplomatic approach first." He leaned across the table. "Some time ago when I was stationed off the coast of Le Havre, I made the acquaintance of Emile Broussard. He's an industrialist. You may have heard of him. "

"I was told he was a criminal wanted by New Britannia."

"I'm not surprised that Cartret persuaded you to take his stance on politics. Where was I? Before we sailed to Aspasia, I secretly sent word to Broussard about your automatons."

"Was that why those French pirates came after us?"

"Yes, though I don't know why Broussard chooses to employ pirates. Incompetent grunts, the whole lot. When Rhys managed to fend them off, I knew I had to take matters into my own hands." Finley clapped once. "So here is an alternative that Broussard will also agree to. If you give him the automatons, he will match the price that New Britannia agreed to, only the money will go directly to you instead of Aspasia."

Lydia didn't know where to start with such an outrageous suggestion. "This Broussard tried to plunder the ship. Now you try to bargain for the automatons since stealing them didn't work?"

Nikolaos nudged her foot under the table.

What did he know about this business? She glared at him before continuing to speak to Finley. "An irrevocable agreement has been made with New Britannia."

"Who's to say that *The Enlightened* ever made landfall in Aspasia?"

Was he delusional? "But you know that *The Enlightened* reached us, and that Rhys drew up the agreement."

Finley folded his hands atop the table. "Ships get lost at sea all the time. With Cartret's pirate past, it would come as no surprise that he and the crew decided to leave New Britannia with the money and go rogue."

"You're very comfortable referring to Rhys as a pirate."

"As he was comfortable being one." Finley slid onto the bench opposite her and Nikolaos. "New Britannia was perfectly happy to condone his behavior despite jailing him for it."

"You're not making the least bit of sense to me. Nor you, Nikolaos." Lydia swung her head in his direction. "But you and Finley seem to share an understanding."

Nikolaos flattened his mouth. "Cartret was convicted on charges of piracy two years ago. He was imprisoned for it and then set free."

"How would you know such a thing?"

"Because I told him the night after Cartret sent him to the brig." Finley rejoined the conversation. "I'm sure Cartret didn't share his history while he was busy seducing you."

Lydia swallowed a lump in her throat. That was why Rhys grew angry with her when she demanded to know more about him. He possessed the background of the very type of man she despised.

But he also changed his life for the better. He was no longer a pirate.

Finley snickered. "How does it feel knowing your charming diplomat is a criminal?"

She wouldn't give him the satisfaction of disgracing Rhys's memory. She drew herself up. "You misinterpret my silence as an admission of shame. I still hold respect for your captain."

"He is not my captain." Finley placed his hands under the table. His shoulders convulsed as anger tightened his muscles. "I am now captain."

Lydia's outrage and sorrow at Rhys's passing gave her courage to voice the truth. "If Rhys did have a history of piracy, his crimes have been paid for. He's not the one committing treason at this moment."

Finley whipped his arm from under the table. Lydia found Rhys's revolver in her face. "You have no idea what you speak of."

Lydia's heart pounded in her ears, almost as loud as Finley's breathing as he bristled up at her. Duncan pressed his gun to the back of her head again.

"Forgive Lady Dimosthenis, please, Captain Finley," Nikolaos interjected. "She's sustained a blow to the head. She's not thinking clearly. Let me guide her in the new agreement."

Lydia always suspected Nikolaos of being disloyal to her uncle. His words now confirmed it.

Hours seemed to go by before Finley lowered his weapon. Duncan did the same, as Lydia felt the pressure of the gun barrel at her skull fall away.

"Listen to your adviser." Finley's voice fell to a vicious rasp as he set the revolver on the table. "This ship is set on a course for Le Havre as we speak. Once the automatons are in Broussard's possession, you and Lord Abeiron are free to take your money and return to Aspasia."

Nikolaos muttered in her ear. "Do it."

Lydia inched away. "What will you do after this is over, Finley?"

"Once I receive my share of the money, I'll take this ship and the crewmembers that choose to follow me. I hear the Americas are hospitable to expatriates."

"I won't stand guilty of treason."

"I'm sick of hearing that word." Finley picked up the revolver again. "I tried being civil with you. I can still sell the automatons to Broussard without your permission."

"May I advise Lydia?" Nikolaos piped in.

Finley kept the revolver pointed at her. "Do so, but remain seated."

Nikolaos spoke in hushed Greek. "Agree to give Broussard the automatons, Lydia. You can claim that it was done under duress. Sabba will understand."

She was forever amazed at how Nikolaos could so deftly weave ruinous circumstances together and come out with perfectly patterned plans of escape. How dare he dismiss everything she worked for Aspasia to gain? She reverted to Greek as well. "This is a lose-lose situation. Aspasia will make an enemy of New Britannia if I disregard the true agreement."

"You have no other choice but to be killed."

Finley cocked the hammer of the revolver, drawing Lydia's eyes to him. "I'm guessing that Lord Abeiron is trying to convince you that dying is a poor alternative. I couldn't agree more. Now, Lady Dimosthenis, you have a decision to make."

Chapter 16

Atlantic Ocean, twenty-two knots out from Portugal

Rhys shook the bars of his cell in aggravation as Thomas administered another round of chloroform to his crew. "How do you intend to make them follow Finley if they aren't awake?"

The deck hand removed a wad of cloth containing the solution from under O'Neil's nose. He let the engineer droop against the wall. "That's Captain Finley's worry. I just do as I'm told and give 'em their hourly dose of medicine." He tucked the rag and bottle of chloroform back in the leather pouch hanging from his belt.

Anger clouded Rhys's vision as he looked again at his unconscious crew. Anxiety soon trumped that reaction when he thought about Lydia. Was she still asleep in her quarters, oblivious to all that took place?

He had to get to her somehow. But first, a way out of the cell.

He studied the lock on the door. If only he had a pick. Unfortunately, he wasn't in the habit of stowing such a handy little tool in his boot while he was on board his own ship. Then again, he and the crew weren't in the habit of being the victims of mutineers, either. New procedures would have to be adapted as soon as he got out of this fix.

"Why are you so quiet?" Thomas's bellow jarred him out of contemplating the intricacy of the cell's lock and his mild lapse in resourcefulness. "You'd better not be thinking of how to break out of that cell."

The deck hand was more astute than he let on. Rhys stepped away from the front of the cell. His back ached something fierce from having to stoop over for so long. "I was thinking."

"About what? Being a prisoner again?" Thomas laughed at his own poor joke.

"The irony wasn't lost on me. But, no. I was thinking about something else."

Thomas came closer to the cell. "What?"

"How poorly you would fare at Coldbaths."

That took him aback. "I'm not going to prison."

"You will when you stand trial before the admiralty courts. Being an accomplice to a crime is just as bad as committing it yourself."

"You would know, wouldn't you?"

Perhaps another approach would yield a more effective result. Rhys waited for the deck hand to finish his second round of chuckles. "You don't have to do this, Thomas. You can end the mutiny."

Thomas wiped his nose on the back of his hand. "Why would I want to do that? Finley said he'll make me bosun. Don't see you offering me no better deal." Shaggy brown hair fell into his eyes when he lowered his head to launch another wad of spittle into the cell.

Rhys stepped away from where the phlegmy trajectory landed. "I can keep you out of prison when I hand Finley over to the authorities." That was if he didn't cause monumental harm to him first, and *that* centered upon whether Finley touched Lydia.

Rhys's blood stilled as Thomas moved towards the brig entrance. If he left, there went with him the only chance for escape.

To his relief, Thomas stayed and leaned against the door. "You've always been a cocky one, haven't you, Cartret? You think you'll make it home? You can't even make it out of that cell."

"Give me the key, and I will see that you aren't subjected to the same punishment as Finley. You have my word."

"Even if I had the key, I wouldn't let you out. You'd try to get one back on me for that fist to the head."

Try wasn't even the word. Rhys wished Thomas would step within reach where he could grab him through the bars and shove his head against them. But that was a bit pointless, seeing as how he'd still be confined to his cell with no way of getting out. "Why would Finley put you in charge of guarding prisoners without giving you a key? He must not trust you."

Thomas's face fell at that. "Not true. I'm stronger than Duncan. Finley said it'd be best for me to guard four men while he and Duncan tended to the woman and Nikolaos upstairs."

Rhys's stomach knotted around itself. "What do you mean 'tend to'?"

"Be a kipper if I knew. Some bother about making a deal with them over those soldiers."

Finley must be forcing Lydia to give him the automatons. The implications of such a move flashed in Rhys's mind. That would instantly make Finley the owner of some of the most advanced weapons in the world.

Rhys's inability to prevent the *Donna Dulce* tragedy slapped him in the face once again. He couldn't live with the weight of bringing destruction to more people. Every minute that he wasted in this cell, Finley had more opportunity to cement a hold on the ship, affairs of state, and the woman he cared for.

Rhys blinked as the realization came to him. From the first time he saw the dancing gleam in Lydia's eyes when she showed him her automatons to that night after the storm when she lingered in his arms, she took up residence in his mind and heart. It was her unique intelligence and deep dedication to make life better for those around her. He couldn't help but be drawn to her. Lydia's very nature was one of progression and hope.

Rhys lowered his head. He dealt too strictly with Lydia, especially in denying her the manufacturing license to profit from her inventions. How could he be so shortsighted and selfish, focusing only on his goals when she aided him twice without hesitation?

He admired her for her persevering spirit. Now he just had to get out of the brig so he could tell her and make things right.

He rapped on the cell bars to get Thomas's attention. The deck hand amused himself by burrowing into an ear with his pinkie. "Thomas, I've always treated you fairly on this ship. Finley will not be so democratic."

Thomas stopped digging in his ear. Hope seized Rhys, and he continued to make his case. "A woman is in danger. Help me see her to safety."

"For the last time, Cartret, you can just go and—"

The room shook without warning. Thomas lost his footing and fell. The chains suspending Rhys's cell to the rafters rattled.

A second rumbling issued through the ship's foundation beams.

"What was that?" Thomas rose on his hands and knees, bilge soaking his chin from where he had fallen face first in the muck.

"Your guess is as good as mine." Rhys reached for his revolver and came up with nothing. A lot of good his instincts did him when he was without a firearm.

He stilled as a third, smaller crash resounded. Wood splintered.

Thomas gained a foothold along the floor beams and listened. "It's coming from the cargo hold. I hear steps. It's the mechanical soldiers."

Rhys heard a series of noises, too. It did sound like approaching footsteps. Heavy ones. "Their engines were disabled before they were taken aboard. This is something else."

The bars on Rhys's cell moved with the vibration. The cell swayed atop the muck. Whatever made such a resonance was not small. "Finley and Duncan must be tinkering with something, but what?"

The heavy staccato beat of the unknown sound grew clearer. It was coming towards them, slow in the advance but nonetheless steady. The steps ended at the door. The door rattled on its hinges.

Rhys shot a look at Thomas. "Is it locked?"

Thomas shook his head multiple times.

Rhys kicked at the padlock of the cell, serving only to make his holdings rock forward like a child's swing. "You still think you're going to be bosun?"

The deck hand gave a shout as the door hinges flew off. The heavy door teetered within its frame before it came crashing onto the ground. Rhys saw an outline of a hulking figure in the entrance.

The entity moved forward. It appeared to have no head as the light from the room lantern highlighted a seven-foot span of torso, arms, and legs, all armor-plated. The frame of the doorway cracked where it applied substantial force to the structure. Metal creaked and bent as rivets sprang loose from their holds.

"She's done it. She's set her machines on us," Thomas's cry echoed in the brig.

Rhys gave the padlock another kick. Thomas was in a much better position. At least he could make a run for it instead of playing parakeet.

The automaton broke through the frame, sending wood and iron fissuring into the room. It ignored the unconscious forms of the crew. It turned its faceless head Thomas's way, eliciting a scream from him.

"Shut your mouth." Rhys attempted to project his voice calmly as he recalled his previous encounter with the automaton in the Machinists Guild. "You're drawing its attention by shouting."

"It's going to kill us."

"Not if you stay quiet and keep still."

Thomas clamped his mouth shut and stood locked in place as a rabbit sighting its predator. Rhys's cell swayed back and forth. The chain creaked and groaned. Despite the noise, the automaton did not turn from Thomas's direction. Rhys squinted. How did it become functional if no one touched it?

But he did tinker with it. Just hours ago, he wound up the gear mechanism in the automaton's back after he shoved it back into place. He remembered that he talked to himself while doing so. The automaton must have made an imprint of his voice. That meant...

"Get away from me. Keep back," Thomas shouted to the automaton as he began running to Rhys's cell. The automaton locked on him.

Rhys's prior cautions to keep still and quiet had no effect on Thomas as he attempted to climb the cell. Thomas grabbed the suspension chain. The chain jerked and broke away from the rafters.

Rhys grunted as the cell made impact with the uneven floor beams and landed on its side with Thomas still clinging to it. Now Rhys couldn't crouch, much less stand. He saw the automaton's crushing metal feet within an arm's length away.

The machine seized Thomas by the back of the shirt and plucked him off the cell as though he were a tick on a dog's back. Free of the extra weight, the cage rolled inches away from the automaton.

Rhys clutched the bars as he watched Thomas dangle in the air. The deck hand's head scraped the ceiling as the automaton suspended him in its iron grasp. It raised its other hand, coming towards Thomas's face. Rhys's pulse sped as he saw that it intended to crush him.

"Stop," he commanded at the top of his lungs.

The automaton's head swiveled down to look at Rhys, but its hand didn't pause.

Rhys told it to stop again, only this time he remembered to say the word in Greek.

The automaton dropped the hand that would have crushed Thomas's face. All the while, it kept its sensors on Rhys, waiting for his next command.

"Drop him," Rhys ordered in the same language.

Thomas landed on his bottom in the muck at the machine's feet. He didn't waste time as he scrambled between the automaton's legs and ran out the brig.

Rhys was trapped in the brig with the automaton. One misstep and the thing could crush him inside the cage. He took moments to decide how to issue another command as it stood waiting to obey.

He crawled to the back corner of the cell first. "Break open the bars."

Rhys sheltered his head and braced himself as the automaton clambered over him. The cell shuddered as it seized the bars and lifted the entire structure off the floor.

Rhys fell against the back of the cell. The ironwork was no match for the machine's mechanized strength. The front bars tore loose in moments. Rhys dove out of his confinement and landed once more in bilge, but he was more than happy to be free.

He wiped his hands on his pants. The automaton continued to work on deconstructing the cell, not noticing that its occupant had been released. "You can stop now."

The automaton registered the word 'stop' and dropped the mangled cell.

Rhys felt a smile stretch on his face. "At least somebody follows orders around here."

Chapter 17

The commotion coming from the third deck did little to unnerve Finley or shake his aim as he kept the barrel of the revolver steadied on Lydia's forehead. "Have you made your decision?"

Lydia swallowed a lump in her dry throat. She couldn't break down, couldn't let Finley intimidate her. She had to stay strong, survive, and find some way to stop him from reaching the French coast, even if Rhys was no longer there to take control of the ship.

"Lydia is capable of reason. Firearms are unnecessary." Nikolaos decided that now was a suitable time to make good on his promise of protecting her. He cozied up to her, a human shield in case Finley fired. Lydia knew it was a useless gesture, seeing what the metal-piercing bullets in Rhys's revolver were capable of doing to the armor of her automatons, much less human flesh.

A chilling wail erupted from two levels below. Her skin prickled. Duncan shivered behind her, judging from how the pressure of the gun slid away from her head.

Finley's trigger finger trembled, his only indication that he also heard the sound.

"Must be the engine," Duncan murmured, uncertainty adding a tremor to his voice.

Lydia knew no engine could make such an eerie racket, but she didn't comment.

"We'll see about it as soon as the lady makes her choice," Finley resumed.

Lydia nudged Nikolaos off of her before looking Finley square in the eyes. "It would do you no good to kill me. I'm the only one on this ship that knows how to make those automatons operational."

"Why do I need them operational?"

"Broussard will want to see if they work before he pays you. What if he asks for a demonstration?"

Finley frowned. "I just told you that if you want to stay alive, then agree to the offer. It really is that simple."

"She's stalling you, Captain," Duncan supplied. "We need to see what that noise was before it comes upstairs."

Just then, Thomas barreled into the galley, puffing. Both Duncan and Finley automatically turned their guns on him.

"Don't shoot." Sweat poured from his head and hit the floor as he stooped over, gasping for air.

Finley lowered the pistol. "What's going on below? I told you to watch the prisoners."

Lydia's ears perked. That meant the crew was still alive. Why, then, did Nikolaos tell her that he saw their bodies being carted off?

Thomas regained enough breath to speak. "One of those machines is loose. It's that woman's fault. It broke through the cargo hold and came at me in the brig while I was guarding Cartret."

"Rhys is alive?" Renewed hope surged through Lydia even as Duncan struck her with the butt of his gun again, this time on her shoulder.

Finley came around the table and seized her arm. He kept the revolver in his other hand. "She'll make the machine stand down. Duncan, take the lantern and the adviser and follow me. You lead the way, Thomas."

They waited for him to get a reluctant head start down the corridor. Lydia hardly had time to process all that was going on around her. An automaton was roaming the ship. Rhys was alive, as were his loyal crewmen, thank God. That was if the automaton didn't get to them yet.

But how did one become operational if its engine was disabled? The only automaton that had that capability was the clockwork hybrid model, but she purposely left its key loose to keep it from being wound up.

Nikolaos stumbled into her as they were hustled from the galley. His voice came out a raspy whisper. "Lydia, Rhys's authority began unraveling days ago. It would do no good to stay on the losing side."

She faced him in the darkened corridor. "The only thing that's unraveling is your agenda. You lied to me. You let me think Rhys was dead."

"You would not have listened to the new proposal if you knew Cartret was alive."

If only King Sabba knew just how plotting and underhanded his chief adviser was. "You worked this out with them long before tonight, didn't you? While you were in the brig."

Finley gave Lydia a rough shake to silence her. Both her shoulder and head rattled from the action.

The mutineers steered her and Nikolaos to the door leading to the third level deck, which Thomas left wide open in his haste to flee the automaton. The engine hummed down below, but the wall light fixtures were still off.

The five of them climbed down the stairs in single file. Finley put Lydia in front of him and pressed the gun to the small of her back.

Thomas's lantern flickered in his hand as he cast light on the cargo hold. "That's where it broke through."

Lydia stared at the demolished door that lay in pieces of broken timber and twisted iron. "None of the automatons could do that unless their engines were started. Even then their voice receiver wiring would have to be activated."

Finley gripped her shoulder. "You were in the hold a few days ago. Did you activate them?"

She winced. "No."

"I don't believe you." Finley's eyes flashed before he barked at Thomas. "Are the other automatons still inside the hold?"

"I don't know."

"Go see."

While Thomas approached the hold, Nikolaos took another opportunity to deliver a babbling whisper in Lydia's ear. "Do everything they tell you."

"I won't hear advice from you."

"I told them I would get you to negotiate. I didn't commit the mutiny."

"You took part in it." Lydia groaned as Finley twisted her arm behind her.

"Shut it, and go help Thomas find the automaton." He shoved her towards the rubble scattered in front of the cargo hold. Lydia moved her right foot just in time to avoid running a twisted iron shard through her sock.

Nikolaos sidled between her and Finley. "We had an understanding. If she cooperated, you and your men were not to hurt her."

Finley rolled his eyes. "Stop putting on a show. She knows you're a coward."

Lydia pulled at Nikolaos for him to move. "Mr. Finley has conceded that shooting me would be pointless, since he needs me to stop the automaton."

"But I don't have to shoot you to prove a point." Finley turned the gun on Nikolaos and fired.

The corridor lit up when the bullet left the barrel. Blood speckled the front of Lydia's shirt as Nikolaos hit the floor.

Lydia screamed and dropped to her knees. The armor-piercing bullet cut clean through Nikolaos's arm and made its mark in his side. She bunched the fabric of his shirt against the larger wound, trying to staunch the bleeding.

The light from Duncan's lantern showed Nikolaos's face turn white as the blood drained from him. His eyes met Lydia's before losing their focus.

Lydia couldn't think. Her ears rang from the gunfire. The smell of gunpowder burned her nose.

Finley yanked her away from Nikolaos. She dangled from his arm and tiptoed around the debris. "Any more glib observations you'd care to share with us?"

She shook her head.

"And that, gentlemen, is how you silence a woman who will try to match wits with you."

***

From his vantage point behind the crates in the cargo hold, Rhys clenched his jaw as he attempted to get a clear shot on Finley. If Nikolaos hadn't decided to be a hero and get in the way, he could've fired on the smug navigator and spared Nikolaos from getting a bullet to the flesh. He picked the wrong time to cultivate a conscience.

Rhys moved his trigger finger as Thomas got in his line of fire. Lying in wait was little better than his original idea of bringing the automaton back to the upper level. To minimize danger and prevent further damage to the ship, he left it outside the brig, anchored by a firm Greek phrase to stay put.

That was if the prior gunfire didn't jolt it to come barraging upstairs. The last thing he needed was a corridor full of screaming people running to keep from being trampled by a machine punching holes in the hull.

Thomas continued to stand in Rhys's line of sight. If he shot him, Finley would have time to duck away with Lydia in tow.

Rhys clutched the handle of the standard service revolver he found in a box. Only one bullet in the chamber. The lantern he picked up in the brig after Thomas dropped it sat by his feet, its oil depleted. What little light there was outside the cargo hold shifted when the men swung their lanterns. He needed to get closer.

"Get in there, Thomas." He heard Finley demand.

Rhys crouched lower amongst the crates, careful not to move suddenly as the light shifted again and Thomas entered the room.

The coward stood less than five feet away from him. Still no good. To shoot Thomas would be to alert the other men. Then he'd face two guns, one of them his very own commissioned weapon. He saw what it did to Nikolaos. He couldn't allow Lydia to be without hope of rescue.

Rhys lowered his head as Thomas raised the lantern higher.

"The other five automatons are still here, C-Captain. They're on the b-back wall."

A smile formed on Rhys's lips. Thomas was too afraid to come closer.

Finley shouted into the room. "Are they activated?"

"No. The one that got out still is."

Rhys rolled his eyes.

"That's the clockwork model." Lydia's voice filled his ears. Her tone was tinged with fear.

A crash issued from the bowels of the ship. Rhys held his breath.

Thomas swung his lantern as he pivoted. "It's still down in the brig."

The sound of steel bending reached Rhys's ears as the automaton moved again. Thomas ran out of the cargo hold. The room plunged back into darkness.

Scuffling occurred outside the door. Wood smashed beneath someone's boot.

"Give her your light, Thomas," Finley commanded. "She brought it to life. She'll go down there to stop it."

Rhys climbed over the crates. The time for lying in wait was over.

He reached the mouth of the cargo hold as the party started towards the steps to the lowest level. Duncan brought up the rear, carrying his lantern. The light was just enough for Rhys to aim his gun by.

He started to squeeze the trigger.

"Captain…"

Nikolaos. Rhys looked down and saw him on the floor, attempting to move his legs. Nikolaos moaned in pain.

Rhys stepped back and pressed against the doorframe, hidden from sight by the pile of rubble.

"Captain, wait," Duncan called to Finley up ahead. "I heard something in the cargo hold."

Nikolaos groaned. "Help. Please…Cartret…"

Could he just be silent for a moment? Rhys listened for Duncan's approach. He crouched down to avoid being in the lantern light.

The deck hand clomped towards Nikolaos. "It's Abeiron. He's moving."

"Handle it." Finley kept going. He all but tossed Lydia down the stairs into the darkness, and then pushed Thomas after her.

Duncan lowered his gun to Nikolaos's head. Rhys fired.

Duncan gasped and dropped the gun and the lantern as he fell backwards. Rhys came out of the shadows. While Duncan still clutched his thigh, Rhys delivered a hook to his jaw. Bone split as Duncan's head hit the wooden floor.

Rhys picked up the lantern and Duncan's gun, discarding his own.

"Cartret," Nikolaos rasped. "I can't feel my arm."

Rhys came to his side with the lantern. Nikolaos's right arm hung uselessly in its rope bounds. The fabric of his shirt was soaked near the lower torso. Every breath Nikolaos took came up ragged. "Lie still. Keep your left hand pressed against your side."

Nikolaos made a dreadful sound when Rhys maneuvered it over the wound. Blood bubbled up over Nikolaos's fingers. His eyes glazed over with delirium. Nothing could be done for him short of laudanum and a surgeon.

Rhys stood. "I have to rescue Lydia. I'll come back. Don't take your hand off that wound." The lantern in his hand sputtered and died, plunging the space into darkness.

Lydia's shouts echoed from below. Three gunshots fired in rapid succession.

Rhys threw the useless lantern aside, stepped around Nikolaos and went down the corridor to descend into the brig.

Chapter 18

Rhys followed the sound of chaos ensuing as he padded down the broken stairs. His foot slipped in the depressions made by the automaton. Sawdust fell onto his head as pieces of the ceiling fell and the rafters shook.

Ahead, the machine loomed above the forms of Lydia and Finley. Thomas lay face down on the ground less than a few feet away, motionless.

Lydia backed into a corner by the brig entrance. The machine had its eyeless face turned her way.

Rhys ran past the center wall, where a section was torn and the steel insulation hung exposed. He opened his mouth to yell for the automaton to stand down.

"Rhys." Lydia's call cut him off. She locked her gaze on him, wide and alarmed. "Behind you."

Rhys dove forward and to the side just before a gunshot added to the din in the corridor. When he came up, Finley stood behind the insulation. Finley lowered his gun again, preparing to fire.

Rhys tucked and rolled to the other side of the corridor. The bullet landed in the wall above his head. Still clutching his gun, he thrust it Finley's way and fired, missing. "That's six bullets you fired, Finley. You're out."

Finley took shelter behind the wall again.

Lydia's shouts prompted Rhys to turn once again to the brig entrance. The automaton had her where she couldn't slide out to the side. She pressed into the corner of the wall. "Stand down." Her tone grew fraught as she learned her commands were not being heard by the automaton.

"Cease."

The floorboards trembled as the automaton moved. Its bulky frame blocked the brig's entrance as it stretched its arms towards Lydia, fingers grabbing for her head. She ducked just before the automaton smashed its hands against the wall behind her. Metal skidded against metal, sending up sparks.

Rhys cupped his hands over his mouth. "Stand down now."

The automaton came to a rough halt, body bent, its fingertips embedded in the wall.

Lydia twisted beneath the automaton's arms. "I'm caught."

He couldn't get close to free her. Finley rammed him in the side, sending him into the brig. The gun flew from Rhys's hand and splashed beneath the bilge water. He fell under Finley's weight.

"This is my ship now." Finley pounded his fist into his ribcage. "You won't take it from me."

Rhys expelled painful gasps of air as he contorted to gain a hold on the hull frame. Finley pressed a hand to the back of his head and forced his face underwater. The cold, foul bilge coated the inside of Rhys's nose. He jammed his elbow into Finley's sternum.

As Finley's hold slackened, Rhys pushed out of the water and countered the next hit with another elbow, shoving him off. Finley dropped Rhys's empty revolver in the water. Rhys picked it up.

Finley staggered back, his breath winded and his nose dripping blood. "I have control of the ship. I neutralized your crew."

"And you call me a thief." Rhys grabbed him by the collar and delivered an uppercut to the jaw, then another punch before offering up a side blow with the butt of the revolver. Finley swayed towards the entrance.

"On your guard," Rhys summoned the automaton.

He heard the gears turn as the machine activated. Lydia crawled out from under its arms when it rose to its full height.

"Catch."

He kicked Finley in the gut. Finley plunged backwards into the automaton's waiting arms. The machine locked him in an iron-fisted embrace.

Finley grimaced as he struggled to break free, blood running down his face. "Fight me fair, pirate."

"As you did when you ambushed me and drugged my crew?" Rhys left him to wriggle in the automaton's arms and went to see about Lydia.

She supported her back against the exposed steel insulation, catching her breath. Alarm spiraled in the pit of Rhys's stomach when he saw the dried blood on her shirt for the first time in full view.

"It's not mine." She read his expression. "It's Nikolaos's. He—"

"He was still alive when I found him." Rhys clutched his left arm, certain his elbow was fractured in several places. The muscles girding his ribcage went into spasms when he drew a ragged breath. "We'll get Nikolaos and Thomas to the infirmary table."

Lydia gave a perfunctory, stilted nod. She rushed to Rhys, and before he comprehended what he was doing, he held her against him with his right arm, not giving his injuries another thought.

"When were you going to tell me that you moonlighted as a tinkerer, Rhys?"

He rested his cheek against her brow, taking in the soft, pleasing warmth of her skin. "I had no idea I was one until tonight. I reset the automaton's windup key. It accepted my voice pattern in the process. That's how it recognized me and came into the brig."

She raised her head, pursing her lips into a pretty frown. "That's not how the voice response mechanism works."

"Maybe it isn't effective."

"I beg your pardon?"

Rhys spoke quickly as he could see her forming a protest. "I mean that perhaps the voice response is in the armor plating itself. You said it contained an alloy that conducted sound. What if that alloy makes the automatons register commands in addition to its wiring?"

"It's possible, especially if you activated the automaton simply by speaking near it. But that's a very dangerous effect. I must find out how to stabilize it."

He touched the knot at her temple, anger rekindling at the mutinous crewmen. "Not until we get to New Britannia. That automaton freed me from my cell. It's now functioning as one for Finley."

A smile passed her lips. "It's about time you appreciated my work."

"That's not all I appreciate about you."

She didn't quite know what to do with his comment. She glanced to the side, bashful. "Finley changed course to Le Havre with intent to give the automatons to Broussard. You'll want to reset your coordinates, unless you intend to pursue Broussard on his shores."

"We'll continue to New Britannia. My first priority is getting you to safety. Then I'll hunt for Broussard."

"What am I doing in the brig?" Malcolm's voice echoed out of the darkness. He staggered forth from the entrance, eyes glued to the decimated doorframe and floor. "Mother's love, what happened to the brig?"

Rhys let go of Lydia. "You missed the mutiny. Finley drugged you and the crew with chloroform and put me in the cell."

Malcolm looked up at the automaton holding Finley and reared back. He saw Thomas's body on the floor. "The machine did that to him?"

"He's still breathing, but he's in need of doctoring. So are two more men. Nikolaos and Duncan are outside the cargo hold."

Finley spat at Malcolm. "I should've done to you what I did to that Aspasian toady."

Rhys marched up to the automaton and delivered a punch between Finley's eyes. He slumped over. The automaton adjusted to accommodate the slackened weight of his unconscious form.

"Thank you, Captain." Malcolm wiped his arm on Finley's shirt without missing a beat. "And how are you, lass?"

"I'm fine, Mr. Clark." She looked to Rhys. "Now."

A slow heat spread through Rhys's veins, doing more wonders for his aching ribs and elbow than a warm compression ever could.

"The engineers are waking up. Don't waste time gawking, you two." Malcolm fussed over his shoulder at Smythe and O'Neil "'Tis the brig you're in. The captain will explain all later. How, I don't know, but get to and follow me. We have the injured to tend to."

He grabbed the two groggy men by the shirtsleeves and hauled them towards Thomas. Once they gained their bearings, they lifted him up and carried him to the stairs. Malcolm looked to Finley. "What are we to do with him?"

Rhys barely spared Finley a glance. "He stays there till the COIC comes to view their choice pick of navigators. We'll keep the automaton wound up to hold him in place. Just find a feeding bowl and a slop bucket."

"I always knew he was about as useless as the foam off a whale's blowhole."

"See that Duncan and Thomas are also restrained after they awaken."

"Aye." Malcolm hustled O'Neil and Smythe up the crumbling stairs.

Lydia wrinkled her nose after they left. "A slop bucket?"

"Would you rather we dispense with one for Finley? Things could get rather distasteful very fast."

"My automaton had better be scrubbed top to bottom before I get it back."

"You have my word, my lady. You should return upstairs and get cleaned up."

She nodded. "It's a shame how Finley corrupted Duncan and Thomas with lies. I've seen plenty tonight to make me sleep with the lantern lit for months."

Not if he was there to kiss her to sleep. Something tugged in Rhys's chest as he thought about spending a life with Lydia. It didn't matter that she came from a different country or had a foreign way of life. With her, he never felt more at home.

She caught him looking at her and cleared her throat. "I'm going to see about Nikolaos."

"You should. He did act as your guardian tonight."

"How do you know?"

"I was in the cargo hold when Finley shot him. I would have got Finley if he and Thomas hadn't been in the way."

"You truly are everywhere on this ship." She gave him one of her reticent little smiles before leaving.

Everywhere on the ship. But now that Lydia embraced him and hinted at some affection towards him, where did he stand with her?

***

New Britannia, August 1837

"Land ahead, gents. Furl the sails. We're coming upon New Britannia."

Rhys's hearty cheer reached Lydia's ears from across the top deck. As the reduced crew hurried to obey, pepped with enthusiasm to get home after a grueling fortnight at sea, she raised her head to welcome the crisp breeze that blew from the crags of New Britannia's rocky shore. Scents of unfamiliar timber filled her nose. She took in the first sightings of her new home ahead, a land mass of dark greens and browns surrounded by gray-blue waters.

"What does it look like?" Nikolaos shifted on his pallet beside her chair. He grimaced from the effort behind his choppy movement.

Lydia took the spare folded blanket at the foot of the pallet and tucked it behind his head. "Better?"

He managed a weak nod. "A finger of rum would complete things."

"You sound just like a sailor." She reached for the bottle on the medical tray at her side. "Malcolm thinks it makes the best curative."

"It numbs the pain of his doctoring, at least."

Lydia glanced at the bandaged stump that was once Nikolaos's right arm. "Malcolm did all he could, but there was no saving your arm." She held the cup of rum to his lips. "But it did keep the bullet from hitting your vital organs."

Nikolaos drank while he clutched his bandaged side with his left hand. "The bosun did a thorough job," he admitted when she took the cup away. "But removing these stitches will not be pleasant."

"You should cease complaining and be grateful he stitched you closed." Lydia craned her neck to see the sail she mended flying overhead. The corner seam at the very top puckered in the wind in sharp contrast to the smoothly sewn ones stitched by Malcolm's hand. "If I had to close your wounds, I would have welded them shut."

"You mean cauterize." Rhys strode up to her chair, carrying a spyglass in his right hand. His left arm was bandaged and wrapped in a sling about his neck. The mutinous ordeal of five days ago still shown in the tired lines around his eyes, but his wind-tossed hair gave him a playful, indolent look that Lydia couldn't help but smile at.

"Cauterize. Weld. The processes are essentially the same."

"Not quite." Rhys's lips twitched.

"How fortunate I am that Lydia did not become a doctor." Nikolaos turned his head away.

"Or a seamstress," Rhys added, his gaze flicking up to the sail with the puckered corner.

Lydia scoffed at their efforts to make sport of her. "A fine thing to say when I've played nurse to you, Nikolaos. And you, Rhys." She narrowed her eyes.

He blinked in picture-perfect innocence, or as much innocence as an imposing, dark-eyed, six-foot-four sea captain could muster.

"I need not begin to tell you what I've done to keep your ship afloat."

"You're beautiful when you're modest." He handed her the spyglass. "Take a closer look to shore. The coastal watch has already alerted the COIC representatives to our approach."

Lydia peered through the spyglass. Everything about the envoys was foreign, from their layered, elaborate dress to the armored carriages their horses maneuvered along the sandy portion of the beach. "They've been expecting us."

"We've been delayed with no form of communication explaining why."

"You have three reasons confined in the brig below." Lydia held the spyglass for Nikolaos to look towards shore.

"The COIC won't be pleased to hear about the mutiny," Rhys said. "But that's nothing you need to concern yourself with. We row to shore in an hour. If you'd prefer to change into a dress, there's time."

Lydia arched an eyebrow. "Are you implying that my mode of dress is not flattering to Londoners' eyes, Captain?"

He took an appreciative study of her pants-clad legs. "Londoners prefer women to wear dresses, but...I am Welsh."

Nikolaos groaned. "And I am an ill man. My stomach hurts to breathe, much less retch from listening to you both prattle like lovesick schoolchildren." He pushed the spyglass away from his eye.

Lydia retracted the instrument. "That's about enough of your melodramatics, Nikolaos." Didn't he realize that his current injuries only served to keep Rhys from giving him new ones?

Rhys held his hand out to her. "You heard him. Mustn't trouble a sick man."

She and Rhys left the foredeck and walked to the ship's stern, away from Nikolaos and the crew.

Lydia leaned on the rails overlooking the waters of the Channel they earlier navigated. "That's how you know Nikolaos is feeling poorly. He usually has much stronger barbs than calling people schoolchildren."

"Lovesick schoolchildren," Rhys corrected.

She bit the inside of her lip as she thought of a comment to deflect from the awkward moment. "He'll have more ridicule for us as the laudanum wears off."

"I've had enough, Lydia."

"You've listened to him for a few months. Try doing it for years."

"I was referring to you."

"What have I done?"

Rhys took his hand off the rail. "You're evading me. I can tell by the way you bite your lip."

She ceased the action immediately.

He took a breath of sea air. "I am not lovesick, but I am in love with you. It's obvious to all but you, since I can't seem to hide it from anyone on the ship."

Lydia kept quiet as she let the declaration sink in.

He went on. "You're far too intelligent to convince me you have nothing to say."

"Well, since you put it so sweetly."

Rhys ran his hand through his hair, the first time she'd seen him make such a nervous gesture. Was Rhys ever nervous about anything? "It's not easy for a man to reveal such things."

"It's not easy for me, either." Lydia stared into his eyes and imagined they possessed a wealth of secrets. "When the mutiny occurred, I thought you were dead. You have no idea what it did to me to assume the worst happened to you."

He reached for her. It amazed Lydia each time how readily she went into his embrace, both sheltering and solid.

"You should know I don't go away so easily." He purred in her ear. She laughed. He drew back slightly, still holding her by the shoulder. "Lydia, what I said before about how I don't discuss my past. It's time that I did."

She put a finger to his lips. "Finley told me about your history as a pirate. He did it maliciously, of course, but it doesn't matter. After all that's happened, I have a new understanding and respect for you. Your actions show that you're not the man you were before."

Rhys drew his brows together. He took her finger away from his lips. "What did Finley tell you?"

"He said he was on the ship that brought you and Malcolm to stand trial two years ago." It embarrassed her to repeat the details. "Finley was probably exaggerating. And if he wasn't, I'm sure what you did to get thrown in jail was nothing in comparison to the gross criminal negligence other pirates exacted at the time. My husband was one of their victims."

Rhys frowned, bemused. "But your husband died at sea."

How did he know the details surrounding Galen's passing? "Yes. The official report is that a gunpowder explosion occurred on the ship he bought passage on in Italy, but I didn't tell you about that. Did Nikolaos?"

Rhys's tanned face paled before her eyes.

Chapter 19

"Rhys, you're beginning to make me worry. Why are you not answering?"

He finally focused his eyes on Lydia and when he did, they shone with wildness that she'd never seen before. "What ship did you say your husband sailed?"

"I never said, but it was the *Donna Dulce*. Why?"

"God help me."

"What is it?"

"Lydia, I'm so very sorry."

The horror in his gaze left her fearful and bewildered. "Sorry about what?"

His tone blackened. "The *Donna Dulce* explosion wasn't an accident."

Her words caught in her throat. "What?"

"A pirate fired upon the ship. He captained *The Neptune*, and…I was part of his crew."

The revelation took the wind out of her. Everything she believed about the circumstances surrounding Galen was confirmed. He was no victim of an accident. He was murdered.

Even so, she looked to Rhys, desperate for there to be error in his recollection. "But you're an ambassador. A COIC agent. You couldn't have been on that ship."

"I didn't take part in the attack, but I was onboard." He lowered his head. "When Malcolm and I accepted positions as sailors, we didn't know the captain turned pirate. He revealed his intentions to steal from merchant vessels after we sailed to open waters. By then, it was too late."

Lydia backed away from him. Rhys extended his right arm, stopping short of reaching her.

"Malcolm and I were chained in the brig when we refused to board the *Donna Dulce*, but we heard everything down below." He grimaced as though someone struck him. "To this day, I can't put the sounds of anguished men from my mind."

Lydia felt the tears well in her eyes. She glowered at Rhys through blurred vision.

"The king's navy caught up with us after they learned the captain recruited a crew in British port. Malcolm and I testified to the captain's crime when we stood trial for piracy. In return for our testimonies, we were given prison sentences and the parole condition that we serve the COIC on matters of maritime intrigue."

Lydia balled her fists. "You were made a diplomat. You profited from crimes that other men hang for."

"No." Rhys set his jaw. "There is no reward in knowing that I couldn't prevent innocent men from dying. Men like your husband."

Lydia heard Rhys's words, sensed his honesty, and still a black rage bubbled up inside her. It filled the spaces of her mind. Made her want to scream. She launched herself past him.

"Lydia, wait."

"Do not follow me." She whirled. "You are a liar. A schemer pretending to be an honorable man."

Rhys didn't retreat. "Lydia, I didn't know that you had a connection to the *Donna Dulce*."

"You think that changes things? I came to trust you."

Rhys appeared torn, but she refused to let herself sympathize when her own heart was beaten down.

"You helped your country," he said. "What you now know about me doesn't change that."

"You'll forgive me for not having the sophistication to pick and choose how I see you because you've thrown money Aspasia's way." She shook her head, disgusted at him and even more at her own bitter sarcasm. "Your entire mission has been a fraud. You're a fraud."

She raced for the topside door. Malcolm and O'Neil worked on the rigging nearby. They halted their progress as they spotted her advance.

"Lass?" Malcolm called.

Ignoring him, she fumbled at the door latch before it gave in to her clumsy handling. Hurling herself into the ship's interior, she slammed it behind her. The tears spilled down her cheeks. Lydia wiped at them in a fury, ashamed that her emotions were laid bare for all to gawk at.

It had all been a fantasy, this whirlwind dalliance. It didn't matter that Rhys said he was in love with her. His connection to the *Donna Dulce* was too much to bear. There was no moving past it.

She played the fool for Rhys. Now she couldn't undo her mistake. She had no choice but to continue onward to New Britannia's shores and live with the consequences of giving her heart to a man who even told her that he couldn't offer her his. Not in the way she wanted. And now she knew why.

***

Rhys stood on the port bow with the Secretary of the COIC and watched as envoys loaded the last automaton on the carriages on shore. Lydia's carriage led the line of transport vehicles. She was to be escorted to an apartment in an estate on the outskirts of central London.

He never got a chance to speak to her after she ran off. She locked herself in his cabin until the envoys came below deck to find her. Rhys pained at the sight of her scrubbed face, still bearing reddened eyes and remnants of tears as she swept past him, following the officials who carried her belongings off the ship.

How would he face her again after this?

"Did you hear me, Agent Cartret?" The Secretary of the COIC snapped shut a brown ledger detailing the ship's estimated damage. "I will see you and Clark in my office tomorrow morning. I expect a full written account of what transpired in the brig, as well as that break in the engine room."

"What do you intend to do with the mutineers?" Rhys pointed to the beachfront where armed agents surrounded the three sailors. They sat in the sand, hands bound behind their backs.

"They're being taken to headquarters where they'll be interrogated by an official. From there, Scotland Yard will escort them to jail to await trial on the charges of mutiny and treason. I still cannot believe a decorated naval officer would stoop to such a low. Finley's credentials were impeccable."

Rhys scoffed at Finley's supposed qualifications. "You have six people to attest to his crime."

The Secretary gave a firm shake of his head. "The Aspasians have diplomatic immunity. Even though Lady Dimosthenis informed me of Finley's intentions, including his plan to contract with Broussard, her testimony in Admiralty Court will not be required."

Rhys's shoulders tensed. He switched his gaze to the quarterdeck, where Nikolaos was being fastened to a gurney to be lowered into a longboat. "Lord Abeiron took part in the mutiny. You're not going to let him walk free."

"*Agent* Cartret." The Secretary bristled as he pulled rank. "Need I remind you of the purpose of your assignment? New Britannia cannot maintain good standing with Aspasia if we hold that nation's representative liable for any supposed misconduct."

"Lord Abeiron's 'misconduct' was not supposed." Rhys ground out through his teeth.

A muscle in the Secretary's neck twitched. "What proof do you have of his involvement? If anything, Lord Abeiron can blame *you* for his sustained injuries. No firearm on this vessel short of a cannon could have cost him his arm save for your custom revolver and bullets."

"Which Finley stole from me and used on Lord Abeiron after he refused to continue taking part in the mutiny."

"The matter is no longer in your authority. Lord Abeiron has already claimed diplomatic immunity and has graciously agreed to not hold you and the crew responsible for the injuries he and Lady Dimosthenis sustained. You know the rules, Cartret."

Rhys knew what the Secretary could do with the rules. Still, he loathed admitting that there was nothing he could do about Nikolaos. International law turned in the man's favor. The fact that he lost his right arm in diplomatic service also bore a great deal of weight.

Lydia probably saw Nikolaos in a better light than she did him at this moment. Rhys moved to fold his arms across his chest, remembering too late that one arm was in a sling. He grunted.

The Secretary went on droning. "For what it's worth, I'd say you did rather well in keeping a hold of the ship. Other than the unfortunate consequences of the storm and mutiny, of course. Let's hope the expense report balances out. Good day, Agent Cartret." He walked to the starboard side and signaled for the crew to lower him down in a longboat.

Rhys clenched his right hand as he marched below deck, intent on finding sustenance in the galley before he made the trip into London. Although, he knew the gnawing sensation in his stomach was not present on account of hunger.

Malcolm was in the galley, clearing out the remaining food in the pantry. He took one look at Rhys and scowled. "What tripe did you say to the lass? She was all in tears when she left." He waved a jar of gherkins at him.

Rhys went to the cupboards and started rummaging. "She knows, Malcolm. She knows we were onboard *The Neptune*. Her husband was on the *Donna Dulce*."

Glass shattered behind him. "What?"

The sharp tang of brine filled the galley as Rhys summarized the last conversation he had with Lydia. When he finished, Malcolm's scowl was gone, replaced by a slack jaw. "I always knew there'd be a day our mistake would come back to haunt us, Malcolm. I just never thought I'd meet someone connected to it. Only fate would allow me to fall in love with a woman who makes me forget the past, yet is forever entwined with it." Rhys stepped over the broken gherkin jar and settled against a table. "And I still want to be with her."

"What are you going to do?"

"What haven't I done? I've taken everything from Lydia. I've acquired her inventions, took her out of her own country, away from family. Now I learn that her husband was one of the victims on that ship." Rhys stood to his full height. "I have to bring justice to this matter, even if Lydia doesn't want to speak to me again. I owe her more than I can ever repay."

Malcolm hung his head. "The poor lass. I don't know what to say. All I know is, I need a drink after hearing this. A tall, long swig of rum."

Rhys left the galley. He didn't need liquid fortification. He needed Lydia, and he was intent to get her to hear him one more time. It didn't matter how long it took.

THE CURIOSITY CHRONICLES: BOOKS 1-3

Chapter 20

London, October 1837

Lydia didn't see Rhys for the next two months.

With no word from the COIC of his whereabouts, she came to the conclusion that he was off on another mission, his involvement with her already forgotten. Given the bitter, angry words she threw at him before they parted ways, why should he want to see her again?

Lydia tried distracting herself from her regret by focusing on her new life in London. New Britannia's capital teemed with people. A jaunt through the COIC building alone indicated that she was not the only foreigner in the city. The agency stood as a beacon of progress, employing people of many nations and races, and frequently seeking contributors of varying schools of thought.

Over time, Lydia found herself letting go of her initial beliefs of New Britannia's citizenry. Those who crossed her path were nothing like the hard, callous pirates who invaded Aspasia. Rhys was correct in that observation.

Rhys. No matter how busy her days, she often laid awake at night in her amply-furnished but lonely apartments, thinking of him.

Rhys was not a pirate. Out of anger and grief over the truth concerning her husband's fate, she treated him as though he were guilty of a crime he didn't commit. She had been given a second chance at love, and she threw it away.

But at least there was one matter she could make right for Rhys, even if he never learned of it. Lydia began the task shortly after her arrival in London. It started with a letter she wrote to King Sabba.

One morning in October at her workroom in her apartment, the doorman announced Nikolaos's presence over the apartment's floor to floor speaker system.

"Send him in," she said into the speaker system as she closed the panel on the second-issue windup automaton model.

"What about the other gentlemen you called for, your ladyship? They're waiting in the parlor room." The doorman's voice came in tinny and muted through the receiver.

"Tell them to go into the hall as instructed. We will speak with them shortly."

Two minutes later, Nikolaos glided through the door, red robes moving at his feet. He never adopted the British men's suit and cravat, choosing instead to retain his Aspasian attire. With his draping garments and new mechanical right arm, he fast received the label of an eccentric.

"I received word from King Sabba." Using his brass and steel arm, he withdrew an envelope from the folds of his robe. "He reports that the coffer stores grow weekly."

Lydia was pleased. "Our efforts proved successful."

"That is not all that has been growing. He writes to say that Her Majesty Queen Eleni is expecting. She is to bring a son or daughter into the world by December."

"No wonder she had bouts of illness during the summer months. She wasn't sickly. She was with child."

"Yes." Nikolaos didn't sound too pleased. "An heir to the Aspasian throne."

"That drops me from the line." The notion of returning to plebeian citizenship brought Lydia relief rather than disappointment. The fate of the Aspasian throne no longer rested on her.

"And there is yet one more thing. My presence is requested in Aspasia. His Majesty informs me that the matter is most urgent."

Lydia tilted her head. "Did the king say why you were being recalled?"

Nikolaos handed her the official document. "He said it involved my role as a state official, but I do not see how. International affairs have added much to my life, despite an initial loss." He wiggled his metal fingers. "I received a tidy sum from New Britannia for the loss of my arm. I am even being paid as a tester of Dr. Valerian's mechanical prostheses. An eccentric and curious man he is, but his designs are quite clever. I should be able to master the movements of this arm in several weeks."

Lydia gave him a smile as he rambled on about himself. "Always the opportunist, aren't you?"

"I hope you learned something from watching me these past several months."

"Oh, I have. Never reveal your hand until the moment your opponent is assured of his fate. Am I paraphrasing correctly?"

Nikolaos closed his metal hand. "I suppose. All matters of past associations aside, we should focus on the future. If I have to take a brief trip home, we should marry to ensure you will have protected status while I am away. I have noticed more than one man at that COIC building looking at you."

Lydia gave a light shrug of dismissal. "They attend my automaton demonstrations. They have to look at me since I'm standing at the front of the room."

Nikolaos's mustache twitched. "What is on your mind, Lydia? Are you still pining over Cartret since he left you straggled on the beach?"

Lydia continued to smile through his attempts to quash her façade. "I hope you learned all you could about that mechanical arm from Dr. Valerian."

"What do you mean?"

Lydia rang the bell for the attendant. Within seconds, four burly constables entered the room. They surrounded Nikolaos.

One jingled cuffs. "We're here on behalf of the Foreign Office, at your king's request. Come along with us, your lordship, and we won't be forced to use these."

Nikolaos looked askance at Lydia. "What is going on here?"

Lydia dangled King Sabba's letter in his face. "This is the result of my correspondence to His Majesty. I made known to him your less than patriotic actions during the voyage to New Britannia. You may be shielded by diplomatic immunity abroad, but the matter is entirely different in our own country."

Nikolaos's eyes grew big and his lips curled. "You told him?"

"You don't listen very well when you're nervous. Let me put it to you in Greek." She met him eye to eye and spoke their shared language quickly and precisely. "I'm grateful you stood up for me when Finley threatened to shoot me, but I won't stand for being a pawn in your greedy schemes. Now these constables will escort you to the docks where a ship is waiting to take you back to Aspasia. There's no sense in struggling. They have official deportation papers."

Strands of Nikolaos's thinning hair fell over his forehead as he struggled against the firm hold of the constables. "Do you really think that I will leave London now that I know why I am being called home?"

Lydia folded the letter and tucked it away. She looked to the chief constable. "Would you prefer to tell him?"

"My pleasure, your ladyship. Lord Abeiron, New Britannia no longer recognizes your diplomatic status. That means you won't be compensated or given room and board. Your accounts have been seized. Your assets will be funneled to King Sabba to do with as he will."

Lydia added, "I suggest you board that vessel immediately. And pray that my uncle deals fairly with you."

She turned her back as Nikolaos was dragged away. His angry shouts echoed down the hall and all the way outside in the streets until she heard the door of a Black Maria shut, cutting him off for good.

It was done.

The confrontation left her tense, but everything went according to plan. Nikolaos would never bother her or take advantage of anyone else again.

She sat down on the workbench to collect herself. Outside the street bustled with the sounds of horses trotting, newsboys yelling, and peddlers hawking. Inside the grandfather clock next to the fireplace struck noon.

"Lady Dimosthenis?" The doorman appeared at the workroom entrance.

She turned from the clock. "Yes?"

"A messenger from the Cabinet of Intellectual Curiosities came by and left a note. He apologizes for the short notice, but your presence is requested, nay, required at their building this afternoon at three."

"That is very short notice. Did they say what it was about?"

He presented her with the calling card. "That is all the messenger told me. I suppose it has to do with those automatons. Perhaps the two manuals you published in the last month weren't enough to answer all their questions." He provided his droll observation.

Lydia turned the calling card over. Nothing on the back side. "Well, if I must make an appearance. Please inform Mrs. Huckabee that I will need her assistance." She referred to the matronly attendant who usually helped lace her into the beautiful yet rigid dresses and underpinnings that were ladies fashion in New Britannia.

The doorman bowed. "Yes, my lady. I will send for a cab as well." He departed from the room.

Despite her display of indifference to the request for an appearance at the COIC, Lydia did wonder what it was about. What more could the officials want her to supply?

She sighed and went to change from her work clothes into something involving a skirt and corset.

***

"And that's how the hydraulic fluid pumps through the engine and powers the automaton. Are there any questions?" Lydia asked at the end of her presentation. When none were forthcoming, she concluded. "Thank you for your time, gentlemen."

The COIC officials politely applauded Lydia. She removed the diagram of an automaton from the easel at the front of the audience chamber.

"Thank you again, Lady Dimosthenis. If you would wait in my office, we'll send for you shortly." The Secretary held the door open for her.

What was left to deliberate? Lydia's curiosity was mixed with a shred of annoyance. She gave the officials the same presentation one week before.

"You'll find tea and refreshments in the office," the Secretary said as she passed him.

"Mr. Secretary, was there anything that I failed to clarify in my presentation?"

The official gave the impression that he had seen and heard every attempt made by those outside of the organization to be privy to its methods. "It is standard procedure for COIC agents to convene privately before decisions are made, Lady Dimosthenis."

"What decision?"

"Control over the automaton manufacture. Now, if you would, do wait in the office. It won't be long."

It was worth a try. Lydia turned right and stopped in her tracks.

Rhys stood at the end of the hall. Dressed in black suit and top hat, he talked with a high-level official, judging from the other man's decorative medallions and ribbons pinned to his coat. Rhys held a black portfolio under his arm.

Every muscle in her body tensed. What was Rhys doing here after two months' absence?

She continued to stare at him. He appeared as the day he stood on the Aspasian beach, handsome and dapper, standing tall over everyone else. Her heart skipped as it did when she first saw him.

He looked her way before walking towards her. Just as she thought he would approach, the Secretary called out to him. "Good afternoon, Agent Cartret. We've been expecting you."

The Secretary ushered him into the audience chamber before he could speak. The door shut behind them.

Most odd.

Lydia proceeded into the Secretary's office. A tea service had been set by the desk. She hurried to pour herself a cup of bergamot tea and sipped the aromatic liquid. Her hands shook so that she spilled several drops onto her dress.

She wished she could hear all that was being said in that chamber.

Lydia reached for a napkin and dabbed the front of her bodice. Ten minutes later, someone tapped on the door. She opened it to Rhys.

He held his top hat and the portfolio under one arm as he stood in the doorway. "May I come in?"

The humble question hung in the air. Something changed in him since she'd seen him on the ship. Though still confident, he seemed more cautious.

"Yes." Lydia set her cup on the tray before she could succeed in spilling the rest of it down her dress. "I was waiting for the Secretary to send for me."

"I just heard about Nikolaos's deportation from the Secretary. I don't know how you got rid of him, but very well played." He gave her a wink that sent her insides fluttering.

"It was a long time coming." Lydia moved to the brown leather Chesterfield. She grew confused as Rhys passed the desk and stopped in front of her. "I thought you said you had official business to tend to."

"I'm here to see you."

The gentle way he said it soothed her nerves. "Didn't we complete our business?"

"Not quite. There was something else that I should have done for you." He presented her with the black portfolio. "This is the manufacturing licensure for the automatons that you asked for in the very beginning. The officials just approved it."

He moved to her side. The lightweight wool of his coat brushed against her arm. Even beneath her long sleeves, the tiny hairs on her arm stood on end. "New Britannia will give Aspasia a share of any profits resulting from the automatons, as well as an annual production fee."

The magnitude of such a gesture washed over her. "Was this why the COIC summoned me today?"

Rhys nodded. "I've been in talks with them since I returned from sea three weeks ago. That's why they kept requesting information from you, to see if granting a full license was a worthy investment."

"I had a feeling you'd gone out to sea again. Not as dangerous as your last expedition, I hope." She found herself bantering with him once more. Whether it was to relive the past or avoid hearing that he moved on from her, she couldn't say.

"I was away for five weeks in France on reconnaissance. We apprehended some of Broussard's men off the coasts of Cherbourg and Le Havre, but they wouldn't give his whereabouts." Rhys set his hat on the Chesterfield and went to the tea service. "The matter is in the hands of another department for the time being. As for the mutineers, well, their days of treason are over. The Admiralty Court found them guilty."

"Where does that leave you?"

"Back to being a merchant until the COIC requires my services again."

Lydia clutched the portfolio. "Thank you for all you've done."

He lifted the lid of the petit fours tray. "Lydia, I was wrong in how I approached you in the first agreement. I shouldn't have dismissed your requests. You deserve to benefit from the fruits of your labor, as should Aspasia." He returned the lid to the petit fours tray without taking a pastry. "I've been wrong about many things. I'm sorry that I didn't reveal my past sooner when it became clear how I felt about you. Those feelings haven't changed."

"I should have trusted you instead of pressing you early on," Lydia acknowledged. "That was wrong."

"I never knew until you mentioned the *Donna Dulce* that you were connected to it. I can't change what happened in Italy. If I could, I would not hesitate to do so in order to spare you the pain. Even if it meant never meeting you or having the privilege of falling in love with you."

Lydia's voice thickened with tears. "I won't lie. I was so angry when you told me you were on that pirate ship, but I've had time to think since then. The circumstances were beyond your control."

He perched on the edge of the desk. "That doesn't negate the damage."

"You have my forgiveness, but that's not what you require. You can't torment yourself forever."

Lydia closed the distance between herself and Rhys. Her fingers touched the planes of his jaw, the lines of his firm, well-shaped mouth. The tension still clung to his shoulders and back, as he held them rigid within the confines of his coat.

"Please forgive yourself." She moved into the space between his arms.

After several moments, he folded them around her. She closed her eyes as a peace settled over her. Being in his embrace again, his cheek touching hers, inhaling his clean masculine scent. She missed him much more than she realized.

He pressed his lips against her ear. "I asked the Secretary if I could present that license to you. I didn't know if you'd want to see me again after this."

"That's not true. I've missed you."

"I love you, Lydia."

"I love you, too."

He captured her mouth with his. She had not forgotten the feel and taste of his lips. The same emotions she experienced during their first kiss increased tenfold as she gave in to his touch, not holding back in fear this time.

Someone coughed. Lydia saw the Secretary at the door.

"Agent Cartret, it appears you and I have different interpretations as to what it means to present Lady Dimosthenis with an important message." The Secretary's prudent tone was laced with prim disapproval.

Rhys stood and shielded Lydia from view. "I apologize. The message was delivered. Lady Dimosthenis will accept the licensure."

"Good. But see that any ancillary messages you have for her don't happen again. At least, not in my office."

"Yes, Mr. Secretary."

"When I return in five minutes, I want you both to have collected yourselves and be ready to meet in the audience chamber."

The door clicked shut. Lydia stepped out of hiding. Rhys's eyes held their mischievous glint again.

"We really must be careful if we're to be working alongside each other," she told him.

"I was thinking of a different arrangement."

"Oh?" She put her hands on her hips. "What did you have in mind?"

His eyes focused on the area of her hips and waist. "Did I say that I preferred you in pants instead of a dress? I may have to side with the Londoners when it comes to that fetching little number."

"You're getting off topic, Rhys."

He took her hands. "I know you've had more than your fill of agreements these past months, but what would you say to just one more? A binding one?"

"I don't know. My experiences so far with negotiating these agreements haven't been the best. What are the terms?"

"They involve a church, a shared home by the sea in Wales…and three automatons."

She all but sputtered. "What in the world do automatons have to do with this binding agreement?"

He gave a rakish smile. "Seeing as how three members of my last crew defected, I want to avoid that happening again on future voyages. Automatons are immensely loyal, even if they make a mess of their surroundings."

She relaxed, laughing. "On one condition. You use the smaller, safer second-issue models that I'm currently designing. And you take me to Aspasia twice a year to visit my parents."

"Those are two conditions, but I will honor both. Does that mean you consent to the full agreement?"

She put a finger to her cheek, pretending to be deep in thought. "You should know that I no longer have a place in line for the Aspasian throne."

"Royal clout is not required for this agreement."

"How long do you intend for it to last?"

He leaned in close. "For as long as we live."

She put her arms around his neck. "In that case, I consent. But I expect this agreement to go into effect as soon as possible."

He kissed her. "I wouldn't have it any other way."

The Armored Doctor
A steampunk tale of mechanical armor, dangerous spies, and the power of compassion
Curiosity Chronicles, Book Two

To those who never give up working for what they believe in.

Chapter 1

November, 1837, London, New Britannia

"Where is Miss Benton?"

Abigail heard the shrill call of the apothecary's wife all the way from the stock room. She hoisted a crate containing empty medicine bottles as she projected her voice in reply, "I'll be there in a minute, Mrs. Macklethorpe."

The floor of the central London apothecary echoed with the clop-clop of stout-heeled shoes before a dour-faced woman launched her matronly form through the stock room doorway. "Why aren't those bottles stocked? That should have been done this morning."

"I had to clear the stock area and sweep the floors first."

"That should have been done the night before. I thought that automaton was supposed to take care of it." Mrs. Macklethorpe pointed to a windup, self-operating machine in the back corner, crafted to resemble a human in body and facial structure, though made entirely of iron, steel, and brass.

"Our service automaton broke down this morning." Abigail set the box on a shelf and dusted her hands on her apron.

Mrs. Macklethorpe pressed her plump hands onto her ample hips. "This store runs on the contributions of paying customers. Go to the front counter. Someone could be here any minute."

Abigail squeezed past the matron and hurried through the store aisles. Behind her, she heard Mrs. Macklethorpe drag a crate across the stock room floor, followed by a relieved sigh as the woman took a seat. *Must be heaven to rest one's feet every now and then*, she thought.

Abigail had little rest since becoming a shop assistant last spring. After her older sister Catherine said she was no longer welcome to live with her and her family in west London, she was forced to accept whatever respectable work was offered in the city. She learned fast that being a spinster of thirty, with no other surviving family or inheritance, left her with very few options for employment.

Still, she thanked divine providence that she had a job. She could accept her lot…if only her sister were willing to make amends and allow her to visit her niece and nephew once in a while.

Abigail arrived at the front of the store, where she helped an elderly couple find a tisane for insomnia. Mrs. Macklethorpe came from the stock room after they left. "I'm going across the street on an errand. Keep to the front counter and don't let those dirty little street urchins in. Last time they stole the ginger chews."

The bells on the door sent Mrs. Macklethorpe off. No sooner did Abigail begin straightening the counter did the bells jingle again.

"Aunt Abigail." A snub-nosed, curly-haired boy burst in.

"Phillip?" Shocked to see her nephew standing before her, Abigail left the counter and went to him. "What are you doing out of school?"

He averted his eyes, looking at the licorice below the counter. "Headmistress Cummings said I could go."

She frowned at the ten year-old, knowingly. "Are you being truant again?"

"No." Phillip bit his lip. "I've been let out of the academy."

"Let out? What did you do?"

He didn't answer.

Abigail would have none of his stalling. "Phillip Evancourt, what did you do?"

"Miss Hinkley, the music instructor, found a dead mouse in her piano."

Abigail's jaw slackened. "Phillip, if your parents knew—"

"You can't tell them."

"I have to. How did you leave the school grounds unseen?"

"I snuck out when the dormitory monitors traded shifts. Are you still going to tell mum and father?"

"Yes. Is your sister still at the academy?"

Sulking, he stared at the floor. "She's outside."

Abigail looked out the shop window and saw a little girl's freckled face staring in. She motioned for the girl to come inside. When Phillip's sister trudged into the store, stockings filthy with street grime, hair ribbons askew, she addressed the eight year-old. "Winnie, did you help your brother frighten Miss Hinkley with that mouse?"

"Yes'm," Winnie squeaked like one.

"Headmistress Cummings didn't release her from the academy." Phillip defended his little sister.

"But I don't want to be in that academy without my brother." Winnie stamped her foot, sending dirt on the recently-mopped floor.

Abigail sighed. They certainly got their stubbornness from the Benton side of the family. "I'll take you both to your mother so she can straighten this out."

"Mum and father are in Switzerland," Phillip revealed. "They won't be back for a week."

"I forgot your parents leave for Switzerland this time of year."

Winnie played with the dirt that fell from her shoe. "Can't we stay here with you, Auntie Abigail? We miss you telling us stories about your travels in India."

Abigail's heart ached. Aside from the children's rare visits to the apothecary to buy candy, she never got to spend more than a few minutes with them before her sister whisked them off. "I miss you and Phillip, too, Winnie, but this…this is how things must be."

The bells on the door clanged, making her jump. A most remarkable gentleman entered. Tall, of lean build, he let the door bang shut behind him as he marched to the front counter with his ivory-handled walking stick tapping the floor in rhythmic urgency. The tail of his navy blue military-style jacket flailed behind him as his pale blond, straight hair came to settle about his strong shoulders. His eyes were concealed by a pair of spectacles with dark lenses.

Abigail herded the children off to the side. "May I help you, sir?"

His cane tapped on the floor one more time as he removed his spectacles. Piercing, ice blue eyes met hers. "Doctor Jacob Valerian. I'm here to pick up an order."

Winnie peered around Abigail's arm. "Are you a soldier?"

"I was once," he spoke kindly to her.

Phillip peered around her other arm. "Silly Winnie. That's just his coat style. Soldiers don't use walking sticks."

Dr. Valerian quirked an eyebrow. Phillip silenced immediately.

Abigail was mortified at their outbursts. "I deeply apologize for the children, Doctor. Let me see if your order is in the stock room. Excuse us." She took Winnie and Phillip each by the shoulder and led them away.

"His hair's quite long for a gent, isn't it?" Phillip remarked, once they were in the stock room. "Father says he hates how some men at the bank do the same with theirs."

"Never you mind, Phillip." Abigail turned two empty crates upside down for the children to sit where she could see them from the doorway. Everything was kept under lock and key in the stock room, save for empty storage containers. Surely they would be safe here for the time it would take to wait on Dr. Valerian. "I will return. Don't touch anything."

She rummaged through the stock room's bin of special orders before locking it and going back to the counter. Dr. Valerian hadn't moved, his posture arrow-straight. She faced him, taking note of his features. The elegant bone structure of his face, combined with his unique silver-blond hair and blue eyes, gave him an attractive, almost otherworldly quality. "Doctor, I didn't see an order in the stock room with your name on it."

"You must not have looked hard enough. I sent a written request for the order eight days ago. Mr. Macklethorpe replied that it would be ready this week. Is he on the premises?"

Abigail bristled at his terse, dismissive tone. "Mr. Macklethorpe made a personal delivery to a client in Hyde Park Corner. He should be back any moment."

"I don't have time to wait. My lecture is at two o'clock and I need the contents of that order." He withdrew a timepiece from his waistcoat and flipped open the case before clicking it shut again.

Why did doctors frequently act as though they were the only ones whose time was precious? Abigail didn't remember her father ever rushing his patients or acting like he was in a hurry. But then, he had also been a missionary. The caring he administered went far beyond prescribing remedies for physical ailments. God rest his soul.

Abigail sought to emulate her father's patience in her current situation. "Perhaps I can find your order if you tell me what it is."

The doctor's blue gaze washed over her, leaving her slightly intimidated by his cool regard and yet oddly invigorated at the same time. She saw that a faint scar crossed over the area of his left eye. "The order consists of a bottle of antiseptic, two bottles of laudanum, a canister of nitrous oxide, and an ether solvent."

A strange mix. Mr. Macklethorpe sometimes received questionable orders from clients, but this one was particularly striking. Antiseptic was used to cleanse wounds. Laudanum was used to dull pain. But what did Dr. Valerian intend to do with the nitrous oxide and mysterious ether solvent? Together, those items could hardly be considered medicinal.

"You seem perturbed." He observed her with that inscrutable gaze.

Abigail looked away, glancing at Phillip and Winnie before turning to him again. "No, I was thinking about your order."

"Well, I should hope so."

She gave a small chuckle. He cleared his throat. Of course he didn't consider that a joke. She straightened. "What I mean is, my father was a doctor, and I don't recall him using the four ingredients you mentioned together. And certainly not the ether solvent. What do you intend to use them for?"

He lifted that pale eyebrow again. Why was his hair such an unusual color? He appeared to be close in age to her. His face had no lines, save for one that creased over the bridge of his straight nose when he frowned. "Your father was a doctor?"

"Yes."

"And what was he a doctor of?"

"He specialized in maladies of the vascular system, but he treated patients for different illnesses when we were stationed in India."

A change came over Dr. Valerian when she mentioned the country, as though it pained him to hear its name. "India?" And even more so to utter it.

"Yes, my family and I were missionaries. Just a moment. I see several orders below the counter here." She checked the names on the neatly wrapped parcels that sat on the shelf. "Ah, here it is. Dr. J. Valerian."

She placed the fairly heavy box on the countertop, but Dr. Valerian was more interested in studying her than verifying his parcel. Abigail took a step back from him, even though the counter provided a barrier. No man stared at her like that, as though she was of deep and profound interest.

She nodded at the parcel. "The tag indicates that payment was made in advance. There is a six pence holding fee for special orders." Seeing as how he still stared, she added, "Dr. Valerian, I apologize if my remarks about my father or India somehow upset you." But why did they? She had simply responded to his inquiry.

"You asked me what I intended to do with the items I ordered." He tucked his walking stick in the crook of his arm and reached in his coat pocket for money.

"It was somewhat bold of me, but I meant no harm. I just assumed that as a doctor, you would be using them on patients."

"And you thought to warn me against using the nitrous oxide or the ether solvent?"

She merely looked at him, embarrassed by her obviousness.

"Assumption without strong basis is practically useless. And assumption in a place of business can be disastrous, especially if you wish to retain paying customers." He set the money on the counter and took the parcel. "You may tell your employer that I'll be sure to place my order with a different apothecary next time."

The curious doctor left the shop. A small limp in his gait had minimal effect of slowing him down as he coursed through the busy street outside.

Abigail put the money in the register, admonishing herself for losing Mr. Macklethorpe a customer. A high-paying customer, judging from the fee Dr. Valerian paid to expedite the order. She pushed the register door shut.

The din of glass shattering resounded from the stock room.

Abigail ran to the back. The floor was littered with glass shards, interspersed with cork stoppers. Her niece and nephew stood in the center of the mess, eyes wide with guilt-ridden fear. "I told you not to touch anything."

"The crate was hanging off the shelf," Phillip explained. "We were just trying to set it back. Weren't we, Winnie?"

Winnie nodded, lower lip tucked in between her teeth.

"Don't move." Abigail reached for a broom. What was she going to tell her employers?

The sound of heels clop-clopping indicated that she wouldn't have much time to think about it. "Seven heavens," Mrs. Macklethorpe exclaimed, once she bustled through the doorway.

Glass broke under the children's hard-soled shoes as they retreated into a corner. Their saucer eyes swung from Mrs. Macklethorpe to Abigail.

"It was an accident, ma'am. I didn't have the crate settled completely on the shelf." Abigail swept glass from the doorway.

"Those children are responsible, aren't they? Shouldn't your niece and nephew be in school?"

"An incident occurred at their academy. They came to inform me of it, since their parents are traveling." Abigail withheld the details of the incident, as it would only serve to fuel the fire of Mrs. Macklethorpe's disdain of Winnie and Phillip. "I would never ask under ordinary circumstances, but may I take the afternoon to see them back to the academy?"

The matron stomped a foot free of glass. "This will come out of your pay."

Abigail couldn't protest, as it was her idea to settle the children in the stock room until Dr. Valerian was gone. "Yes, ma'am."

Mrs. Macklethorpe clucked her tongue in disapproval. "The husband certainly won't like this when he hears about it."

Abigail was certain she would just as equally not like the consequences.

Chapter 2

Headmistress Cummings of Cummings Proprietary Education Academy raised a wire-thin eyebrow at Abigail from across the heavy oak desk in her office. "Very well, Miss Benton. The children may remain here for one week until their parents return from Switzerland. If their parents do not come forth to readmit them, they will be promptly released. Is that understood?"

"Completely." Abigail sighed with relief as she shifted in her uncomfortable chair.

"If those children misbehave in the slightest manner, you will be summoned at once to retrieve them."

Abigail rose, taking her coat under one arm. "That won't be necessary. They'll be on their best behavior."

"Let us hope so."

"Thank you and good day." Abigail closed the door to the headmistress' office on her way out.

Winnie and Phillip sat on wooden chairs in the hallway. Winnie dozed with her mouth open. Her brother whittled a design into the back of his chair with his thumbnail. Winnie woke from her doze and sat up.

Phillip ceased carving into the chair. "What did that old biddy say?"

"Her name is Headmistress Cummings," Abigail answered. "I asked her to let you stay at the academy until your parents come to readmit you."

Winnie folded her little arms. "I don't want to stay here. Momma and Papa make us. I want our tutor again."

Abigail knew that her sister and her brother-in-law Hammond

dismissed the children's tutor and forced them to attend the expensive, though strict, academy in hopes that it would better serve Phillip and Winnie. Unfortunately, the decision seemed to have worsened the children's propensity to misbehave and made them miss their parents. "Your parents will be here next week, so I suggest you both start being on your best behavior. That means no backtalking, no disruptions, and especially no mice. Is that clear?"

Phillip nodded, grudgingly. "Yes, Aunt Abigail."

"Winifred?"

Winnie cringed at the use of her full name. "Yes, Auntie Abigail."

What was she going to do with the two of them? A better question was, what she was going to do when Catherine and her husband returned? She hadn't spoken more than a few sentences to her sister in months. How would Catherine receive her when she showed up on her doorstep?

Abigail took her nephew and niece and escorted them to their respective dormitories. Once that was done, she was forced to address another important task. Her shift at the apothecary wasn't scheduled to end until eight that evening. If she hurried back, she could earn enough to recoup some of what she loss during the afternoon.

With a collective breath, she buttoned her woolen coat up to her neck and exited the academy.

*****

Both Mr. and Mrs. Macklethorpe were waiting for her at the apothecary when she returned. Mr. Macklethorpe, a medium-built, thoughtful-looking man with an intelligent brow, was usually pleasant when he greeted her. This evening, no smile graced his mustachioed face.

"Miss Benton, we need to speak with you. Put the closed sign up on the window, please."

She did as she was told, even as an uneasy feeling settled in her belly. The Macklethorpes never closed the apothecary during normal business hours unless there was very good reason.

She went to stand before the counter. "Yes?"

Mrs. Macklethorpe scowled at her before casting an expectant look upon her husband. Mr. Macklethorpe smoothed his cravat. "It's come to our attention that your work in the shop has suffered lately. This afternoon you took leave without proper notice."

"Mr. Macklethorpe, I informed your wife that I had no choice but to escort my niece and nephew back to their academy. Their parents are away, and I'm the closest relative they have."

"Yes, Mrs. Macklethorpe told me." He glanced at his wife, who started busying herself by wiping the counter of fingerprints. "You know the rules about visitors during work hours. The children were here for more than ten minutes, and they broke store merchandise."

"But I cleaned it up. It won't happen again."

"Miss Benton, this not only concerns your niece and nephew. A customer had a grievance against the way you treated him."

Abigail's palms sweated. Dr. Valerian must have spoken to Mr. Macklethorpe about her. She must have left quite a foul taste in his mouth if he had already taken the time to return to the apothecary and voice his complaint, especially after saying that he had a lecture to attend. "If I may ask, who had the grievance?"

Mrs. Macklethorpe stopped wiping fingerprints from the counter. "It was the gentleman who came in with his wife shortly before one-thirty this afternoon. He needed an insomnia remedy and you sold him castor oil to put in his tea instead of chamomile."

"Oh, dear." Could she really have been that careless?

Mrs. Macklethorpe continued. "His wife came back while you were out, and oh, did she give us a piece of her mind. Her poor husband will be shut in the privacy of his privy for days."

"I'm so sorry." Abigail looked from the apothecary owner to his wife, but neither was receptive to her imploring gaze.

"It's clear that you're distracted, Miss Benton." Mr. Macklethorpe reached for an envelope on the counter beside his hand. "And you have been since we hired you last spring. These incidences with your family keep you occupied more than your work here. That's why it's best for all that we end your employment. Here is your severance pay." He held out the envelope.

Abigail stared at it for several seconds. "Mr. Macklethorpe, please. Today was simply a trying one. I can do better than this. I know I can."

"Today you caused a man to be in some discomfort, but what if you had given him a stronger medicine by accident? He could have suffered severely or worse."

Abigail shuddered to even consider that possibility.

"Take the envelope. It doesn't please me to do this, but the welfare of our customers is of utmost importance."

With shaky fingers, she grasped the envelope that held the last of her wages. Mr. Macklethorpe smoothed his cravat again before leaving the front of the store.

Mrs. Macklethorpe stayed, but never ceased to wipe the now sparkling, immaculate glass countertop. "On your way out, don't forget to turn the sign over from Closed to Open."

Abigail waited for her to raise her eyes, but when that didn't happen, she left the store as a paid employee for the final time.

***

Jacob left the lecture hall New Britannia College of Science and stepped outside in the dim of the evening. Overhead, charcoal-colored smoke streaked the sky, wafting from the factories further east down by the river. The cold frequently made his right leg hurt. This fierce winter looked like it would offer him only more of the same.

Clutching his parcel from the apothecary, he used his walking stick to hail one of the oncoming hansom cabs. The driver guided his horse near the curb and pulled on its reins.

"Where to?" The driver hopped from his perch with enviable ease and proceeded to open the cab door.

"Nineteen Locksford Lane in Bloomsbury. I'll pay you an extra shilling if you get me there fast enough." Jacob sank into the plush interior of the cab. Once the driver started the cab off, he unwrapped the parcel and lifted the box lid.

There it was. The ether solvent. He lifted the small bottle gingerly in one hand, being careful to cradle its base in his palm. At last, the final key to his experiment.

Most apothecaries never carried ether solvent in stock, but had to place a special order with a small chemical manufacturer in Scarborough. The druggist Macklethorpe worked a miracle to get his order of the solvent to London in less than a fortnight. Jacob considered using the apothecary to purchase his supplies from now on, despite what he uttered in haste to that inquisitive, green-eyed female store clerk.

He couldn't recall if she told him her name. She did, however, tell him just about everything else about her life in a span of five minutes. Her father had been a doctor at some point in his life. She once worked as a missionary in India.

Jacob turned the ether solvent bottle in his hand as the cab's wheels rolled over cobblestone below. Even though he left India four years ago when his country's army sent him back home on a ship, injured, he still remembered his time spent there as though it were yesterday.

The pain and loneliness resulting from the campaign wouldn't let him forget.

The wheels struck a hole in the road, jolting the cab. Jacob closed both hands around the ether bottle and shifted to block the rest of the items from tumbling out of the box on the seat beside him.

Spilling the ether solvent on the floor of the cab would have made Jacob become well-acquainted with the bricks used to pave the street. Spilling the nitrous oxide would have made him too riotous with laughter to care about being trampled under the cab's wheels.

Jacob placed the ether solvent back into the box and secured the lid until the cab came to a stop. He heard the driver jump to the ground.

"Nineteen Locksford Lane. Made it here in under fifteen minutes, I did."

He paid the man an extra shilling as promised and hurried to the two-story property that housed both his residence and practice, where he outfitted amputee patients with artificial limbs. His valet Struthers opened the door just as his hand touched the knob.

"Good evening, Doctor."

"Good evening, Struthers. Where is Maria?" He referred to the valet's wife, who worked alongside her husband in Jacob's employ as a cook and housekeeper. Both employees were longstanding, and Jacob treated them as his family.

"In the kitchen, preparing supper," Struthers answered. "Will you be dining with us?"

"Not tonight. You and Maria may have the evening off."

"Very good, but what of your practice?"

Jacob paused. "I didn't forget an appointment today, did I?"

"No, sir, but the area still has in prominent display your papers and the steel plates you assembled this morning. Shall I remove them?"

Jacob forgot to clear the space in his rush from the house. He pictured what the practice looked like. His notebooks sat piled on the examination table. Tools and prosthetic models lay in groups on the floor. "I really must place an advertisement in the *Times* for a new assistant. It's a shame my last one gave his notice. What did he say it was about?"

Struthers placed his hands behind his back. "I do recall, as you said, 'some nonsense with the physicians' practices in Cavendish Square being less cluttered'."

"Oh, yes. Right. Well, the young medical student should have realized that my specialty is not one of convention . Prosthetic devices take immense patience and time to craft."

"Indeed, Doctor."

Jacob realized that he had still to answer Struthers' inquiry about tidying up the practice. "Before you leave, if you would please see that the area is fit to receive patients, I would appreciate it. And I will place that advertisement tomorrow."

"I've already taken the liberty of doing so. It's been listed in the *Times* for six days. Let us hope someone will answer it soon."

Struthers' reliability never failed to impress. "Thank you."

"Is there anything else, sir?"

"No, Struthers. I'll see you and Maria in the morning." Jacob continued on his way, without handing Struthers his coat to put on the rack.

With walking stick and box in his hands, he traversed the hall and opened the door at the end of it, leading to the cellar. Down the steps he went, his right leg protesting the journey after a full day traversing lecture halls and the streets of London, but he soon arrived to his workroom.

In the dimness of light seeping through the doorway above, Jacob flipped a switch on the wall to turn on the lamps. Their experimental electric coil bulbs crackled on.

Everything was where he left it. Glass tubes and containers sat on the long table. Across the room, the door leading to the blast furnace on the rear lawn, where he forged the mechanical prosthetics, remained locked. On a shelf beside the door, notebooks lay scattered, evidence of his prior assistant's departure over two weeks ago. He truly could do with a new one soon.

Jacob approached the table. The sample he had worked on yesterday evening remained covered under a piece of cloth. He lifted the cloth. A six-inch square of copper resided on a steel tray. Now that he had the final ingredient, he could complete his experiment.

Jacob set his walking stick and box to the side, removed his jacket, and began to work. He took a knife and started cutting through the edge of the metal. Once he had a sliver, he set it inside a glass bowl.

Jacob then took the ether solvent out of the box. He removed the wax seal and cork stopper, tilted the bottle over the bowl, and let one drop fall on the metal sliver. He held his breath as a single wisp of smoke arose. The ether drop bubbled and spread over the metal, merging and penetrating through the layers until there was no longer a solid mass, but a liquid that coated the bottom of the bowl in a viscous layer.

"It works." Jacob's whisper matched the soft rasp of the ether solvent as it finished its work. He put the cork back on the bottle and set it aside. Then he lifted the bowl and brought it under the lamplight. What he saw brought the corners of his mouth upward. "I knew there was something about the properties of this Aspasian metal."

He didn't care that the statement was directed to no one. His theory proved true after weeks of speculation.

In the previous autumn, he learned of a Mediterranean island called Aspasia that produced iron and copper that showed excellent conductivity of sound, far better than ordinary metals. These Aspasian metals were already being experimented with in automatons. The metals granted the machines the ability to respond to the human voice.

News of such a marvel gave Jacob an interesting theory to test: What if the metals could improve functions of other devices, such as weapons or prosthetics worn on the body?

If his theory proved true, it had the potential to help many people, especially his patients. Then the real work could begin.

Chapter 3

The female desk clerk at the employment office of east Holborn shut the book containing the weekly job postings. "So sorry, Miss Benton, but there isn't any work available for ladies at the moment."

It had been four days since Abigail was dismissed from employment at the apothecary, and how long she spent seeking another place to work. She remained optimistic at first, but as she prepared to leave the desk of yet another employment office empty-handed, her buoyant mood began to sink.

"There must be some work available. Christmas will be here soon. Do any shopkeepers have need of an assistant to help with additional customers?"

"We've already fulfilled requests for more store clerks. The last one was filled yesterday."

Abigail looked over her shoulder at the line of men and women behind her who were also seeking work. She knew it wouldn't do to stall the line's progression, but she had to make sure to explore all prospects. "I do have some experience in supervising children. Are there any positions for a tutor or governess?"

The desk clerk shook her head. "You may have better luck if you come back next week."

Abigail slipped from the front of the line. In the corridor outside the office, she saw two people reading the advertisement spread of the *Times* on the wall's job posting board. She inspected it once they left.

The desk clerk was right. Hardly any positions available were suitable for women. Abigail skimmed a column until her eyes caught a notice for a physician's assistant.

Ambitious and skilled person needed immediately for physician's practice. In addition to normal business hours, must be able to work some evenings. Pay to start at 18 shillings a week. Inquire within at 19 Locksford Lane, Bloomsbury.

She kept her finger on the address. She had experience helping her father keep records of his patients. She even made rounds with him in the local Indian villages. This job would undoubtedly have similar responsibilities. And at eighteen shillings a week, it was worth applying for.

Abigail had nothing to lose, save her lodgings at the boarding house if she didn't come up with rent money in the next week.

She committed the address to memory before leaving the employment office.

***

Locksford Lane was a respectable neighborhood of middle-class professionals, but like most addresses of central London, it was not far from the outskirts of industry. As Abigail navigated the populated street of drays, cabs, and fellow pedestrians, she saw the smokestacks of the paper mills rising above the residences.

Abigail walked further up the lane. The roofs of the houses held dustings of fine snow. Tiny icicles laced the edges of windowsills and clung to the gaslights lining the cobblestone street.

She stopped in front of a large, two-story residence at the very end of the street, spaced apart from the neighboring houses by an acre on each side. Abigail saw the engraved numbers 1 and 9 on the sidewalk in front of it. She cast her vision to the rooftop and saw a thin trail of smoke that appeared to be coming from the back of the house.

The path to the residence was swept clean of snow. A layer of coarse salt crunched under Abigail's shoes as she drew up to the door. She shifted her eyes to the window on the door's right. Drawn curtains discouraged passerby from peering inside.

Abigail lifted the brass knocker and let it fall. Then she noticed the small plaque beside the door. *Doctor Jacob Valerian, physician and prosthetics outfitter.*

She snatched her hand back. Could this really be the residence of the harried doctor that came to the apothecary four days ago? Was it he who placed the notice in the paper?

Abigail questioned whether she had taken down the correct address. If memory served, this was the right place. But what would Dr. Valerian make of her standing at his door, especially after she had unwittingly succeeded in irritating him only a short time ago?

Instinct prompted her to leave before someone answered the door, but she needed a job. This was the only one available. She had to try. Perhaps the doctor's mood had improved.

The door opened. An older man, dressed in a dark uniform of neatly pressed trousers and suit coat, regarded her with a calm, genteel air. "Good morning, Miss. Do you have an appointment to see Dr. Valerian?"

"No, sir." She folded her cold hands together. "But I am here in answer to the advertisement."

The man's flicker of surprise went nearly undetected, save for the twitching of his right eye. "You're applying for the assistant position?"

"Has it been filled?"

"No, but," he trailed as he regarded her with obvious thought, "I believe the doctor was expecting the position to be filled by a man."

Abigail was prepared for just such a reaction. "I understand, but I have prior experience assisting in a physician's practice."

"That may be so, but Dr. Valerian's practice requires somewhat of a liberal outlook to work in. More liberal than what you may be used to."

What did he mean? Since he went to such trouble to cloak the details of the job, Abigail doubted that he would be more straightforward if she asked. "I can be very open-minded, sir. May I please speak with the doctor?"

"He's not present at the moment."

Of course any proper domestic servant would say that to be rid of unwanted visitors, whether or not the master was at home. But she wouldn't give up that easily. "I'm willing to wait."

"He won't be back until noon. If you would leave a calling card, I'll make sure he receives it."

"I don't have a calling card."

The man gave a mild frown. "Do you have a reference letter from your previous employer?"

A cold wind made Abigail's ears burn. "To be honest, I hastened here from the employment office in east Holborn as soon as I saw the advertisement."

The wind painted rouge on the tip of the man's nose. "I can take your name and your request for Dr. Valerian. But it's quite cold out here. Would you care for some tea inside while you wait?"

Abigail nodded. Dr. Valerian's domestic servant, though very dutiful in screening his master's visitors, was courteous. "Thank you. I would."

She stepped inside the house. Immediately her feet sank in the plush rug near the door. The interior of Dr. Valerian's foyer was not filled with elaborate décor as was the current style, but it was clean, well-lit by gas lamps, and most important of all, warm.

His servant directed her into the parlor and to an armchair in front of the hearth, where a fire crackled below the mantle. "Wait here." He walked down another hallway.

Abigail sat for no more than a few minutes before he returned. He held a leather-bound book in his hands. "This is Dr. Valerian's ledger. Since you don't have a card, I thought this would suffice to, oh dear, this isn't good."

"What is it?"

He lifted several sheets of paper from the ledger. "The doctor forgot his notes. He's giving a demonstration of one of his armored devices today. In less than thirty minutes, in fact."

Abigail looked at the grandfather clock beside the mantle when it struck eleven. "Where is he giving the demonstration?"

"The lecture hall at the New Britannia College of Science. But my wife and I must remain at our posts in case the first afternoon patient arrives early." The domestic servant broke into a brisk pace for the door. "I must find a courier to bring this to him at once."

"I'll do it."

"I beg your pardon?"

Abigail left the cushioned embrace of the armchair and the fireplace's warmth. "I'll do it. I'll take Dr. Valerian's notes to him. That lecture hall is walking distance from here." Her father spoke at the college several times when he sought to raise funding for his missions.

Dr. Valerian's servant gave a vehement shake of his head. "I cannot simply give the doctor's notes to a stranger and trust they will be delivered safely."

"But you are giving them to a stranger, the courier. That is, if you can find one in time. I can make it to that college before eleven-thirty if I leave now."

The man's right eye twitched again. "Young lady, what did you say your name was?"

"I'm Abigail Benton."

"Why should I entrust you with these notes?"

"I've come here seeking work. It involves making sure Dr. Valerian has everything he needs, including his notes. Let me demonstrate that I'm a suitable candidate."

He cast a second worried glance at the clock. "You're right. There isn't time to send for a courier. Remain here." He left the waiting area again and returned with an envelope. He placed the notes inside. "This may be the most confounded thing I have ever done, but I trust you to personally see that this gets to Dr. Valerian. If you fail in any way, I can lose my position."

"We won't have that." Abigail took the envelope from him. "I spent an hour standing in line at the employment office. I couldn't bear to subject anyone else to the experience."

Without waiting to be shown to the door, Abigail saw herself out and started her brisk pace for the lecture hall. She pulled her scarf tighter about her neck with one hand while clutching Dr. Valerian's notes with the other.

She passed people on the streets, darting between pedestrians and newsboys still selling the morning edition on the corner. She hurried up three blocks, breezing through a standing flock of pigeons and sidestepping a pile of rubbish spilling from the gutter before the college stood before her across the street. She walked through the door of the lecture hall.

An attendant met her inside. "Your ticket, Miss." He looked about her as though he were searching for her escort. Of the handful of ladies that were present, all of them hung on the arm of a gentleman.

She raised the envelope before the attendant's eyes. "I'm Dr. Valerian's acting assistant. I'm here to deliver his lecture notes."

"He's in his office. Next hall, fourth door on your left. Say, what happened to Ollie Pickens?"

"Who?"

"Valerian's first assistant."

"I wasn't told. Excuse me." Abigail left the lobby and followed the attendant's directions to Dr. Valerian's office. She knocked on the fourth door.

"Yes, what is it?" The now familiar voice answered from the inside. Abigail imagined she saw a flurry of small movements through the frosted glass window.

She opened the door and stuck her head in. The movements turned out to be papers. Sheets of them, flying in the air, falling to the floor, getting caught in the crevices of the bookcases and furniture. "Dr. Valerian?"

One last sheet made its descent before his silver-blond head appeared from behind the desk, though his back was towards the door. "I said, what is it? The demonstration begins in five minutes and I can't find my notes."

Abigail stepped inside. "I have your notes."

Dr. Valerian finally turned. He stared at her for a moment before recognition settled upon his refined features. "You're that clerk at the apothecary."

"I no longer work there." Raising on her toes, she tiptoed through the spaces between the sheets of paper blanketing half the floor. She extended her hand to give him the envelope.

He took and opened it. "How did you come by my notes?"

"I visited your address this morning in answer to your advertisement."

"You wish to be my assistant?"

She nodded in the face of his disbelief. "Your manservant saw that you left the notes and permitted me to bring them to you."

"Struthers allowed you to—" He stopped and thrust the notes in his jacket pocket. Like the one he wore the first time she'd seen him, this one also possessed brass embellishments and a close fit that suited his tall, trim frame. "I'll question him later." The limp in his right leg was noticeable today as he went past her and grabbed his walking stick and a long metal case by the door. He locked the office after she exited behind him.

She walked alongside him in the hallway. "Should I wait in the audience?"

He shoved his spectacles over his eyes. She noticed the lenses were now clear instead of dark. "Really, Miss…?"

"Abigail Benton."

"Miss Benton, my practice requires someone with a hearty constitution. Many of my patients are victims of horrific accidents. I cannot be hindered by delicate, feminine reactions of weeping and fainting. "

Abigail steeled against his insult upon her gender. "That is most unfair of you, Dr. Valerian."

"I disagree. Now if you'll excuse me." He turned a corner, where he slipped into the side entrance of the auditorium.

Abigail placed her hands on her hips. Dr. Valerian was stinging, a difficult man to please. But he paid well. She could handle his fussiness. She just had to make him see that she could perform the job of physician's assistant as well as any man.

She darted into the auditorium's side entrance, hoping that the next hour of the demonstration would give her an opportunity to do just that.

Chapter 4

How did Miss Abigail Benton manage to talk Struthers into letting her personally deliver his lecture notes?

As Jacob entered the auditorium, his mind still reeled from the sight of her in his office. Her cheeks were pink from the cold and probably exertion from running. The casualness with which she handed him the notes and the confidence in her voice, why, one would think she really was capable of being his assistant.

She brought the notes in the nick of time. He was grateful for that, despite her being a near perfect stranger in possession of some of his most guarded documents. But that had to be dealt with after the lecture. For the next hour, his full concentration needed to be on educating students and members of the public about his new device for self-defense.

Attendees filed into their seats as he neared the stage steps. Professor Markel, one of the lecture's organizers, hastened to take the case containing the device from Jacob in order for him to grasp the stair rail and his walking stick at the same time. Jacob nodded in appreciation, but refused to grip the rail. He ascended the steps slowly and with deliberation as the lecture attendees watched.

Jacob ground his molars, willing his face to not show the painful strain that the seemingly ordinary action of climbing the steps caused him. Some days his leg barely hurt at all. Others were agonizing, with lightning pains shooting up into his thigh and hip with every step.

Today fell into the latter category. Even with the specially-designed reinforcement steel plates he strapped on this morning, his right limb repeatedly protested being put into use.

At last he reached the stage. He adjusted his spectacles against the bright stage lights and took his chair beside the table that held the metal box. Behind the table, on the back wall of the stage, a target circle had been positioned.

Professor Markel clapped twice for the audience to quiet. "Ladies and gentlemen, thank you for coming to the College of Science's weekly lecture series. Today we have speaking…"

Jacob scanned the auditorium while the organizer introduced him. The crowd was modest, about fifty attendees. However, there was someone else among them that he sought to leave a good impression .

Alistair Kidman, head administrative official of New Britannia's premier scientific agency, the Cabinet of Intellectual Curiosities. Known simply as the Secretary, he was in charge of placing new inventions on the agency's roster for acquisition and funding. Jacob received an inquiry from him in late summer, when one of Jacob's prosthetic devices was needed for a visiting diplomat. Since then, the Secretary sought a commission from Jacob to design a wearable weapon that the COIC's agents could use in their missions of espionage and defense abroad against New Britannia's rival, France.

The Secretary gave a nod to Jacob from the right side of the auditorium. Jacob had to succeed in this demonstration. It was the first step towards getting the money needed to better fund his practice and help all of his patients.

"May I present Dr. Jacob Valerian," Professor Markel concluded the introduction.

Jacob waited through the polite round of applause. He projected his voice to reach the back of the auditorium. "It is my pleasure to unveil the newest model in my wearable weapons line." With that, he opened the lid of the box and lifted the device from its cushioned slots. "May I present the gauntlet gun."

He heard a collective murmur as attendees leaned forward to get a better look. Ignoring the pain in his leg, Jacob walked to the stage front with the gauntlet. "To the naked eye, this is a contraption reminiscent of what our ancestors may have worn while riding into battle. But looks are deceiving. This is a modern weapon of defense."

"Looks like a glorified piece of jewelry to me." A student whom Jacob recognized from the school's chemistry wing heckled from the front row.

How such dull-minded fellows gained the attention of the college's admissions board was beyond him. "You can be certain that this device is no trinket. It can mean the difference between life and death on the battlefield or even in a back alley skirmish. I'll provide the demonstration, but first, I need a volunteer to wear the gauntlet."

The room became silent. Jacob looked in the direction where the sound of a man's coughing originated. "Is there a show of hands?"

More coughs and nervous throat clearing commenced. Then a slender hand arose from the middle row of the auditorium. Jacob peered over the rims of his spectacles and saw that it was *her*.

Abigail remained bundled in her coat as she sat between two elderly men. No doubt she intended to approach him again about the assistant position after the demonstration was over.

Jacob looked to the left side of the audience, though he could still see her hand in the air. "I assure you, it's quite safe to volunteer. We will all walk away from this demonstration in one piece."

His comment produced a few chuckles, but no hands except the one he turned away from. Through his peripheral vision, he saw Abigail wave as though she were flagging down a visiting relative at Paddington Station. For goodness sakes, now she rose and stood on tiptoe. Couldn't she see that he was deliberately ignoring her, or at least trying to?

The heckling student had no trouble seeing it. "There's a volunteer for you, Doctor. Let the lady wear the bracelet."

"I'd as soon give her your seat in the chemistry wing, since I hear you're one letter grade away from no longer occupying it."

While the audience laughed, Jacob tightened his grip on the gauntlet. Abigail could not be ignored now. He had to call her to the front. "Would the lady wearing the paisley scarf come forward?"

She practically climbed over the other people in her row before Professor Markel directed her to the front. She accepted his offered hand and proceeded to spill out in the aisle.

As Jacob awaited her approach, he took additional notice of her appearance. She was somewhat tall for a woman, and of slim build. She walked with precise purpose, quick and light.

Under the auditorium lights, her hair showed dark auburn, a flattering hue against the rose tone of her creamy skin.

Professor Markel took her coat and scarf before she climbed onstage. Jacob straightened as she came to stand before him. Where most people would very noticeably stare at his scar, she didn't seem to be interested in focusing on that area. Instead, her soft green eyes were steady as they looked into his.

"You don't take 'no' for an answer, do you, Miss Benton?" he remarked in a voice that only she could hear.

A smile budded on her pink lips as she gave a tiny shake of her head.

***

Though Abigail smiled directly at Dr. Valerian to show him that she possessed the necessary confidence to be his assistant, inside she was shaking. She had never spoken or done anything before an audience. Now she was to help him demonstrate the use of a peculiar, wearable weapon that looked as though it belonged in a museum collection of medieval armaments.

She stared at the gauntlet gun as he provided the audience with an explanation of its structure. The device bore the traditional structure of a knight's protective armor for the hand and wrist. The cuff even extended upward in a chevron pattern, but where the gauntlet differentiated from its medieval predecessor, it did so greatly.

Wires protruded from the wrist to connect to copper fixtures attached to the top of the cuff. The fixtures housed small aluminum vials containing some unnamed liquid or gas component. A small lever extended from the heel of the hand. Abigail supposed that the lever, when force was applied, activated the panels along the cuff's sides.

Dr. Valerian was a physician and prosthetics outfitter. She failed to see how the weapon he held could be considered a medical contribution.

"Your arm, Miss Benton," he prompted.

She extended her right arm, unbuttoned the sleeve of her blouse, and rolled it up as though presenting it to him to draw a sample of blood. He looked at it and then at her before he slid the glove on her fingers.

Was it the coldness of the metal or the surprisingly warm, comforting touch of his fingers as he eased the cuff onto her wrist that caused her to tremble? The soft wool of his jacket sleeve gently brushed against her bare skin, making the hairs on her arm stand on end. She held her breath as he adjusted the buckles of the cuff.

"As you can see, the gauntlet can be adjusted to fit the arms of both sexes." Dr. Valerian raised her arm high for the audience. The gauntlet was heavy. Once he took his hand away, Abigail worked to keep her arm from dropping at her side.

She came upon an observation that prompted an immediate utterance. "I see that I have a true firearm now."

The audience chuckled at her unintentional play on words. Dr. Valerian remained stone-faced. Did he never smile? Even if the pun was rather weak, it still made the audience pay attention.

He certainly would do well to smile. Even sculpted features as his couldn't soften the effects of such a sour frown.

Dr. Valerian displayed that frown directly at her before once again addressing the audience. "Now we will demonstrate how the pistol mechanism works. There is no need to worry about the fatality of the projectiles. For the purposes of the demonstration, they are made of vulcanized rubber."

Dr. Valerian turned from the audience, retrieved his walking stick from where it rested against the table, and walked six paces closer to the target. "The lady will now attempt to fire upon the bull's-eye."

Either he was the most maverick of medical practitioners or very confident in the failsafe construction of his invention. Abigail deemed it to be a combination of both. She went to him, the heels of her shoes echoing across the stage. "I didn't think I would actually be discharging a weapon indoors," she murmured.

"You did see the target onstage, Miss Benton. Surely you didn't think it was strictly décor?"

Abigail raised her arm at the target, supporting the heavy weight of the gauntlet with her other hand. The audience ceased its soft stirring behind her.

Dr. Valerian leaned in close. His scent was crisp and masculine. "Have you fired a pistol before?"

"Yes. In In—abroad." She caught herself before she could say the name of the country, knowing what reaction it produced in him the last time.

"The actions are essentially the same, only the pocket pistol will discharge from a compartment at your wrist. Keep your fingers in front to catch hold of the pistol. When you're ready to fire, take your other hand

and pull the lever straight back. Understood?"

Abigail managed a nod. Dr. Valerian must have read her lack of complete and total confidence. With a grumble, he raised his voice for the audience. "The lady will now attempt the first shot." He stepped away to give her room.

Abigail shifted, so that her line of fire was directed at the target's middle. She pointed her fingers out, as Dr. Valerian instructed, and pulled the lever towards her wrist.

Her entire arm jarred under the recoil as a pocket pistol sprang from retracted coils and landed in her palm. She pulled the trigger. A bullet shot out. She saw the target shake from the impact as the bullet lodged itself in one of the rings.

She lowered her arm as smoke and the scent of gunpowder and rubber issued from the bullet chamber. Dr. Valerian came forward and inspected the target, pointing to where the bullet lodged in the third ring from the bull's-eye. The audience clapped.

"Press the button on the right above your wrist to activate the safety mechanism," he instructed her. While she did that, he went forward with the demonstration. "Now we will show another feature of the gauntlet. In the event of the pistol having no ammunition, the gauntlet has stores of smoke deterrents. These provide distraction, allowing the wearer to flee. These deterrents are housed in small vials until activated."

Abigail tilted her arm to look at the aluminum vials.

"We will demonstrate with a harmless gray smoke. Miss Benton, if you would push the lever to the right to release the corresponding vial."

Abigail did so, but the lever jammed halfway.

"Return the lever to the original position and try again."

She tried moving the lever, but now it wouldn't shift left. She heard the audience snicker. Dr. Valerian allowed her to volunteer. She could not let him be mocked because of her inability to control the device. Grasping the lever with thumb and forefinger, she tugged it sharply to the left.

One of the vials flew from the copper fixtures in a fissure of smoke. Abigail caught a whiff of the slightly sweet scent before it sailed across the stage and landed within the audience. People rose from their seats as thick gray smoke rose from the floor.

"Everyone, leave the auditorium immediately," Jacob shouted before covering his nose and mouth with a handkerchief.

Abigail looked at the gauntlet and saw that she released the left vial instead of the right. "Oh, dear."

Shouts came from the audience as they rushed for the exits, but their cries didn't sound like anything remotely of panic.

An odd chuckle came from Dr. Valerian. "Now you've done it." Although his mouth was covered, she saw that his eyes crinkled in a smile.

Seeing him suddenly cheerful put her in a good mood, too. At least he wasn't angry at her for releasing the wrong vial. The sweet scent of the smoke filled her nose. She felt an irrepressible urge to giggle. "What have I done?"

Dr. Valerian coughed. "You released the vial of nitrous oxide." He chuckled again as he rushed to her. "Laughing gas."

"Oh." She stood on tiptoe and looked over his shoulder even as he pulled her off the stage. The auditorium was a scene of smoke and hilarity as people doubled over in laughter. Some even fell to the floor in their artificially-rendered mirth, clutching their stomachs, guffawing as tears ran down their cheeks.

Abigail tried holding her breath, but the smoke tickled the back of her throat. She coughed, inadvertently inhaling the laughing gas again. Suddenly the auditorium appeared filmy and sparkled at the corners, as though in a dream.

She heard Dr. Valerian's voice in the distance, even as she registered that he was right beside her, his hand grasping her arm firmly. "We must get out of here."

But why must they leave? The auditorium was a world of happiness and gaiety. Outside was nothing but silly little problems. So silly that she couldn't help but laugh at them.

Chapter 5

Abigail's reaction to the gas was worse than Jacob thought. Even as its effects wore off him shortly after he entered the hallway outside of the auditorium, she did nothing but giggle as he led her to his office. Now, as he attempted to step over the correspondence he scattered over the floor in haste earlier, he grew concerned over her behavior.

"What a funny picture." Voice inordinately high and giddy, she giggled at a painting of a pastoral landscape hanging on the wall above his desk. "The leaves on the trees look so crinkly. Did you paint it yourself? I like to sketch, you know."

He knew he should never have picked her out from the audience as a volunteer, but how could he ignore her when she pumped her hand in the air and stood on tiptoe? He reasoned that letting her assist him would cause less of a scene than her attempting to leap over the heads of the other lecture attendees.

How wrong he was. She hit the lever on the gauntlet gun and sent the whole lecture hall into a cloud of nitrous oxide. Students fled the hall, leaving books and overturned chairs in their wake. Judging from the cacophony of chortles outside due to the laughing gas, it would be several minutes before anyone could reach his office. Surely by then he could get Miss Abigail Benton to stop giggling.

Perhaps.

"Miss Benton, I think you should sit down." Jacob pulled out one of the chairs in front of his desk.

His words dissipated in the air, as she didn't hear him in her induced state. She kept her gaze transfixed on the painting. "Those branches look like squirrel tails. Bushy squirrel tails." She let out a loud snort while tottering on her feet. One hand came dangerously close to knocking a glass globe off his desk.

Jacob hissed as the globe wobbled on the edge. "Miss Benton, if you would be seated, please. I insist."

She seized upon the globe like a cat pawing a ball of yarn. "What's this? Is it a child's toy?"

"It most certainly is not. That was given to me by the Cambridge Dean of Medicine. Put that down."

She gave it a shake. Her green eyes widened as the tiny snowflakes swirled inside. "Why, it's Christmas inside."

"Put that globe down and sit in this chair now." Jacob hoisted the chair off the Indian rug and set it down with a thump. "I shan't say it again."

"I shan't say it again." Abigail dropped her voice an octave in mimicry. "Well, alright, then, since you asked so nicely." She set the globe down. It promptly rolled off the desk and cracked once it hit the floor. "Oops."

Jacob gritted his teeth. *Oops* couldn't begin to summarize this continuing debacle.

Instead of walking to the chair, Abigail plopped herself on the desk, oblivious to the stacks of papers that spilled under her. She wobbled, her shoulders tilting. "Oh, my, I feel quite dizzy."

Jacob steadied her with one hand while touching her forehead with the other. "You're a bit warm. You're experiencing a side effect of the gas."

"You have lovely eyes." She raised her chin and gazed at him with large, dilated pupils. "They're light blue and clear as icicles."

"I—" Jacob pushed his spectacles higher on the bridge of his nose. "Icicles?"

"You really shouldn't hide them behind those spectacles." Abigail swiped at them with a clumsy hand, leaving three fingerprints on the lenses.

Jacob thought about the accident that made his eyes sensitive to bright light and forced him to wear them in certain environments. "It's not something that can be helped."

"I can help. Allow me." She tugged the spectacles off his face.

"Give those back."

Shaking her head with a lopsided smile, she put them behind her.

"I am not in the mood for games, Miss Benton. Ouch."

She caught a portion of his hair between her fingers and tugged. "How peculiar your hair color. You're too young to have gray."

Jacob winced as she tugged again, attempting to keep his neck straight. "That hue is the result of a trauma experienced during the field campaigns in India. As is the scar over my left eye."

Her features contorted as sympathy competed with the residual giddiness on her face. "You poor man."

Despite the effects of the gas, Jacob sensed that her response was genuine. To which, he didn't know what to say.

"I find your hair quite fetching." Her fingers glided through the strands to land gently on the scar over his eye. "And your scar."

He closed his left eye and froze as her warm touch caressed his brow and slid down the length of his scar to his cheek. She hadn't the foggiest idea what she was saying. His injuries made him repulsive, not fetching. And the ones hidden underneath his layers of clothing were far worse. "Miss Benton, I think that you ought to lie down until the effects of the gas wear off. But first I need to take back that gauntlet."

He took her hand from his face. She found the lapels of his coat to grab instead. With surprising strength, she pulled him down for a very passionate and unexpected kiss.

Abigail's kiss was just as warm and fevered as her brow. Her soft lips moved under his as she pulled him further down. Jacob caught the edges of the desk before he could fall on top of her. Unaware of his flailing, Abigail continued to press her mouth against his, still holding him by the lapels in an iron grip.

Her scent enveloped him in soft vanilla. Jacob found his eyes closing, his tactile senses coming alive as he felt her creamy-soft skin and the tickle of her hair against his cheek. He had been without the touch of a woman for so long that he almost believed that Abigail's contact was real, that she welcomed him with open arms.

But her embrace was only the nitrous oxide talking.

Jacob broke free and came up for air. "Get a hold of yourself." He spoke for himself as much as he did for her.

Abigail threw back her head. Auburn hair, loosened of its severe knot, tumbled over her shoulders in tangles and embedded pins. Hardly a caption of coiffed glory, but the absence of structure lent a playful edge. A blush crept onto her cheeks.

"You need a glass of water." Jacob extended his right arm to grab hold of the pitcher on a side table.

"Such a gentleman," she uttered before slumping against his shoulder.

"Miss Benton?" He shook her. Her cheek squashed against the epaulet of his coat as she sank against him. Her eyes may as well have been welded shut. She passed out like a furloughed sailor on a tavern spree.

Jacob grabbed her around the waist and supported her weight as he pulled her off the desk. His right leg buckled under their combined weight, but he retained balance as he backed up to the armchair by the curtained window. The COIC Secretary's alarmed voice sounded at the door.

"Valerian, what in heaven's name are you doing to that woman?"

The Secretary invited himself into Jacob's office. He closed the door, shutting off the din of people crowding the halls.

Jacob shifted Abigail in attempt to put her in a more dignified position. A little muffled noise issued from her lips. "Mr. Secretary, this isn't what it appears to be."

"Well, I certainly don't know what to make of it." The Secretary helped him get Abigail seated on a chair. "What was in that smoke capsule?"

"Nitrous oxide. A relatively harmless compound under normal circumstances." Jacob bent over Abigail and checked her vitals. "When inhaled, it brings a sense of relaxation and euphoria. In small doses, the effects usually last no longer than a few minutes. Miss Benton must have inhaled a large amount as it launched from the gauntlet gun."

"Mm." Abigail's head fell back.

"Now she's fainted. Bring my medical bag from the bottom desk drawer." He fanned Abigail's face.

The Secretary retrieved the bag. "Is what we've seen today an accurate portrayal of how that gauntlet will work in the field?"

Jacob fished inside the bag for smelling salts. He worked to uncork the bottle. "As I said, the nitrous oxide is a last resort to be employed when one wishes to make an escape."

"Good." The Secretary studied Abigail. "The COIC needs effective weapons to fight against Monsieur Broussard. That criminal industrialist is the true reason why we stay in conflict with France. And now there's word of a spy ring he has running about somewhere in London's streets."

Jacob got the cork out of the bottle. The Secretary's mention of Broussard gave him a fleeting thought for the COIC's current domestic and foreign agendas, but his concern for Abigail trumped both. He positioned his hand behind her neck and cradled her head. Soft strands of her hair tumbled over his fingers. He brought the smelling salts under her small nose.

Her eyelids flew open and she blinked rapidly. Jacob allowed her to sit up as she gasped once. "Miss Benton, how are you feeling?"

She turned her eyes on him, wide, wild, and green as forest mist. She looked ready to spring from the chair any moment. "Where am I? I was on a stage with this striking device. Oh, who are you?" She pointed at the Secretary with the hand that still wore the gauntlet. He reflexively drew back.

"He's an associate of mine," Jacob explained while swooping quickly to unbuckle the gauntlet and remove it.

The Secretary crept out from where he shielded himself behind the desk. "That was quite a demonstration you performed, Miss Benton. I don't think I've seen anything so engaging in a lecture hall."

Jacob looked at him. Surely he wasn't encouraging her.

"Tell me, where did you learn to shoot?"

"My mother taught me," she replied, rubbing her wrist where the gauntlet's straps left their mark. She rolled her sleeve down. "She always stressed to my sister and me that a lady should know how to defend herself if the situation calls for it."

The Secretary's eyes flicked from her to the gauntlet in Jacob's possession. "Perhaps Dr. Valerian will consider letting you help him test that gauntlet gun until it's ready for another demonstration."

He was encouraging her. Jacob stifled a groan as a hopeful smile graced her face. As much as that smile warmed the cool interior of his office, he couldn't allow her to get her hopes up. "Miss Benton, I think you should go home and rest. I'll find you a cab."

"But I feel more enlivened than when I arrived here." She planted both feet on the floor and stood. Jacob and the Secretary moved to support her in case she became unsteady, but she shook her head of unraveled hair. "Whatever you put into that vial seems to have given me much pep."

She already had more than enough to begin with. Perhaps that was why the laughing gas' effects took so long to wear off, Jacob thought wryly.

"You will go home to recover. Doctor's orders." A knock came from outside the door. "Come in."

Professor Markel entered and instantly focused on the collage of correspondence on the floor, as well as the shattered globe. "Dr. Valerian, I still have the lady's scarf and coat. I came to see if she was here with you."

"Indeed, she is. Are there any drivers waiting outside?"

"Just one, I believe. Most people have already left."

Fled the premises, was more like it. Jacob doubted any of them would return for next week's lecture. "Miss Benton will be taking a cab home. Here's money for her fare. Would you please see that she is situated?"

"Of course, Doctor." The professor took the money from Jacob. "If you will come with me, Miss Benton." He held Abigail's coat open for her to put on.

Jacob leaned against his desk. The euphoria effect of the nitrous oxide had eased a little of his leg pain, but now it returned. "Thank you for your help with the demonstration today, Miss Benton."

She turned a glare up at him. Those wide, wild eyes he compared to green forest mist now begat a layer of frost. She put one hand behind her neck and her expression turned surprised as she realized her hair had come undone.

Jacob averted his eyes politely as Abigail attempted to make something orderly of her tangled strands and the pins that remained in them. The other men did the same.

Professor Markel still held her coat. She jabbed the last hairpin in place before she thrust her arms in the coat sleeves and slipped her scarf around her neck. The ends flew in the breeze she made when following the professor out the office.

Jacob turned to the Secretary once the door closed. "I sincerely apologize for the mishap with the gauntlet gun's deterrent smoke capsule, but that will be fixed promptly."

"I'm not sure I believe you, Doctor."

Jacob grew anxious. Did that mean the end of his chances to get the COIC commission? "May I ask, why?"

"You have a lecturing contract at this school."

"It's temporary, in order to supplement my practice. My patients are mostly of the laboring classes and unable to pay full price for their prosthetic devices."

"And your practice consists of a good number of patients. How will you have time to work on the commission? I've heard nothing from you on the sample of Aspasian metal I sent."

Jacob found his spectacles on the desk. Abigail's prints blurred the right lens. "I just completed a full report. I'll send it to your office at COIC headquarters this evening."

The Secretary stopped him from going on. "My point is, your schedule is full. Our agency is trying to stop Broussard from getting the best and brightest inventions. We cannot afford to wait much longer. Can you put your theory of the Aspasian metals into practice with that gauntlet gun by March?"

"I'll do my absolute best." How could Jacob say no, even if he wasn't sure that he could make such a deadline?

The Secretary remained unconvinced as he tossed his gaze from one end of the floor to the next. "Why is your office in such a state?"

Jacob moved several sheets of paper into an untidy pile with the tip of his walking stick. "I was looking for my notes before the lecture."

"How did you find them in this mess?"

He stopped attempting to make the office look presentable. "Miss Benton brought them here."

"She's your assistant, then?"

"No."

"Someone needs to help you organize things. What happened to your former assistant?"

"He resigned. I'm in the process of finding another."

"Miss Benton seems keen for the task. She's not too bad of a markswoman, either."

"Yes, but a woman in this line of work—"

"We've several female agents and affiliates within the COIC. If a woman can handle a weapon and assist you in your demonstration without prior instruction, I say she's more than fit to help you construct this project. Unless, you have something against the fairer sex."

Jacob did not like being referred to as a chauvinist. He had nothing against women, really he didn't. He just found that most were unable to abide with his habits, which, he admitted, were a little unconventional. But they also did not take too well when they learned of the full extent of his battle scars. Especially that.

But Abigail did see one scar up close. And she did not recoil. In fact, her reaction was most pleasant…

He forced himself to stop thinking of Abigail and her kiss for a moment. "Mr. Secretary, does this mean you have decided to go ahead with the commission?"

The Secretary's nod was halting. "I'll give it my approval, but only if you show you can handle the task. You need an assistant. Miss Benton is available for immediate hire. I see no one else jumping to volunteer for the job."

Abigail did practically jump. And stand on tiptoe. And wave.

"Hire her or find another," the Secretary continued. "But if you don't find someone in the immediate future, the COIC will be forced to refuse to fund you."

Jacob acquiesced. "I will see if she's still nearby."

The Secretary nodded, satisfied. "Remember one of the first lessons of working with the COIC. You never do so alone."

Jacob nodded as the agent left. He followed him out, then locked the office and left the building in search of Abigail.

THE CURIOSITY CHRONICLES: BOOKS 1-3

Chapter 6

Abigail pulled the curtain closed over the carriage window as it pulled away from New Britannia College of Science. There went her chances of getting employed as Dr. Valerian's assistant.

She rested her head against the cushioned seat. What happened between the time she accidentally released the laughing gas from Dr. Valerian's gauntlet gun and after she found herself sitting in his office? And why had her hair come undone?

She knew she fainted. The sharp whiff of smelling salts still burned her nose. But that wasn't what made Dr. Valerian so eager to send her home. He was on edge in that office, even more so than he was in their interactions before the demonstration.

And why were her lips tingling? She touched them. Was this also a side effect of the laughing gas?

A shout came from behind the carriage. Abigail felt the force of the carriage's forward motion as it came to an abrupt stop. She grasped her seat and righted herself.

She moved over to the door and opened it. The carriage traveled less than one block from the college. Abigail looked back at the lecture hall and witnessed Dr. Valerian's approach.

"Miss Benton, I must speak with you." His walking stick rapped on the cobblestones as he increased his pace. He reached the carriage and thanked the driver for waiting before he climbed inside. "Thank goodness I caught up with you. I worried you would be well on your way."

He worried? Abigail regarded him on the bench across from her as he closed the door. The carriage resumed its sojourn. "Forgive me, but you were the one who sent me on my way."

"Yes, I know. I was somewhat hasty."

He was always hasty, always rushing, Abigail began to realize as he pulled his spectacles off. The lenses were dark, not transparent anymore. Did he have two pairs?

"Miss Benton, what exactly is your experience in the medical field?"

The carriage hit a bump in the road. Abigail, conscious of her appearance before him, pushed the hairpins back into place where they worked their way out. "I've worked briefly as a nurse after I returned home from abroad. Before then, I assisted my father, as I said previously. I helped him administer medication to his patients and made visiting rounds to see them."

"My patients are laborers. They've had their limbs amputated out of surgical necessity. They require considerate professionals to treat them. What I'm asking is, do you possess a strong constitution?"

She raised her chin. "Six years stationed in Calcutta hardened my nerves, Dr. Valerian, but not my compassion."

He seemed not to notice her confident reply. He polished his lenses with detached interest. "I, too, was stationed in India for a time. As a medic, not a missions doctor. I will tell you that some of the cases here in London are much more atrocious than what you may have seen abroad."

Was he implying that her family's mission work was substandard to his medical practice? Abigail drew close to sputtering her indignation, but then considered that Dr. Valerian's arrogant stance may not have been completely genuine. "You're testing me."

He looked up. "Sorry?"

"You're testing me." She repeated. "You want to see if I really possess the fortitude to be your assistant. But you must already believe I do, else you wouldn't have rushed from the college to stop me."

He pocketed his spectacles. The way he sat across from her and said nothing made her restless. She felt like a patient who knew she had a grave illness, but was only waiting to be told the official diagnosis. "Dr. Valerian, I've demonstrated my interest in the position. I'm very sorry for the misfire of the laughing gas, but I can do better."

"It's not that I think you undetermined. I see you as feminine."

What was she supposed to do with that explanation? "I suppose my gender is somewhat apparent to you, but a number of women are nurses and physicians' assistants. I've even heard that in some countries, a few of them are doctors like you."

"There are no doctors like me."

Abigail had just about had it. Did he practically run down her carriage just so he could boast of his exclusivity? "I could name several doctors who specialize in the outfitting of artificial limbs. They regularly visit the apothecary."

"You never did explain why you left your position there." Dr. Valerian stretched his legs, hand resting lightly on the carved handle of his walking stick. He waited for her to answer.

"I was dismissed."

Up went the eyebrow. "For?"

"For filling an order incorrectly. A gentleman wanted something to ease his insomnia. I meant to give him chamomile extract, but I mistakenly sent him home with castor oil."

Dr. Valerian sounded an *ahem*.

"It only happened once," Abigail added fast. "It was an unusually hectic day."

"The day I came into the apothecary?"

"Yes."

The carriage slowed. Abigail surmised they were nearing the ladies boarding house. Thoughts of returning to her little room once more with no job prospects made her sigh.

"Answer one more question for me, Miss Benton. You said your father is a doctor. Why not work for him again?"

"He was a doctor. He and my mother contacted cholera during the outbreak in Calcutta two years ago. They didn't make it back to New Britannia."

Dr. Valerian gazed at the door. "I see. I'm sorry."

"None of us anticipated the risks."

"No British man or woman does until it's too late."

Abigail stirred to ask just what he implied, but something told her that he wasn't speaking solely to her circumstances.

"I'm willing to take you on as my assistant on a trial basis. If you learn the operations of my practice quickly and manage to stay on for thirty days, then we will evaluate whether to proceed on a more permanent basis."

Abigail was speechless, even as the driver announced from above that the carriage reached its destination.

Dr. Valerian went on. "But I will warn you, this is rigorous work. I have a practice, lectures, and monthly rounds at a laborer's hospital near the St. Giles parish. I also have an onsite blast furnace where I forge the mechanical prosthetics and weapons devices."

So that explained the residual smoke Abigail had seen wafting behind Dr. Valerian's residence earlier. She wavered at that. She knew next to nothing about metallurgy or smithing. "Will I be expected to cast metals, too?"

"I do the forging. Struthers assists me in operation of the furnace when necessary. Your duties will remain mostly within the practice. But," Jacob warned, "Do not expect to sit at a desk in my office all day."

The door whipped open, bringing a gust of November chill and garish winter light. Abigail partly rose as Dr. Valerian put on his spectacles. "Thank you. I will work hard."

"No castor oil."

"No castor oil." She witnessed the lenses of his spectacles darken as sunlight filled the cab interior. Happily, Abigail set her feet on the snow-dusted ground.

He escorted her to the door of the boarding house. "Good day, Miss Benton. I will see you at my practice Monday at nine-thirty sharp."

"Good day, Doctor." She sailed inside, past the front desk where the landlady sat and went to her room down the hall and around the corner.

Monday, no matter what it entailed with the mysterious Dr. Valerian, had to be the start of better days. She'd give her best to make sure that it was.

***

No sooner did Abigail disappear inside the slightly worn-looking boarding house than the carriage driver's smile deteriorated worse than its sagging front steps. "I need an additional ten pence."

Jacob balked at the driver. "That's outrageous."

"I had to stop the carriage so you could get in. 'Sides, the fare doubles for two passengers."

"You mean triples. Take me back to the college and I'll pay you."

The driver grumbled. Jacob closed the door, his thoughts on Abigail rather than the driver's complaints.

She didn't remember kissing him before she fainted in his arms. If she did, she wouldn't have been at ease speaking to him afterward. He had been nothing but uncomfortable in her presence, even when he feigned detachment while putting her resolve to work to the test.

Her vanilla scent lingered. Jacob closed his eyes. Could she truly be up to task for this? Abigail was determined in mind, but her demeanor was pure, unsullied. How would she handle being around his patients, or him? Once she began working at his side, she'd be privy to the pain that he dealt with for years.

No. Jacob opened one eye and looked down at his right leg. He could not allow her to see that side of him, to know the cause of his pain. For however long her term of employment lasted, Abigail Benton could not see him for what he truly was.

***

Abigail woke early Monday. Today was to be her first day of work as Dr. Valerian's assistant. But she had another task to tend to that morning, and it had to be done before she went to his practice. Her sister and brother-in-law should be back in London. She needed to tell them about Phillip and Winnie before the children were released from the academy.

In the dim light of an oil lantern, Abigail washed and dressed in her best work skirt and matching jacket. Once assembled, she searched for her reticule on the table in front of the bed. It lay nestled among a stack of sketchbooks and a pencil case, supplies for one of her favorite pastimes. She found the reticule, put on her coat, and left the boarding house.

Abigail braced herself against the early morning chill as she traversed the streets to reach her sister's house. There was no money to spend on a cab or omnibus today.

Twenty minutes later she arrived at Catherine's residence in Paddington, a location that was home to some of London's growing middle class. Catherine and Hammond left a more humble abode and moved there last spring when Hammond's position as a bank loan officer was promoted to branch president.

Abigail stopped before their impressive columned house. A festive holly wreath on the door beckoned her to come forward and knock, but she knew the reception she would receive when Catherine answered. After she had rejected her sister's match in a potential suitor, she was ordered not to return again. "But I must speak to her on behalf of the children," Abigail told herself as she pushed one foot in front of the other.

The holly wreath came in full view. Abigail peered around the layers of red ribbon and green sprigs for the chain that would sound the doorbell. She rang twice before Hammond answered.

A man below average height, Abigail was able to look him eye to eye without raising her chin. He blinked several times, as though he didn't fully trust his eyesight. "It's you, Abigail. I don't think I've seen you in, what has it been, six months?"

Eight, but she knew to correct him would only bring more awkwardness between them. "Good morning, Hammond. I need to speak with you and Catherine. It's about Phillip and Winnie's school."

Her brother-in-law adjusted his stark white shirt cuffs. "I must be getting to the office soon. Can it wait until a better time?"

"I'm afraid there is no better time. May I come in?"

Hammond shut the door on the cold once she stood in the entranceway. "What is the matter?"

Abigail smelled sausage cooking in the kitchen. "Where's Catherine?"

"Still asleep. We arrived home very early this morning. " Hammond put on his suit coat. "The children aren't ill, are they?"

"No, but they got themselves into a spot of trouble." She summarized the story for him, dead piano mouse and all. "The headmistress agreed to let them stay at the academy until you came to readmit them, but that ends today. You must go and speak with her."

Her brother-in-law scolded at the clock on the wall. "I told Catherine that the children should have a tutor at home, not attend the academy. It appears I'm right." He took his hat off the peg by the front door. "Tell my wife I can't linger at breakfast. I have to settle this before I'm late for work." He pulled open the door and left.

Catherine's voice carried down the stairs. "Hammond, who are you talking to?" Seconds later, she appeared at the top of the stairs in a robin's egg blue dressing gown. Her curly russet hair was braided. "Abigail. What are you doing here?"

Abigail heard the change in her older sister's tone. Eight months later, the anger was still there. "I came to inform you and Hammond about Phillip and Winnie. He left to see about them."

"Are they in trouble again?"

"Headmistress Cummings almost expelled them. They scared their music teacher with a dead rodent."

Catherine gave a high-pitched squeal as though the deceased vermin was now sprawled atop the banister. "The academy was supposed to correct their bad behavior." She placed her hands on her hips, emphasizing her slim waist, tiny even without the aid of a corset. "Is that the only reason why you stopped by?"

Abigail folded and unfolded her hands. "We haven't spoken in a long time. I think it's time we try to put our past feud behind us."

Catherine relaxed her arms. "Perhaps you and I do need to speak more often."

Abigail looked up, hopeful. "Yes, we do."

A maid came from the kitchen, bearing a steaming platter of eggs and sausage and a pot of coffee. There had certainly been no maid when Abigail lived with them.

"Eleanor," Catherine addressed the maid. "I will take breakfast in my room this morning."

Eleanor nodded and went back in the kitchen.

"Come, Abigail. I must show you how I decorated the upstairs."

Abigail followed her sister into a room that closely resembled a hotel suite than it did simple sleeping quarters. The floor was cushioned by several expensive rugs. One side of the room that housed the bed was concealed by an Oriental screen while the other half displayed a boudoir set, complete with couch, matching chairs, and a dressing table with a vanity mirror.

"Isn't it marvelous?" Catherine spread her arms.

"It's very lovely." Abigail looked at the figurine clock on the dressing table. The hands rested on eight and six. "I can stay but for a few minutes. I must be at work in an hour."

"The apothecary's only a short walk from here." Her sister sat at the dressing table and picked up a hairbrush.

"I don't work there anymore. I found more gainful employment." Abigail skipped over the exact reasons for her having to leave the apothecary. "I start work today as a physician's assistant."

Catherine wrinkled her pert nose. "Father's office always smelled of medicine. You want to breathe in those vapors again?"

"Dr. Valerian is an outfitter of artificial limbs. I don't think he keeps much stock of medicinal tonics."

"Even worse." Catherine stopped brushing her hair. "Those patients are not like you and me."

"They are exactly like us, except they've suffered accidents. That doesn't make them indecent."

"Still preaching on the missions field, I see. Sometimes I think you and our parents held it against me because I chose the more conventional route of marriage instead of charitable work."

"Not at all. You have a beautiful family." Abigail heard the maid come up the stairs with breakfast. She waited until Eleanor set the trays on the table and left to speak again. "I believe this new job will be good work for me, Catherine."

"Yes, yes." Catherine flitted to the tray to nibble on a scone. "I'm curious about your employer, this Dr. Valerian. Didn't I read something in the papers about him? It was right before the society section…oh, yes, he presented an invention at a lecture hall on Friday. Caused quite a stir when it went awry."

"There was a mishap. Fortunately, no one was harmed."

"You were there?" Catherine paused chewing to shrug. "It figures, I suppose. You always did have an interest in scientific things."

Abigail guessed the article did not mention her name as Dr. Valerian's assistant during the lecture, or else Catherine would have remarked upon it. For now, at least, she decided to keep mum of it to her sister.

"I shall ask my husband about Dr. Valerian. Care for some eggs and sausage?"

Abigail's mouth watered at the smell of the savory breakfast dishes, but knew she must be going. "Dr. Valerian's practice is a long walk from here. I need to go."

"You can't go with nothing on your head. And I recognize the skirt of that drab, dark dress you're wearing. You used to enjoy being fashionable. Let me see what I have to liven it up."

"I really don't have the time." Abigail protested as her sister marched in bedroom slippers to a wardrobe on the room's right wall.

"You always fuss with me. This will only take a moment." Catherine pulled a hatbox from the top shelf of the wardrobe and carried it over to the bed. Abigail expected her to present some frilly topper of flowers and silk netting. To her surprise, her sister lifted the lid and presented a tiny black hat, complete with white band, bow, and flowers that looked too small for even Winnie to wear.

"It's the latest in hat styles. I saw all the ladies wearing them at my neighbor's party last week." Catherine affixed it to the side of her own head to demonstrate. "Isn't it adorable?"

"It looks like a doll's hat."

"You can be fashionable as well as intelligent, you realize." Catherine removed the hat and put it on Abigail, affixing it with a comb and hat pin. Her hazel eyes danced as she set the hat to a jaunty perch.

For a moment, it felt like no argument had ever ensued between the two of them. If a simple hat was the start to putting them on speaking terms again, then perhaps Abigail could wear it for a while. What would it hurt?

And besides, Dr. Valerian was not one who adhered closely to the prim and fastidious clothing norms of physicians. Everything about his appearance, from the cut of his suits, his color-changing spectacles, the carvings on the handle of his walking stick, to the way he wore his hair, was different. He most likely wouldn't blink a piercing blue eye at her miniature topper.

"Abigail, I don't think I've ever seen you contemplate an article of fashion so deeply."

Abigail caught herself staring into the vanity mirror. Her thoughts were not upon her reflection, but Catherine thought they were.

Her sister beamed into the mirror. "I told you it was adorable."

The slight weight on the side of Abigail's head made her feel lopsided. "Thank you, Catherine. Now I really must run or I will be late." She paused upon reaching the door, her hand on the frame. "I hope we can talk again soon."

"Oh, we will. I want my hat back." Catherine wrapped a scone from the breakfast tray in a napkin and gave it to her. "Shoo. Mustn't keep the good doctor waiting."

Chapter 7

Jacob heard the grandfather clock chime downstairs. With eyes still closed, he reached for his pocketwatch on the table beside the settee he fell asleep on the night before.

He opened his eyes to the dim interior of his study. Morning light broke through the curtains in a vain attempt to penetrate the room. He flipped open the watch case.

Nine o' clock. Abigail would be there in half an hour.

He sat upright. Blood rushed to his head, though it did little to clear the heavy drowsiness that refused to dissipate. The laudanum was to blame for that.

Jacob rubbed his face. He hated dulling his senses with medication, but from time to time, he had no choice. The pain had gone on for two full days, rendering him unable to leave his residence.

He moved his hands away from his face to stare at his right leg—what remained of it— beneath the wrinkled, slept-in fabric of his trousers. Strange how something that was no longer there could still make its presence known. He rolled the trouser leg up, stopping at a few inches below his knee, the site of amputation.

His sacrifice for the India campaigns. He had been fortunate. Some men lost their lives. At least he returned home. That was what he told himself when the memory of his trial returned in full force.

But there was no time this morning to think on it or the trace aches that lingered in his joints and bones. Abigail was coming. He must get cleaned up.

He reached for the steel and aluminum prosthetic limb beside the settee. The series of buckles and straps presented a challenge to him in the early days when he first fashioned the device. Now he barely gave it thought as his fingers worked quickly to attach it at his knee and buckle the straps along his thigh and waist. He stood once it was on and walked from the study to the water closet in his bedroom.

"Please." He talked at his reflection in the shaving mirror. "Let her be late."

***

Abigail arrived at Dr. Valerian's door with one minute to spare. Struthers let her inside.

"The doctor said to expect your arrival this morning, Miss Benton." He took her coat. "If you will follow me to his office."

Abigail rubbed her arms as she trailed him down a brief hallway. A fire blazed in the front room of the house, but the adjoining corridor was cooler.

"Dr. Valerian will be downstairs shortly." Struthers led her into the office, a room furnished with a large desk, divan, and armchairs.

Abigail's eyes wandered from the rows of glass display cabinets lining the walls to an exam table with lampstand that resided in the room's right corner. She returned to the cabinets, where items of which she could only describe as pieces of armor, occupied the shelves. One shelf held gauntlets that resembled the device Dr. Valerian demonstrated at the lecture hall. Most of them were prosthetics instead of weapons, judging from the straps inside that appeared as though they were meant to be attached to the amputation site.

Another shelf held what reminded her of knights' greaves, armor designed to protect the wearer's legs. They were fashioned with gleaming plates of silver and brass. All of them resided in various stages of completion, with hooks and wires protruding from the joints connecting the plates.

She moved to another cabinet before she saw Dr. Valerian's reflection in the glass. She whirled as he entered the office, noticing that Struthers had left.

"Good morning, Miss Benton." He went to the desk, where he opened the patient ledger at once. "We have our first appointment in fifteen minutes."

That didn't give Abigail any time to acquaint herself with the office and procedures.

His eyes rested momentarily on her hat, though he said nothing. He left his walking stick by the desk and walked to the cabinet on the left which contained the gauntlets. His gait was smoother today. "The patient we are about to see is a train conductor. He suffered the loss of his hand during a derailment this past August. If I can outfit him with an artificial one, he may be able to return to work soon." He opened the cabinet and removed one of the items. "This is a basic model."

Abigail didn't think anything Dr. Valerian crafted could be called basic. The prosthetic hand was forged of silver metal, with linked joints that appeared to be able to move through a complicated series of interconnected wires extending through the wrist and up into the hollow forearm. The forearm capped off with four straps to connect it to the wearer's elbow and upper arm.

"The gauntlet gun was heavy. Is this made of a similar metal?" she asked.

"The steel is hollow for the wires to go through, and I used brass sparingly. It's lighter than you think." He gave her the prosthetic to hold. "While the metal does weigh more than an arm of flesh and bone, the wearer will eventually get used to it through exercise and practice."

Abigail pressed a plate down inside the forearm's cap, where the amputation site would depress it. She watched the fingers close into the palm. She released the plate, and the fingers unfurled once more.

Dr. Valerian took the prosthetic hand again. "Depending on how the plate is pressed, the hand can curl into a fist, one finger can point, or the digits can be used to hold an eating utensil." He depressed the plate to demonstrate all three movements. "But as I said, it takes practice."

Abigail pointed to another model in the cabinet. "You make armored devices for people who don't require artificial limbs."

"I have clients as well as patients. My clients are wealthy sporting gentlemen who commission weapons that are extensions of their hands and legs. Catering to their occasional order allows me to provide services for some patients that could not otherwise afford an artificial limb."

Struthers came to the open door of the office. "Doctor, Mr. Carney is here to see you."

"Send him in." Dr. Valerian closed the cabinet. "Miss Benton, you'll find a brown leather-bound notebook on my desk along with a pencil. See that you take notes."

Abigail went to retrieve the items. When she turned around, a man of stocky build, dressed in a brown suit, stood at the door.

Dr. Valerian greeted him. "Mr. Carney, do come in."

The man ambled into the office. Abigail saw the gleam of a metal hook extend from his right coat sleeve. "Hope I'm not late for my appointment, Doctor." His voice belied an Irish lilt.

"You're on time. Have a seat."

Mr. Carney noticed Abigail. "I haven't met your missus, have I?"

She started to correct him, but Dr. Valerian beat her to it. "Miss Benton is my new assistant."

"You don't say?" Mr. Carney settled into an armchair. "What happened to your old one?"

"Mr. Pickens put in his resignation. But Miss Benton has worked both as a nurse and physician's assistant before she came to my practice. She is very dedicated to the field of medicine."

Dr. Valerian's statement sounded almost like a compliment. Abigail decided to take it as such. "How do you do, Mr. Carney?"

The man nodded to her. "Improving bit by bit. I'll be even better when I find something to replace what the surgeon gave me." He displayed the hook and made it open and close. "Hurts my arm every time I move. What do you think, Doctor?"

Dr. Valerian had him remove his coat and roll up his shirt sleeve. He inspected the hook and the straps that clamped the man's arm. "The prosthetic is ill-fitting. See how the straps must be tightened to the point where they chafe the skin?"

"The surgeon said that the skin would be red for some months."

Dr. Valerian shook his head as he removed the prosthetic. "That shouldn't occur once the amputation site is healed. Miss Benton, bring me that model we just looked at before Mr. Carney arrived."

Abigail stopped writing in the notebook to go to the cabinet. She lifted the prosthetic metal hand from its place and brought it to him. She observed him adjust it to fit the train conductor's forearm.

"Now, Mr. Carney, in the same motion that you used to open and close the hook, I want you to move the fingers of this model."

He curled his new hand into a fist. "Well, look at that."

"Good. Try to grab your coat off the chair."

He was successful after two attempts. "I can go back to directing the trains, I can." Laughing, he dangled his coat in the air by its sleeve.

Abigail couldn't help but smile as she witnessed the man regain some of his dexterity and much of his confidence. Dr. Valerian nodded with satisfaction, but he remained sober.

"It will take time for you to master the movements, but after that, you can return to your work. You'll need to have a model custom made."

He proceeded to schedule his patient for a second visit for measurements. Abigail recorded the date in the ledger.

Mr. Carney reluctantly gave the prosthetic model back to Dr. Valerian and returned his hook to his forearm once the visit was concluded. "This visit was worth the trip from Birmingham. I'll see you next week, Doctor." He set payment on the desk. "And you as well, Miss Benton."

"A pleasure to meet you, Mr. Carney," Abigail replied.

The train conductor gave Dr. Valerian a conspiratorial look. "I like her better as your assistant. Much nicer to look at."

Dr. Valerian cleared his throat. "Have a good week, Mr. Carney." He saw him to the door.

Abigail hid a smile as she finished recording the last of her notes. She looked in the record book and saw that another patient was due to arrive in the next ten minutes. She straightened the chairs in preparation for his arrival.

The second patient was a former admiral in the Queen's navy. Having lost his left leg to a case of gangrene at sea, he arrived to get the custom artificial limb that Dr. Valerian made for him. Abigail took note of how he expertly fitted the former admiral with the mechanical limb and gave instructions on how to walk with it, a task that took patience, considering how the limb's pressure plates and pulley mechanisms needed to work in tandem to allow the wearer to move.

Yet, at noon, the admiral stepped out of the office a contented man, on his way to no longer being inhibited by the stilting movements of a wooden leg.

"That concludes the morning patients," said Dr. Valerian after he had left. "We'll break for noonday meal."

Abigail followed him out of the office. She smelled something savory coming from the front of the house. Expecting Dr. Valerian to go that way, she was surprised when he pivoted in the opposite direction.

"Appointments will resume at one o' clock. I have four more patients and a client to see," he said as he stopped before another door and unlocked it with a key. Without further word, he vanished behind the door and left her standing in the short hallway. She heard his footsteps descend stairs.

Abigail went into the vanity closet to wash her hands and returned to the hallway, all the while wondering why Dr. Valerian had left so quickly.

"Pardon me, Miss Benton. Lunch is served. Follow me."

She looked to the doorman Struthers after he addressed her. Abigail left the hallway. She saw that he and another domestic employee, a cheery-faced, middle-aged woman of medium height and stout build, set a tray in the dining room.

Abigail took her seat in front of the table, stealing a glance behind her to see if Dr. Valerian would reemerge from the door of what had to be the cellar.

Struthers introduced the other employee. "This is Mrs. Struthers, my wife. She is the cook and housekeeper."

"Pleased to meet you, Mrs. Struthers," Abigail greeted Struthers' wife.

"Call me Maria." The woman's warm smile was in stark contrast to her husband's detached air. She poured tea into Abigail's cup.

Abigail unfolded her napkin and set it upon her lap. "Should I wait for Dr. Valerian?"

The skin crinkled around Maria's brown eyes as she squinted down the hallway. Struthers made a sound and she promptly shook her head. "The doctor takes his meals while he's at work," she replied quickly.

Abigail thought that work was over, at least for an hour. What was he doing in the cellar?

Maria lifted the tray to reveal soup and a Cornish pasty of beef for one person. She and Struthers departed, leaving Abigail alone with her food and the soft crackling of the fireplace. Abigail noticed that they did not venture to the cellar with a second tray of food.

She ate and lingered over her tea for the remainder of the hour. At five minutes to one, she heard Dr. Valerian emerge from the cellar and open his office again. She folded her napkin on the tray before she stood up to join him.

The afternoon brought more visitors to his practice. One of them was a member of a prominent London banking family, seeking to purchase a Christmas gift for his son, an avid gun collector. He chose an iron wrist cuff that allowed a hidden derringer to unfold.

Abigail recorded in the ledger the very lofty sum he paid before proceeding to prepare the office for the next visitor.

As the afternoon wore on, she became very tired. Dr. Valerian meant what he said about her not being able to sit longer than a couple minutes during business hours. She rubbed the small of her sore back when she was sure he wasn't looking.

"Business hours are concluded for this evening, Miss Benton," he said, after the final patient departed. "I will see you tomorrow morning at eight-thirty. Tuesdays and Fridays I lecture at the college and I must be there early to assemble my presentation."

Abigail lengthened her stiff spine when he came to take the ledger from her. "You don't see patients on Tuesdays and Fridays, then?"

"In the afternoon. The office remains open for an additional two hours." He began locking the cabinets. The day's activity did not appear to leave him fatigued, but rather energized. He moved quickly, his back straight. Miraculously, his clothing remained starched and pressed as it appeared at the start of business that morning.

Abigail positioned her borrowed miniature hat back into place where it began to droop over her ear. "I will be here promptly at eight-thirty."

Dr. Valerian said not a word as he locked the last cabinet. Did he even hear her?

"Have a good evening, Doctor."

"Yes, good evening." Distracted, it seemed, he returned to the middle display cabinet to unlock it. He removed one of the incomplete mechanical arm models and brought it over to the desk to inspect under the lamp.

Abigail slipped from the office and went to the front of the house, where Struthers waited with her coat. She thanked him, donned the coat, and ventured outside. Her back and feet ached as she started the walk home. She wondered what the next twenty-nine days of being in Dr. Valerian's employ would have in store.

Chapter 8

Christmas Day

Nearly a month passed since Abigail came into Dr. Valerian's employ. In that time, she attended four lectures, straightened both his home office and the one at the college at least ten times apiece, learned how to take measurements of patients being fitted for various prosthetic devices, did the bookkeeping, and became acquainted with several of his more frequent visitors.

All this, and Dr. Valerian still remained taciturn, as though he merely tolerated her being in his employment. Would she still have her job after tomorrow, when he was supposed to give her an evaluation on her state of permanent employment? She wondered what all he was storing up to evaluate her on.

But today was Christmas, and she could rest from work. A week before, Abigail received an invitation from her sister to visit on December 25th. She welcomed the opportunity to see family again and celebrate the holiday.

Hammond answered the door when Abigail came by on Christmas morning. He called back into the house, "Catherine, Abigail is here."

The sound of little feet pattering ensued. Instead of Catherine coming to greet her, Phillip and Winnie burst past their father and all but leapt onto Abigail like a pair of capuchins. Laughing even as she sought out her balance, she wrapped her arms around the children. Her hands clung to a tied parcel and two wrapped packages, one in red and the other in green.

"Merry Christmas." She handed the red gift to Winnie and the green to Phillip.

"Open them in the sitting room," said Hammond, ushering them back inside. "They've been this rambunctious ever since the academy let out for winter holiday."

"This is for you and Catherine." Abigail handed him the wrapped parcel, which contained a loaf of gingerbread, and stepped over the threshold. She beheld the interior space decorated with holly boughs, ornaments, and wreaths of pine and fir. The festive display continued with the mistletoe-strewn entryway of the sitting room and up the bell-laden banister of the staircase. She inhaled of the crisp greenery of pine, mixed with the warmth of plum pudding wafting from the kitchen.

"Abigail." Catherine emerged from the sitting room, flashing teeth as white as the lace on her taffeta dress. "I thought you wouldn't make it, with your new work and all."

"Even medical practices take holidays."

"Speaking of which," Catherine said, steering her over to the bottom of the staircase. Her voice dropped to a conspiratorial whisper. "Hammond has brought us news of your employer."

"He has?" Abigail didn't really think Catherine would trouble herself to learn more of Dr. Valerian. Obviously, she was wrong.

Hammond joined them. He glanced at the children in the sitting room before he spoke. "Abigail, I've done some inquiring among my bank clientele and club associates. They had a few remarks about Dr. Valerian."

"You sound worried."

"I am." Hammond tilted his head. "According to other physicians who went to school with him, Valerian is more metal worker than medical practitioner. He doesn't follow conventional practices."

"If by that you mean his methods are more inventive, then I suppose you're right."

"I mean he's an eccentric. He doesn't frequent the gentlemen's clubs or take part in society as others of his profession do."

"He's very busy with patients and college lectures."

"Does that explain why he's let his hair grow long, or dress in loose trousers?" Hammond leaned forward, lowering his voice. "One of his Cambridge classmates described his appearance to me. He also said that before Valerian accepted a position as a field medic to India in '32, he looked like any other gentleman. Since he came back, though, he grew obsessed with metalworking, even building a blast furnace in the back of his house. He's thrown himself into nothing but his work. A recluse, estranged even from his own family in Sussex."

"Egad," said Catherine. "What do you think it could be? Brain fever?"

"In India's heat, perhaps." Hammond shrugged a thin shoulder. "I talked with another associate, a railroad investor. Valerian was engaged to the man's youngest daughter before he left. Needless to say, she didn't marry him. He must have gone mad over there and scared her upon his return home."

Abigail stepped out of the circle of confidants, uncomfortable with what they were telling her and the free manner in which they did so. "I think I've heard enough gossip."

"Hammond only means to tell you this for your own protection," said Catherine.

"Yes," Hammond affirmed. "I know little of Valerian's marvel mechanical devices, but judging from what I've gathered of his eccentric work habits and unsociable demeanor, you need to be careful."

Abigail acknowledged that there was an air of mystery surrounding Dr. Valerian, one that left her bemused and sometimes daunted, but she grew impatient with her sister and Hammond's summation of him. They didn't know him, but merely relied on the gossip of others to form their opinions. How could they be sure any of it was true?

"I don't see why you can't simply go back to working at the apothecary," Catherine voiced after her husband left to be with the children.

"I'm afraid that's not an option."

"What happened?"

"I made a mistake with a customer's order, but that's all past. I found new work as Dr. Valerian's assistant."

"Oh, I do wish you had taken my advice in the beginning and found yourself a well-to-do gentleman to marry. Then you wouldn't have to support yourself by seeking this kind of work."

Abigail proceeded to speak in what she hoped was a calm manner, not wanting to spoil the holiday bickering with Catherine over her choice of employers and reigniting their old feud. "I'll be careful as you and Hammond asked, but I intend to keep this job. Now, can we please continue with Christmas?"

Catherine's lips thinned in a pink line, but she nodded. Abigail followed her into the sitting room, where Winnie and Phillip played with their new toys. The tension between the three adults remained, leading Abigail to speculate sadly that she had been invited to her sister's house only for the children's sake. And to hear Hammond's findings on Dr. Valerian.

She wondered if the doctor was in his cellar working even now. She hoped that her small gift would give him a moment's respite from his work, at least.

***

Jacob followed his nose out of the cellar and into the dining room, where the warm, spicy scent of cinnamon finally succeeded in tearing him away from his research. There, he found Maria setting a pot of tea on the table. Beside it rested a tray of freshly baked cinnamon bread, his favorite.

"Maria, you didn't have to do this. I gave you and Struthers the day off."

"It wasn't my doing, Doctor. This cinnamon loaf came from the bakery. The boy that delivered it said it was paid courtesy of Miss Benton."

How did Abigail know he liked cinnamon bread? He looked at Maria.

She shook her head of gray hair. "I knew nothing of it."

"I shall thank Miss Benton when she returns to work tomorrow." Jacob approached the table and prepared to cut a slice. He truly didn't expect Abigail to present him with anything for Christmas. She only started working at the practice a month ago, after all. He paused, holding the breadknife over the cinnamon loaf.

"Something wrong, sir?" Maria asked.

"No, I was just considering." He began to cut a sizeable slice. Abigail's small gesture of the Christmas spirit was the first of such he had received in years from someone other than his patients. His estranged family never sent Yuletide greetings.

Images of them shot through his mind, the father that disowned him upon learning that he lost his leg in India. *You're a cripple, unsuited to inherit the familial estate*, Jacob remembered his exact words. His mother and two brothers stood by the Valerian patriarch, not arguing in Jacob's defense.

"Beggin' your pardon, Doctor." Maria cut through his thoughts. "You said you were considering something."

Jacob brought his faculties back to present. "I was considering the pleasant aroma of this cinnamon bread."

"Ah." Maria nodded with the demeanor of one who knew better.

"And," Jacob continued as he poured himself a cup of Darjeeling. "I would be pleased if you and Struthers took the holiday to rest. You needn't spend the day here with me."

"Our friends have taken holiday outside of London." Maria pushed the sugar cubes and small pitcher of milk his way. "And if you don't mind my saying so, the husband and I don't think anyone ought to be alone on Christmas." She raised her head upon hearing a rustling in the kitchen. "Ah, speak of the husband, I hear him now. He's returned with roasted ham. We'll get it on a platter. Enjoy your tea and bread, Doctor." She bustled back into the kitchen, shutting the door behind her.

Jacob chewed on a warm morsel of cinnamon bread when the doorbell rang.

He heard Struthers and Maria talking in the kitchen, their words interspersed with the clattering of dishes and the clinging of silverware. They did not hear the doorbell. Jacob pushed his chair back and went to the front of the house to answer it himself.

"Hello, Dr. Valerian." A giant of a man stood before him. He had the appearance of the Welsh, black of hair and dark-eyed, and spoke with the lilting cadence of one who made his home near the Swansea docks. He held a large box in his arms. "I'm COIC agent Rhys Cartret, and this is my wife, Lydia. I know the Secretary briefed you on her work."

"The celebrated machinist." Jacob's eyes fell onto the woman at Rhys's side. She had olive skin, dark curls, and unusual gold-green eyes. "Come in please." He stepped aside so that they could enter. "Lady Dimosthenis, I read of your work with the voice-responsive automatons. Most extraordinary."

"A pleasure to meet you, Dr. Valerian, but my name is Lydia Cartret now." She spoke in a Greek accent. "My husband and I just wed Saturday." She trained a smile at Rhys, who lifted his eyebrows suggestively. The silent exchange between them spoke volumes.

"Congratulations." Jacob felt like he was intruding, even though they came to see him. "To what do I owe the occasion of your visit?"

"We come bearing gifts." Rhys raised the large box. "The Secretary approved of your findings from the ether solvent test of the Aspasian metal alloy sample. Here's a larger supply for you to work with."

Jacob indicated for him to set the box on the settee in the parlor. While Rhys and his wife removed their coats, he raised the box lid. "There's enough of the copper alloy and cast iron here to craft a working armor device."

"We thought you'd be happy," Rhys remarked, with a droll smile.

"I'm impressed with your findings, Doctor." Lydia came beside Jacob and lifted one of the small samples of the copper alloy. "When I created the automatons, I thought the voice-responsive function worked simply because sound can be conducted through metal. I had no idea that the compounds of the copper alloy were what actually allowed the automatons to follow orders."

"Compounds that can only be found in your country of Aspasia," Jacob added.

"Yes. Fortunately, it takes just a very tiny portion of the alloy to make use of the function." Lydia held the copper alloy sample between her thumb and forefinger. "I would say this is enough to give that capability to half a dozen devices, depending on their size."

Jacob lifted a sample of the cast iron, about the size of his fist. "And this will provide a conduit. I'll have to find a way to incorporate as small amount of iron as possible in the armor. COIC agents have enough heavy firearms to carry."

Rhys stood behind the settee and looked down at the sample case. "Do you think voice-responsive weaponry will give our agents stationed in France the upper hand against Broussard's men?"

"It's working with the automatons in India. Based on COIC reports I was granted access to, they're defending the mercantile holdings in Madras and Bombay against French mechanized forces. The need for infantrymen has been reduced."

"My hope is to do the same for London's factories," Lydia said. "Having an automaton operate the boilers or some of the more dangerous machinery would reduce the number of accidents."

Jacob agreed. "We could surely do with a change. I'll be visiting one of the laborer's hospitals in January. Each month the factory-related injuries get worse. But I digress." He closed the lid on the metal samples. "Thank you for these. Now I can begin crafting."

"You should ask the Secretary for clearance to work at headquarters," Rhys ventured. "My wife may even lend you an automaton to assist you. Of course, you'd have to instruct it beforehand."

"The offer is generous, but I have already invested in training an assistant. Last month, I hired her."

Rhys looked up and to the side as though he were consulting his memory. "Is she the same lady you chose from the audience to assist you during that demonstration?"

"She is. I take it you were there or are an avid reader of the papers?"

"I wasn't there, but the Secretary commented on the potent mixture of nitrous oxide she deployed from the gauntlet gun. See, Lydia, yet another woman who's not afraid to make a statement with a firearm." Rhys teased his wife.

Jacob straightened his collar. "It caused more alarm than anything else. I should have better explained to my assistant how the weapon worked, but there wasn't enough time onstage."

"Pay no attention to my husband, Doctor." Lydia gave Rhys a mock scowl. "He enjoys bantering with me."

Her husband's eyes twinkled at her. "I've had my own share of firearm mishaps. That's how she and I met. It was on a beach. White sand, sun high in the sky. And this lovely woman comes up to me, but before I can doff my hat and greet her like a proper gentleman, I find myself staring down the barrel of a very big blunderbuss."

Jacob witnessed a bronze blush creep upon Lydia's cheeks. Again, he felt as though he were intruding upon the couple's unusual, though humorous, flirtation. "Well, things have improved for the two of you, I'm sure."

Rhys and Lydia continued to stare into each other's eyes. Jacob was certain that he and the settee were the only things keeping the two of them from embracing.

An odd sensation sprang within him. He recognized it as loneliness. Seeing the newlywed Cartrets, with their display of love and playful affection, served as a poignant reminder of an aspect of life that managed to elude him.

Thank heaven for the ringing of the dinner bell. The sound broke through the trance of the spell the Cartrets had upon each other, and allowed Jacob to change the subject without seeming rude. "My housekeeper and valet have Christmas dinner ready. Would you care to join us?"

Rhys regarded the grandfather clock. "We were going to find a food vendor at the rail station before leaving for our honeymoon. What do you think, Lydia? The doctor's kind invitation to dinner promises better than what the station has to offer."

"I would enjoy sampling British holiday cuisine." Lydia smiled. "And we can finish discussing the properties of Aspasian metals. Please lead the way, Dr. Valerian."

Jacob showed them into the dining room, pleased now that he, Maria, and Struthers would have additional company.

For the first time in years, his dining room was filled with the sounds of lively conversation. But even as the wine flowed and the Christmas ham was passed amongst them, Jacob thought of Abigail.

"This cinnamon bread is delicious," Lydia said, after taking a bite.

"My assistant had it sent from the bakery." Jacob consumed his first slice and was onto his second.

"She had good taste. I look forward to meeting her if she comes to the COIC."

"Miss Benton would complete our gathering." Jacob spoke the words before he fully comprehended them. "For our discussion of the metal properties, that is." He raised his glass to his lips to relieve his suddenly parched throat.

The Cartrets and the Strutherses continued to dine as though nothing odd was said. Jacob attempted to do the same, but his mind now filled with thoughts of his slender, auburn-haired assistant, with her warm smile and kind nature. Whatever caused his minor lapse in semantics, he hoped it wouldn't occur again tomorrow with Abigail, for he had much to discuss with her on the day that marked the end of her trial employment.

Chapter 9

Abigail returned to Dr. Valerian's residence the day after Christmas at eight-thirty. Struthers greeted her and took her coat. "I saw Dr. Valerian go into his practice early this morning," he said.

Could that mean her evaluation was set to start immediately? Abigail smoothed the front of her dress before traversing the short hallway. All month long she had done her best. She hoped it was good enough.

The door to Dr. Valerian's practice was locked. Through the window panel, Abigail saw that no one was inside. The gas lamps were on, as though someone recently entered and then departed. Abigail wondered if he simply hadn't made it downstairs from his upper rooms yet. She returned to the front of the house. "Struthers, he isn't in his office. The door is locked."

Struthers was gone.

A loud clang made her turn towards the hallway again. It sounded like it came from the cellar.

A softer noise ensued from below half a minute later. It repeated itself thrice, calling to Abigail's mind the sound of sharp metal striking and scraping against another metal. Long-winded hissing followed.

She went towards the cellar door. It was not fully closed. The hissing began again, just before the space below the door shone a bluish light.

Was Dr. Valerian in the cellar? She'd never heard such sounds emitting from the house's foundation when he was down there any other day. A prickly sensation crept along Abigail's arms. What was behind that door that kept the doctor tirelessly at work?

She touched the door handle as the blue light flickered again, following the hissing. She shifted her eyes to the well-lit practice and to the parlor. She could still choose to wait up here and see from which direction Dr. Valerian would appear. She could still wait by the door of the practice and not venture into parts of the residence that she was not given access to.

She could still pretend to not be curious about the mystery and eccentricities surrounding Dr. Valerian.

The continuous flashing of blue light beneath the door put a stop to her hesitation. She opened the door and went down two stone steps into the cellar just as the light disappeared and plunged her surroundings in black.

Abigail clutched the cold iron railing as she remained on the step, not daring to move in the dark. The cellar smelled of copper, iron, and something recently heated. The tiny sliver of light from the hallway above offered her one last chance to venture out the way she came.

Abigail waited for the blue light. It came, enabling her to view the brick inlay of the walls encasing the stairs and above her head, cementing the foundation of the house's first floor. She counted eight steps. The rest beyond that remained in darkness.

She learned the timing and pattern of the light. It flashed roughly every six seconds, lasting for four. She took two steps down each time it came on, pausing when it disappeared. Her foot found the bottom of the stairs in shortly under a minute. Abigail waited for the light, but this time, it flashed at three seconds, much brighter than previously.

Less than ten feet away, a shower of sparks sprayed from a hunched figure.

Abigail clambered back, tripping on the hem of her skirt. Sparks continued to fly, reaching the stairs. She slapped at them as they landed on her dress.

The cellar retuned to black and stayed that way. Abigail blinked rapidly in the dark to make the starbursts from the blue light dissipate from her eyes.

Where was the hunched figure? Did it see her before she retreated? She listened for footsteps. Nothing. But the person knew she was there. That's why the light stopped flashing.

She twisted to find the railing. Light suddenly engulfed her as the lamps in the cellar came on at once. Abigail looked up to a figure looming over her with large, black, empty eyes. A cry rent through her throat before the figure raised a big hand and peeled back its face.

Dr. Valerian's familiar intelligent features and keen eyes appeared. His finely etched mouth drew a hard line. "Are you lost, Miss Benton?"

The remaining starbursts fell from her eyes. She saw his protective leather duster, gloves, and welder's mask. A workbench and table were situated to his right, a small portable coal burner on the floor. The frantic fear she experienced moments before fizzled to chagrin.

"Of course you're not lost," he answered for her, "Curiosity got the better of you and so you found your way down here."

"I saw light flashing. I heard noises."

"From welding instruments. I'm constructing a component for an existing device." He peeled the gloves and duster off next until he stood before her in his normal attire of shirt, pants, and waistcoat. "But tell me, exactly what was it that you expected to see?"

He had every right to react the way he did. She intruded upon him. Anything she said now to defend herself would come out foolish and unjustified, so she opted for speaking the plain truth. "I don't know what I expected to see."

"Graveyard spoils and lightning conductor coils, perhaps?"

"I'm not one for macabre horror stories, Doctor." Abigail finally let go of the iron railing. "I'm in the wrong, I know, but I wished to learn why you spent so much time down here. You never seem to rest."

"Are you concerned for my health now?"

"What an odd question."

"It's called sarcasm, Miss Benton. You'll find it typically employed in situations where one's boundaries are encroached upon." He returned to his workbench. His walking stick rested against it. "To ease your concerns, this is where I start constructing my ongoing projects. I have one now that must be completed by spring. That's why I am at constant work."

Abigail came down to the cellar floor again. The foundational level of Dr. Valerian's house was a craftsman's work area, with cutting tools, hammers, welders, and rivet guns of varying sizes lining the cork-boarded walls. Shelves housing an assortment of glass bottles and storage containers rested in the back corner. Another large shelf gleamed with raw materials of steel, brass, and copper. "Is your project for a patient or client?"

"Neither. It's for a scientific agency."

The loftiness of his statement gave Abigail pause. What could he be making? "Did your former assistant work on it, too?"

"No, this is very new. Besides, my former assistant didn't dare to even venture to the cellar without being accompanied." Dr. Valerian tilted his head for a moment to regard her. "Which I can't say is true, in your case."

Abigail saw the hard line of his mouth soften, one corner slightly raised. One minute he was angry, and the next he seemed to be laughing at her. She folded her arms, frustrated. "Does my daring amuse you?"

"It hasn't escaped my notice. You've shown yourself to be persistent and inquisitive. In other realms of society, such traits in a woman would be scorned."

Surely he wasn't drudging up this tired bit about her sex again. Abigail ventured to ask, "And in your realm of science and medicine, Doctor, what would be the conclusion of your findings about me?"

Her challenge made him scrutinize her. "Such traits lend themselves useful. I cannot have a timid assistant."

Perhaps she didn't wreck her chances of keeping this job after all. "Does that mean I'm to remain in your employment?"

"I promised you an answer at the end of thirty days. The day isn't over yet." He picked up a small hammer and chisel and went to work on a fist-size chunk of rock.

He was going to force her to wait. Abigail took a seat on the bench across from him at the table. He didn't object. She noticed a saucer on the far end of the table, along with an empty teacup. The saucer bore the crust of cinnamon bread.

"Did Maria inform you that I liked cinnamon bread?"

She'd been caught staring. "No. Was it satisfactory?"

"It was very good. Thank you." And as abruptly as that started, it ended as Dr. Valerian launched back into chiseling. "This is cast iron that I'm preparing to put into an armored device," he explained. "It has properties unlike any other composition of iron as we know it."

She watched him chip away at the cast iron before she reached for the sketchbook and pencil on the table. "Do you mind if I use this to make notations?"

"Go ahead, if you can find a blank sheet."

Abigail flipped through the pages. Sketches of various armament and prosthetic models filled the book. A few she recognized from seeing in the display cabinets in Dr. Valerian's practice, but most of the drawings were very rough conceptual designs. Eraser smudges and hastily scrawled notes filled the edges of the paper.

"As you can see, the design stages are much cruder than the end product. You said you did some sketching as well."

"I do sketch, but I don't remember saying so to you. Was it before you hired me?"

"The time wasn't important." Dr. Valerian waved dismissively. "How would you rate your ability to draw?"

"I don't say this to boast, but I believe I can fashion presentable drawings. I usually do them from memory."

"Show me."

Abigail found a blank page in Dr. Valerian's sketchbook. She took the pencil and made a rough sketch of one of the prosthetics in the display cabinets upstairs. The process took several minutes. She presented it to Dr. Valerian. "Do you recognize this?"

Dr. Valerian studied the sketch. His eyebrows lifted. "That's the prosthetic device for Mr. Carney's hand. You sketched quickly, but the details are still there." His eyes moved from the paper to meet her own. "I'm impressed."

Abigail became strangely bashful under his frank and steady gaze. "Thank you."

Now," Dr. Valerian said, picking up a piece of the cast iron he chiseled, "this metal is from Aspasia, an island nation near Greece. The Aspasians have used the iron for centuries, but it was recently discovered that when an automaton is built with this combination of iron and copper alloy from the same region, it can interpret sound."

Abigail put down the sketchbook. "I knew metals conducted sound, but what do you mean by interpret?"

He picked up another piece of metal. It was reddish-gold in the light. "If crafted properly, these metals make a mechanical device register vocal commands through resonant vibration. Somehow, when particular tones and pitches are recognized, the device reacts. No one yet knows why the metals can make it do this, but I have a theory that the soil properties where the metals are extracted play a role."

All she could do was stare at him.

"I knew you'd be skeptical." He offered an accepting smile that produced in her an interesting inner excitement. "I was, too, at first, but I tested my theory. You remember the ether solvent I ordered from the apothecary." Instead of waiting for her to respond, he rose from the bench and walked to the back of the cellar. Abigail followed him.

He removed a box from the shelf and withdrew two stoppered vials. "I added one drop of solvent to these cast iron samples. See how the Aspasian iron's components were broken down compared to the locally sourced iron on the left."

Abigail peered into the vial. The iron had liquefied under the solvent's harsh chemicals to subsequently solidify into a penny-sized corrosive mass. The edges had a prismatic effect of light blue, green, and violet. She turned to the local iron sample. The ether solvent reduced it to a flat mass as well, but its corrosion was the normal ruddy color of rust. "I do see the difference."

Appearing pleased to hear so, Dr. Valerian returned the vials to the shelf. "Just think, Abigail," he didn't notice that he addressed her by her first name, "if I could find a way to embed the Aspasian metals into armor and prosthetic devices. A weapon could discharge upon an assailant with just a word. Or in the case of prosthetic limbs, instead of the harnesses and springs used to maneuver them, a voice-responsive metal could make for ease of movement."

"Your patients would be enthralled by the improved use of their devices."

"Yes. Very." He looked down momentarily at something on or near his right leg.

She couldn't tell what it was.

"But you said this project was for a scientific agency."

"Correct. Once a working weapon is complete, the Cabinet of Intellectual Curiosities will let its agents test it."

"I've never heard of such a Cabinet."

Dr. Valerian returned to the worktable and began putting the Aspasian metal samples away in a box. "The COIC doesn't engage widely with the public. It's comprised of inventors and scholars who seek objects of scientific value."

Abigail turned over in her mind what she just learned. "Like the automatons from Aspasia. And now your work with mechanical prosthetics."

"Yes. When the Cabinet learned of my practice, they commissioned me to not only build a weapon, but find how the Aspasian metals worked when worn on the body as opposed to being within an automaton."

A British agency, a relatively unknown Mediterranean island, and the astounding properties of supposedly ordinary metals. It all sounded like strange fiction. Hammond's words about Dr. Valerian came back to Abigail: *He's an eccentric.*

But eccentricity didn't have to be the bedfellow of instability. Abigail wanted to give Dr. Valerian the benefit of the doubt. "When in the spring does the COIC want this project?"

"The third week of March, to be exact."

"That's not much time, considering all that must be done. But aren't you scheduled to go to the college today?"

"The college is still on holiday." He looked at his pocketwatch. "Today we'll visit the laborer's hospital near St. Giles. This is the final rounds of the practice that you haven't seen. But we must leave now if we're to be there on time."

And before Abigail could catch her breath, he whisked her away from the ether solvent experiments, rough sketches of mechanical armor, and unfinished welded metal.

Chapter 10

Now that he told Abigail a little about the COIC project, Jacob wondered what she thought of him and his practice. Maybe he should have waited to see how she handled herself at the laborer's hospital first.

Jacob looked at her from across the surgeon's ward, where she talked amiably with a patient at his bedside. Already those in the ward had warmed to her pleasant demeanor, which was good. The men and women, and sometimes the occasional child, that found themselves within the hospital's crumbling brick and plaster walls needed to see a friendly face.

Life inside a laborer's hospital was overcrowded and grim, with frequent need of cauterizations and amputations from factory machine accidents. Outside the building, a few blocks within the parish of St. Giles, life was grimmer still. Even after four years of traveling through it in order to care for the hospital patients, it never failed to unnerve him that progress brought with it so much poverty and filth.

And pain. Jacob looked away from Abigail and finished changing the bandages on a female patient's arm. She gave an agonized moan, even with the small dose of morphine he administered to her. "There's no sign of infection, but if the area of amputation continues to bleed, it will have to be cauterized again."

Her eyes, glazed over from pain and medication, produced a veil of tears. "I can't take much more."

"It is an ordeal," Jacob acknowledged, quietly. "But you must do what is necessary."

"You got two workin' hands. Look at this." She raised the bandaged stump of where her right hand used to be, and promptly let out a sharp cry.

"Madam, please." Jacob helped her ease her arm back down upon the bed. The dingy threadbare bedcovers rose and fell with her rapid breathing. "You must keep yourself reposed so that you can heal."

"I was one of them silk weavers at the mill." She turned her head away from him on her thin pillow. Her brown hair, cut short for her to work around machinery, matted with sweat against her neck. "Got my hand caught in the loom and now I've got no way to care for my wee ones. My husband'll be next. He works in the mill, too."

Heaviness fell across Jacob's shoulders. Nothing could be said to console her. He knew from experience how trite and useless even the most well-meaning words of comfort could be, especially when the pain of losing a limb drove a searing hole through the mind's ability to cope.

"I will help you." He hoped that she still listened. "With every resource at my disposal, I will help you and the other patients in this hospital to regain their health."

"But not my hand." Her bitter, mournful words were muffled against the pillow.

No, that he could not do. The silk weaver, poor and already living without, was now forced to sacrifice more. Jacob rubbed his leg at the knee, where the straps securing his mechanical limb dug into his skin.

The subtle warmth of vanilla rose above the hospital's smell of unwashed linens and its ill inhabitants. A gentle touch fell upon Jacob's shoulder.

"She's in much pain," he said to Abigail, as she approached a rolling cart near the silk weaver's bedside. "The hospital won't receive another shipment of morphine until tomorrow."

Abigail gave a solemn nod. She took a clean cloth from the cart and dipped it into the cart's attached water basin. "I'll stay with her while you visit your other patients."

Jacob picked up his medical bag and went to the next patient's bedside, wishing he had brought his own supply of laudanum to the hospital. It wouldn't have been nearly enough for every patient in the ward, but it would have offered some respite for those suffering the most.

He checked the new patient's vitals as he heard Abigail speak to the silk weaver in gentle, dulcet tones as though she were her own mother or sister. She applied the damp cloth to the woman's fevered brow.

Jacob finished making his rounds at the ward at six o'clock, one hour later than he expected. The hospital windows showed the backdrop of the paper mill and garment factory buildings. Between the steam and soot clouds billowing from their roofs, the sky darkened from gray afternoon haze to a brown dusk.

He needed to get Abigail out of that part of London before nightfall. Assistant or not, there were certain parts of the city that were very unsafe for women after hours.

Jacob took his bag, coat, and walking stick and went to find Abigail. She was at the front of the ward, walking alongside a mill boy who was learning to maneuver on crutches. "It's six o'clock. We should be getting back to Bloomsbury."

Abigail helped the boy to his bed before she put on her coat and joined Jacob at the hospital door.

Outside, the temperature and the late hour had sent most people indoors, including those leaving the day shifts at the factories. Jacob viewed the street from left to right in search of a hansom cab to ride. None were to be found. He tapped his cane against the curb, regretting his continuous lapse in punctuality. "It looks as though we'll have to walk until we find a cab, Miss Benton."

Abigail buttoned her coat up to her neck. "The cold isn't as bracing today."

"It's not the cold that concerns me. This quarter is dangerous at night." Jacob cast a glance at the nearest gas light as an automaton lamplighter wheeled along and, raising half its body with the use of a metal ladder apparatus, lit it. The automaton's gears creaked as it lowered itself down and went forward. It repeated its procedure on three more coal gas lights on the row before the street settled into a gritty dimness. Additional illumination was provided by the glow from fires that stoked the machines of the mills. The automaton rolled along to complete its task on the next street.

Abigail watched it depart. "At least the streets are not crowded. That is in our favor, isn't it?"

Across the way, two men stumbled out of a drinking establishment. They turned their faces towards the hospital, and then lingered on Abigail.

"It's time we leave," Jacob said, maintaining eye contact with the men to let them know that their presence did not go unnoticed.

He felt Abigail slide her hand into the crook of his arm. She took his medical bag and fell in step with him. The two men continued to watch until they were up the street.

Jacob gripped his walking stick defensively as he moved first around the corner. The street itself lay bare before them, but three men stood huddling along the sidewalk. They walked past a waif and an old woman who warmed their hands over foul-smelling flame, stoked with rubbish. The boy looked up at them with large sunken eyes. The old woman sneered.

"Leave 'em be, lad. They's better'n us."

Abigail shook her head and moved as though she were going to search her reticule for some coin. Jacob stepped into the street, taking her along with him.

"Why did you do that? She wouldn't have hurt me."

He waited until the three men passed by. "Giving money at this hour only draws more attention. Didn't you learn that during your missions to India?"

"I see no harm in helping one woman," she protested, looking back.

"You may not see the harm, but that doesn't mean others are not watching you from the alleys." Jacob heard his voice becoming harsh, but it fell upon him to protect her. She could be annoyed at him for it if she wished.

They walked seven blocks, getting closer to the outskirts of Bloomsbury, but still near to the St. Giles parish, as well. Another factory building took up the street's north end. Thick black smoke churned from the chimney, blanketing the moon from view. The street and buildings surrounding the factory were covered in a film that lent the area a stilted, dull appearance.

The smoke got into Abigail's lungs. She coughed.

"Does the lady need a glass of water?" a voice mocked.

Jacob instinctively pulled Abigail closer to his side as he surveyed the area. Three shadowed figures emerged from the smoke-filled path ahead of them as they came into the pale light emerging from the factory windows. He assessed the men.

Dressed in dark, ragged trousers and patched, frayed coats, they possessed a lean, hungry look. They came closer until they stood less than ten steps away. It dawned on Jacob that they were the three men who passed him and Abigail just minutes before.

"Look wot we got here, lads," the one who stood in the middle spoke. "A bloke out on an evenin' stroll with his lady."

"Yeah, Tim." The man on his left, looking barely older than twenty, joined in. "Looks like he's a rich bloke, judgin' from the handle of that walkin' stick. Is it ivory, Perry?"

"I don't know." The scraggly-bearded one on the right shrugged, hands in his pockets. Jacob knew he had a weapon in one or both of them. "The skirt hangin' on his arm is wot I got me eye on."

Abigail tensed under his leer. Jacob drew himself up, moving his walking stick from his side to the front of his feet. His fingers moved over the carved handle until they found the smooth depression at the base. He maintained them there. "Gentlemen, we want no trouble with you." He kept his words civil and spoke calmly, but he intended for the men to hear the warning in his tone.

Tim, the leader, laughed. "Who said there'd be trouble, chum? Do you see any trouble, lads?"

Perry gave Abigail a gap-toothed smile before he raised a brass-knuckled hand to scratch his whiskers. "Not in the least."

"I agree." Tim patted his pocket. "All I see is a wee woman and a cripple."

Jacob bristled at the term. The gang leader saw it and laughed. "We'd be willin' to let the lady go, provided she hand over the coin she was gonna give to that old hag." Tim advanced towards her. "We know she has money. You both do."

Jacob got in front of Abigail. "Leave her alone. I will give you money."

A hard glimmer reflected in Tim's black eyes, like the crows that scoured the streets in the daylight hours. "I want her money. Then she can go." The flash of a knife appeared in his hand.

Jacob felt Abigail's grip on his arm tighten. He needed her to be as calm as possible right now, and to follow his instructions. He prayed she would listen. "I hate to ask, Miss Benton, but it seems we have no choice. Your reticule, please."

He moved his right hand behind his back and turned it over. He waited. He heard a rustling of wool and muslin lining, and two moments later, he felt the weight of her small reticule land in his palm. He closed his fingers around it and presented it to the gang leader.

"That wasn't so hard, now was it?" Tim jingled the coins in the reticule. "And to show you that I'm a man of my word…the lady paid her toll, lads. Let her pass."

The other two men stepped apart from each other. Jacob got a bad feeling. What were they up to? But as long as he could get Abigail away from them, he would be willing to bear the brunt of what they had in store. "Go, Miss Benton," he said, never turning to look at her, but keeping his face always towards the men whose desire to rob appeared to remain unappeased.

Abigail hesitated. Jacob sensed that she didn't want to leave him alone to face the three men. Along with their combined strength, they possessed knives and brass knuckles. He had a walking stick. But he would use it. "Go," he repeated to Abigail. "It will be alright." He gave her hand a gentle squeeze.

Abigail started forward. Perhaps if she reached the Bloomsbury outskirts ahead, she could find a constable to intervene. But Jacob doubted they would make it back in time.

Perry and the youngest gang member stepped back for her to pass. They wouldn't allow her to go around them. She stared straight ahead. The men stayed put as she went between them. She tightened her grip on Jacob's medical bag that she still carried in her possession.

Something didn't look right. "Abigail, look out." Jacob's shout reached her just as one of the men seized her arm.

Jacob saw no more of her as Tim descended upon him, knife extended. Jacob pressed the button on his walking stick. Immediately, the casing fell away from the handle and its blade. Before Tim could drive the knife home, Jacob deflected with his cane sword, sending the small blade sailing through the air. He then drove the sword deep into the man's shoulder, cutting through muscle until the blade bit into bone. Tim let out a cry of pain, diving to the ground. His hands outstretched, he grabbed onto Jacob's right leg. Before he could do anything, Tim's grip on the mechanical limb tightened.

"What the—?" The gang leader exclaimed as he realized that his grip came upon steel, aluminum, and brass. "*What are you?*"

Jacob kicked him off before his right leg became completely unhinged. He fell backwards as his center of gravity shifted. Tim also fell, landing on his back. Tim scrabbled along the cobblestones to regain his footing.

Jacob looked to Abigail. She struck Perry with his medical bag, sending the man back. She turned it onto the youngest one, striking him in the jaw. Perry, meanwhile, righted himself. Jacob saw the flash of Perry's brass knuckles before they came into contact with Abigail's temple. She dropped the bag. Perry picked it up and ran off with it, followed by his young accomplice.

The brawl was over as quickly as it commenced. The leader Tim scuffled to his feet like an injured dog. He grappled for his knife in the slush.

Jacob pointing his cane sword at Tim's throat. "Leave."

Tim backed away clumsily, clutching his shoulder. He followed after the two men. They went down the street and right before disappearing in an alley next to an abandoned storehouse.

Jacob's focus turned elsewhere as soon as they departed. "Abigail?" He saw her on the ground. She rolled onto her hands and knees. "Answer me."

Shakily, she got to her feet. A look of horror permeated her features as looked at Jacob's mechanical right leg.

Chapter 11

The look on Abigail's face summarized everything that Jacob spent the past several weeks trying to avoid instilling in her.

Shock. Fear. Confusion. Her lips parted as she stared at the steel and aluminum apparatus that was his mechanical limb situated on the ground beside him. Was it horror? Disgust?

"Are you injured?" he asked.

"I don't think so," came her small reply.

Jacob dragged himself through the grime and coal dust-encrusted slush of the street to get to his mechanical limb.

Abigail started forward. "I'll get—"

"No." He snatched the limb by the boot before she could come closer. His rebuke stopped her short.

In the sting of humiliation, he turned his back to her, set the cane-knife down, and worked furiously to attach the limb back on his knee. He shook his head as he went through the process of rolling up his trouser leg, searching for the straps that were attached to a belt at his waist, yanking them past his thigh, and hooking them through the prosthetic's closures. All with the indignity of having to do so in the middle of the street. Finally, he cinched the band that strapped over his knee and pulled his trouser leg back down over the top of his boot last.

Jacob pushed himself to his feet, his back still to Abigail. He dared to turn. She remained standing in the same spot. Her eyes were large as she stared at him. "Those men will come back with reinforcements. We're almost to the main road where we can find a cab."

He picked up the cane-knife and found the shell of his walking stick nearby. The knife slid in with a small click. But then he noticed that Abigail brought her hand to the corner of her brow and kept it there.

"Abigail, what is it?"

She shook her head, wincing. "Nothing. I thought…that man with the brass knuckles…he grazed me with the side of his fist."

Jacob crossed the space between them and took her hand away from her face. "You're bleeding." He saw the dark wetness that stained her gloves. She winced again as he moved back the hair that stuck to her forehead. Blood trickled from a bludgeon wound.

"Is it bad?" she asked.

"There's not enough light for me to see the extent of it. Are you dizzy, disoriented?"

"No…" Her halted speech told him that she was still reeling from the shock of being attacked. He had to get her back to his practice. "We're closer to my residence now than we are the hospital. We can't linger here." He withdrew his handkerchief and placed it against her brow. "Keep this pressed to your temple."

She followed his instructions and started walking beside him again, matching his stride. Jacob's knee ached from where the gang's leader Tim pulled him down. *If I had both my legs, I could have been faster. Then Abigail wouldn't have been injured.*

But the fault was still his. He took too long making his rounds at the hospital. They should have left earlier. Then they would have had the afternoon light and a cab waiting to take them back to the practice.

Jacob kept a close eye on the darkened alleys and street corners as he and Abigail went up New Oxford Street. He saw a cab on the adjacent corner and hailed it, increasing his pace even as the driver acknowledged him.

He made sure Abigail got inside the cab even before the driver hopped down from his perch. "Nineteen Locksford Lane. And hurry." He climbed in and shut the door himself.

Very little of his tension eased as the cab started to move. He turned to Abigail. "Lift your hand."

The gaslights they passed did little to let him see the exact site of the wound, or even how big it was. "Continue to keep it compressed." He remained on the edge of his seat, studying her.

"I didn't realize I was injured when you asked the first time," she said. "I was surprised to see—I'm sorry."

She didn't have to say it. He knew why she was distracted from noticing the full extent of her injury.

The cab sped through town and stopped at Jacob's address. He opened the cab door to see his valet and housekeeper hurrying from the house.

"We were worried something happened to you and Miss Benton," Struthers said. His expression turned to distress when he saw Abigail clutching the bloodstained handkerchief to her head. "My God."

"Struthers, pay the driver from my despatch box on the console. Maria, if you would help me get Abigail into the office where I can treat her."

His housekeeper took Abigail's arm as Jacob helped her step down from the cab. "There now, dear." She put a supportive hand on Abigail's back as well. "It's going to be alright. You'll see. The doctor will take good care of you."

Like I did in the industrial district. Jacob bitterly recalled, as he helped Maria take Abigail to the examination table. Then he threw off his coat and went to wash his hands before coming back.

"Is there anything else I can do for Miss Benton?" Maria asked, holding Abigail's coat in her arms.

"Prepare the guest room. Tell Struthers to get the fireplace working in there. Miss Benton will not be going home in this state tonight."

"Right away, Doctor." Maria exited the office.

"I can't stay here," Abigail voiced. She took the handkerchief away from her head.

"Now is not the time to be concerned with propriety." Jacob lit the lamp next to the table. "You have a head wound that needs looking after." He cupped her chin and tilted her head in the path of the light. A portion of hair was matted over her left temple. He brushed it back with his fingers as gingerly as possible.

She tensed under his touch. "How is it now?"

"The bleeding stopped." He spotted the origin of blood just below her hairline. "The skin broke neatly. Some bruising and swelling, but I don't think you'll require stitches."

A shudder went through her.

"I didn't mean to startle you." He went to a cabinet for antiseptic and cotton gauze. "I'm used to speaking plainly to my patients."

"It's fine. I'm a patient tonight."

"And that's my fault." He closed the cabinet after getting what he needed and placing the supplies on a tray. He found her reflection in the cabinet mirror staring at him.

"You didn't know those men were going to ambush us."

"It could have been avoided had we left the hospital earlier."

"Perhaps. Or perhaps we could have been attacked in daylight."

"It's not as likely." He carried the tray to the examination table. "I won't be inattentive like that again, not when you're with me." Jacob dotted antiseptic on the gauze. "This will sting."

He touched the gauze to her brow. Her eyes welded shut. Her jaw clenched. Still, she made no protest as he wiped at the blood and cleaned the wound.

"Almost done," he said.

She opened one eye suddenly. "I didn't thank you for fending off those ruffians."

"If I still had my—forget it." He set the gauze on the tray and reached for a fresh one and bandages. He felt the weight of her contemplative stare.

"Why didn't you say anything about your leg?"

"Should I have?" He secured the fresh gauze to her temple and proceeded to wrap the bandage around her head.

"Yes. I would have understood, then, why you avoid the topic of India." She held her hair up in back for him to tie the bandage. "Is that where it happened?" She forced him to look directly into her eyes, eyes that held compassion and not the horror he misinterpreted in her expression before.

"Yes." Jacob knew where this was leading. He did not want to venture there, but after what Abigail went through, she deserved to know why his past influenced him to work as he did. "I don't tell people about my amputated leg because I don't wish to be pitied."

"You defended me tonight. You have my gratitude, not pity. Do Struthers and Maria know?"

"They are part of a very small group of friends and associates who do. Having a walking stick is one thing, but even among my patients, it's quite

222

another to know that the physician treating them is without one of his legs."

"I must disagree with you, especially if you haven't ventured to reveal that fact to them." Abigail must have seen his surprise at her spirited declaration, for she promptly toned down her voice and added, "What I mean is, I think your patients would respect you all the more, knowing that you've gone through what they're experiencing. Others would, too, if they knew of your sacrifice for New Britannia."

"It isn't as though I haven't considered your point. My life changed after I came home from India. I was expressly told by my father that no permanently disfigured son of his would inherit the family lands."

Abigail shook her head. "That is regrettable as it is reprehensible."

Jacob agreed, but he was long past the anger towards his family that she now displayed. "But it was understandable. I was the eldest son whose pastimes involved chemistry and metalworking, not learning how to run an estate. I left Sussex for London to become a doctor and eventually joined New Britannia's armed forces, where I could at least put both my skills to practical use. I was given orders for Madras."

"When I was in India, New Britannia and France were still fighting over Madras' surrounding provinces."

"That's where my injuries occurred. I was a medic at a combined soldier and civilian hospital camp outside the city. A handful of rogue legionnaires disregarded the rules of war and released mortar rounds into the camp." He paused as the memories rushed back.

The air whistled with the sound of mortars flying. Screams tore through the camp. Gunpowder burned Jacob's nostrils before he saw black smoke rise.

He was on the ground, his hands riddled with broken glass. He could no longer feel his right leg, only immense pain. His skin stung and his eyes burned from a liquid that splattered across his face. He could feel the heat from the burning tent flaps as he crawled away from them. But he heard the patients still trapped inside. They were dying even as they screamed for help. And there was nothing he could do to save them…

"Doctor? Doctor, can you hear me?"

Abigail's voice and her touch penetrated his senses. The vision dispersed. He was in his office again. At his address in London, thousands of miles away from Madras.

"You should be seated," he told her.

"I got up because you looked like you didn't know you were here." She slowly loosened her fingers from his. Jacob felt the absence of her touch just as poignantly as he did the initial contact of her hand. He wanted to reach for her and keep her close, but controlled the urge.

"It doesn't happen often, but the past comes back to me. I can't predict when it does."

"It must have been brought on by our discussion." Abigail sat on the divan. "That attack was a terrible thing you suffered."

He felt like every secret he had was laid bare before her, but as uncomfortable as that was, it also brought a sense of release. She surprised him by her unwavering resolve to listen without being frightened off. "Not many in the camp survived the legionnaires' incendiaries and the experimental weak acid they used. A mortar round shattered my leg. The acid, originally used to dissolve vegetation surrounding the provinces, got near my eyes and weakened the retinas. It's where the scar comes from." He touched the faint webbing of scar tissue on his face. "That's why I must wear lenses that tint in bright light."

Abigail's eyebrows curved in confusion. "I feel as though you told me some of this before, but I can't remember when."

Jacob remembered. She had been in his college office, where the effects of the nitrous oxide still coursed through her system. He didn't think she would be able to recall aspects from that day a month ago.

What if she remembered that kiss she gave him while under the laughing gas' influence? Or worse, that he returned it while completely sober? Surely it would disrupt their current arrangement. Abigail would be beside herself for embracing him, a near stranger at the time and now, since she learned of his amputated leg, a disfigured man.

She could extend sympathy towards him, yes, but Jacob thought it impossible that she would ever exhibit such passion towards him again in her right frame of mind.

He'd spare her the indignity of resurrecting the memory. And himself from experiencing her rejection if she were to find out. He changed the subject. "Abigail, you should eat. I'll see if Maria can cook something."

Abigail played with the thread of a missing button on her sleeve, probably lost from the scuffle. "You often call me by my first name when you're tense or excited."

"Oh." He grew embarrassed. Her presence was making him forget himself more often than not these days. "I'll see that it doesn't happen again."

"I don't mind."

"You may call me Jacob in private, but we'll maintain formal titles in front of patients."

Her eyebrows lifted high. "Does that mean my evaluation went well? I'm to stay on?"

Is that what he just told her? He supposed he did. "Yes, but the choice is ultimately yours. I can't ask you to accept the dangers inherent with visiting the laborer's hospital."

Hesitation and a note of caution swept her face, but then it disappeared in resolve. "You explained the work to me before I started. I accepted that there would be risks. We'll simply have to be more careful next time."

Yes, they would. Jacob began to think of ways to ensure Abigail's protection. She needed a device to defend herself. He should get on that right away.

"Jacob?"

"Yes?"

"You have that faraway look again."

He shook his head to clear it. "I'll see what's keeping Maria."

Out in the hallway, he heard Struthers descend the stairs. He met him at the bottom.

"Have you kindled the fireplace in the guest room?"

"Yes, sir, and Maria put fresh linens on the bed."

Maria came down the stairs. "How is the young lady, Doctor?"

"She has a cut and some bruising on her forehead, but it will heal within a week."

"How did she come by such a brutish injury?" Struthers asked.

"We were met by three men close to the laborer's hospital near St. Giles."

"That area is no place for a lady," Maria scolded Jacob. "What were the two of you doing there at such an odd hour?"

"Maria." Struthers was clearly embarrassed by her outburst.

Maria caught herself too late, putting her hands over her mouth.

"Pardon me, Doctor. I meant no harm."

"You're concerned for Miss Benton. I take no offense." Jacob put her at ease. "Miss Benton's injury was due to my negligence. We left the laborers' hospital later than we should because I didn't mind the time."

"Please have care for her, Dr. Valerian. She might be capable and brave enough to do a man's job, but she's still a woman."

"You have my word."

"Will Miss Benton be staying on as your assistant?"

"She will."

"Wonderful." The housekeeper beamed. "I've never seen that office runnin' so smoothly or you so…" She averted her gaze. "I'll be in the kitchen."

Struthers' composed, austere appearance was in the process of unraveling as his wife left. "I must apologize for her, Dr. Valerian. I ask her not to speak every thought. It's the Celtic blood that makes her so inquisitive."

"It's quite alright, Struthers." Jacob casually wondered if Abigail possessed a similar ancestral line as Maria. The two women were high-spirited and apt to speak their minds to whoever would listen. Which, in Abigail's case, especially, he was beginning to find refreshing. "We'd better see to Miss Benton's supper."

Chapter 12

Abigail awoke in a room that she didn't recognize.

"Good morning, dear," Maria's voice sounded from a wooden chair by the door. Abigail then remembered where she was, in a guest room at Jacob's residence. The night before, Maria brought her supper to the room and lent her a nightgown to sleep in after she had a bath.

"The doctor told me to keep an eye on you during the night." Maria yawned as she stood up to stretch, still attired in her gray dress and white apron. "He came to peek in on you around six this morning."

Abigail shifted under the blankets. "What time is it now?"

"Eight. Time for me to bring you breakfast and let Dr. Valerian know you're awake." Maria slipped out the door.

Abigail sat up in bed. An ache began at her temple. She tested the area. The swelling had gone down, but it was sore and would be for some time. But things could have turned out much worse if Jacob hadn't been there to prevent those men from doing her further harm.

She sank back into the pillows, recounting all that she had learned of him last night. If she had not seen the mechanical limb, she would never have guessed Jacob lost his leg. Due to a small limp and his use of a walking stick, she assumed that he sustained a field injury, but nothing as he had described to her the night before.

And it made her respect him all the more. From what she knew of amputations in the field, not many people survived them. The fact that Jacob returned home and opened a practice to help others who had lost their limbs was nothing short of admirable.

She hoped that her initial surprise upon seeing his prosthetic leg didn't convince him that she felt otherwise.

A tap sounded upon the door. Jacob entered, bearing his walking stick. "How do you feel today?"

"The ache is bearable." She burrowed under the covers until only her head and neck were visible. Being abed and in a nightgown made having a conversation with him quite awkward. "How are you?"

"It's been some years since I've had to employ martial skills, but I'll be fine. Not to worry." A bit of humor crossed his face as he chased away her concern. He dragged the wooden chair Maria previously sat on and put it by the bed. "Let's see how your temple looks today."

Abigail stilled as he untied the knot of her bandage. Her skin heated where his fingers touched. Was she turning red? Oh, she hoped not.

He leaned close. The smell of soap and green, lingering notes of bay leaf aftershave pleased her nose. A temptation emerged, a subtle coaxing to reach up around the back of his neck and draw his face down, where she could feel his skin against hers, press her lips upon his.

Where did such an ardent notion come from? Abigail pressed both hands into the mattress. And why was the thought of it so vivid, as though she had once engaged in such an exchange with Jacob before?

Perhaps her head injury was more serious than she thought.

"Your injury looks better today," Jacob said.

She watched the sun's soft rays filter through the curtain to shine on his hair. Pale blond strands mixed with a touch of silver produced an intriguing, otherworldly coloring. Angles of shadow and light formed along the clean planes of his face. He was a handsome man, even with the faint scar that patterned over his left eye. In a quiet way, Abigail thought it grounded his refined features.

"You won't be assisting me today," he said, while he tied her bandage again. "You're to rest here. Then, if you feel better, you can go home in the afternoon."

She gave him no argument. Even if her head didn't hurt, his patients wouldn't know what to think if she were to appear before them all bandaged up.

"I also want you to refrain from work for a while."

"How long?"

"Until Friday. In the meantime, since you're the better artist, you can start sketching the COIC project. We need to find the best place to embed the Aspasian metals into that gauntlet gun."

She liked that he said *we*. At last, he included her in every aspect of his practice. "I'll get started as soon as I can."

"But not until you feel up to it." The clock chimed downstairs. He rose. "A patient will be here early. I'd better go. I'll be back to check on you in a few hours."

He left as Maria returned with breakfast.

***

Abigail did feel well enough to leave that afternoon. After Maria was kind enough to lend her a hat that concealed most of the bandage, she took a cab back to her boarding house. Struthers accompanied her, at Jacob's insistence.

Despite putting on a brave face for Jacob, Abigail was left somewhat unnerved by last night's attack. Even from the safety of the cab, she felt compelled to watch the street closely. An odd feeling settled about her as she tried to relax. She got the feeling that she and Struthers were being watched.

"Your residence, Miss Benton," Struthers announced, after the cab stopped at the corner. He saw her to the door.

Even as people hurried by on their late afternoon jaunts, she still felt eyes on her. It had to be her nerves. Struthers hardly looked discomfited. "Thank you, Struthers. I'll see you tomorrow." She went into the boarding house, tugging the hat brim over her brow.

The chair at the front desk was empty, but a cup of tea sat steaming beside a ladies domestic magazine. The landlady must have only gotten up a moment before to tend to an errand.

Good. If Abigail didn't have to suffer through looks as to why she was just now coming home after nearly thirty-six hours, in the same dress she had on yesterday, then she would count it a blessing. She kept her head down as she passed another female tenant and tiptoed around the hall to her room.

Her room was the same as she left it yesterday morning. The bed was made. The washbasin and pitcher were arranged neatly on the stand. Nothing looked out of place.

She picked up a charcoal pencil from the floor and return it to the case on the table. The afternoon sun got in her eyes. She went to the window to draw the curtain.

Abigail's fingers halted on the curtain as she took in the view across the street. Below the sign of a storefront, a man dressed in a well-worn suit and brown topper flicked his cigar stub in the gutter before walking away. Abigail found herself shying away from full view in the glass.

Goodness. She pulled the curtain closed. Was she to be spooked at the sight of every man she saw on a street corner from now on?

She removed Maria's hat from her head and sat at the table. A quick sketch would calm her before she had to rearrange her hair to conceal her wound and change clothes for supper in the dining hall. She took the charcoal pencil out of the case and put it to her sketchpad.

Only then did her unease subside, but traces of it remained, hiding, in the corners of her mind.

***

January, 1838

Roughly one month passed since Jacob offered Abigail permanent employment. Once month since she suffered an injury at the hands of the street gang. He resolved to maintain the former and prevent the latter from happening again.

The overhead lamps provided light in the cellar as he watched his assistant inspect the newly refurbished gauntlet gun. Abigail turned it over and saw where he embedded a steel plaque into the forearm portion and inserted the Aspasian iron and copper alloy. The plate connected to wires above the wrist.

"It looks just as how I sketched it," she talked, as she admired his handiwork. "I'm glad that I was able to illustrate the concept you described to me."

"The gauntlet couldn't have been completed without your help." He was pleased when his sincere compliment brought a smile to her face.

She turned the gauntlet over again. A flash of copper peeked out from the sleeve of her blouse. Jacob was glad to see that she wore the cuff with the retractable pocket pistol that he fitted for her. The pistol it contained was discreet enough to be hidden beneath a shirtsleeve, but capable of injuring a would-be assailant if he got too close. All with the press of a button.

He hoped she would never have to use it, but if the situation occurred, she had a weapon to protect herself.

"Now that you have the voice-responsive metals and copper wires affixed, how exactly does the gauntlet work?" Abigail caught one of the wires between her fingers.

"That, I'm still working on." And with less than two months before he was scheduled to present the device to the COIC, he had little time for extensive experimentation. "I did some tests before you arrived this morning." He directed Abigail's attention to the wires again. "When I put the gauntlet on and spoke aloud, the wires moved. They conducted the sound of my voice, but nothing registered with the device. I wonder if I need a larger amount of the Aspasian metals."

She eyed the steel plate. "Perhaps the metals don't register voices when they're worn close to the body."

"That would defeat my theory, then. And my chances of getting the commission from the COIC."

"Perhaps not." She tucked part of her lower lip between her teeth and placed a hand on one hip as she continued to study the gauntlet. She looked so charmingly deep in thought that Jacob's dismay over his potentially debunked theory was temporarily eased. "The Aspasian metals might register other sounds besides your voice." She brought his attention back to their work, "What if it heard your heartbeat instead?"

"My heartbeat?"

She nodded, moving the wisps of hair that escaped the bun at the nape of her neck. "This may seem far-fetched, but if the metals are worn close to or on the skin, can it be possible that they're, I don't know, able to sense pulse and muscle movement?"

"It's possible, but even if that's the case, the weapon is useless if it can't be activated by speaking."

"It may not be. Would you mind putting the gauntlet on again?"

Jacob rolled up his shirtsleeve. "What are you hoping to find?"

"I'll know in a moment." She held out the gauntlet for him to put his hand through the glove. She cinched the cuff around his wrist and buckled the straps along the inside of his forearm. Her soft, light fingertips tickled as they moved quickly over his skin, adjusting the steel plate containing the Aspasian metals over the pulse point of his upper forearm.

The connecting wires began to move. Jacob turned his arm over and saw the wire's movement carry upward to the small unit containing the spring release mechanism for the pistol. He turned away from Abigail and went to depress the switch to make the firearm unfold. His fingertips barely flanked the switch's surface before the unloaded pistol sprang from its compartment to land in his hand. "That didn't happen before."

Abigail moved to his right. "You didn't have the plate lined up on your brachial artery." She looked up flittingly and provided, "Your pulse point."

"I know what it is." He retracted the gun. "I'm just surprised that veins and arteries found their way into our discussion of sound-conducting metals."

"I suppose it was bound to happen when you hired an assistant with a background in vascular medicine."

"I'm glad I did."

The tawny glow deepened in her cheeks. Jacob felt a nervous clench in his stomach. He spoke too freely. What if she took that to be a flirtation? Was it?

Abigail smoothed her hair and resumed with the original topic. "But as I was saying, I wonder if the gauntlet gun would work better if you incorporated more pulse points on the body for the wires to connect."

"That's going to be a challenge. The COIC commissioned a weapon and light armor for its field agents."

Her light green eyes darted to his torso and her brow immediately furrowed.

Jacob followed the path of her gaze, wondering if he spilled tea on his waistcoat at breakfast. "What is it?"

She tilted her head, now appearing to disapprove of the color of his necktie. "My sister once said that gentlemen don't concern themselves with fashion as much as women because their clothing hasn't changed much in the past two centuries."

"Come now. I've had this tie and waistcoat for a couple seasons, but they don't look that old."

She chuckled. "No, but your waistcoat is descended of the iron breastplates men wore to protect themselves in battle. What if you made one now, using light steel? Would it hold up against a weapon?"

"It could deflect a knife and possibly a bullet from a small gun fired at medium range. But how would the Aspasian metals detect pulse if an armor plate is in the way? "

"You could embed a second set of copper wires in the plate here." She touched two fingers on the pocket of his waistcoat, over his heart. "They could extend to your scapular artery." The fingers of her left hand traced a pattern across his chest to his right shoulder. "And finally travel to connect with the wires and steel plate of the gauntlet."

Jacob's pulse sped in every place that she touched. What was wrong with him? Abigail's touch was not as a lover, but merely to show how the armor was to be crafted. Had he been without a woman's affection for so long that he began to imagine that she could feel that way about him?

He pleaded with the gauntlet's wires, hoping they didn't jump to match his heart's erratic beat. Sure enough, they were moving. "This has all been very interesting." He pulled his arm away from Abigail and pressed it to his side. "Should we get to work, then?"

Abigail dropped her fingers from his chest. "Pardon me." She rushed to speak, her voice sounding flustered. She rubbed the creamy skin of her neck. "I got carried away."

As did he, only Jacob was certain that her departure was much more scientifically-related. He removed the gauntlet. He did a fine job of making her uncomfortable. But Abigail was too gracious to add to the already awkward situation by telling him so.

"I'll begin sketching the armor plate." She went away from him, towards the worktable. The sound of her rummaging for a pencil echoed the din in his mind as he hastened to return himself to reality.

He must uphold professional decorum. He had to stop thinking about that silly kiss between them that occurred two months ago. Just like the nitrous oxide Abigail had accidentally breathed in that made her forget herself that day, so had she forgotten her actions as soon as the smoke dissipated. It was high time he did the same.

Or else he'd miss his deadline and lose the chance to earn funding to help his patients. He thought about it as he rolled his sleeve down. He still had other people to care for. He hoped he could return to feeling that work was enough, but with Abigail so near, that notion became increasingly difficult to recapture.

Chapter 13

March, 1838

After being in the missions, there were very few things in life Abigail prided herself on besides her faith and work ethic. Being attracted to her intelligent, brave, and persevering employer certainly wasn't one of them.

In fact, it was most improper, she thought, as she watched Jacob test the newly improved gauntlet gun on the grounds in the back of his house. A patient cancelled an appointment, and the unseasonably warm overcast March day allowed them to take the hour to work on the COIC-commissioned project.

When did it start? , she wondered, while Jacob aimed at a target he set up beneath a wizened oak. Was it a month before, when, in her efforts to explain how breastplates were precursors to waistcoats, she kept her hand steadily affixed to his chest?

She groaned at the embarrassing memory of such liberty she took upon his person.

Jacob fired the gun at the target.

Or was it a little before then, when he drove off that street gang and got her to safety? They hadn't run into them since.

Maybe it was when he started being candid with his patients and telling them how he lost his leg in India. The courage it took for him to reveal that only endeared him to her even more.

Or did her attraction form in the very beginning, when he first entered the apothecary, and his avant-garde appearance and piercing blue eyes caught her attention?

He turned those eyes to her after shooting the target a second time. The sun was not bright enough for him to need his lenses outside today. She liked that. "What do you think?"

Of his eyes? How ice blue they were? "Oh, that I cannot say," she murmured.

"Sorry?"

Heavens, her mind did nothing but wander these days. He was asking her about the gauntlet gun's trajectory, not her opinion of his features. She strolled up to the target and found the bullet lodged in the middle of the board. "Yes, a very good shot."

He strode up beside her. His gait was noticeably smoother today. "The Aspasian metals practically interpret my next move. I barely have to press the switch on the cuff to release the gun, and it has improved the pin trigger response. Of course, it could be from the extra wiring in the metal vest." He lifted the lapel of his coat and inspected it.

Amazing what he could make from just a few of her sketches. In a short time, she'd seen it go from paper to forged metal. Now the vest rested smartly beneath his jacket like an armored waistcoat.

Abigail brought her eyes to the gauntlet on his arm. "I hope the theory works just as well on prosthetic devices as it does weapons. Should we start work on a model?"

"I already have, actually. I finished it late last night."

"Oh." Abigail looked towards the house. "Did you use one from the display cabinet?"

Jacob gave her one of his little smiles that indicated when he had a new discovery and could not contain himself any longer. "I decided to go with my own. I used the same process, only I connected a wire beneath the limb's pressure plates."

Abigail remembered how pulse points traveled to the knee area as well. "And did you think it was an improvement?"

"Yes, I don't have to depress fully on the plates anymore, which means less pain. But, I should do more tests with it." He started to disassemble the target's stand.

Abigail folded the board. "Your last patient arrives at two this afternoon. We can come back out to the yard, then."

"I was thinking of something more challenging."

She noted that the yard spanned a good half-acre. "What else did you have in mind?"

He looked towards central London. "It's a warm day, Abigail. Would you like to go for a stroll in the park?"

***

Regent's Park was rife with more than a few of the London gentry's well-to-do out to take advantage of the pleasant afternoon. The sun decided to emerge from the clouds after all.

Abigail observed the pedestrians as they took to the path that wound about the gardens. Courting couples, fashionable ladies, and gentlemen dandies walked ahead of her and Jacob. A few people walking in the opposite direction offered stares at the two of them. Abigail supposed she and Jacob did make an eccentric pair, he with his long hair and tinted lenses, she with her somber brown work dress. But she enjoyed being with him, putting her hand on his arm as they walked.

"I don't think I've been out to Regent's Park in years," Jacob said. His head turned left and right as though he were taking it all in for the first time. Abigail had never seen him in such a lively mood. She noticed that he relied far less on his walking stick as well.

"I've only been once or twice in the past year," she supplied. "But I used to walk here all the time with my niece and nephew."

"I do recall you mentioning that you had a sister. Is she in London?"

"My older sister lives in the Paddington district with her husband and two children." Her stomach constricted as she thought of her strained rapport with Catherine.

They passed a group of ladies who stopped along at a pavilion. The ladies' backs were towards them, but Abigail could have sworn that she had seen Catherine's russet curls.

"You never said why you and your sister were estranged."

Her gaze flew up. "How did you know?"

"Both of your parents are gone. Your sister is your closest surviving relative. She lives in London with her husband and children, and yet you reside in a boarding house."

She turned her eyes towards the bare trees. "I suppose it does appear obvious. My sister and I had a disagreement last year because I refused to be matched with a suitor of her choosing. She said that she and her husband could not afford to maintain a spinster in their household."

"That seems to be a unique way of getting someone to marry. But, I see that it proved unsuccessful."

She laughed at his irreverence. "My sister did what she felt was best, but she's not to be completely blamed. I shouldn't have imposed upon her two years before when I came home from the missions. I overstayed my welcome." She diverted her conversation. "But enough about that. I see a lady selling flowers. Do you think Maria would like one?"

"Why didn't you marry?"

Abigail was struck by the bluntness of Jacob's question, but she answered him, anyway. "As you noted before, I can be quite unconventional. Even though my work overseas is through, I still wish to be of service to others. I can't be content to sit still inside a house. That was what the gentleman wanted of me. What most men tend to require, actually."

"Not all men."

"Oh, and I tend to make pencil drawings. Most odd for a lady."

Jacob's mouth tilted in a contained smile. "I hadn't noticed."

She returned his smile before shyness made her look away. "We've been walking for some time now. Perhaps we should rest."

"If you're worried about me walking a long distance, I've never felt better."

"That's good, but my feet are starting to feel fatigued."

"There's a bench along the evergreens to your left." He escorted her off the promenade path and down the smaller path away from the pedestrians.

She passed under the tree and sat on the bench. "That's better."

Jacob stood close to her and removed his spectacles in the shade. Abigail took notice of his stance and the angle of his face, even though she couldn't understand why.

He saw her stare. "Yes?"

"I believe I've looked up at you from a similar angle as this before."

"You probably have. I am taller than you."

She tossed off the glib remark. "That's not it. We were someplace I can't remember, but I recall either sitting on or leaning against a piece of furniture." A murky image crept into her mind. She saw bookshelves, papers strewn about the room. "We were in an office. Yours, at the college." More images came. "You stood before me. Your face was close to mine. One moment you had your spectacles on, the next they were off."

"You shouldn't worry over a random memory," he said, coolly, pocketing the spectacles as the sun disappeared behind clouds overhead.

"That look. You gave it to me before. You were agitated."

"Abigail, really."

But she persisted. "What did I say to make you uncomfortable?"

He sighed. "It wasn't what you said. Not entirely."

"Please don't be cryptic." She left the bench to come to him. "Something happened in that office, didn't it?"

He remained silent.

Abigail's pulse jumped. What was he withholding? "I'm right, then. Something did happen."

"It doesn't need mentioning."

"Jacob, tell me."

Strands of hair moved about his shoulders as he turned to look directly at her.

Abigail reached out, but let her fingers hover in the air. "Why do I feel as though I've touched your hair before?" The question was impertinent, but she knew she must risk asking it to get to the truth.

"Because you have," he answered. "You wanted to know why it bore traces of silver."

She couldn't remember asking that question, but her fingers did remember the feel of his skin under them. "And did I touch your face, too?"

"You wanted to know about the scar. I told you, after you pulled my spectacles off."

"What came over me to do that?"

"A cloud of nitrous oxide. The effects were prolonged in your system. It happens to some individuals."

"I was giddy?"

"You were very elated. I asked you to sit down to calm yourself, but you—I would spare you the details."

"No."

"As you wish." He paused. Not for dramatic effect, she thought, but what looked to be in an effort to fortify himself for a revelation. "You kissed me."

A current of surprise jolted through her. "I—"

"You caught me off guard at first, but I kissed you back."

She let her back fall against the evergreen's trunk. "Why am I just now hearing about this? Were you also under a cloud of nitrous oxide?"

"It wore off after I got you out of the auditorium. I didn't mention the kiss to you later because I didn't think it was appropriate. You weren't in your right frame of mind when it happened."

"Yet you were in yours, and you returned the kiss."

"I shouldn't have," he admitted. "But I didn't want to turn away. After a few moments, though, I knew I had to."

Abigail vaguely recalled him doing so. "Yes, I do remember you suddenly drawing back." She couldn't help but glance at his mouth and think back to the time after she left the office. No wonder her lips tingled as though they had been kissed. They had been, and thoroughly.

The sensations of it came back in her mind and sent pulsing waves along her body.

"You see why I wanted to say nothing." Jacob alternated between watching her and fiddling with the handle of his walking stick before letting it rest against the tree. "You needn't suffer by revisiting my appalling actions."

"I cannot imagine being appalled by you kissing me. Then, or at this moment." Abigail was so nervous by her admission that her teeth began to chatter. She bit down her lips and averted her eyes from him, but when she swerved back, she found his countenance locked upon hers. His eyes were intense, his jaw set. She spoke again, despite a knot that formed in her vocal chords. "I-I would hope that you weren't too offended by me." She looked down.

He raised her chin with his finger. "What I felt was nothing close to offense."

She tried to breathe deep, but air remained trapped in her ribcage. Her chest felt constricted, rising up and down. "I would do it again if I could."

"Permit me." He lowered his lips to hers.

His kiss awakened her body. This was what she felt before, what her senses remembered even as her mind's memory had failed to recall where or when.

He covered her mouth with his, not forcefully, but with a soft, slow coaxing that made her lift her neck higher and arch her back away from the tree. She felt the warmth of his hand come to her waist, his gloved fingers as they came through the tiny space between the small of her back and the tree and settled upon her.

He gently drew her to him. Abigail's hands went to his straight shoulders, felt them gradually relax under her touch. She returned his kiss, letting the realness of it envelop her as she delicately pressed her lips to his top lip, then his bottom. The warmth of his breath tickled her skin. She smiled against his mouth. He gave her another tender kiss, long and sweet.

The sound of heeled shoes clicking on the brick-lain path jolted Abigail from her pleasant interlude. Someone gasped very loudly.

"Abigail!" Her sister's voice rang across the clearing.

Chapter 14

Abigail and Jacob's embrace shattered as Catherine continued her exclamation. "Abigail! Is that you?"

Abigail was right when she saw a woman with russet curls before. It was Catherine in the park. And now Abigail was in a fix. "My sister is here," she whispered to Jacob. Smoothing her appearance, she went around the tree.

"Catherine. Good afternoon."

Catherine's miniature hat bobbed on her head as she swung her gaze upon Abigail. "I thought I saw you and a gentleman leaving the promenade to come down this way."

Jacob came around the other side of the tree. Catherine's jaw slackened and tightened again in instant succession. Abigail knew she recognized him based upon Hammond's description.

"Jacob—Dr. Valerian, I mean." Abigail wanted to sink into the base of the tree. "May I introduce you to my sister, Mrs. Catherine Evancourt."

Jacob tipped his hat. "A pleasure to make your acquaintance, madam."

Catherine only gave a slight nod. Abigail folded her hands in front of her. "I didn't expect to see you in the park today, Catherine."

"I'm sure you didn't. My neighbor and her daughter invited me to come along for a walk." She turned her head towards two other fashionably dressed ladies who remained just off the side of the promenade. Their velvet and lace-flounced hats touched as they conspired with each other, no doubt concerning the salacious scene set before them.

Catherine returned to glaring at Abigail. "It seems none of us could

AVA MORGAN

pass up the opportunity to frolic in this unusually balmy weather." She set the glare upon Jacob. "Wouldn't you agree, Doctor?"

Jacob remained laconic as he answered, "Indeed, madam. Miss Benton and I were enjoying the pleasant air, but it seems to have taken a frigid turn. We will be leaving for a more hospitable atmosphere."

Catherine's eyes widened. Abigail was impressed by Jacob's polite, but sharp deflection of her sister's double entendre.

And Catherine was not used to being deflected. She tugged at a lace sleeve peeking out from her velveteen coat. "Dr. Valerian, would you mind terribly if I had a word with my sister?"

Abigail nodded when he looked at her.

"Not at all, Mrs. Evancourt, but I'm afraid it will have to be brief. Miss Benton must be getting back home."

Catherine's gaze froze over. "I shall be very clear and concise with my sister."

"Very well." Jacob took Abigail's hand and gave it a reassuring squeeze. "I will be at the bench near that statue on the north end of the park. Good afternoon, Mrs. Evancourt." He tipped his hat again to Catherine and strode off.

Abigail watched him walk away. She had to admit that he did cut a dashing figure in his military-style coat.

"If my sister is done with her ogling, perhaps she will be able to hear me."

"I hear you fine now, Catherine."

Her sister was positively put out. Her cheeks and forehead flashed red, her mouth completely downturned in a frown that stood in comical juxtaposition to her whimsical puffed coat sleeves. "You forget yourself, Abigail. Our mother taught us better than to prostrate ourselves like platters of sweetmeats for strange men to lap over."

How dare she speak so vulgarly? Abigail met her sister's accusing eyes with both hands on her hips and bridled anger in her tone. "She also taught us not to fight. But if we were not in public, I think I would battle the temptation to strike you for that horrendous insult. I am no slattern, and Dr. Valerian is no predator."

"Then what has made you become so fiery? Kissing in public! What more would have happened if I didn't see you earlier and decide to come walking down the path?"

242

"He and I would have kissed and continued on our walk. I'm tired of you exaggerating."

Catherine's reticule flounced in the air when she jerked her hands up. "I don't know what to make of you anymore. You refused to be courted by that esquire friend of Hammond's. I thought you would come to your senses if I made you live on your own as a true spinster, but it only made you more independent and headstrong."

"What else should I have done? I wasn't going to be bullied and ordered about by my older sister."

"No, but you would rather sweep floors and hand out cough syrup at an apothecary. Now you're in the employ—not to mention the arms—of an eccentric physician. You see why I worry."

"You concern yourself about Dr. Valerian because of rumors and half-baked tales cooked by Hammond's associates. They don't truly know Dr. Valerian. In fact, they shunned him after he came home from India."

"And you know him, after spending only three months working for him?"

Abigail conceded to some of her rebuttal, but not all of it. "He's shared things with me that I will not repeat out of closed confidence. But if you could just see what he has overcome and what he's doing to aid those that most of London tends to forget about, you wouldn't say those things."

"You're in love with him." Catherine stared at Abigail as though she were a strange and foreign object.

Abigail didn't flinch. "I suppose I am."

"Egad, if I didn't believe in Heaven, I'd say our mother and father must be spinning in their graves."

"They're looking down on us now and shaking their heads at our relentless bickering. I'm trying to put a stop to it. I don't want us fighting anymore."

Catherine maintained silence.

Abigail looked to the promenade behind her sister. "Your friends grow impatient, and Dr. Valerian waits for me. If we can't reconcile, then let's at least go our separate ways peaceably."

She started walking up the path and looked back to see if her sister would follow. When Catherine remained, she fought a rise in her throat and went on to the promenade alone.

She found Jacob at the statue where he said he would be. He wore his spectacles in the face of the afternoon sun as it began to lower. He stood, offering his arm, which she took, knowing that Catherine and her friends were in all likelihood watching. Abigail didn't bother to look behind her to confirm it.

"I apologize for my sister's behavior."

Jacob escorted her to the park entrance. "She was just trying to protect you."

"I don't need protecting from you. I wish she could see that."

"Abigail, I know that I am not the most well-received of gentlemen in London. I've come to accept that many will never understand the choices I've made. I can live with their disdain, but I would rather you didn't."

Did he call himself protecting her now? Abigail tired of being discouraged from making her own decisions. "What do you mean?"

Jacob hailed a carriage driver across the street. "You're bright, resourceful, and your presence is filled with light. Have you considered what type of life you will have after we complete this project and you continue as my assistant?"

They crossed the street as Abigail answered, "One that has purpose and meaning beyond earning a wage. Isn't that how you also feel?"

"It is."

"Well, then," she said, as he assisted her into the vehicle, "you should know that I, too, won't have my life dictated by the rumor mill."

He got in and the carriage started off. "But you may be isolated."

"You're not isolated. You have the friendship and loyalty of Struthers and Maria. You have patients, colleagues, and the COIC who seek your consultation."

"True, but there are those who avoid me because of my injuries. Your sister sees that, and doesn't want you to be ostracized by association. I know that you care for each other, even while you argue. I do not wish to cause a permanent rift between you."

Abigail saw what he was doing. "You're testing me again, trying to protect me by pushing me away. Why, Jacob?" Her voice strained with frustration. "I've shown you that I care. I'm not like those that rejected you because of your injuries. I'm not your former fiancée."

His eyebrows slanted. "How did you know that I used to have a fiancée?"

Abigail silenced as she scrambled to contemplate what she just uttered.

Jacob's features formed a stone mask. "You've been listening to the rumor mill after all." His voice cooled as he audibly began to distance himself from her. "Even though you say you're not influenced by it."

"Jacob—"

He cut her off. "I never told you about my former fiancée because our engagement ended before I even left for India. I didn't know how long I would remain abroad, and she wished to be married immediately. But our parting was amicable."

Abigail felt as though she swallowed a mill stone. She sank deeper and deeper into the realization of her error. She criticized Catherine and Hammond for relaying gossip, yet somewhere along the way, she relied on their words as fact instead of coming to Jacob and inquiring about his past. "I'm sorry."

But already, she saw the hurt and anger in his eyes. She saw through his protective mask of calm resignation that he employed to deflect emotion.

He crossed a foot over one knee and traced his fingers around the carvings on his walking stick. "We'll continue to test the gauntlet gun as planned tomorrow. As for this discussion, it's finished."

An invisible wall went up around him that Abigail did not begin to know how to penetrate. Their combined silence lasted until the carriage reached her address. She got out. Jacob saw her to the door and returned to the vehicle. She watched it drive off.

Now she had a rift with Jacob as well as her sister. What was she going to do?

***

Jacob slept poorly that night. Whether it was the knowledge that he deepened the rift between Abigail and her sister, or Abigail's revelation that she delved into the rumors surrounding his past, both circumstances created a draught of insomnia.

He tossed in bed.

The former he should have seen coming. His reputation preceded him as an unconventional physician and a castaway son of one of the landed families. Of course Abigail's sister would be wary of him. It didn't help things a bit, either, that he forgot himself and kissed Abigail in public.

The blood heated beneath his skin as he thought about holding her, breathing in her scent. She had been so warm in his arms. Her slender body fit perfectly against his. Her lips were soft. Their taste was sweet. The response of her kiss was equal in passion to his, but with an innocence that made him break. And this time, she gave it freely, with full clarity of mind and heart, unrestricted of pity. It was too much for him to break away. On that, he took full responsibility that he should have been aware of the chances of them being seen by others.

He threw the covers aside, for the room had grown too warm.

But did he have a right to be angry with Abigail for listening to rumors? He didn't share much of his past with her beyond the details surrounding his injuries. She showed her willingness to learn more about his life. He had chances to tell her, but settled on his usual way of dealing with the curiosity of others. He kept himself guarded, irritable, even, when Abigail extended her hand to him gently. Yes, her inquisitiveness got the better of her at times, but never had she forced the issue well beyond the bounds of propriety.

She was right about him testing her. In his mind, hidden deep below his conscious thoughts, that was what he had been doing since they met. All because he wondered if and when she would flee like so many other people because his condition, his work, *he*, would get to become too much.

Jacob shook his head at his own misdirected reasoning. Assumption without strong basis is practically useless, he once told Abigail. He would have done well to bear that in mind all along when he assumed Abigail wanted nothing to do with him because of his injuries.

But she didn't have to be tested. She did not run away from challenge or adversity. Abigail had proven herself to be exactly what he needed well before she knew anything about his amputated leg, his family troubles, or his broken engagement. She appreciated and respected him. She wanted him as a woman desired a man.

And in return, he certainly had much more to offer her than a lonely, isolated life. Everything he had, he wanted to give to her.

Was it too late to tell her? Was he too far beyond correcting his mistakes?

Jacob rose from bed at first light and was dressed even before Struthers entered with his first cup of tea. Thoughts of Abigail spurred him on. Even though he had no appointments until the afternoon, he was downstairs and in his practice going over the ledger before the grandfather clock struck seven.

"You're up and about early this morning, sir," Maria observed, as she went into the practice and dusted the end tables. "Are you expecting patients in the next hour?"

"No, Maria, but I want to put some things in order before Miss Benton arrives."

Her feather duster stopped moving. "She's not in any trouble, is she?"

Jacob saw anxiety pass over her usually cheerful face. "Of course not. Why would you think that?"

His housekeeper twiddled the handle of the duster between her fingers. "It's not really my place to say."

"Maria, you've never been one to hold back on your words before."

She fidgeted with the handle some more. "It's just that I noticed you and Miss Benton have seemed to reach a friendly accord as of late. But she didn't come back to the practice with you yesterday afternoon. I thought something happened while you were out."

"Miss Benton and I did part ways after our sojourn to Regent's Park. But she will be here as we can expect this morning, with five minutes to spare." At least, he hoped she had not come to a decision overnight to put in her resignation. He knew he certainly gave her enough reason to.

The doorbell rang, followed by a terse knock.

"Perhaps that's Miss Benton now," Maria said, brightly.

Jacob rose from his desk with his walking stick. "If it is, then she's terribly early." Perhaps she didn't sleep well last night, either.

He went to the front of the house and saw Struthers standing at the open door. The COIC Secretary had one foot over the threshold and looked as though he intended to barrel past the valet any second.

"You'll forgive my unannounced arrival , Dr. Valerian, but it was most urgent that I come to you."

Jacob nodded to Struthers that it was alright for the gentleman to enter. "What brings you here?"

"A most alarming event has occurred concerning your work and your assistant. You must come with me to the agency headquarters at once."

Chapter 15

A disturbing knot formed in Jacob's chest at the thought of Abigail. "Is Miss Benton alright?"

The Secretary's face belied his urgency, but was otherwise unreadable. "I can't tell you more outside of headquarters. My driver is waiting to take us there now. Bring the project."

"I'll get your coat and hat, Doctor." Struthers hurried to retrieve the items from the rack.

Jacob turned and found Maria peeking from the door of his practice. Her frantic expression mirrored what he felt inside. She stepped out of his way as he marched into the room. He unlocked the cabinet containing the gauntlet gun and attached breastplate and put the weapon in the black case. "Maria, close the practice, please," he said, upon leaving.

Struthers returned to the door with his outer garments and assisted Jacob in putting them on.

"Struthers, if I have not returned in three hours, you're to send word to my patients that they will need to reschedule."

"Yes, Doctor." Even Struthers' normally stoic face betrayed itself with the furrowed brow of concern. "I hope this matter will be addressed quickly."

"As do I." Jacob donned his hat, picked up the case, and his walking stick. "After you, Mr. Secretary."

The Secretary led him outside, where the blustery March cold returned after yesterday's uncommon warmth. The wind blew against Jacob's neck as he climbed into the coach. Immediately, his eyes took to the armored interior. Steel rivets lined the walls. The window had iron bars over the panel.

"You see that within our agency, we keep even the personal transports heavily guarded, Doctor."

Jacob's gaze shot back to the Secretary. "Now will you tell me what this is about?"

The Secretary remained on the edge of the seat as the coach rolled forward. "I already said that it must wait."

"Then at least tell me that Miss Benton is not in any danger."

"I cannot."

Jacob gripped the handle of his walking stick so hard that the carvings dug into his palm through his glove. "Cannot or will not?"

The older man was clearly surprised at being spoken to in such a demanding fashion. "There are things at stake here that go beyond you and your distress over your assistant, Doctor. Well beyond."

The Secretary turned his aristocratic, aquiline nose to the window, refusing to say more. Jacob gritted his teeth as he tried to tamp down his anger, control his anxiety over where Abigail was and what was happening to her. The frustration of not knowing made his mind race, and the possibility that something terrible occurred to involve her made him sweat beneath his clothes.

The coach finally stopped. The driver opened the door and saw the Secretary out immediately. Jacob moved to stand. Every muscle in his body was locked and tense.

The COIC's headquarters looked like any other government building in London: austere, both impressive and intimidating, and entirely unreadable as to its function simply from a glance. Jacob had been to the headquarters several times in the past year for discussions involving his work. But today, Jacob was unimpressed with the COIC building, its diverse mix of agents both male and female, and its collection of acquired scientific oddities.

He just wanted to know if Abigail was safe.

He kept up with the Secretary as he was taken past room after room of conferences being held, intelligence-gathering, presentations being put on, and experiments being conducted.

The Secretary came to a door at the end of the corridor and tapped a set of buttons into a metal panel on the wall that sounded remarkably close to the new Morse code. The door opened on its riveted iron hinges, reminding Jacob of a bank safe. He entered after the Secretary. They stopped short at another door. A large window beside it showed two agents standing over a man seated before a table. The man appeared to have his hands restrained behind him.

"Dr. Valerian, what you see is a French spy our agents caught around two this morning near St. Giles parish. I told you of the spy ring Broussard has crafted within our own city. This spy admitted to being his liaison. We're interrogating him."

"While I applaud your efforts to ensure London's security, what does this have to do with me or Miss Benton? And why did you have me bring this along?" Jacob raised the box containing the gauntlet gun and breastplate.

"The weapon must be strictly safeguarded after what we have uncovered. As for Miss Benton, our agents confirm that she is safe at her address. We had better go inside."

Why were agents even at her address?

The Secretary keyed in the code to open the door. Jacob entered the room with the agents and the captured spy. He took a look at the spy's rumpled, worn suit and bowler. The spy glanced at Jacob and the Secretary before turning a grizzled cheek.

"We think he's been operating in London for the past four or five months, disguised as a vagabond," the Secretary explained. "We also think he may be paying members of the working classes and vagrants to secure information for him. Doctor, this is why I brought you here." The Secretary signaled to one of the agents, who reached for a folded document behind his coat lapel. The Secretary took the document and unfolded it.

Jacob recognized Abigail's early sketch of the refurbished gauntlet gun.

"We found this on the spy. We have reason to believe that your assistant has been stealing and trading your armor designs."

***

"I'm telling you, I am not a thief."

Abigail sat at the small table in her room under the watchful eye of a female COIC agent and the agent's male partner. The landlady stood at the door and shrugged helplessly at Abigail as the male agent searched through her closet and hope chest.

Ransacked was the better term, Abigail thought. She cringed as she heard fabric ripping. The agent tore through the pocket lining of one of her best skirts. The next minute he ran a knife through the inner seams of her finest dress. Boots, jackets, blouses, and her spare reticule all were thrown out of the closet for the chance to find more supposed evidence to support the COIC's outlandish claim.

"Why would I steal from Dr. Valerian and trade to a criminal spy ring?" she asked the female agent standing over her.

The agent, severe in her prim black skirt and jacket, shook her head. "It's not for me or Agent Ford to say why you've done anything, Miss Benton. What our fellow agents found on that French spy is enough evidence to warrant a search of your room."

"You still haven't told me what it was you found."

"A sketch of the weapon that Dr. Valerian commissioned for the agency. The shading technique looks much like those on the table." She pointed to the sketches Abigail worked on for leisure.

Abigail was speechless. She couldn't figure out how any of her sketches could wind up in the hands of a spy. She went to no places other than Jacob's residence, the college, and the laborer's hospital. Of the last, she went there but three times, and she never carried a sketchbook and pencils with her.

"You're silent now, Miss Benton. Is that an admission of guilt?"

She met the female agent's superior gaze. "Absolutely not."

"What were you hoping to gain for trading that sketch over to one of Broussard's men?"

"I did no such thing. In fact, I have no idea who this Broussard man is. How did a spy get his hands on my drawing?"

The female agent didn't respond. Abigail assumed it was because she didn't know the answer to the question, either. She asked the agent another. "Have you spoken to Dr. Valerian about this?" Abigail knew that he was the best person to help her fight the charges.

"I haven't spoken with him. Now, you must tell me, where do you make most of your sketches?"

"At Dr. Valerian's residence. Sometimes here, as well, but I turned over all the work-related sketches to him since the project finished completion."

"Did you overlook one?"

"Not that I'm aware of. I kept everything in one portfolio that I gave him."

Abigail turned as Agent Ford moved from laying siege to the closet to now pillaging her hope chest. Petticoats and other unmentionables, as well as her books, all fell victim to his haphazard rummaging. "Please tell him not to do that."

Agent Ford dug up to his elbow in the chest and came out with a sketchbook. "Agent Donald, I found something." He opened the book, flipped through the pages. "Never mind. It's blank."

Abigail sighed. "Agents Ford and Donald, I respectfully ask if you are finished."

"For the moment." Agent Donald opened a small notebook suspended from a chain about her waist and proceeded to jot notes. "We've found nothing here to have you placed under arrest. You haven't been officially charged with theft yet, but this investigation is ongoing. I would advise you not to try to flee the city."

Theft. Investigation. Arrest. Abigail's blood pressure elevated with the growing list of words associated with criminal involvement used to describe her. She tried to breathe through her alarm. "I won't flee the city, but I need to leave this room." Jacob was probably irate with her for being an hour late. But once he heard her of the ordeal she was going through, he would move immediately to provide his assistance.

Or would he? A nagging thought penetrated her mind. Did Jacob think she stole from him? Did he contact the COIC to investigate her?

"You won't be going into work today, Miss Benton." Agent Donald finished writing. "Dr. Valerian is one of the COIC's contributors, and it's our right to protect him and the commissioned project. Because you're the main suspect, we're suspending you from Dr. Valerian's employ, effective immediately."

***

Jacob sat across from the French spy and looked him directly in the eyes. After hours of listening to the COIC agents and the Secretary interrogate the spy to no further avail as to how he came into possession of the weapons sketch, at last Jacob had his turn.

"How did you get this?" He set Abigail's sketch on the table between them. The agents and the Secretary lined the wall, observing.

The spy, who had previously revealed his communication skills in the form of expletives, hurled a string of them at Jacob.

"Let's try this again, and if you answer me well, perhaps I'll pardon your French."

The spy sneered and made a sound of contempt through his nose. "I do not have to tell you anything, crippled man."

Jacob crossed the right foot of his mechanical leg over his left knee while he regarded the unkempt man. " Perhaps I can persuade you to speak." He swept his hand towards the men along the wall. "These agents know you're in New Britannia illegally as a spy. Those are grounds to be tried, thrown into jail, and even executed. If you answer my questions, an unfortunate end could be avoided."

"I work for one of the most visionary of men, Monsieur Emile Broussard. I am not afraid to die, even at the teeth of New Britannia's dogs."

"How does one man who's rarely seen or heard from, even from within your country, inspire so much loyalty in his followers?" voiced the Secretary.

The spy swiveled his head to look at him. "Broussard sees to the needs of those who aid him."

"He doesn't seem to be doing that well of a job." Jacob pointed to the man's suit and hat. "You could make do with a better wardrobe. I thought the French were very meticulous in that regard."

"I have higher things to concern myself with."

"Is stealing from women one of them?" Jacob asked to determine whether Abigail had sold the sketches to the spy, or if he took them from her. Jacob didn't believe that Abigail would betray him, but he needed proof for the COIC agents.

The spy answered him with sarcasm. "I cannot help if your *femme* employee is careless with her work."

"I can assure you she is not careless. How did you take the sketch from her?"

"Her room at the boarding house has a window. I've watched her from across the street when she sketched at her table." The spy smiled suggestively. "She is pretty, *non?*"

It took all of Jacob's reserve to keep himself from launching at the man's throat. The spy wanted to ruffle him. He needed to keep calm and get answers. "You broke into her room and stole the sketch when she wasn't there. How were you not seen or heard by the other tenants?"

"Why do you assume that I had to force my way into her room? Perhaps *la mademoiselle* freely invited me."

Jacob couldn't keep from displaying his disgust this time. "She would never associate with the likes of you."

"But would she favor you, a man in need of a cane? Young, but with silver in his hair?" The spy made that nasal sound of contempt again. "You talk about my clothing, *monsieur*, but I can change my suit. You cannot take the scar off your face."

Jacob rose. The COIC Secretary put a hand on his shoulder. "Enough. I'd have a word with you." He pulled him to the side.

"I'm trying to get this man to confess how he got Abigail's sketch," Jacob spoke polite words, but his voice came out low and even in response to the Secretary's unwanted intervention.

"Can't you see he's leading you on a red herring? Look how he's trying to make you vexed."

"He's not the only person. You've accused my assistant of theft. You brought me to headquarters while you left her unprotected."

"That's not entirely true. Our agents were with her. They went to her room at the boarding house this morning and did a search. They found nothing."

"Now I'm vexed. By what right do you have to intrude upon her?"

The Secretary's back stiffened. "By right of the agency's commission. We sought out a weapon to use against Broussard. I won't have it stolen by his spies and sympathizers."

"Abigail is not a sympathizer." Jacob saw movement over the Secretary's shoulder.

The French spy was up from his chair, his restraints broken. One of the agents rushed at him. The spy pulled free of his grip and made for the door. He shook the handle, then he glanced up at the code panel and wires.

The second agent caught him by the shoulder, forcing him to turn around. The French spy's body went slack and doubled over as he did so. The agent dropped his hold as the spy sank to his knees and fell face forward.

Jacob cautiously approached the spy's form and turned him over. The spy's suit jacket parted to reveal an object protruding from his shirt in the upper left corner. Crimson bloomed around it. "He stabbed himself."

"Through the heart, it looks like," said the Secretary. "Where'd he get the knife? He was searched."

Jacob saw a vent in the spy's jacket sleeve. He peeled the worn, dirty fabric back to see a pocket sewn into the lining. "He kept it hidden there."

The Secretary proffered a grim sigh as the two agents gathered the man up. "He knew he wasn't getting out of here, so he made sure that we wouldn't get our answers."

"I still intend to get them." Jacob rose with the aid of his walking stick. "But first, I'm seeing to Abigail's safety. Broussard's spy ring will come looking for her if her address was one of the last places this man visited before he was caught."

"You can't go to her. Until the investigation is complete, she's suspended from working with you."

Jacob gripped the walking stick tighter while his other hand closed into a fist. "I am not a COIC agent. You do not have the authority to suspend my employee or keep me from going to her, commission or no commission." He took the box containing the weapon. He walked out the door after the two agents opened it and carried out the dead spy.

As Jacob expected, the Secretary came after him as soon as he was through the second door behind the agents. "Doctor, I want to believe Miss Benton is innocent, too. I was the one who recommended that you hire her."

"And it's because of her that there even is a finished project. Why do you turn on her and treat her like a criminal when you have little to go on?"

"New Britannia has powerful enemies within and beyond her borders. As one of this agency's top officials, I can't afford to give suspects a wide benefit of doubt."

Jacob pained at Abigail being called a suspect. "If you want to protect the citizenry, then you shouldn't assume its members are guilty until proven innocent."

They emerged into the main lobby of the near empty building. Most of the agents and officials had gone home for the evening.

"You're right, Dr. Valerian. I'm going to get to the bottom of this and see if Miss Benton's name can be cleared."

Jacob didn't have time to hear the Secretary's good intentions. His only concern was for Abigail, and he was going to her aid tonight. "If that's the best I can hope from you, then I must take it. Good evening." He exited the building.

But the Secretary followed him outside. "I'm coming with you. We'll take my coach."

"Good." Jacob rerouted to the vehicle.

The Secretary followed. "You're actually glad I'm coming with you, then?"

"Yes, but only because I'm in a terrible hurry and can't be bothered to wait for a hackney cab."

Chapter 16

Abigail returned the last ruined dress to her closet. Torn clothing and a room in shambles were the least of her worries, but they certainly added insult upon injury.

Her mind still whirled from being accused of theft. So much that she had to steady herself by picking up the mess left behind by the COIC agents. Yet it took forever, and the agents left that morning. It was now going on suppertime.

And she had yet to see or hear from Jacob. Abigail imagined that if she hadn't come to him by now, he would have come to her. After all, he fretted for her safety for weeks after that gang attacked them. Did the COIC take it upon itself to make sure that he didn't contact her?

Someone knocked on the door. Hope rose in Abigail's chest as she went to answer it, only to have the emotion dissolve once she saw who the person was.

"Catherine." She saw her sister's tight-lipped expression and relived the angry episode they had in the park yesterday afternoon. Her sister looked as though she was still upset. A repeat of harsh words was the last thing Abigail needed at the moment.

"The landlady told me your room was this way. May I come in?"

"You'll excuse the mess." Abigail pulled the door back.

"Goodness, you certainly weren't expecting company." Catherine's eyes enlarged as she entered the room. "What happened in here?"

Abigail shut the door behind her. "An investigation and interrogation took place."

Her sister pivoted. "Have you broken the law?"

"No, but I've been accused of doing so. The Cabinet of Intellectual Curiosities believes that I've stolen the works of Dr. Valerian."

"Sister, I have no idea of what you're talking about."

"Right." Abigail forgot that Catherine never heard of the COIC. "Suffice it to say that a government agency commissioned Dr. Valerian to fashion a weapon for them. I drew the concept sketches. Now someone has somehow gotten their hands on one of them."

"Who?"

"I don't know. I was told it was a spy who worked for a French industrialist named Broussard. Have you heard of him?"

Catherine sat on the bed. "The name may have come up when Hammond and his friends talk foreign affairs, but I've never listened much beyond that. I find the subject to be so dry and tedious."

Abigail began stacking a pile of books in her arms. "But as it goes, this Broussard has an established spy ring running about London. Someone in their midst managed to get a hold of my sketch. The COIC thinks I gave it to the ring in exchange for money or whatnot."

"Where might the spy have gotten hold of your sketch?"

"Again, I don't know, and I don't feel safe."

"You can stay with me."

Abigail set the books on the table. "I couldn't impose."

"You're my sister. How could I let you face this alone?" Catherine's gaze fluttered down as soon as the words were uttered. "Abigail, I listened to what you said yesterday. I was monstrous for casting you out of my home in order to make you see things my way. I thought that after our mother and father died and you came home from India, you no longer had the luxury of living life as a spinster."

"It's no luxury for me, Catherine, but all the same, I didn't want to be with a man I couldn't love, and know he wouldn't love me in return. And rather than cause you and Hammond difficulty by supporting me, I thought it best to leave."

"Well, you've shown that you can take care of yourself. I thought working for the Macklethorpes would change your mind in no time."

"You know I'm headstrong."

"Your head is as hard as a rock."

"And yours was forged in an iron foundry."

Catherine smiled. "I'm sorry. Forgive me?"

"Only if you forgive me."

"Done."

Abigail embraced her sister after a year from refraining. It was good to put the past to rest. "Help me pack. I don't think those agents wrecked all of my clothes."

"They'd better not have touched my hat. You still haven't returned it to me."

"It's over by the window." Abigail crossed the floor and went to the small shelf below the window sill. She bent down and froze.

"What is it?" Catherine came over.

"I've never seen that scuff mark before." Abigail pointed to it on the top of the shelf.

"Could the agents have done it in their search?"

"No. It looks like the heel print of a man's shoe." Abigail rose and looked at the sill. "The latch on the sill has been raised. That's how the intruder got in and no one heard him."

"How could he have raised the latch from the outside?" Catherine leaned in to inspect the latch and test it.

"This window's always been a bit loose. There's just half an inch of space at the bottom. The intruder must have found something—a piece of bent wire, perhaps—and forced it through the space to turn the latch. That's how he was able to raise the window." Abigail shivered as she realized how easily the spy was able to enter her room. "He could have done this any time in the past two months that I started sketching designs for the project."

"And more than one spy could have been watching you, too." Catherine stifled a nervous reaction, but part of it displayed in the tic of her jaw.

"In December, I remember seeing a man standing in full view of my window from across the street. He wore an old suit and bowler. I knew something wasn't right about him."

"Where did you keep the sketches at that time?"

"I usually keep them on the table as I'm working on them. The spy must have come during one day while I was out, rummaged through the portfolio, and took a sketch. I wish I knew which one."

"I can't believe there's a spy ring in our very own London." Catherine shivered.

"That's what the COIC says." A

chill went through Abigail's body, too. "Catherine, I just thought of something. That French spy was caught today. What if the other spies soon discover him missing and go out searching for him?"

"This would be the first place they'd look."

"We have to leave now." Abigail drove her hands into the hope chest and found her empty valise. Catherine took it from her and tossed it back.

"Leave it. You can wear my clothes. There isn't time to waste." Her sister pulled her towards the door.

They bustled through the hallway. Abigail heard the other female tenants having supper in the dining room a few doors down. She took a left past the front desk where the landlady started to rise from her chair.

"Will you be joining the ladies for supper tonight, Miss Benton?"

Abigail kept walking towards the front door, hesitant to stop. After spies breaking into her room and agents searching it, she didn't know who to trust anymore. "My sister and I will be taking supper elsewhere this evening."

She and Catherine left the boarding house and started their brisk walk up the street. She heard the landlady call out to her from behind, but had no idea of what she said.

"I see a hackney carriage on the right," said Catherine, already flailing her arms to hail the driver. "You hurry and get in. I'll tell the driver where to take us."

Before they reached the vehicle, the driver hopped down to open the door. He was back on his bench seat as Abigail and Catherine arrived. Abigail stepped on the pedal and practically vaulted into the carriage as she heard her sister call out her address to the driver.

"I promised him a guinea should he get us there posthaste," Catherine said, as she climbed across on the other seat and shut the door. "My, but this is the shabbiest vehicle I've ever been in. Look at the state of these cushions. And the cloth on the ceiling is practically molting."

The carriage lurched forward. Abigail held onto the edge of the worn seat. Once the ride became smoother, she settled back. "Thank you for your help, Catherine."

"Nothing to thank me for. But I must ask, with all these accusations flying about, where is Dr. Valerian?"

Abigail was assailed again with a feeling of confusion and loss. "I don't know. I haven't been able to reach him."

"Or he has been out of reach deliberately."

"Catherine, please. You and I have just reconciled. Besides, Jacob's absence could mean any number of things."

"But he's not here in your hour of need." Her sister sighed and wrung her hands. "I know you are fond of this man, but what if he brought the charges of theft against you or supported the investigation?"

"That doesn't make any sense. Jacob knows I wouldn't steal from him. And if he even thought that I would do such a thing, he would ask me himself. He wouldn't send COIC agents to do it."

Catherine still appeared doubtful. A frown settled into her delicate features. "If he really cares for you, he will defend you against the charges and restore your good name."

"He will. He's a good man."

"I'll believe that about him when I see it. But right now, I see that he has left my sister to fend for herself."

Catherine's cold appraisal of Jacob stung. Abigail wished she could show her differently, but knew that her older sister was only going by the evidence set before her. And to Catherine, it looked as though Jacob had put the safeguarding of his work above Abigail. But something must have happened to keep Jacob away this long. If only she knew what that was.

"The carriage is stopping." Catherine leaned forward to look out the window. "This isn't Paddington."

Abigail peered out. The sight of an abandoned feed storehouse came into view at a corner of a darkened alley. Above the roof loomed the smoke chimneys of factories. The smell of offal assailed her senses. "We're near St. Giles." Her stomach dropped as she saw a group of men in stained and tattered clothing emerge from the storehouse and begin to approach the vehicle.

"I distinctly told that driver my address. He won't be getting that guinea now." Catherine raised her arm to pull the string to alert the driver.

"No." Abigail stopped her, lowering her arm. "Catherine, what did that driver look like?"

Her lips pouted in thought. "I don't know. He wasn't particularly clean, I'll give you that. He had his shoulder drawn in and kept scratching at it."

Abigail's blood came to a sluggish halt as she heard the driver jump to the ground.

Catherine started to say something, but silenced immediately as she saw Abigail roll up the sleeve of her blouse.

The driver's footsteps came around to the carriage's side. Abigail pressed the button on the side of her cuff to release the pocket pistol. Its springs gave a soft click as the weapon flew forward to rest in her palm. Catherine gasped.

She whispered to her sister, "When I tell you to run, do it."

The driver slapped his hand on the door handle. Abigail kept aim on the door and waited.

***

"Here we are." Jacob pulled on the string to alert the driver once they arrived at Abigail's boarding house. He didn't wait for the Secretary as he got out and marched inside the building.

The tiny lobby was empty, including the chair behind the front desk. Jacob hit the bell on the desk.

A woman in her fifties came scurrying from the corridor. She looked worried and distraught. "May I help you?"

"Miss Benton resides at this address. I know it is late, but I wish to see her."

The woman narrowed her eyes. "State your name and purpose, sir, or I shall alert the nearest constable at once."

The Secretary entered. "There will be no need for that. My name is Alistair Kidman, and I am an official with the Cabinet of Intellectual Curiosities."

The woman's eyes grew as they fastened on him. "You people again. Why can't you leave that poor girl alone? Hasn't she been through enough in one day?"

Jacob glared at the Secretary before addressing the woman again. "We are not here to cause Miss Benton any distress. We merely wish to see if she is doing alright."

"I wouldn't know. She left this evening with her sister. She said they were going to have supper out, but they've yet to return."

"Did they say where they were going?"

"No, but they were in a mad haste to catch a cab. Miss Benton neglected to lock the door to her room behind her."

The unease that already gnawed at Jacob grew into a fierce bite. "Take us to see her room now."

She nodded at his firm command and grabbed the oil lantern off the desk. "Follow me."

Jacob trailed her past the identical closed wooden doors of the other tenant rooms until she stopped before the last room around the corner. She gave the lantern to Jacob before she pulled a key from one of many on the ring she wore at her waist.

"I locked the door for her." She unlocked it and pushed it open. Jacob went inside and held the lantern to the darkness.

The room looked as though a storm blew in. Books and papers lay spilled across the narrow bed and on the table. Two of Abigail's dresses stuck out through the half-closed closet doors, their seams torn.

Jacob turned to the Secretary. "There had better not have been a struggle in here."

"I was in the room with Miss Benton when those agents did their search," the landlady volunteered. "They combed through here slapdash, but they didn't touch her."

Jacob headed to the window.

"What are you doing?" asked the Secretary.

"Trying to find how the spy got in. I assume you generally remain at the front desk during daytime hours, don't you, madam?"

The landlady fidgeted. "I sometimes get up, but it's never for more than a few minutes. Certainly any of the ladies here would notice if an intruder were to come in."

The Secretary scoffed. "But that's just it. No one did. But I do see that you have a key to all of the rooms."

She gasped. "I hope you're not accusing me of going into Miss Benton's room and snooping about?"

While the two of them went back and forth, Jacob found that the latch on the window was broken. "You can stop frightening the landlady, Mr. Secretary. I just found out how the spy got in. Look at this window. It won't close all the way. There's enough space at the bottom for someone to get a hook or wire through."

The Secretary went to see for himself. "You're right. And once he got the latch free, he could climb in. There's a heel print on the shelf."

"We know how he did it. And why. It was easier for him to watch Abigail's room here in east Holborn than it was for him to attempt a theft at my residence. Not much good this information does us now. Thank you, madam." Jacob gave the lantern back to the landlady and went out Abigail's room, through the lobby, and outside. He took a deep breath of the cold air. It was all he could do to control his frustration as the Secretary came after him.

"Maybe she went to her sister's residence," he suggested.

Jacob shook his head. "If so, I don't know the address."

"Look. A cab approaches."

Jacob saw the hackney driver bring the vehicle down the other side of the road and pull on the horses' reins. A thin man of medium height burst out, paid the driver, and came rushing up to the boarding house.

Chapter 17

"Is this the ladies' boarding house?" the thin man asked Jacob. Despite the cold, his face was sweating.

"It is," Jacob answered. "Are you looking for someone?"

"My wife. She told me that she was going to pay a call to her sister who lives here. She's been gone since."

Jacob fitted it all together. "Is your wife Mrs. Catherine Evancourt?"

"That's her name." The man looked at him with suspicion and unease. "I'm her husband, Hammond Evancourt. Do you know where she and her sister Miss Benton are?"

"I do not. According to the landlady, they left around suppertime, but haven't returned."

Hammond pushed his hands through his hair. He wore no hat, possibly having forgotten it in his distress. He raised his eyes up at Jacob. "You're Dr. Valerian, aren't you?"

"Have we met?"

"No, but your appearance and reputation precede you." Abigail's brother-in-law did not spare Jacob his direct appraisal. "What have you to do with my family's disappearance? Speak quickly."

Jacob had no time for this. "I'm trying to find your wife and her sister. This man beside me is the Secretary of the Cabinet of Intellectual Curiosities." Jacob left it up to Alistair to volunteer his actual name.

Hammond looked confused. "The what Cabinet?"

The Secretary cleared his throat. "I'll explain later. Right now, we must find those women. I fear they may be in danger."

"Why were they in such a hurry? Where were they going?" Jacob fought against the tide of volatile emotions sweeping through him. He had come too late. He had failed to protect Abigail again. And this time, he had no idea of her whereabouts. London was a sprawling city. She and Catherine could be anywhere.

He left Hammond and the Secretary standing in the street as he went back inside the boarding house. The landlady was in the process of locking the doors for the night. "Did you see anyone or anything out of place on the street when Miss Benton and her sister left?"

"There were few pedestrians out due to the cold."

"You said the two women ran to catch a hackney. Did you see what the cab and the driver looked like?"

"I tried running out to tell Miss Benton to make sure to eat supper, but she didn't hear me. Come to think of it, I did see that carriage they took when it was situated out front before it went up the street. Didn't look very up and up. Almost like those jarveys down in the factory district."

Jacob paid attention. Now they were getting somewhere. "Did you get a look at the driver?"

The landlady put a finger to her cheek. "I saw part of his face. He had a hungry look about him. And he kept leaning one way with his shoulder. Must have damaged it bad recently."

"Tim." Jacob remembered the gang leader.

"I beg your pardon?"

"Thank you again." Jacob hurried back outside, where the Secretary and Catherine's husband looked at him in bewilderment.

"What did you say to her?" asked the Secretary.

"I asked her about the carriage Abigail and her sister took. She saw the driver. From her description, I know who he is. He's a gang leader near St. Giles and likely, part of Broussard's spy ring."

The Secretary whistled. "Of course. He must be a cab driver by day trade in the work districts. The perfect occupation for a man who needs to see and not be seen."

"Precisely. Now we mustn't waste any more time. I remember the gang running down an alley off New Oxford Street towards an abandoned feed storehouse. That may be their hideout."

The Secretary nodded. "Get in the coach. I'll find a telegraph office and alert my agents to meet us there." He went off down the street to the nearest office.

"I'm coming with you," Hammond said.

Jacob turned to him. "It'll be dangerous. And we don't know how many men are in this spy ring."

"Catherine needs me. I won't abandon her."

Jacob nodded. "And I won't abandon Abigail."

The Secretary came back a short time later. "The reinforcements are on their way. What are you men waiting for? Let's go."

The three men got into the armored carriage and set out for the factory smoke in the distance.

***

Abigail pulled the trigger as soon as Tim opened the door.

The bullet shot out of the tiny pistol with force, jolting her hand. Still, she kept her arm steady. Tim let out a cry and grabbed his right shoulder, staggering back as the carriage shook from the scared horses.

"Run," Abigail commanded her sister.

Catherine hustled in front of her and jumped down from the cab. She stumbled as she landed near Tim's feet. The hem of her dress caught on the cab's foot pedal. Tim, one hand still clutching his shoulder, made a grab for her.

Abigail tried to take aim for a second shot, but Catherine's back was in the way. Suddenly, the carriage rocked. Abigail tripped and fell on the carriage floor. She heard laughter over the horses' neighing as she saw faces of the men through the window. They pushed the vehicle again, pitching it sharply to one side. Abigail spilled out onto the cobblestones beside her sister.

Someone seized Abigail from behind. Brass bit into her throat as a coarse hand closed about her neck. She recognized Perry's voice and scraggly beard as he spoke against her ear, whiskers scratching her lobe. "Miss my touch, did you, love?" He pressed the corner of his brass knuckles into her windpipe.

Abigail choked and flailed her arms. She lifted her right and succeeded in bringing her steel cuff into Perry's head, hard enough to make the springs of the pistol retract the weapon into its compartment. He growled, seized her arm, and wrenched it painfully behind her back.

Tim, blood staining his hand and the front of his shirt, grunted as he

267

seized the back of Catherine's coat and shoved her against the cab. "Get these two bitin' cleavers into the storehouse."

Abigail gasped as Perry released his hand from her throat. He still held onto her arm behind her and pushed her towards the house. She saw a rangy man in crushed tophat drive her sister along in similar fashion.

The steps of the abandoned feed storehouse creaked and protested under the combined weight of the men as they shoved her and Catherine up and into the structure. Kerosene lamps provided light to the front room. The stench of urine and unwashed bodies pounded Abigail's nose immediately. She nearly vomited at the sight of human waste on the floor near the entranceway where the door was supposed to be.

Perry stepped around the filth and positioned her in the center of the bare space of the room, still restraining her. The man in the tophat brought Catherine beside her.

"What do we do?" Catherine, face white with fear, leaned toward Abigail. Her captor drew her back by the hair. She yelped in pain.

"Stop." Abigail moved instinctively to protect Catherine, even though Perry made sure she stayed put.

The rest of the men entered the house. They came one by one and in pairs, until Abigail counted twelve. All of them were dressed in worn or ragged clothing, but she noticed that they weren't all wearing the usual assortment of motley apparel thrown together in effort to keep warm. Some wore the collarless, tough canvas shirts of factory and mill workers. Others had caps and thick cable knits worn by fishermen and loaders down at the docks, and still others wore the fingerless gloves favored by newspaper and tract salesmen.

Abigail recognized multiple representations of the industrial district's working classes as they assembled before her. Tim cut a path through the men, his hackney driver uniform a stained mess.

He came to stand inches from her face. She smelled his rank breath as he took in forceful, pained gulps of air. The look in his dark eyes spelled murder. "You whore." A knife whipped in front of her nose.

Abigail screamed before Perry put his hand over her mouth. Tim seized her right arm and slashed through the sleeves of her coat and dress. The blade scraped against the cuff of her retractable pistol. He forced the ruined sleeves of her garments up past her elbow. She trembled as he turned her wrist over and drove the blade through the thin leather straps of the cuff. He nicked her skin as he worked. The cuff fell to the floor.

"A new toy of that mad doctor's." He stooped to pick it up. "Langlais will pay a pretty penny for this."

"Broussard, you mean," Catherine's captor said. "He's the one backin' the ring an' all."

Broussard's web of spies. Abigail understood now. All of these men, by virtue of his line of work, were able to ply their trades while gaining information for Broussard without anyone in London taking notice. The working classes, after all, were seen and yet often not observed.

Broussard took advantage of the men's hardship and supplied a need that most of London's officials failed to address. Now she and her sister were going to witness firsthand the consequences of such a slip.

She wiped the blood that trickled from the small cut on her wrist on her torn sleeve. Perry's voice rumbled over her head. "Where is that Frenchie? He makes us do all his spyin' while he gets to sit and stare at the dollymops 'round the city."

"He's been watchin' this one at her boardin' house." Tim gestured to Abigail. "He said, go to her address if he went missin' for more'n twelve hours. So where's he?"

Abigail leaned away from his knife. "I don't know who you speak of."

"Langlais' been watchin' your room for the past three months. He's always come back here, though, to see wot news we've collected 'round London proper for 'im. No one's seen 'im since yesterday."

So that was the spy's name who had stolen her sketch. "I don't know him or where he would be."

"She could be speakin' true," said Perry. "Langlais looked like any other workin' class gent in that bowler."

Abigail stiffened. Tim noticed. "You know where he is?"

"I spotted him once in December, but I haven't seen him since."

"I think you're fibbin'." He drew closer. The coppery scent of blood was in the air as his gunshot wound bled. "Where's Langlais?"

"I'm telling you the truth. I don't know."

Perry interrupted. "You should get that hole patched up, Tim. You're bleedin' like a trout."

"I will. The cleaver just grazed me with her pea shooter." Tim glared at Abigail. "I should shoot you wit it when Langlais gets through talkin' to you."

He turned to address the other men of the spy ring. "We'll wait another hour to see if Langlais comes back. He'll pay us for gettin' this cuff gun an' for nabbin' the shrew."

"What about this one?" Catherine's captor pointed down at her. Catherine gave a little whimper.

"He might also see wot she knows about that doctor's business. Put the two o' em in the dry room upstairs."

Catherine's captor picked up a lamp and led the way. Perry nudged Abigail onward. She and Catherine walked between the two men. They climbed the small flight of rickety stairs, with its protruding floorboards. On the second floor, the man leading took them through the first door on the right.

They were deposited in what must have previously been the dry room to rid feed grains of moisture before they were bagged. Large and spacious, with shelving and generous window panels on both sides and in the back that were once meant to let in the sun, the room was now bare. A cold wind blew in from the glassless panes. Abigail looked down and saw piles of old burlap feed sacks and rubbish lining the side of the building before spilling into the alley. Instead of cheerful light, the windows let in the red-orange glow from the factory coal fires. Smoke drifted towards central and west London.. Abigail prayed this wouldn't be her and Catherine's final view of home.

"Think you can keep an eye on 'em?" Catherine's captor asked Perry, once he set the lamp down.

Perry nodded. "Better'n lookin' at you and the boys downstairs." He lowered his eyes upon Abigail and Catherine. "Much better."

Abigail and her sister backed near the windows and stayed there.

"Tim didn't say you could touch 'em. Best leave 'em as is for now. Wouldn't want them to clam up 'cause you got their skirts wrinkled." The man with the crushed tophat went towards the door and proceeded to close it behind him.

"Don't worry, Silas. I'll be on me best behavior with these upstandin' ladies." Perry puckered his lips at Abigail and Catherine.

Abigail fought off another reflex to vomit. She felt the draft from the windows. They were only on the second floor. If she and Catherine could climb out, then they could make an escape through the alley. The drop was somewhat sizeable, but the piles of feed sacks and rubbish would break their fall. The only other way out was back down the stairs where the spies were gathered.

They had to attempt escape through the window. But first, Perry had to be convinced that their intentions were to remain in the room. He watched them from the door.

Abigail counted one minute and then took a seat on the hard wooden floor. She motioned for Catherine to do the same. Her sister gave her a quizzical look, but obeyed.

"Good to see you makin' yourselves comfortable." Perry chuckled from the doorway. His posture relaxed instantly in what Abigail perceived was his assumption that they had accepted their captivity. She continued to wait.

Two minutes. Three. Abigail listened to the factory noises surrounding the block. Four minutes. She heard the murmurs and occasional outbursts of swearing or laughter coming from downstairs. Five.

Catherine shifted closer to her as a cold breeze swept through the window again. Six. Perry dug into his pocket and came out with an envelope. He pulled something from its contents and stuck it into his mouth.

Seven minutes. Abigail spoke. "My sister and I have need of the water closet."

"There ain't no indoor privy here." Perry chewed.

"What are we to do, then?"

He shrugged. "Lift up your skirts right where you sit for all I care."

Catherine gasped with indignation, but Abigail hoped Perry would say that. She imitated her sister's horror. "Sir, we are respectable, civilized ladies. Surely you cannot expect us to tend to our relief in such a way."

Perry found a round container on a shelf. He launched a stream of tobacco juice inside before setting it in the middle of the floor. "Use that."

Abigail pretended as though she would approach it. Then she stopped midway. "Again, sir, we are respectable. Would you allow us a few minutes of privacy?"

He looked disappointed. Abigail remained waiting. She raised her chin to a haughty angle for more effect. Finally, he nodded. "Five minutes. But I'm comin' back in as soon as the time's up. I'll be on the other side of this door."

The door opened, he slipped out, and closed it behind him. Abigail waited until she heard it fully shut against the frame. She tiptoed back to Catherine and whispered, "Out the window. Now."

Chapter 18

"Climb out the window?" Catherine whispered back, astounded. She took view of the distance down and violently shook her head. "It's too high."

"Come on. You first." Abigail sat her down upon the ledge.

"Why me first?" She swung one leg over and cringed.

"You have a family to return to."

Catherine looked back at her with tenderness. "You're also my family."

Abigail reached out to steady her sister as she began to position herself for the drop. "We'll both leave here safely. I promise." A veil of tears blurred her vision. "But you're getting out of this storehouse first."

***

Jacob and Hammond waited in the alley behind the abandoned storehouse for the Secretary to return from surveying the front.

"Do you think this is where the spy ring is located?" Hammond asked. "They could just be vagrants inside."

Jacob felt the weight of the armored waistcoat against his chest. He tugged his coat sleeve down to conceal the gauntlet gun that he strapped on before they left the armored carriage a few blocks behind. "An old jarvey was alongside the curb. It matched the landlady's description of the one that took Abigail and Catherine."

Hammond groaned. "I pray the ladies are in there, and those men haven't touched them."

"Yes, I've prayed, too. And now I'm going to pass the ammunition." Jacob handed him one of the two revolvers he tucked in his belt. "Courtesy of the Secretary's weapons store from the carriage."

Hammond's eyes widened, clearly unused to being around or seeing so many firearms. "But I already took a pocket pistol from there."

"You're going to need a bigger weapon than that if there are more than three men inside that storehouse."

Hammond took hold of the revolver just as the Secretary returned from his reconnaissance.

"Did you see the women?" Jacob and Hammond asked, almost in unison.

"No, but I counted eleven men," the Secretary said, returning his six-shot pistol to the holster beneath his jacket. "There could be more upstairs. We have to wait for the COIC agents now."

"I'm not waiting any longer," Jacob said. "There's no telling how far or near your agents are."

"You can't just waltz up in there alone, Doctor. I obtained your service record. I know you lost your right leg fighting the French in India."

"I wasn't planning on waltzing, but that is an ironic choice of words," Jacob remarked.

"I meant no offense, but you need to consider that there are three of us and so many more of those spies inside that storehouse."

Hammond looked down at Jacob's feet. "You lost your leg? That means, you're wearing an artificial one?"

Jacob met his stare of incredulity. "Yes, Hammond."

"But how are you not...er, you don't make heavy use of your walking stick."

"I made a new construction that enables me to depend less upon it. Forgive me if I don't explain more, but we do have two women still in need of rescue."

"I didn't see them on the first floor," said the Secretary.

Jacob raised his eyes to the second floor of the storehouse. "There. Do you see that light from that large window?"

Hammond craned his neck. "I think I see movement. Good heavens. Someone's coming out on the ledge."

Jacob looked again. He saw a woman sit down on the ledge and dangle one foot over. She did the same with the other. Her skirt and petticoats fanned about as she dropped into the darkness below.

Hammond raced down the alley, followed by the Secretary and Jacob. Jacob's blood ran cold as he considered the drop from that height. If that woman didn't have anything to break her fall, she could easily have suffered a broken spine. He prayed he would not see what he expected.

"It's Catherine." Hammond tore through the feed sacks and moldy rubbish to get to his wife, who had landed on her side.

Jacob climbed over the refuse, using his walking stick to move objects out of his path. He reached Abigail's sister just as Hammond put his arm under her neck.

"Are you alright, Catherine?" Hammond asked. He supported her as she wobbled to her feet.

"Abigail's still on the second floor," she cried, pointing upward.

Jacob saw Abigail through the second floor window. She grabbed onto the ledge and started to swing her leg over. Her eyes were on him the entire time. "Hurry, we'll catch you," he said.

Something made Abigail's head turn towards the room. She cried out just as a large man seized her and pulled her off the ledge. Jacob saw his face and scraggly beard.

"I'm going in to get her." Jacob turned past the Secretary and moved fast around the building's corner.

"Wait, I'm right behind you."

Ignoring the Secretary's shouts, he proceeded towards the front of the storehouse.

The men inside began moving as they heard shouts from upstairs and outside. Jacob aimed his right arm at one of the broken windows of the first room and flicked a switch under his wrist. A smoke capsule launched through the window and landed on the floor inside.

Curses and calls for evacuation ensued as the smoke flared. Jacob pulled his revolver and fired off two warning shots. Six of the men scrambled out immediately. The Secretary came up with his pistol and cornered them, ordering them to get on the ground.

"I've got these," he shouted. "Go inside before that smoke gets too high."

Jacob climbed the stairs into the house. He pushed past a seventh man that blocked the entrance, hitting him in the gut with his walking stick when the man attempted to fight, and shoved him out of the way.

The remaining members of the spy ring scrambled for their bearings in the thick veil of smoke. Their outlines remained barely visible. Jacob saw the flight of stairs on the right and moved there.

The smoke continued to rise, heavy and opaque against the light of the lanterns. He heard Abigail shout again as he ascended, climbing two steps at a time. Pain shot up through his right thigh, but he kept going.

Perry and Abigail struggled with each other in the doorway of a large room. Perry had trouble keeping hold of her. Abigail kicked, thrashed, and scratched at the man. He let go of her with one hand and reached into his pocket.

Jacob fired the revolver.

Blood sprayed from Perry's face as he fell away from Abigail. His sudden weight gone, she teetered before correcting herself. Then she saw Jacob and ran towards him.

Perry was still alive. He shuffled in a blind crawl, moaning, but still moving. Jacob saw him fumble for the kerosene lantern in the room. Perry clawed for the handle and, as the last of his life fled, scrabbled to toss it at Jacob in the hallway.

Jacob pushed Abigail against the wall and sheltered her as the lantern shot past him and over the stair rail. Glass shattered. Flames broke out instantly on the old, dry wood in the middle of the first floor. Jacob looked to Perry again and saw the man fall back, still.

Jacob dropped his walking stick and pocketed his revolver in order to pull off his jacket. He threw it over Abigail's head. "Move downstairs and out the house." He took her hand to lead. Just as he turned, he heard gunfire and felt a strong hit in the chest.

Abigail screamed as he fell to the floor. His revolver clattered somewhere on the ground. He saw Abigail's distressed face over him before her gaze turned towards the stairs. Jacob fought to move.

"Look, it's Crutch come back." Tim reached the top of the stairs, carrying Abigail's retractable pistol in his right hand. The cuff, too small for his wrist, dangled in mid-air. "I owe you one in return for that nick in the shoulder." He shoved Abigail aside.

Jacob struggled to get air back into his lungs. The combined smoke from his deterrent capsule and the flames of the thrown lantern sucked at the remaining oxygen in the storehouse. Abigail was already choking. He put his hand over the dent in the waistcoat where the bullet struck. It remained lodged there.

Tim pulled the trigger of the pocket pistol again. A click resounded.

Jacob tried to reach around for his revolver before Tim realized that Abigail's pistol was out of bullets. But Tim rushed at him, using the metal cuff of the weapon to beat his face, his arm.

"You're a freak of nature," he said, as he continued his assault.

Jacob drew his gauntleted arm inward and delivered a punch to Tim's ribs.

The man doubled over as the wind got knocked out of him. Jacob crawled to his left knee and pushed himself off the floor.

Tim spat blood. "You're just half a man." A knife appeared in his hand. "Weak with that metal leg."

"I prefer to see it as a strength." Jacob lifted his right leg in a kick.

Tim slashed with the knife. The knife ripped through the fabric of Jacob's pant leg but only slid against the metal body of his mechanical limb beneath. The momentum of Jacob's kick continued, uninterrupted. His foot caught Tim under the chin. The man's neck snapped back as he went flying down the stairs. His body landed with a heavy thud.

Jacob bit back pain as the top of his leg absorbed the impact from striking Tim. He limped to Abigail and drew her up. Her face was covered with the sooty film that rose from the floor below and began to cover the walls of the storehouse. She coughed and gasped.

"My eyes are burning." Her lids were squeezed shut as tears streaked gray down her face.

"Hold onto me. We're going downstairs." He pulled his jacket over her again as he held her firmly to his side. She stumbled on the broken floorboards as the wood began to heat and warp beneath them. Jacob could feel his right leg buckle as he tried to steady his balance and keep her from falling at the same time.

The heat from the flames blasted on his right side, hotter than the fires started from the mortar rounds that injured him permanently. He kept Abigail to his left as he descended the stairs with her, step by step. He heard the explosions again, heard the screams of the dying in the camp.

But I'm not in Madras anymore. I'm in London. And I have to get Abigail to safety. He fought his rising panic as the flames chased him, lapped at his heels and reached for the flesh at his neck.

The flames burned near the front door. Jacob kept Abigail along the opposite wall and shielded her as they stepped past and outside, away from the storehouse.

The bracing night air was like a balm that cut through the sting of smoke burning his lungs. Abigail gulped in deep breaths beside him in the street. Shouts were all around them. Jacob rubbed his eyes and saw the additional COIC agents swarming in around the ten men that escaped from the burning storehouse.

He saw the Secretary's armored carriage a safe distance away, with its driver and Hammond tending to Abigail's sister.

"Where's Catherine?" Abigail blinked through her tears. "Did she make it away from the building?"

"She's in the carriage over there. She's safe. You're safe." Jacob spoke soothingly as Abigail began to shake, her pent fear finally showing itself in full force. He held her as the emotions racked through her body.

"I knew that you'd find the gang. That you'd seek the truth for yourself. I didn't steal from you." Her words spilled one after the other in quick succession.

"I never once believed you did. But it's all over now. The men have been caught. Broussard's spy ring is defused. Your name is cleared."

She continued crying. Whether it was from the smoke still in her eyes, tears of relief, or a combination of both, Jacob could not pinpoint. But her breathing began to return to normal and her tremors slowed. She looked up at him through wet auburn lashes. Though the smoke dirtied her face, it did nothing to sully the gentle green eyes that took hold of him.

"I'm so sorry I hurt you by believing those rumors."

"Abigail, you already apologized. I'm sorry for not telling you more when I should have."

"I'm here with you. Don't shut me out."

"I won't. Not now. Not ever again." He kissed her until her trembling stopped for good.

Epilogue

June, 1838

"Catherine, help me with this side button."

Abigail stood before the full-length mirror of her sister's boudoir as she tried to fasten her wedding dress. She twisted as Catherine's reflection came up behind her in the mirror. "I can't seem to get a hold of the fastenings for these sleeves."

"Those sleeves are the peak of ladies fashion." Catherine straightened a seam at Abigail's shoulder. A smile crossed her face. "You look so lovely. I cannot believe my little sister is finally getting married."

"You don't have to stress that word."

"Married?" Her sister teased.

"You know which one. We'd better hurry. Everyone's at the church. I'm sure Hammond and the children are waiting restlessly."

Catherine started to help her button the dress. "Actually, Phillip and Winnie have been behaving very well since we decided to reinstate their tutor. I guess just because the academy offered an expensive education didn't make it the most suitable for them."

"Your children didn't like being away from you and Hammond."

"Speaking of my husband, I must admit that I haven't been able to keep myself too far away from him, either, these past few months. Ever since he heroically came to my rescue after I dropped from the window of that storehouse, well, let's just say getting to work early each morning is no longer his pressing priority."

"Catherine." Abigail looked down at her white satin slippers, mortified. "That's a bit much."

"Oh, honestly, sister. You can pretend to be so prim when you want to, but don't forget, I've seen you and Jacob kiss before. And if that's any indication of what he has planned for you tonight—"

"Dear me, look at the time. The wedding starts in half an hour. We must go this minute."

"I guarantee it won't start without you. Calm yourself." Catherine laughed. Then she smoothed Abigail's veil over her shoulders. "Our parents would have been so proud of you. You continued in your humanitarian efforts for others, and you've found a good man who loves you."

"They would have been proud of us both. We've each found men who love us."

Catherine curled her fingers over each other in nervous motion. "I was wrong about Jacob in the past. Hammond and I both judged him wrongly. I hope you can forgive us."

Abigail stilled her sister's hands. "I already have. The past is in the past. Why don't we keep moving forward?"

Catherine nodded, then looked at her vanity clock and jumped suddenly. "My goodness, look at the time. We must get to the church." She grabbed the train of Abigail's dress and shuffled her sister out the bedroom door.

***

Jacob looked at his pocketwatch again as he stood at the front of the church.

"Try not to fret so, Doctor," Maria said, seated beside Struthers in the first pew. "Brides are notorious for not being on time. I was late to my own wedding." She nudged her husband, who stilled her elbow with a gentle pat of affection.

"It's past the time the ceremony was supposed to start. I hope Abigail didn't get cold feet." Jacob looked to the minister in apology. "Give her a few more minutes."

"I'm in no hurry," the kindly minister reassured him. "I'm sure the lady will be here any moment. In the meantime, try thinking good thoughts. You'll keep calm that way."

"Yes." Jacob supposed he was rather a bundle of nerves that summer afternoon. He looked out at the intimate gathering of people there to witness him and Abigail join hands in holy matrimony. In addition to Maria and Struthers, Hammond was there with Abigail's niece and nephew. The children waved to him, and kept waving to him at the expense of their father's parental control, until Jacob was past the point of containing his laughter.

The COIC Secretary came to the wedding as well. He sat in the second row behind Maria and Struthers. After clearing Abigail's name from the spy ring investigation, he granted her and Jacob status as COIC contributors. He also fully approved the gauntlet gun and armored waistcoat. The sizeable payment granted was well beyond the original commission price, enough for Jacob to supplement his practice and improve conditions at the laborer's hospital. The Secretary completed his benevolent actions by apologizing to Abigail in person for wrongly accusing her.

Jacob smiled at that. The gesture certainly warranted the Secretary a wedding invitation.

He came out of his recollections as Catherine entered the church and took a seat beside Hammond. She nodded to Jacob. Abigail was on her way.

Jacob's bride did arrive a few minutes later, as the minister had predicted, but she was more than lovely. The guests stood as Abigail walked down the aisle, a vision in white. Her hair was rich auburn against her glowing complexion.

She's so beautiful, Jacob thought, *and she wants to marry me.*

She came to stand at his side. He went weak as she offered him a shy smile beneath her veil. He gave Struthers his walking stick to hold in order to take her hands. Her skin was warm and soft. This time, it was she who gave his hands the gentle squeeze of reassurance.

What did he do to deserve her? Jacob never imagined his life could take such a good turn after all he'd been through. But the past was in the past, as Abigail would say. Here was the present, and Abigail, his beautiful, intelligent, and irrepressible love, was there to share his future.

The Industrial Spy
A romantic steampunk tale of secret agents, eclectic engines, and surprising alliances
Curiosity Chronicles, Book Three

For Suzume, whose encouragement and wise counsel inspired me to explore the freedom that comes from trusting my own creativity.

Chapter 1

Northern France, August 1838

Dominique lined up along with the other female flour mill workers as they prepared for Broussard's inspection. She adjusted her apron before the French industrialist sidled up to the front of the line to begin what had to be the most tawdry employee evaluation in all of French industry.

"Too scrawny." Monsieur Emile Broussard gave his first verdict to a meager slip of a woman. Dominique watched in anger as one of Broussard's cronies took the woman by the arm and dragged her away.

The industrialist proceeded to the second female. Towering over the petite mill worker by at least a foot and a half, he looked down his fleshy nose at her. "Too pale."

Another crony came forward to take her away. Broussard stepped heavily to the third. Possessing a barrel chest and thick limbs, he had to weigh as much as two stout men. He assessed the third woman and sniffed. "Too ugly."

She immediately burst into tears, not because he wasn't fond of her looks, but because she was now out of work.

"I do not employ unattractive female workers in this mill," he announced over her growing sobs. The remaining female workers cowed in fear for what his razor assessment would bring each of them.

Dominique only became disgusted. Ever since she began working undercover at the mill for the French government agency Bureau de l'Industrie, she'd seen violation after violation of employee rights and machine safety procedures. As if endangering his workers wasn't enough, now Broussard wanted to transform the mill into a brothel to increase his profits in the sleepy villages outside Le Havre.

It was up to Dominique to dismantle his scheme and bring him into custody. But first, Broussard had to decide if she was pretty.

She placed a hand on her hip and waited for the pompous industrial crime lord to strut his way down the line. He rejected two more workers.

Just as he reached her, Monsieur Delacroix, the mill overseer, burst out of his office. "Monsieur Broussard, you must see this."

Broussard looked away from Dominique. "I instructed all of the men to wait outside. What is it?"

Yes, Dominique wondered. What could make the normally unaffected overseer look as though he were ready to jump out the window and into the Seine River?

Monsieur Delacroix stopped short before Broussard. "The bolting machine is fit to burst. Our new engineer says he saw cracks forming."

"I didn't give you license to hire an engineer. Where is this man?"

Delacroix jabbed his thumb backwards.

Dominique turned and saw a man emerge from the office. With confidence, he strode forward. Dominique heard the women behind her murmur as he passed them, tall and steady in his gait. He stopped beside her.

He matched Broussard in height, but that was where the two men's physical similarities abruptly ended. The newcomer was built lean and strong. Muscles shown in his forearms where he had rolled up the sleeves of his cambric work shirt.

Dominique's gaze rose higher to the engineer's face. A square jaw sat firmly anchored below a sensual mouth, a small nose, gray eyes, and a wide, creaseless brow. What was most striking was his hair, a thick shock of copper.

He must have been hired only today or she would have noticed him long before, the way he stood out from among the other male workers.

"You say you're an engineer?" Broussard demanded, sizing up the man that stared him eye to eye.

"*Oui*, monsieur."

Dominique listened to his French carefully. He had the words correct, but something was wrong with his regional accent.

The engineer saw her stare and boldly returned her gaze. Strength and resolve were in his eyes, as well as a hint of youthful rebellion. He was a grown man, but couldn't have been past his mid-twenties, only a few years older than she was.

She felt a heavy hand come down upon her shoulder.

"You look like a man who knows his women," Broussard said to the engineer. "What do you think of this one?"

"She's not too plain."

Well, then. Dominique found herself reacting. Why did she suddenly care about a perfect stranger's estimation of her appearance? The engineer turned his attention away as swiftly as it had been directed towards her.

"Monsieur Broussard, the bolting machine," Monsieur Delacroix reminded.

Broussard's hand slid off Dominique's shoulder. "I'll get to it. *Un moment.*"

But Dominique heard a shrill whistle from the back of the mill. Seconds later, she saw flames burst from the bolting machine.

The mill workers fled for the door leading downstairs in a collection of shrieks. Broussard exited with surprising speed for his formidable size, flanked by the overseer.

Dominique didn't know how that fire started, but now was her chance to raid the overseer's office and get what evidence she could find to incriminate Broussard. She darted forward.

Right into the arms of the engineer.

"You should be running," she said.

"As should you, in the opposite direction."

"I must see if other workers remain inside." She pushed against him, but his grip was strong and sure.

"They've all fled, Dominique Fontaine."

She ceased struggling. "How do you know my name?"

"Every agent has secrets." He refused to let her go as he pulled her with him to the nearest window. "I'm Colton Smythe. I'm with New Britannia's Cabinet of Intellectual Curiosities. And you, mademoiselle, are wanted by my agency for questioning."

Before she could respond, he put his arm around her waist and tilted her backwards, out the window.

Dominique experienced a moment of weightlessness as wind rushed past her ears and she plummeted from the mill. The engineer still held onto her. She saw his expression of calm determination just before she smacked the cold rolling surface of the Seine.

Dark water covered her face and submerged her body. Her skirts quickly became weighed down as she struggled to right herself. The engineer's arm tightened about her waist as he came up from his dive. Dominique pounded his hand to get away, but the buoyancy of the water absorbed the impact of her fist. Remembering her defensive training, she pinched the area of skin between his thumb and index finger. His hold slackened. She pushed his arm off and began swimming away from him.

She couldn't see where she was going underwater, but the current moved against her. She heard the continual grinding motion of the mill's motorized waterwheel as it turned nearby. The coal-powered engine within the mill itself made it churn faster and draw more water to power the machines within. The wheel was six yards away. Her skirt and apron were being drawn into its wake.

Dominique fought to swim against the river current. Her hands pushed through underwater brush and reeds as she tilted upwards. She began to see the daylight at the water's surface.

Her head broke the surface. The river's churning, the wheel's grinding, and the crackle of the flames as they licked at the mill produced a roaring noise in her ears. Water roiled into her nose and got into her mouth when she tried to take a gulp of air. She headed for the riverbank on her left.

Her arms burned as she forced her muscles to pull her to safety. She heard something break and turned to see that a section of the mill's roof had crashed into the water. Part of it was still engulfed in flames.

Dominique's foot touched the silt bottom of the riverbed. She pushed forward, leveraging herself to go higher to the bank. She found more ground with the other foot and moved until she was standing in the shallows. The rocks were uneven and slippery as she stumbled to shore.

The reeds parted easily enough for her to cut a path to higher ground. Dominique fell upon the dry grasses before she glanced back at the river.

The engineer—no, undercover COIC agent—was nowhere to be seen.

Did he drown? As rude a man as he was for tossing her out of a three-story window, she didn't wish such a fate upon him. Did he swim to the opposite shore? She saw the last supply wagon rolling off in the distance with mill workers. Maybe he was on it. Whatever the case, she hoped he was safe, even if it was just for the chance to shake him silly later.

Dominique pulled herself to her feet, flung off her soggy apron, and wrung out what she could of her skirt. One thing was clear. Broussard was long gone. The interim between the bolting machine catching on fire and the panicked evacuation gave him enough time to distance himself. His wagon was probably well on its way down another route away from Le Havre, transporting him from the eyes of the port authorities and the Bureau de l'Industrie yet again.

She groaned as she heard the flames cackle at the mill. By the time anyone returned to investigate, the building will have burnt to the ground. And Broussard would have no reason to go there again.

There went all of her work to catch the robber baron. She spent six months conducting industrial espionage at the mill, waiting for the rare chance that he should visit. Her efforts were completely botched, thanks to that one lone engineer. If she ever saw that forceful, self-assured agent again...

"Looking for someone?"

Dominique whirled and saw him standing in the clearing.

Chapter 2

Hands on his hips, back straight, the engineer looked none the worse for wear, even with his clothes drenched.

"*You*," Dominique muttered.

"*Moi?*" he asked.

"Do not pretend that you speak French. Your accent is *tres terrible.*"

"That's not good to hear. I had to spend eleven months learning French since the COIC sends me to Le Havre so often," he said in English.

His accent was not clipped and precise as those she heard among the wealthy New Britannia citizens that often came through Le Havre's ports on their way to Paris or the Cote d'Azur. Instead, it was peppered with a saucy tone associated with the British sailors and tradesmen that worked down at the markets and fishing docks.

"Your agency should have provided you with a French tutor," she said in his language, having learned it long ago from helping her family sell baked goods to tourists in the Le Havre marketplace for years.

"I got the job done, didn't I? I got Delacroix to hire me and I convinced everyone at the mill that I was French, even Emile Broussard. Now, as I was saying before we parted ways..." He started to come towards her.

"Stay back," Dominique ordered. She moved away, going up the side of the bank and into the clearing. "You said you were a COIC agent."

He slowly walked where she previously stepped. "My agency needs to know what information you have on Broussard. He's wanted for crimes in New Britannia, too."

"That may be so, but I won't be handed over to your agency for questioning."

As a result of living so close to the Channel, Dominique was well aware of the various disputes between New Britannia and France over the years, both great and small. For the moment, the two nations participated in an industrial rivalry for the latest scientific inventions. Their respective procurement agencies, the Cabinet of Intellectual Curiosities and the Bureau de l'Industrie, were no different.

Dominique heard stories from the more experienced agents of the Bureau de l'Industrie about what happened if they were taken in by a COIC field operative. Aside from the forced journey to New Britannia, there was the long series of inquiries to endure at COIC headquarters in London. Afterwards, the Bureau agent was made to wait in a London embassy while diplomats negotiated his or her return home.

It was no secret that the two nations enjoyed sparring and quibbling with each other. The process of returning home to France was painstaking and deliberately slow. Dominique had no intention of taking such an extended holiday abroad.

"Agent Fontaine, we have to talk," the engineer persisted, pausing in his advance upon her.

He introduced himself as Colton Smythe before he had stopped her in the mill on her way to Delacroix's office. A strong yet strange-sounding name. It reminded her of coals, industry, and all manner of fiery, combustible things.

Hmm, perhaps the name was fitting, given his red hair and potent manner. Dominique posed a question to him. "You caused that fire, did you not?"

"That's what happens when machines aren't well-maintained. The mill's equipment was old and not up to standard."

Dominique chafed at his elusive, irreverent tone. "You ruined my mission."

"*My mission* was to find you and shut that mill down. Broussard wanted to turn it into a secret brothel. I saw my chance for sabotage when the men were outside and you ladies were gathered in the middle of the main floor, away from the machines."

"I've worked undercover at that mill for six months, waiting for Broussard to come inspect it. I could have brought him to the Bureau today if not for what you did."

He cast a doubtful glance at her. "I don't see how you would have got past his bodyguards, unless you were hiding a spring-loaded net beneath that corset." His gaze lingered upon her torso.

Dominique saw that her blouse was plastered against her skin, allowing him prominent view of her figure and its corseted underpinnings. Embarrassed, she deflected his cheeky statement. "I have something better." She reached into the space between her corset and blouse and pulled out a weapon. She pressed a button on the glass handle and a blade released at the metal hilt.

"Touche," he remarked, raising both eyebrows in goading jest rather than the fear that she would have preferred.

Nevertheless, Dominique held the switchblade knife out. "I do not wish to use this, but I won't be taken anywhere by you. Stay away from me."

He regarded the blade with mild interest. "I hoped that you'd come along willingly." He stepped closer.

She moved away again. "Was pitching me from a three-story window your way of asking politely?"

"I was saving you from the fire."

"The one that you started."

"Yes, we've already established that. It was best the mill be destroyed."

She kept the blade extended, ready to move it in any direction that he might choose to spring. "You burned evidence against Broussard and Delacroix along with it."

The engineer shook his head, his hair dark red from a dousing in the river. "The mill's records are kept somewhere offsite. I searched Delacroix's office when he went out to survey the floor this morning. There was nothing in there for either of our agencies to charge Broussard with."

If that was true, then it meant that Dominique's mission was an inherent failure. She couldn't accept that. Wouldn't accept it, not from a British man who simply blundered his way in and then demanded that she come along with him into COIC custody. "Why should I take your word for it?"

"Well, you can't go back to the mill to see for yourself, now can you?"

A loud snapping and a crash interrupted him.

Dominique looked beyond him to the mill. The rest of the roof and top floor caved in to the second floor. The flames hung from every window of the building. Black smoke rose off what remained of the roof.

Distracted by the sight, she was unguarded as Colton seized upon her wrist and made her accidentally press the button again to drop the blade portion of the knife. He kicked it in the brush. "Now, Agent Fontaine, we really should be on our way."

That scoundrel. Dominique wouldn't let herself get manhandled and dragged away by him again. She dropped the glass knife handle to the ground and stepped hard on it. A gaseous cloud began to rise beneath her foot.

"What the—" Her would-be captor coughed, unable to finish his sentence. But he still managed to keep her wrist in his grasp.

Holding her breath, Dominique employed another defense technique. While he held onto her, she turned her wrist at an angle. Then she jabbed her thumb down as though she were giving a sign of disapproval. The motion freed her from his grasp. He staggered as the gas rose in the air. Dominique hitched up the heavy wet hem of her skirt and ran from the clearing.

Shortly after, she heard his boots pound the ground in pursuit.

Zut alors. He didn't breathe in enough of the aether sedation gas to fall into a deep sleep. There was enough of it in concentrated liquid form to affect a group of people, but most of it absorbed into the dirt when she broke the knife handle. At least it slowed him down and gave her a head start.

Dominique thought to lose him in the woods. She had grown up in the area outside Le Havre, and knew every paved path and dirt road like the back of her hand. She doubted that the engineer had been in the region long enough to become acquainted with its intricate little paths.

Dominique balled her skirt in her arm, hating how it slowed her movement. Ducking in an area of trees, she zigzagged her way around fallen branches and dips in the terrain, hoping to lose Colton in the process. She reached one of the dirt roads that led to her home village of Chay Oiseau.

She expected to see someone to call out to for help, but no one was on the back road in midmorning. She gulped clean air into her tired lungs. The fire and smoke had yet to reach this area of the woods.

Air rushed from her lungs as Colton caught her around the waist.

Losing her balance, she felt her feet starting to give out from under her.

He drew her back to him before she could fall forward. "I stand corrected," he talked in beats as he caught his breath. "I do see how you would have attempted to take Broussard into custody."

"Not attempted. I would have succeeded." She fought to get away, but he wouldn't let go.

"You wouldn't be able to drag a man his size."

She struggled again. He still held on.

"I've had about enough of this, Agent Fontaine. Come peacefully with me to Le Havre or I'll be forced to use restraints."

Dominique bent over suddenly when Colton shifted his stance. She tilted to the right and smiled with satisfaction as he inadvertently went with her momentum. His upper body traveled past her shoulder and went first onto the ground, followed by his upended legs.

She started to flee, but he swept his leg in front of hers. Dominique lost her balance and pitched forward. He caught her as she landed on top of him.

"I didn't want to do that." He rolled over, pinning her to the ground. Irritation wrinkled his brow as he restrained her arms from flying up to strike his face. "If you'd just calm down, you'd see that I'm not trying to harm you."

"I do not care what your agency wants. You'll have to carry me kicking and screaming if you want me to come with you."

"That's a bit much." He gently brushed a speck of dirt from her cheek. "I'm an engineer. I prefer to be efficient as possible." Still restraining her under his greater weight, he reached into a leather pouch at his belt. He produced a set of cuffs, connected by a finely-hammered, silver chain. The cuffs looked as though they could be bracelets, so polished and refined in their design. He put one on her right wrist and the other on his left. The chain dangled between them, glimmering like jewelry.

Dominique instinctively tugged to test the chain's integrity. It held strong.

"Don't let its delicate beauty fool you. That chain's made with Toledo steel and a silver-iron alloy with the strength to haul a galleon."

The chain winked as it caught the sunlight sifting through the trees. "I don't know if I should be insulted for you restraining me with this or comparing me to a sailing vessel."

His lips formed a smirk. "I work on a ship. She's not as pretty as you are, but she cooperates much better." Colton rose and helped Dominique to her feet.

"You told Broussard I was 'not too plain'." She regretted mentioning their initial encounter just as soon as she uttered the words. It made her sound as if she cared about his opinion. Which, of course, wasn't true, Dominique insisted to herself. They had only just met, and he made an outrageous first impression.

"Broussard was ghastly in his intentions towards you ladies at the mill," Colton responded. "I wasn't about to encourage him by mentioning your looks. Let's go. We can reach Le Havre in about an hour on foot."

Dominique, out of knives, aether sedatives, and escape plans for the moment, walked alongside him on the dirt path. She had an hour to think of a way to get out of her restraints and alert her agency of a COIC agent's presence in the area.

They walked on the road for about a half hour before they met an approaching cart that carried two matronly women. They came from the direction of Le Havre. Dominique assumed they were coming home from a morning at the market. Their cart was pulled by one horse.

Colton grabbed Dominique's hand, concealing the cuffs' chain between their palms. She shied at the sudden intimate touch and tried to pull away, but he held onto her firmly. "*Bonjour*," he greeted the women, as though he and Dominique caught them while out on a simple stroll.

The woman holding the reins tugged, bringing the horse to a stop in the middle of the road. She gave Colton and Dominique a one-eyed stare. Her other eye was concealed beneath the brim of a floppy, worn hat. "*Bonjour, monsieur et mademoiselle.* We saw smoke in the distance. I think it's coming from the mill. Did you come that way?"

"*Oui*," said Dominique.

"*Non*," Colton said, at the same time, his deeper voice overshadowing hers. "We went for a swim upstream. Pay us no mind," he stated, lightheartedly in French to the women. "We didn't think anyone would find us returning home at this hour."

Dominique twisted and saw his gray eyes twinkle with mischief. She then watched in disbelief as the matrons started giggling like schoolgirls.

"I remember those days, swimming in the Seine with my young beau," said the one who held the horse's reins. "Don't you, Giselle?"

Her travel companion Giselle nodded, enthusiastically. "Oh, *oui*, Bernadette. I wish my Pierre still were able to do so. Alas, he has arthritis, and my legs aren't as good as they used to be."

"Well, we had better get home to tell the young men to see about that mill. The smoke is black. It has to be fire."

Dominique tried to wiggle out of Colton's iron grip. "Madames, I need your help."

But Bernadette and Giselle were too busy eyeing the smoke in the distance. Bernadette dismissed her statement with a light wave. "Oh, *ma cherie*, you have everything you need beside you, holding your hand in his. Isn't that right, monsieur?"

The engineer gave her a rakish smile that could melt the heart of winter, were it January instead of August. "Of course, *demoiselles*."

The old women giggled again, delighted at being referred to as young, virginal damsels.

"We must return to our village. The men may be on their way to douse the fire now. *Bonjour*, young lovers." Giselle waved as the cart started off again. The other woman drove faster, now that she knew the flour mill was on fire.

Dominique wanted to stamp in a fit of frustration.

The engineer leaned in and spoke low in her ear. "That's what I love about you French women. So passionate and romantic."

She ignored how her ear tickled upon hearing his strong tenor spoken so closely and how warm and solid his body was against hers. She wiggled her hand out of his and stomped on his foot. "That is a tale for tourists."

He drew in air, then exhaled through the pain. "Those sweet older ladies proved you wrong."

"You fooled them into thinking we were lovers. That is the very last thing I would ever consider of you, especially after what you've done to my mission."

The chain linked them a bit too closely. Every time his arm brushed hers, a heated sensation warmed her still-damp skin. He took her hand again, concealing the chain between their palms. "Hand in hand, we'll stroll through Le Havre and down to the docks like the young French lovers we pretend to be."

"That is one cover I will not assume." Dominique unlaced her fingers from his, hating that she was still attached to him nonetheless. "I'll be sure to introduce you to more ways we Bureau agents deal with unexpected embraces."

"As much as I look forward to your instruction, we have a ship to catch." He quickened his pace along the path.

Chapter 3

When the COIC ordered Colton to sabotage Broussard's flour mill and track down Bureau agent Dominique Fontaine, he thought the latter would be a breezy let-up from his last days of apprenticing as a ship's engineer. How little he knew.

Based on the intelligence information that he read about her in the COIC dossier, she seemed like a pleasant enough mademoiselle. Age twenty-one, born and raised in the quiet French village of Chay Oiseau, eldest daughter of a family of bakers. Studied cooking—*culinary arts*—it was so fancifully called, briefly in Paris. Quaint description. Charming, all of it.

She even looked charming in person when he spotted her leaving Chay Oiseau early that morning to go work at the mill. About average height, with generous curves tucked into the dull mill uniform of white blouse, dark skirt and apron, that did little justice for her winsome form, she walked a proud carriage through the village center.

It'll be a piece of cake to bring her to Le Havre for questioning, Colton had thought, as he watched her from behind a firewood cart before following her to the mill.

Of course, that was before she pinched the dickens out of his hand, nearly broke his foot, and tossed him in the dirt like a wrestler twice her size. The COIC dossier might have mentioned that she was schooled in the defensive arts.

He didn't even want to get started on the sleep gas in the glass handle of that knife she kept stored in her corset.

Ah, well. At least he got control of the situation eventually.

He spared a glance at his newfound acquaintance as she walked beside him on the road to Le Havre. Chin-length black hair framed a heart-shaped face that was bottled tight with unexpressed emotion, all of it vexed and bothered. A frown marked her high, ivory brow. Her red lips set in a firm line of aggravation. The effect dimpled her small chin as she stuck it out.

"I much liked your face better when you were at the mill. It was all business and no anger."

Dominique hooded her large brown eyes and looked up at him through sooty lashes. "You mean, before you bungled my mission?"

And so it went again. "You must get past that. It'll make the trip to town go faster if we can speak civil to each other."

She stared ahead at the road. "Do you always feel the need to chatter so?" she asked in her velvet-laced accent.

"You might want to get used to talking. The COIC Secretary has many questions to ask you."

Sunlight dappled through the tree canopy overhead, making patterns of light play across her hair. "I don't understand why your agency wants to question me. I am no criminal. All of my work has been centered on finding Broussard and bringing him to justice."

Colton wanted that, too. Badly. He recently learned things about Broussard's involvement in London industry that shed light on his own past. It explained why Colton had been forced to live the life he did without his mother, staying in orphanages until he was seventeen.

If he had known Broussard would be making an inspection at the mill today, he would have attempted to capture the industrialist instead of sabotaging the mill's machinery. But even then, he would have needed to find a way to go up against the passel of lackeys that formed Broussard's bodyguards. Colton hated coming so close to capturing him and demanding answers, but failing just the same. Broussard seemed to always get away.

He hoped Dominique and her agency would provide the COIC with their collected information to help find and capture Broussard, but as of that moment, Agent Fontaine did not appear to be in any mood for conversation. "Your agency and mine share the same goal," Colton told her. "They both want Broussard behind bars."

"For completely different reasons," she rebuffed him, as he expected. "The Bureau de l'Industrie wants to stop Broussard from creating poor working conditions and cheating people out of a fair, respectable living. The

COIC wants Broussard only to stop him from discovering inventions before they do. I heard about your agency's race to dismantle his spy ring in Liverpool."

Apparently, her agency also maintained up-to-date dossiers, even if they got the names a little confused. "You mean London."

She lifted her free hand loosely in indifference. "My point is that New Britannia has been rivals with France since the turn of the century."

"You have that reversed. France renewed the age-old rivalry. Your country's been chomping at the bit for New Britannia's industry ever since Napoleon saw our steam-powered artillery in the wars."

She shook her head. "Your understanding of politics is flawed, Agent Smythe."

"Call me Colton."

She called him nothing by saying just as much in reply.

Colton tried again, this time attempting to leave behind the sore topic of rival nations. "Dominique, your meeting the COIC Secretary has nothing to do with our nations' histories."

"Why should I trust you?"

That was one of her favorite questions, he noted. It was also a good one. Colton tried to think of an answer to it, one that took his actions of chasing and handcuffing her into positive consideration. He couldn't come up with anything. "Suffice it to say, you have my word. You'll see when you get there."

She *tsked*. "You will have to do better than that."

Best leave her be for now. Maybe once they reached the ship waiting for them at Le Havre's port, she'd see things differently. Or maybe not. She was quite stubborn. Either way, he completed his mission by bringing her to the COIC Secretary.

Colton reached for Dominique's hand as they arrived at the outskirts of Le Havre. The coastal French city bustled with commerce as merchants and sailors conducted business in the markets and loading docks. Making sure the cuff chain was hidden snugly, he circumvented the main thoroughfare and led her to the port. They walked past the throng of citizens and foreigners.

"There's the ship, *The Enlightened.*" He pointed with his right hand to a three-masted carrack tied to the third landing at the docks.

Dominique's hand grew rigid in his.

"As I said," he attempted to reassure her, "we only wish to talk to you. You won't be harmed or taken to London headquarters."

"You bring me here in restraints and then tell me your agency merely wishes to have a *tete a tete?*"

He didn't know what that last phrase meant, but it sounded awfully sarcastic.

He met the captain of *The Enlightened*, his friend and fellow COIC agent Rhys Cartret, at the landing. "Captain," he greeted.

"I was just about to come after you. You're late."

"I had a bit of resistance at the mill."

"Your appearance is somewhat telling." Captain Rhys gave a nodding glance to his dirt-stained, damp clothes. "You made sure that none of the workers were harmed, didn't you?"

"Yes, all were out before the flames spread. But my delay actually had to do with another fiery sort. Captain Rhys, may I present Agent Fontaine."

"*Bonjour*, mademoiselle," the captain greeted her diplomatically. "If you would follow me to the navigation room onboard the ship, we can begin the discussions."

Dominique didn't immediately follow Captain Rhys as he turned to go up the gangplank. Colton had to give her hand a tug to coax her along. He surmised that they made a funny pair to onlookers, holding hands as they went single file up the gangplank.

Colton's fellow crewmembers observed him on deck. The bosun Malcolm Clark had a telling look of annoyance on his face about bringing a woman on board. The salty sailor considered all members of the fairer sex to be bad luck at sea, including the captain's wife, who was stationed somewhere about the ship.

McNamara, Colton's fellow engineer with whom he was apprenticed, shot a grin as he looked from Dominique to him. *This is not what you think*, Colton wanted to say aloud.

Across the deck and up the quarterdeck they went to the navigation room. Inside the small space that housed charts, maps, and navigational instruments, the COIC Secretary waited at the table. Seated next to him was a man with salt and pepper hair, dressed in an inconspicuous morning suit of light gray. Colton didn't recognize him.

But Dominique did. She drew to attention immediately.

The COIC Secretary spoke. "Welcome back, Agent Smythe. This is

Agent Joubert, head of the Bureau de l'Industrie. He's here to take part in our discussion with Agent Fontaine."

Colton felt the chain on the handcuffs become taut as Dominique freed her hand from his grasp and stepped in front of him. She was forced to stand at an odd angle.

"*Agente* Joubert, what is going on?" she asked her superior in French.

Colton wanted to know as well. He had assumed that the COIC would be speaking alone with Dominique aboard the ship. To let the head of a rival French agency onto what accounted as British soil was a risky exercise.

"My apologies for being unable to give you advance notice of the change in situation, Agent Fontaine," Agent Joubert replied to her in English. Colton guessed he did so out of respect for everyone else in the little room. "We're in a hurry. Please, sit down so we can begin."

Captain Rhys closed the door. "It's going to get a little stuffy in here, but we can't have anyone on the docks overhearing."

Colton suffered another terse tug upon the chain as Dominique presented their linked wrists to Agent Joubert. "Would you please tell this man to release me immediately?"

Agent Joubert, the COIC Secretary, and Captain Rhys saw the cuffs for the first time. All three men looked upon Colton with disapproval.

The Secretary, a seasoned agent himself, remarked coolly, "Agent Smythe, I thought you would have informed Agent Fontaine as to the reason for her visit. The use of those new standard issue restraints is unnecessary."

Colton defended his choice to utilize them. "With all due respect, sir, she didn't believe me when I told her that you wished to talk to her peacefully. She refused to come along."

Dominique swung her gaze to him. "Not only are you an agent of New Britannia, but you are a complete stranger. I can't trust you to be who you say you are after you impersonate a civilian engineer and set fire to a mill."

Colton fished in the leather pouch at his belt for the key to the handcuffs. "I already told you why I did it, but I'll say it again for your superior's benefit."

"I already know," said Agent Joubert. "The COIC Secretary stated that in addition to finding Agent Fontaine, your orders were to sabotage Broussard's modes of commerce."

Colton freed Dominique's hand from the cuffs. He pulled out a chair for her and remained standing behind it. "I found more reason, sir. He wanted to give the female workers additional labor by turning his flour mill into a secret brothel."

Agent Joubert shook his head in disgust. "When we catch Broussard, I will make sure that his abused workers have justice. The ones that aren't purposely engaging in the schemes with him, I should say. My agents seized the mill overseer Delacroix upon his arrival into the city just before you two arrived. He's being interrogated at Bureau headquarters."

Dominique rubbed her wrist. "What about Broussard? He and Delacroix left the mill at the same time."

"Broussard was there?" The Secretary's eyes shot to Colton. "How did you let him get away?"

"Uh-oh," Dominique mumbled, realizing that she got him in trouble.

Sometimes the COIC official rode on such a high horse that Colton was tempted to remind the man of how long it had been since he'd seen action in the field. Times had changed since the days of criminals pillaging villages with axes and pitchforks.

However, he kept his voice level as he explained his actions. "Broussard had bodyguards with him. I couldn't stop them on my own, much as I wanted to. My guess is he's taken one of the back roads into the surrounding villages. He may have already left the area by way of the river."

"But why are we conjecturing when we could be pursuing him?" asked Dominique.

"It's time for all of us to reevaluate our strategies, Agent Fontaine." Captain Rhys folded his arms, leaning against the door.

"Agent Cartret is right," said the Secretary. "Both of our agencies want to capture Broussard because of the industrial crimes and robber baron practices he's committed within the past year, but neither France nor New Britannia has been able to do so."

"Your agency dismantled his spy ring in London a few months ago, if I understand correctly," said Agent Joubert.

"The COIC has defused Broussard's hold in London, but it hasn't stopped him from trying to gain more of our scientific and industrial pursuits abroad. His agenda has reached a scale that spans the Continent and the Mediterranean."

"Is he still after our holdings in the Mediterranean?" asked Colton, intentionally not mentioning the specifics in front of the two Bureau agents.

"You may speak freely before our French collaborators, Agent Smythe. I've already informed Agent Joubert of the matter." The Secretary gave an inclusive nod to the Bureau official and Dominique. "If you mean the automatons and the voice-responsive iron ore and copper alloys from Aspasia, then yes. Broussard's hired men stole a shipment of them from one of our other trade ships en route from the island this past July."

Colton groaned, having clear recollection of all that he, Captain Rhys, and the rest of *The Enlightened* crew endured last year in order to procure those self-operating machines and their parts from the small island kingdom. The ordeal involved an attack by pirates, a storm at sea, an untrustworthy diplomat lord, and a broken ship's engine. That wasn't accounting for the brief mutiny that persuaded Captain Rhys to replace several members of his crew with automatons.

"How big was the shipment?" he asked.

"One automaton and about five hundred pounds' worth of copper and iron ore," Captain Rhys voiced, with regret. "Broussard's men let the crew go after taking the one thing they needed."

They were much nicer to that crew than they were to *The Enlightened,* Colton mused, wryly. Must have been a different set of pirates. "No telling what Broussard could build using the metals, especially now that he has one of the automatons."

Dominique turned to frown specifically at him. She shook her head in confusion. "I'm afraid I am lost. I've never heard of Aspasia. What are these strange vocal metals you speak of?"

"Voice-responsive," Colton corrected her. "It's a little complicated to explain."

"But what does it have to do with Broussard's illegal business practices and attempt to create a brothel right here in northern France?"

The COIC Secretary answered her. "There was a scientific discovery in Aspasia last year that enabled New Britannia to make automatons that could interpret vocal commands. Also, one of our affiliates was able to use the metals to design weapons and body armor that respond to the wearer's vitals."

"Broussard wanted to get a hold of these devices and the metals to exploit them," Agent Joubert said. "You've only been handling this from a limited domestic theater, Agent Fontaine. I haven't briefed you or given you clearance to pursue Broussard on a wider scale. Until now. France will partner with New Britannia's Cabinet of Intellectual Curiosities to stop Broussard once and for all."

Colton watched Dominique's expression go from confusion to surprise. He was sure his face did the same. Work with the French? The Secretary said nothing before about an international partnership. He thought it was just going to be a trade of information.

"The rivalries between New Britannia and France are still strong," Agent Joubert continued, "but it's time we put our differences aside, at least for this task. We will need agents who've already succeeded in going undercover and infiltrating one of Broussard's mills. That would be you and the COIC's Agent Smythe."

Chapter 4

Dominique glanced over her shoulder at Colton before addressing her superior. Did she just hear what she thought she heard? Work with the British? "Agent Joubert, what are you proposing exactly?"

Agent Joubert clarified. "I'm proposing an alliance that may enable us to finally capture Broussard. You and Agent Smythe will pool your resources and work alongside each other to infiltrate another suspected facility."

Colton put his hands on the back of her chair. "Where? Here in Le Havre?"

"*Non*, west of here in Bretagne, near Saint-Brieuc. *Capitaine* Rhys, if you would assist me with a visual."

Dominique watched as the captain came away from the door. He stopped near her seat. "Agent Fontaine, if you wouldn't mind moving your hands from the table."

She withdrew her hands and placed them in her lap. The captain hit a button underneath the table's mahogany panel. She heard a soft scrape of wood before the table's plain surface turned over, revealing a sprawling map of the known world.

Agent Joubert thanked the captain and continued. "My Bureau outpost agents are located in a small hamlet about three towns west of Saint-Brieuc. They've reported seeing more shipping vessels sailing past the bay." He pointed to the specific area of northwest France on the map. "They have reason to believe that increased productivity has occurred in a small nearby metal foundry along the Gouet river valley. That is the only production facility in the area for miles."

She gazed at the map, recognizing Saint-Brieuc from having visited there a few years ago on holiday with her parents and younger brothers. The rest of the territory was unfamiliar. "Do you believe the increased productivity may be because of Broussard? I wonder what he's making now."

"Whatever it is, he has been known to favor manufacturing facilities outside of villages and hamlets where there are less people to take notice. There is little more outside of Saint-Brieuc than smaller towns, pastoral lands and coasts."

"Saint-Brieuc is also far enough from a large city," Captain Rhys added. "Ships can slip in and out of the bay easily."

"If Broussard is secretly moving goods from there, we don't want to alert him by having the ships inspected. They carry multiple goods to different businesses, anyway. Do you understand why we must find out what is being made in that foundry, and for whom?"

Agent Joubert posed the question to both Dominique and Colton, but Dominique was the first to respond. This was her first mission away from home. It was also her first mission where she had to work with someone else, a man from New Britannia at that. She had more than a few reservations. "It could take time for us to establish ourselves in the area."

The COIC Secretary puffed. "Let's hope it doesn't call for too much of an extensive stay. We've wasted enough time already. You both need to make sure you report your findings regularly. I assume you are familiar with Morse code and telegraphy, Agent Fontaine?"

Agent Joubert came to her defense. "You have nothing to worry about. Agent Fontaine is very proficient in the use of modern communications devices. She's shown adept learning in all her training since she has been with the Bureau."

Dominique appreciated her superior's gracious comment. It managed to unravel some of the Secretary's brusqueness towards her.

"What comes after we report our findings?" Colton asked his superior.

"Leave that to us. We'll send further instructions." The Secretary rose from his chair. "But I'll caution you. This mission will have you working in the field without immediate access to the COIC or the Bureau. Maintain your cover at all times. You'll be issued field equipment for defense, in case it becomes necessary to use."

Even though Dominique was anxious about the new mission, she couldn't let her feelings get the better of her. She looked up at Colton. He didn't appear to harbor the same unease as she did concerning their shared assignment.

"Guess you'll have to deal with me for longer than you thought," he remarked, with a carefree smile. Dominique refrained from expressing her choice words in the respectable company of both their superiors.

Agent Joubert stood alongside the COIC Secretary. "You've both been briefed. Captain Rhys will proceed from here. Go back to your village and gather what you need for the journey, Agent Fontaine. You and your new partner will set sail for Saint-Brieuc tonight."

***

"I am deeply and thoroughly confused."

Dominique walked into her village of Chay Oiseau that evening, flanked by her new partner. The smell of smoke from the mill fire lingered in the air from where it blew upwind. On the way home, she had spotted only the faint glow of dying fires in the distance. At least most of the flames had been doused sometime prior that afternoon, thanks to the mill's proximity to the Seine and the efforts of local villagers.

"One minute I'm following orders to expose one of Broussard's illegally-run mills," she continued talking to Colton. "The next minute I'm being told by my superior that I must work with you to go undercover and gather intelligence."

Colton shrugged. "*C'est la vie.* Agency officials are prone to surprises."

Did nothing unnerve him? He possessed a laissez faire attitude that she wished she could cultivate to ease her worries about their new mission. "Aren't you the least bit confounded?"

"It's simple." Colton swung his head left and right to take in the surroundings of the picturesque, quiet village she called home. Dusk began to paint the sky in blush tones. "The Secretary and Agent Joubert want us to work together. I don't see what else there is to be confused about."

"This talk of Aspasia and its metals, for one. Or is that two? Anyway, whatever your agency found on that Mediterranean island, you certainly did a good job of concealing it from the rest of the world."

"Word died down after the initial discovery. The COIC has a way of making news disappear or seem like a passing fad."

"And they only give away just enough information for the Bureau to work with them." Another reason why she didn't fully trust the idea of collaborating with the COIC. Or Colton. He may give the impression of a nonchalant engineer just doing his job and following orders, but something told her that he knew more about this Aspasian puzzle than he let on. More about Broussard, for that matter. A quiet intensity burned behind those mischievous gray eyes of his. Colton possessed a jovial spirit, but he was certainly no laughing fool.

Dominique hated feeling out of sorts when it came to her information, and right now, Colton, his agency, even Agent Joubert, all possessed more knowledge of Broussard's criminal footprints than she did. "If you would, bring me up to speed about Broussard's activities abroad."

"We can talk more about it later onboard *The Enlightened*, after you tie up all your loose ends here," Colton replied. "But you need to pack your bags quickly. The longer we linger, the more the locals will get suspicious. They're already gawking at us."

"I am a local, Colton. They're gawking at you, not me."

"Most of it's coming from the ladies." He returned a wave to one woman who pumped water from the village well.

Dominique knew her as the butcher's wife. The woman giggled before resuming her task. Her action was repeated by another impressionable young lady that Colton passed.

"This isn't a bad spot, really. I think I could like French provincial life. I've never gotten this kind of reaction before in London."

Dominique wanted to roll her eyes. "They are paying attention to you because of how you look. No one in Chay Oiseau has ginger hair."

"Was that a compliment as to my uniqueness?" A corner of his mouth tilted up in a boyish smirk.

Dominique looked away. "Don't flatter yourself. It was a simple fact. My family's house is up ahead." She indicated to a modest red-roof structure with a stone and brick façade, situated between two buildings that formerly housed the village's cheese shop and dressmaker's.

A brief sadness passed over Dominique as she allowed herself to look at the addition to her residence, a dormant building that once was home to the Boulangerie Fontaine, the family bakery. "You should probably wait in the square until I get back."

Colton's smirk disappeared, replaced by a serious countenance. "We're supposed to stay together. I'm still not convinced you've warmed to the idea of us being partners."

"I am not going to run off. I may prefer to work alone, but I will follow Agent Joubert's orders."

Colton's drawn brows showed that he remained unconvinced.

Dominique employed another attempt at persuasion. "I live with my parents and two brothers. My family cannot see you."

"They don't know that you're an agent?"

"They know I work as an industrial spy for the Bureau de l'Industrie."

"Well, then they know how an agency's plans and missions for you can change." He started to walk towards the house.

She put a hand to his chest, stopping him in his tracks. "Still, it's better that I go to the door alone. I wouldn't want them to think that I was suddenly packing to run off with a man I just met."

"But that's exactly what you're doing, mademoiselle."

So it was, to an extent. Dominique returned her hands to her sides, though the warmth from coming into contact with him didn't leave her fingertips. "You know what I mean. Let me say my temporary goodbyes without causing more disruption than I have to. You can watch me from the front windows, if it will put your mind at ease."

"Fair enough." Colton went to the cobblestone square and took a seat on one of the iron-wrought benches. He tossed a casual glance at her family's house. "I'll be watching."

"Or you could busy yourself by thinking of matrons to flirt with and call damsels again."

"You almost sound as though you envy the attention I gave kindly Giselle and her companion Bernadette."

"I've already received more than my fair share of your attention. I'll be back. Please do not talk to the butcher's wife. Her husband is very good with an axe." Dominique left him in the square and walked up to her residence.

She spared yet another wistful glance at the building next door. Her family members weren't the only business owners whose stores had closed. The same was repeated throughout the village. She looked at the apothecary shop and the former tavern beside it, all bought out by Broussard through cunning and trickery.

She put her key in the lock and turned it. Her sixteen year-old brother Fabian greeted her when she opened the door.

"You're safe," he breathed a sigh of relief. "Antoine and I went to the mill this afternoon in search of you when the fire struck. Everyone else returned to their villages except you."

Dominique embraced him. "I went to Le Havre to talk to Agent Joubert." That was very true, even if she did leave a few things out. She stepped through the door. Expecting to smell fresh-baked bread to go along with supper, she noticed that the dining table was empty. "Where are *maman* and *papa*?"

"Still selling food at the market in Le Havre. They left early this morning before the fire started." Fabian shut the door. "What happened to you? You look like you've been doused and left to dry outside."

Dominique could always count on her youngest brother to provide the cold, honest truth, even when she didn't ask for it. She pieced together an explanation of her condition without mentioning her run-in with Colton. "The bolting machine caught fire at the mill. It should have been cleaned and repaired a long time ago. I had to swim through the river to escape the mill flames."

"Why didn't you come back home soon afterward then?" Her other brother Antoine walked in from the kitchen. "Did you get lost in the woods?"

"No, *mon frère*, I didn't get lost in the woods." Dominique ruffled his curly hair, knowing how much he detested her doing so.

He swatted her hand away. "You ran off to complete another mission, didn't you?" he stated, with all the gravity and sage knowledge of his seventeen years. "I bet the Bureau set the mill on fire, don't you think, Fabian?"

"It's possible," said Fabian.

Antoine finished smoothing his hair. "We wanted to help the Bureau find Broussard, too, and get back at him for what he did to our family's business."

"It's not revenge as much as it is about bringing him to justice," Dominique reminded.

"Your words and mine mean the same thing. But we still wanted to be agents." Antoine wouldn't let it go.

"You'll have to be content to be bakers for now. You know that the

Bureau doesn't hire children. Now, I have to pack some things and be off." She made for her bedroom.

Antoine blocked her from going forward. "Where are you off to? The mill just burnt to the ground. You're out of work."

"I can't tell you."

"It's another secret mission," said Fabian. His brown eyes got large as he looked at Dominique. "Tell us where you are going."

"You know I can't. Agency orders." Dominique dodged Antoine and went to her room. She got on her knees beside the bed and pulled a leather satchel out from underneath the mattress. It was her supplies that she always kept packed in advance with clothing, toiletries, and money for leaving at a moment's notice.

She went to her wardrobe chest and pulled out her folded travel dress and stuffed it into the satchel as well. No time to change out of her mill uniform now, but hopefully, there would be somewhere private on *The Enlightened* to do so.

Her brothers barged into the room. "Why can't you tell us where you're going?" asked Antoine.

"You know why."

"What are we to tell our parents?" Fabian queried.

"The truth." Dominique hoisted the satchel over one shoulder. "When our parents return home, tell them that I went on a mission for the Bureau. Also tell them I love them and will be back soon." *I hope soon*, she added silently. "I love you both." She kissed each brother on the cheek before going to the front door.

She went out and shut the door behind her before she had a chance to look back. She didn't know when she would see Antoine or Fabian again, nor did she want to fully consider how dangerous her new mission truly was. The uncertainty of what she was going to face, and how, left her with an uneasy feeling.

"Take care of each other," she whispered, as though addressing all of her family members. Dominique wiped her eye where a tear came to the brink of falling.

Chapter 5

Gathering herself and her belongings, Dominique returned to the village square.

Colton remained on the bench where she had left him. He reclined on it as though it was a hammock, his long legs taking up the full length while his boots hung over one side. "I was about to come in after you when the door closed."

"I had to get my belongings and say goodbye to my brothers. I'm ready to leave if you are."

He jumped to his feet. "I'll carry your bag."

"*Merci.* How kind of you." She handed it to him as they began walking out of Chay Oiseau. Dominique smelled supper coming from the ovens of the other village homes. She took in the scent of the regional herbs of rosemary and lavender used to season the food.

"I noticed most of the shops in the village have closed down," Colton said.

"You have Broussard to thank for that. About two years ago, he bought out most of Chay Oiseau's shops from its local owners. We were told that he needed the coal supply of the village diverted to power the light and machines of the new flour mill. In return for our contribution," Dominique heard the bitterness in her tone upon using the word, "we were to receive a share of the mill's profits. I'll leave you to imagine how well that went."

"Broussard didn't keep his word," Colton ventured to guess, as they started out again on the road to the coastal city.

"That is putting it mildly. My family refused to sell their business but had to close it anyway. We owned a boulangerie, what we like to think was the best bakery in this part of France. Our breads and pastries would sell for a high price in the markets of Le Havre every day. Now my parents go there once a week, if that, and sell whatever we can bake from our small oven at home." Dominique looked back at the village as she put more and more distance between it and herself. "Some of our neighbors were forced out of their homes. They left the village for other parts and we've not heard from them since."

"Why didn't your family leave?"

"Where would we have gone? It costs more to establish a permanent business in Le Havre rather than it does to sell at a stall in the market. Besides, we couldn't bear to leave Chay Oiseau."

"You did briefly. You went to a cooking school in Paris."

She blinked and looked up at Colton in surprise. "How did you know that?"

He gave her a side glance. "I read your dossier before I went to the mill. I guess the COIC Secretary got it from Agent Joubert earlier."

Why didn't she receive Colton's dossier, then? Dominique was starting not to like his agency's official. The Secretary seemed terse and withholding. She didn't know how Agent Joubert was going to deal with him. "I went to cooking school last year to become a pastry chef. I wanted to enhance my skills for the family bakery, but I had to come home early when my family no longer had enough money to pay for my room and board."

The evening shadows began to form in the woods, but Dominique was still able to see Colton's face. "I guess the bigger industry gets, the more men like Broussard can take away all people have," he commented softly. The poignancy of his statement made it sound as though he knew from personal experience what it was like to lose something highly valued.

"The Bureau has done well to catch other robber barons, but it's never been able to charge Broussard with a crime. He makes sure that little can truly be traced back to him."

"But everyone in your village knows that he cheated them out of their businesses. That's not enough proof?"

Dominique moved her head side to side. "Broussard sent a representative to Chay Oiseau to buy some of our businesses and rights to use of our coal. No one protested at the time because the payment was large. That is, until we learned that it would be the only payment we would receive from him. This was before his criminal mark became well-known as it is today."

"What did the Bureau do about it?"

"It could do nothing at first because some of us in the village agreed to sell. Broussard left no contracts, no papers to trace. That's why I volunteered to assist Agent Joubert when he came to the village last year and questioned the business owners. I want to restore Chay Oiseau's way of life."

Colton said nothing. Dominique wondered if she went on for too long.

They walked in silence on the main road to the city, passing merchants who were leaving the Le Havre markets for the day. Her mother and father were usually two of the very last to leave their market stall. Still, she looked for them among the passerby, wanting to see them again before she went on her mission, even if she couldn't draw attention to herself in the open by stopping to tell them goodbye.

Her parents were not among the other merchants. Dominique resigned herself to continuing into the city without a parting glance at them.

Once she and Colton passed the outskirts and headed for the docks, she said, "I'm sorry."

Colton turned his head away from the gaslights along the boardwalk. "For what?"

"You've come all the way from London to catch Broussard for widespread crimes, and here I am, telling you how he caused my family to lose business and shut down our bakery. You must think I'm very simple and provincial."

"No, he robbed you of your business. I'd be angry, too."

His understanding and the way he gave validation to her cause made her feel a little more comfortable about working with him.

Colton looked out to the water as the darkening sky turned its surface an opaque gray. "Broussard ruined lives in many places." His voice trailed as though he recalled a memory of old.

Dominique noticed another telling sign on his face. The subject of Broussard did hold personal significance with him. "Why did you take part in this mission?"

"I'm a COIC agent. I dedicate my time and service to New Britannia."

"I know, but I meant when it comes to Broussard. Did he take something from you, too?"

A steam whistle sounded from the landing where *The Enlightened* was docked.

"The ship's about to cast off. We'd better get onboard." He switched her satchel to his other shoulder and trod faster onward.

"Slow down." Dominique picked up her feet as well. He knew the ship wasn't going to cast off without them. What did she say to make him abruptly take off?

The Enlightened's engine idled at the landing. Dominique felt its dynamism as she walked up the gangplank. The wood carried a soft vibration, thrumming with the energy transmitting from the merchant ship. Dominique looked across the deck and saw what looked to be part of a black motor exposed. At the stern of the ship, she spotted Captain Rhys and another figure at the wheel. The figure looked strange from the back, as though it wore a suit of heavy armor plates.

"We're back," Colton announced to the captain, making his way to him. Dominique followed, her eyes still on the armored man.

Both the captain and the armored man turned after Colton spoke. Dominique recoiled with a cry. The man in armor was not human at all, but a machine. Its face was a mask of solid metal, eyeless, with no features. Its hands and limbs were all fashioned of iron and steel, with joints of brass winking in the glow of the deck's small, iron-caged lights.

"Don't tell me you've never seen an automaton before." Colton returned to a state of good humor. An amused smile appeared on his face.

Dominique straightened, where, in reflex, she had altered her stance in preparation to flee.

Other crewmembers of the ship had stopped their activity upon her outburst and now observed her. Some had laughing expressions. Others had annoyed ones, for her having startled them. She cleared her throat and pretended to ignore the sudden attention placed upon her.

"There are no automatons in or near Le Havre," she explained. "I've heard that most are abroad aiding the legionnaires' campaigns, or in large factories in central and southern France."

"No automatons to help shape the bread dough in Paris cooking schools?" Colton asked, clearly enjoying himself.

She wrinkled her nose. "Do not be silly. What person in their right mind would eat something made by a machine?"

The automaton's head moved as it followed the sound of her voice. Dominique stiffened as she saw her reflection in its face plate.

"I apologize for the Aspasian automaton frightening you," Captain Rhys took control of the embarrassing scene. "New Britannia has continued widespread use of them in factories and front lines of the battlefield, too. Now we're testing them to function as part of a ship's crew. They can mop the decks, move crates, man the wheel."

"But we haven't tested them in the engine room yet," Colton added.

"I suppose you would want someone who's not highly flammable." Dominique heard the gears turning fast inside the automaton. Did the crew not worry about the machine overheating? She wanted to back away from it, but stayed her ground. She already revealed that she had never seen an automaton before. There was no need to make the COIC agents, Colton, especially, think her inexperienced and unfit to take part in the mission.

Captain Rhys said lightly, "Just don't let my wife hear you discussing the limitations of her machines."

"Don't let your wife hear what?" A feminine voice interrupted.

Dominique saw a tall, brunette woman of Mediterranean descent emerge from the door leading below deck. Dressed in a linen shirt, a workman's vest, black pants, and boots, she walked across the deck and came to stand at Captain Rhys' side.

He put a possessive arm about her slim waist. "May I introduce Lydia Cartret, my wife, better half, brilliant machinist, and inventor of the revolutionary voice-responsive automaton you see before you."

"Rhys, I think she got the point." Lydia's cheeks bronzed at his lavish praise. She leaned into him in a small embrace. It was obvious that she and the captain were very fond of each other.

Dominique was surprised to meet the inventor of the automaton. She was even more surprised—and pleased—that the inventor was female, something that was relatively unheard of in France. "You invented an automaton that hears orders?" she asked. "I thought that they could only be wound up like a clock and set loose."

She thought she saw Colton hide a smile.

"It not only registers orders, but obeys them," the captain's wife replied, her Greek accent making Dominique think of the automaton's Aspasian origins.

"They obey orders most of the time, is what she means to say," Captain Rhys added. A teasing look passed between him and his wife before he turned and shouted an order for the crew to cast off.

Colton set Dominique's satchel down. He went to a series of levers on the wall beside the topside door and raised one. The ship's engine went from a hum to a steady rumble.

He pulled another lever and cranked a handle. A chain wench built into the deck began to retract until the anchor emerged from the water. The other crewmen went to their stations, securing loose items on deck and unfurling the sails. Dominique watched as they all functioned as one efficient unit.

The ship gave a small heave as it began moving away from the landing. Dominique shifted to regain her balance as she bumped against the rail.

The captain told the automaton to steer. The machine obeyed, gripping the wheel and turning it at quarter intervals. Slowly but surely, *The Enlightened* began making its way from the port of Le Havre to the open waters of the Channel.

Dominique rubbed her elbow. She was now in New Britannia's water and on its soil, represented by the ship. Even though her country was still in view just behind her, it didn't change the fact that she was the sole French citizen on board.

"And what is your name?" Lydia asked Dominique, while the men were working.

Dominique realized that she hadn't introduced herself. "I'm Dominique Fontaine. I'm an agent with the Bureau de l'Industrie."

"Rhys told me that the COIC Secretary and a French official met in the navigation room to have a discussion about Broussard."

Dominique stole another glance at Colton, who now helped another crewmate. "The French official is my commanding officer, Agent Joubert. I was at the meeting, too. I'll be working with Agent Smythe."

Lydia nodded. "Broussard's tactics keep getting worse. I had no idea who he was a little more than a year ago, but since I've left Aspasia, all I hear about is how he's stolen inventions, bought out factories, and hired more criminals."

At that last statement, Captain Rhys turned back to the two of them. "Lydia is quite familiar with Broussard's schemes. Upon her first trip from Aspasia, he hired pirates to steal the automatons she brought aboard *The*

Enlightened. We nearly lost the ship fighting them off."

Dominique raced to piece everything together. "So, if I'm to understand, Broussard wanted your automatons. He just stole one last month."

"Correct." Lydia nodded. "And I hate to think of what he can do with such a powerful machine."

If it was anything like the automaton steering the ship now, Dominique didn't want to think about it, either. "But what is all this talk of Aspasian alloys and iron ore, then? What do they have to do with anything?"

"They have to do with everything," Colton said, rejoining them at the stern. He dusted his hands on his pants. "Those metals can make mechanical devices respond to sounds. Broussard wants to put them into his own machinery and make a profit."

"I'll explain to her how the metals work," Lydia said. "But shouldn't Agent Fontaine be offered something to eat and a chance to refresh first? I'm sure all this talk is tiring, especially after what she went through today."

Dominique smiled at her in gratitude. Food and a hot bath would be welcome. She hadn't had anything to eat since breakfast. She appreciated Lydia's call for hospitality. Knowing that there was another female presence aboard the ship put some of her nerves at ease.

She caught Colton watching her. His eyebrows pulled down in concentration. "You look worried about something. Is it about going to Saint-Brieuc?"

She raked her thumbnail against her palm. "That may be part of it." What else could she say? Even though the captain was being civil towards her and the crew seemed to keep to themselves for the most part, she could tell that taking part in this shared mission wasn't easy for any of them.

It was also hard for Dominique to dispense with her long-held reservations about the British. As of that moment, her countrymen were battling soldiers of New Britannia in settlements abroad. Agent Joubert and the COIC Secretary may have pooled their resources together for this one mission, but theirs was still an uneasy truce.

And she and Colton were the ones who had to do all the work by carrying it out.

Dominique stilled her hands. *Zut alors,* she had a job to do. If the Bureau trusted her enough for the task, then she couldn't spend her time dwelling on national rivalries.

"You're not worried about me finding information first, are you?" Colton asked, humor lightening his countenance as he teased her.

But...a little friendly competition certainly wouldn't hurt.

She could show the COIC that the Bureau's agents were just as capable of nabbing Broussard. And she'd start with showing Colton. She lifted her chin high and answered his rousing question. "I was thinking about how best to complete the mission, not about soothing your pride when my information leads us to Broussard first."

He appeared as though he couldn't think of a quip fast enough to match hers. Her comment elicited a tiny laugh from Lydia.

"There will be time enough for you both to discuss your agenda," said Captain Rhys, struggling to contain a smile himself. "We won't arrive in Saint-Brieuc until the morning. Take my wife's advice and rest, Agent Fontaine. Smythe, I need you to work your shift in the engine room before you prepare to leave again."

"Aye, Captain." Colton turned on his boot heel to go below deck, but not before tossing a final look Dominique's way. "We'll speak later. I still have to issue you your field equipment."

Dominique could only guess what she was going to be issued from the COIC's coffers. If it was anything like the inventions and materials that had already been described to her, she'd better find a way to learn their methods of operation quickly or get left behind. She couldn't let France get left behind.

And as for her own pride, she certainly wouldn't let Agent Colton Smythe leave her in the dust on his way to catching Broussard.

"Come, Agent Fontaine," Lydia directed. "I'll show you where you may refresh yourself."

Dominique bent to pick up her satchel. When she rose again and looked back at Le Havre, the port city was a mere darkened smudge on the horizon.

Chapter 6

Colton turned his wrench to release the valve on the engine. He waited for the deluge of debris, kelp, and silt to come pouring out in the recess pipe. Maintaining a ship's engine was constant work.

The Enlightened's engine room was not a place for the fainthearted, or even simply for those who were prone to fainting. Steam constantly rose from the bottom of the grated metal floor to the ceiling as the engine churned to convert water into a source of power. The temperature in the room remained balmy at best, sweltering at worst.

Colton wiped his brow with the back of his protective leather gloves before pulling a switch to pump most of the bilge water out from the lower rungs of the ship.

"You're mighty quiet this evening," McNamara, his fellow engineer and mentor, yelled over the churning of the bilge pump.

"Just working, is all," Colton yelled back. His mind was elsewhere. On the mission. Broussard. Dominique.

McNamara started conversing as he tended to the cover on the air vents. "Malcolm's just about had it, I can tell you that. He's gotten used to having the captain's wife aboard every so often, but now, you bring another woman on the ship? Ha, I'm sure every tale of ruinous luck is swirling through his head."

"Dominique will be off the ship in a couple of hours. Then he can go back to complaining about the automatons working as part of the crew." Colton switched off the pump and picked up a mop and water bucket. He started to clean the floor of residual debris from the engine.

"No, Malcolm doesn't like automatons. Can't say I much do, either. Those faces with no eyes in them give me the shivers, they do. It would help if Mrs. Cartret had glued some glass ones on them, don't you think?"

"So long's they do what they're told and don't break down, I don't care what they look like."

"But you do care about how that little French agent girl looks. I've seen how you stare at her, boy." McNamara, twenty years his senior, gave a knowing smile and laughed.

Colton came up with a logical explanation for his actions. "She's liable to run off if she's not watched closely." And brandish sharp, pointy weapons that released sedation gases, but he let that point remain unspoken.

McNamara hooted with laughter again. "I'd believe that if we were on dry land. I don't think she wants to risk drowning in the Channel just to get away from you."

"She did try to get away from me by swimming upstream in the Seine."

"What?"

"Forget it." Colton wrung out the mop. Maybe he did stare at his new partner a little longer than he should have before. "I didn't think the crew would keep paying that much attention to us."

"After a year with us, you should know better. We sailors notice everything, particularly when a new person comes aboard."

And especially when that new person happened to be a pretty woman, Colton mused.

"You'll be having your hands full with her. I can tell already." McNamara tightened a bolt on one of the engine's ventilation hatches.

Colton dumped the dirty water down the recess drain and returned the bucket and mop to the room's corner.

"What's wrong, Smythe?" McNamara dropped his wrench back into the pocket of his leather apron. "You usually toss barbs right back. You know me and the crew only rile you because you're the youngest."

Colton sighed. "It isn't that. I've just got my mind on something else. And it's not Dominique. Well, not just on her, anyway."

"Is it the mission to track the scalawag Broussard?"

Colton paused at the industrialist's name. "It might be. And that report last week from the Scotland Yard archives I told you about."

"The report." McNamara let out a reflective sigh as he stood against the wall. He put all jesting aside. "I don't know how you remember that canning factory in London. You said you were only a boy at the time."

Colton removed his gloves and hooked them on the wall with the rest of the engineers' tools and protective gear. "But I was old enough to know Broussard owned the machine in the factory that caused my mum's accident."

McNamara halted at that. "Apologies. I was only asking about your mission. Didn't mean to stir other things up from the past and whatnot."

"You didn't. It's something that I've been thinking about." Colton stopped himself as he sensed something long-contained being dredged up. Anger, hurt, a bitter mixture of both. He made fists to suppress the emotions.

"Easy, Smythe. This is why I should've kept my yip shut."

"It's not your fault. You just asked a question." Colton slowly released his fists. He could tell McNamara didn't know what to say, and he felt bad for putting him in that spot, even if he hadn't intended to.

"You'd better get cleaned up and ready to go on your mission. We'll be reaching Saint-Brieuc in a few hours," the older engineer remarked, quietly.

One step closer to finding Broussard again. One step closer to confronting him. "I still have to issue Dominique her field equipment before we set out." Colton set one foot on the stairs.

"Smythe."

He turned.

McNamara paused, weighing his words. "You and Agent Fontaine do what you have to do for the mission, then come back in one piece. Don't risk your life to chase after the past. It's over."

He knew McNamara meant well, but it wasn't over. He'd barely gotten started tracking Broussard, and if he had known how he was tied to one of the man's earlier injustices, he would have gone after the robber baron a long time ago.

***

Dominique stretched her freshly-scrubbed limbs after putting on her ironed travel dress, still warm from its pressing.

She sat at the mahogany desk in the cabin. Captain Rhys and Lydia had

THE CURIOSITY CHRONICLES: BOOKS 1-3

graciously lent the room to her for a chance to rest for several hours. Residual steam from her shower filtered from the cabin's built-in water closet, complete with faucets. Only the most lavish of transports possessed such modern amenities. Dominique had to hand it to New Britannia's COIC in that regard. They spoiled their agents.

But the food was another story.

She looked down at a tray of food on the desk, dropped off by the ship's gruff bosun Malcolm. *Salmagundi*, he had called the unidentifiable, gelatinous mass on the plate as he handed it to her at the door almost an hour ago. Perhaps she should have consumed it before she bathed and changed clothes. Dominique stuck her fork into the middle of the mass and came up with a brown, wobbly substance that looked remotely of beef but smelled of old fish.

She dropped the utensil and the wobbly meat back into the middle of her plate and took a sip of water instead.

A knock sounded at the door. Dominique opened it. Lydia came in.

"Rhys says we've reached the northwestern region of France. We'll be at Saint-Brieuc at dawn if the ship keeps moving at this speed." Her gaze came to linger on the plate on the desk. "Did you want something else to eat?"

Dominique became embarrassed. "I'm not really that hungry."

Lydia nodded with understanding. "Sometimes I think Malcolm forces the newest person aboard to eat salmagundi as a rite of passage. The only person who seems to truly enjoy the dish is Smythe."

Dominique watched as the fork slowly began to tilt and sink into the salmagundi. "He's certainly not a picky eater, then."

"As much as he and the other crewmen eat, none of them can afford to be. But I promised to explain more about the Aspasian metals. We need to go to the cargo hold for me to do so."

Dominique followed Lydia out of the cabin and through the hallway. Sconce lights lined the wall. She could hear the waters of the Channel lapping the ship's hull from outside. Dominique looked to the walls, lined in metal. Water would have a hard time breaking through those rivets of steel and iron.

They reached the door to the second lower deck and went down the short set of stairs. A constant motor humming came from behind a vaulted door on Dominique's left. She guessed that to be the engine room.

323

Lydia pulled open a set of doors on the right. "This is the hold. When *The Enlightened* isn't on mission, it operates as a merchant ship."

Immediately, Dominique's nose filled with the fragrances of teas and spices, wood, and leather. She stepped through the door and saw crates upon crates stacked along the walls, as well as metal and wooden chests lined neatly along the floor. The low ceiling graduated into a dome apex at the room's center. Along the back wall, two faceless automatons stood dormant.

Lydia went to the first one on the left. "These automatons were crafted using iron and copper from Aspasia."

Dominique stood before the automaton and looked at her reflection through the machine's shiny face plate. "Why Aspasian metals and not those of other countries?"

"Aspasia's soil contains properties that enhance iron and copper's ability to conduct sound." Lydia reached around the automaton and came back with a thin copper wire in her hand. "The automatons register commands through a set of wires in their back panels."

Dominique would have been skeptical of the claim had she not seen Captain Rhys command an automaton before her very eyes. "The COIC Secretary said that Broussard stole copper and iron ore from Aspasia."

"And he wants much more than the supply he stole. Last month, the king of Aspasia sent word that more pirate ships were sailing near the island."

"They haven't succeeded in getting on the island, have they?"

"No. I left a few of these to guard the shore." Lydia tucked the wire back into the automaton and shut the panel. "But I'm going home to see my family. I'm worried for them. Aspasia's had pirate encounters before. If those men Broussard hired are brave enough to come so close to the island again, then they may planning an attack or raid in the future."

Dominique sighed. "Illegal mills in France. A spy ring in New Britannia. An interest in Aspasia. Broussard has too many cogs in his wheel."

"I hope you and Smythe get the evidence you need to lead us to him."

Dominique heard footsteps approach.

Colton came to stand in the doorway. "We're coming upon Saint-Brieuc in thirty minutes."

He had changed out of his former clothes into a white button-down shirt, navy pants, and utilitarian leather waistcoat. The waistcoat looked a bit stiff, as though it were lined with a coarse material. He donned a pinstriped engineer's cap. Although he was dressed for travel, his attire still indicated his profession, and, Dominique admitted to herself, a masculine, industrial appeal.

And yet, something was different. She studied him closely when he came into the cargo hold. "You changed your hair color." She viewed the strands peeking out behind his ears.

He removed his cap, granting her full view of his hair, now dyed brown. "Couldn't have anyone recognize me. Word may be traveling that the mill burned down after a new engineer was hired."

"What did you use?" asked Lydia.

He shrugged. "Some tonic the COIC chemists cooked up and wanted to test in the field. It's made with indigo and a plant from India. Starts with an 'h', they said. I have to apply it every week."

A pity that they were working undercover. Dominique had begun to like Colton's coppery hair.

"Are you ready to go?" he asked her.

She nodded. "I still need my field equipment."

"I'll leave you both to pack." Lydia went to the door.

"Lydia explained how the Aspasian metals work," said Dominique, after she left. "No wonder Broussard's after them."

"New Britannia reached an exclusive trade agreement with Aspasia." Colton went to one of the metal chests and started fiddling with the lock. "But Broussard pays no mind to such things. He is not one of your country's finest."

"I agree, but he doesn't represent all of us." Dominique placed her hands on her hips. Colton seemed a bit prickly. The joviality he displayed hours before apparently had been washed out of him when he put the hair tonic in.

He lifted the lid of the chest. "Try this on. It's a ladies version of a bullet-resistant waistcoat." He produced what looked to be a brown leather corset vest. Brass hooks fastened the front closed instead of traditional lacing.

It must have weighed at least ten pounds in Dominique's arms. She felt a heavy, though finely woven chainmail beneath the supple leather. Under Colton's alert gaze, she slipped her arms through the openings.

The vest settled against her securely, like the armor it was designed to be. She tried to pull it closed over her dress. The hooks stopped within half an inch of each other. "Uh-oh."

"There's a strap that adjusts in the back. Turn around."

Dominique reversed. She froze as she felt his hand on the small of her back. "I suppose this is the result of training to become a pastry chef."

The leather gave when Colton found the strap. "Your waist is slim. It wasn't what kept the vest from closing."

She knew exactly what part of her he was referring to. She hurriedly fastened the hooks on the front of the corset vest and smoothed her dress before facing him.

He wore a contained smile as he rubbed the back of his neck. "It suits you."

She liked that he approved, but pretended that his comment had no effect on her. "As long as it does its job."

"Next item." Colton reached into the chest for another object, a small bag on a strap. The leather matched that of the corset vest. It was meant to be attached to the hip.

"A lady's reticule?" Dominique guessed. The bag was heavier than it looked. She opened the flap and withdrew a silver metal cuff. It reminded her of jewelry, but was unlike any bracelet she had ever seen. "I'm beginning to wonder about your agency's collection of restraining devices."

"It's not a handcuff. It contains a retractable pistol. Go ahead and press the button on the side. Be careful, though. The gun's loaded."

Dominique turned aside from him. She put the cuff on and pressed the button underneath that sat inside her palm, near her pinkie. A lid snapped open, and a pistol, small enough to be concealed in the palm of her hand, landed there, sprung from its attached coil.

"It can pierce through metal at close range with the right bullets. The Bureau did teach you how to shoot, didn't they?"

She returned the pistol into its original position and closed the lid. "I'm sure I'll figure out the business end sooner or later, *non?*"

"Such sass." Colton gave a small shake of his head. "I miss Giselle and Bernadette already. One last thing." He grabbed a smaller item from the chest. "Soldier's knife. You'll find two blades, a file, lock pick, and saw. No vials of sleep gas, though."

Dominique stuck the knife in one of the pockets of her corset vest. "I was wondering when you intended to replace my old knife."

"I'm not sure I should have now."

A whistle sounded from top deck of the ship.

"We've arrived." Colton shut the chest.

"What about your field equipment?" Dominique went out in the hall with him.

"It's on deck." He closed the cargo hold doors.

"I still have to get my satchel. I'll meet you topside." Dominique traversed back to her borrowed cabin, passing two crewmen on the way as they ran to get above deck. She grabbed her satchel by the desk.

At topside, Colton stood talking with the captain while the crew prepared *The Enlightened* to go inland. The night sky was just beginning to show the first faint light of dawn on the horizon. The ship's deck was alight with lanterns. A single automaton stood near the longboats.

"We're coming upon the town by way of river estuary," Captain Rhys said, when Dominique joined him and Colton. "This is the quickest way to the foundry, according to the charts, and keeps us from being sighted in the bay."

Dominique cast her eyes towards land, represented by a darkened mass. The town of Saint-Brieuc was somewhere further inland, but several gaslights along the river docks were lit for travelers. *The Enlightened*'s speed slowed as it turned in their direction.

Malcolm steered the ship along the estuary instead of the automaton, Dominique noted.

"Agent Fontaine, have you ever been to this town?" asked the captain.

"A few years ago, when there wasn't a foundry. I don't know what it looks like now."

"We're stopping here. Malcolm will take you and Smythe to shore by boat."

Captain Rhys took hold of the wheel so Malcolm could free one of the longboats chained to the deck. Colton went to help him. At the captain's order, the automaton assisted the men in lowering the boat over the side of the ship's rail. Malcolm climbed into the boat first, situating himself in the front.

Colton looked back at Dominique. "Ready?"

Dominique put her satchel in first and then allowed him to take hold of her hand and assist her into the longboat. His hand was large, engulfing her own as his fingers curled over her palm.

Dominique lowered herself into the middle seat and held tight to the boat's side. Colton climbed into the back.

"Lower," Captain Rhys called to the automaton manning the cable wench.

The longboat gave a frightful wobble twenty feet over the black water when the cable chain wench started to descend. Dominique grabbed the boat's sides, instinctively bracing herself.

The bosun let out a curse, his Scottish brogue deepening with anger. "What does that automaton think we are, an anchor to just toss in the river as it pleases?"

The longboat settled into the water and bobbed, reminding Dominique of the lure of a fishing reel. Malcolm and Colton unhooked the cables. Malcolm took the oars and started rowing to shore.

Minutes went by. The dawn began to stretch its orange mouth in a yawn over east. Dominique saw the outlines of the modest docks ahead.

Malcolm glanced back at the ship as he pushed the oars forward. "Did you remember the captain's instructions, Smythe?"

"Telegraph the COIC in Le Havre when I find something." Colton pulled the brim of his cap down lower on his head.

Dominique surmised that Agent Joubert must have granted the COIC access to Le Havre's telegraph station. The Bureau had agents employed there, where they rotated shifts around the clock.

"I'd imagine the Bureau will want you to do the same for them, Agent Fontaine. I tell ye, it'll take the life of me to learn how men got those telegraph wires to stretch under land and up the Channel." The bosun wagged his head.

"Monsieur Clark, what of you and the crew of *The Enlightened?* Will the ship remain in a nearby port?"

"No. We go south for a month to see about the pirates raising their flags in the Mediterranean."

Dominique considered how she and Colton truly were on a mission of their own.

They arrived at the docks, where Malcolm tied the boat to one of the posts. Colton got out first. Dominique placed one foot on the pier and held her hand out to him, thinking he would simply offer a bit of leverage. He bent down and lifted her out of the longboat as though she weighed little more than a feather, even with the addition of the chainmail-lined corset vest.

Dominique grasped his broad shoulders until he set her feet down upon the dock. She murmured a *merci*, glad that the sun was not yet high enough to reveal her bashfulness as he held her in his arms.

"Keep an eye on each other." Malcolm hoisted their satchels on the pier. He untied the boat. "You especially care for the lass, Smythe."

"Agent Fontaine will be fine in my keeping. She and I will have this mission completed by the fall harvest."

"Big talk for an agent who recently completed his engineer's apprenticeship." Malcolm managed to grunt and laugh at the same time. He picked up the oars. "See that your mission is completed. France and New Britannia are counting on you both."

He started rowing, and the longboat drifted away from the docks and the two of them, back out towards the ship.

Chapter 7

"An apprentice? That is very interesting."

How did Colton know that Dominique would latch onto that bit of information as soon as Malcolm uttered it?

He traversed the dock with his bag of clothes and field equipment. The mail beneath his bullet-resistant waistcoat added to the weight he carried. "The COIC makes every engineer apprentice with one of their own first, no matter the years of work they did before."

The sun began to dawn fully, enabling him to see the tickled glances his fellow agent kept frequenting his way.

"You should talk. An agent with prior experience as a pastry chef."

She gave a cool, Gallic shrug. "What better training to pose as a worker at a flour mill? But I am curious. What did you do before you became a COIC agent?"

"I built engines for a locomotive company in London. Did it since I was seventeen."

"Is that where the COIC found you?"

"They came to do a building inspection. When they saw that I could assemble engines well enough, they wanted me to help them with their own."

"That must have made you and your family proud."

Colton only nodded. He knew his mother would have been proud that he made something of himself, had she been able to see his success.

The morning sun highlighted parts of the town of Saint-Brieuc. The steeples of old medieval churches made a picturesque scene as they rose above the rustic homes and the little shops in the square.

As Colton and Dominique continued on their walk into town, the merchants and the stall vendors started to open their shops and set up their wares along the old cobblestone road. The citizens of Saint-Brieuc gave the two of them passing glances before resuming their morning tasks.

Colton liked the little town immediately. Unlike London and its noisy bustle, it was quiet and frozen in time. He could get used to the COIC sending him out in the field to places like this. "Based on Captain Rhys' map, we should reach the foundry if we stay on this road."

It didn't take long for them to clear the main stretch of the town. Soon, the cobblestone roads turned to dirt paths. The old houses grew interspersed with gaps of pastoral land, until they too gave way and the pastures merged with the knobby grasses along the riverbank. Colton saw an outcropping of small buildings ahead. Beyond them, he thought he saw the moving surface of water stretch along their border.

"The river Gouet," voiced Dominique. "And I see smoke on the horizon."

"We should be getting close to the foundry, then."

They followed the road until it gave way to a large building structure along the river. Dominique halted in the middle of the road. Dust rose above her round-toe boots. "This is it."

Colton craned his neck to look at the cylindrical brick tower rising high above the foundry. Wisps of white smoke puffed out of the tower. The building was not as large as the factories he was used to seeing in New Britannia, yet its length spanned a quarter of the road and served as the most prominent sight along the riverbank.

Noises came from inside, indicating that work went on throughout the previous night.

Colton saw the morning shift of workers coming down the road. Men dressed in battered hats and roughspun shirts and pants began to file into the building. "We should visit the foundry overseer before he gets busy."

Dominique spoke when the last man closed the foundry door behind him. "I didn't see any ladies going in there. I need to come up with a reason for accompanying you."

"Easy." Colton had already given that considerable thought over the course of the walk from Saint-Brieuc. "You're my wife."

She blinked twice. "Your wife?"

"Yes, you're traveling with me because I'm looking for work. There's no better cover, unless you believe you can think of one."

No answer came from her normally quick tongue.

He walked on ahead. "We'd better move before someone wonders why we're standing out here."

Dominique caught up to him. "What if I pretend to be your sister instead of your wife?"

He studied her cropped dark hair, straight and thick, her black eyebrows, and chestnut eyes. "We look nothing alike."

"That is true." Her eyes drifted downward in thought. "Your half-sister? Or one by adoption?"

"It'll be much easier for you to pass as my wife than any other relation." Did she really find the idea of pretending to be married to him so objectionable? Colton thought they made a convincing, jolly good pair. And if Dominique would stop wrinkling her cute little nose whenever he uttered the word *wife*, maybe others would believe it, too.

"Husband." She spoke the word as though trying it on her tongue to see how well it settled there.

It established itself quite nicely, in Colton's opinion. "There. Was that so hard, wife?"

She didn't wrinkle her nose that time. Good. There was hope for them working undercover after all. "What is our shared name?"

"Hmm." They were ten paces from the front entrance of the foundry. "Smith?"

She gave him a look.

"Not Smith. Too close to my real name. What about David? It sounds French if you accent it right."

"A French surname draws less attention than a British one."

"Pick one, then." Colton touched the door handle.

"Roland." Dominique gave a very enticing roll of the 'r'. "After my grandfather."

"After you, Madame Roland." Colton held the door open for her.

The heat of the furnaces within the foundry surprised even Colton. The air was clammy and hot, rank with coal and rife with steam that reached to the rafters in the ceiling and fogged the grimy little windows along the wood-beamed walls.

Men crowded the main floor, going to and from the work stations.

Cranes and hoists hung over their heads. Colton counted two grindstones, four feet wide, one in each corner of the foundry. At the far end of the building, an iron crucible, eight feet high and about as wide, hung suspended from the ceiling by a system of pulleys and ropes. It heated above a blast furnace, of which men ran back and forth to stoke the dying flames, shoveling coal into its red mouth.

The cavernous foundry interior filled with the sounds of tools being sharpened, hammers clanging against anvils, flames roaring, men shouting, steam hissing, and iron being smelted.

Dominique rubbed her nose and visibly drew deep breaths. Colton was used to heat and the smell of iron and burning coal, but even he found it harrowing to stifle a cough.

"Monsieur." He tapped a man on the shoulder before he could walk past. "Where is the overseer?" he asked in French.

The man shook his head and cupped his ear. "*Pardon?*"

Colton shouted the question.

The man pointed to a balding figure standing under the crucible. He and a shorter, stocky worker lined up a mold casting directly beneath the crucible's tipping point. The overseer stepped out from beneath and signaled to a pulley operator overhead, who stood on a permanent scaffold built into the foundry wall. The operator pulled a lever and the crucible tilted forward. Molten metal poured white-hot into the molds. The overseer signaled to the operator again when the molds were near to full. The operator returned the crucible into an upright position.

If Broussard did have connections to this foundry, it was with good reason. The facility was equipped with modern machines, something that Colton did not expect in this town so far removed from large industry.

"You should stay back here while I go talk to the overseer," he told Dominique.

She shook her stubborn head. "I would hear everything you say to him."

"Watch where you step, then."

Colton started picking his way through the swarm of workers at their stations. The men paused to let him and Dominique pass, their gazes fixed on her since she was the only female present.

Colton made sure that she kept at his side, instinct making him want to protect her even from their stares.

He reached the balding man as he left from beneath the crucible. "Are you the overseer?"

The man turned Colton's way. Pockmark scars left ruts in his ruddy cheeks. "I'm the day shift overseer. My name is Monsieur Louis. What do you want?" His French was rough-sounding.

"I'm an engineer. My wife and I are looking for work."

"We'll talk in my office. Too loud here." The overseer moved his arm in the direction of the office, a closed door towards the front of the foundry, on the right.

Once again, Colton and Dominique passed the workers, led by Monsieur Louis. He held open his office door and they went inside.

Coal and grit left its mark on every inch of that room as well. The single window was streaked in a gray film, so that the view of the Gouet was perpetually dim and overcast. The floor bore multiple black marks from the overseer's large shoeprints that went behind and away from the rickety wooden desk and two chairs. A half-eaten sandwich, left over from the day before, judging by the current time of day and the bread's soggy, wilted look, was cast to the top of a wooden file cabinet.

Colton exchanged glances with Dominique before the overseer shut the door. He gestured for her to sit in the chair before the desk. She refused, eyeing its grimy surface, and remained standing.

If she was going to be that picky, she was going to have a rough mission.

"You said you need work," the overseer stated. "So what can you do?"

"Repair and maintain machinery. I've also put engines together. My wife, she's worked in mills before." He left it at that.

Monsieur Louis narrowed his already close-set eyes. "You don't talk with some of the Breton words usually spoken around here. Where are you from?"

"Granville," Dominique provided. Colton had no idea where that town or city was located in France. He hoped her short answer would be enough for the overseer.

"Not much work with machines to be found in Granville," the overseer replied. "I see why you came this far. I'm from one of the hamlets in Normandie myself."

Colton introduced himself, giving the new name he thought up. "I'm Carl Roland. My wife's name is…" He glanced at Dominique. She had such a fancy name. She needed something short and jaunty, befitting her new station as an engineer's wife. "Minnie."

Her eyes became glowering coals. Oh, he was going to hear it from her later.

"Let me see." Monsieur Louis tapped his dirty fingers on the desk. "I already have enough engineers working the morning and afternoon shifts. Can you work in the evening and at night?"

"Whatever you have, I'll take."

"There is a vacancy on the nightshift. On the good side, it's quieter at night and easier for the other overseer Monsieur Totou to see how you fare at the job. On the not-so-good, the work will be difficult and plenty. There's no Sunday respite for you since you work nights, but it pays twenty francs a week."

"I don't shirk from hard work."

Monsieur Louis looked at Dominique. "We don't have labor at the foundry for women, but some of the workmen's wives are laundresses and cooks at the lodging house up the road. Take her there, and then come back early at six this evening. I'll be here until eight to show you the routine."

"*Merci.*"

"Tell the desk clerk that I sent you."

Colton shook his hand, never minding the dirt. He figured he'd soon be covered in it himself, anyway.

Dominique picked up her bag and went out of the office with him. When Colton closed the door of the foundry behind them and they were back outside, it all came bubbling up from her.

"*Minnie?*" She spoke the name as though it were a hushed curse.

"What's wrong with Minnie? It's a fun little name for a girl."

"*Exactement.* A girl. I'm grown. I keep thinking of the word 'miniature' when you say it."

"Don't you French prefer names that way? Colette for Nicolette. Minnie for Dominique."

She sighed, conceding the matter to him. "Well, now I should find employment in this lodging house."

She walked past him. So precise and fetching was her sashay that Colton almost didn't want to catch up with her.

The two of them reached the lodging house. The sign for the three-storied tenement structure stood out past the building. The weekly and monthly rates of the rooms were painted on the sign in faded black letters.

They went inside. The lobby was dark and smelled stale. A man sat at the counter. Attired in an old brown suit, he flicked his gaze up from across the room. "All booked out of nightly stay rooms."

"Let me talk to him," Dominique said.

Colton set his bag on the floor. His aching shoulder thanked him. He followed Dominique's French as she spoke to the desk clerk.

"Monsieur, my husband has just gained employment nearby. We need lodgings."

"Who told you to come here?"

Dominique appeared taken aback by his tone. "*Pardonnez-moi?*"

The clerk huffed with impatience. "Who told you to come here?"

"Monsieur Louis of the foundry."

"Should have said that in the beginning." The clerk opened a drawer and pulled out a large ring of keys. "The foundry workers give us the most business, so they receive the best rates. You can pay when you get your first wages." The clerk removed two keys from the ring. "There's a room on the second floor."

"Did you say, *a* room?" asked Dominique.

"*Oui.*" The clerk's moustache twitched. "You said the two of you were married, didn't you?"

"I-I did."

Sharing a room with his partner was one thing that Colton didn't consider. He thought the lodging house would be similar to the workhouses in London, where men and women slept in separate quarters. This was going to make things very awkward, to say the least.

Poor Dominique. She was stunned into silence. The clerk looked at her as though she were daft.

"My wife's tired from traveling," Colton supplied.

"Maybe you should take the keys, then. The room is upstairs, number eight. Washrooms are at the end of the hall. The dining hall is open now for breakfast and again for supper at five." The clerk tossed Colton the keys.

He caught and pocketed them. He picked up his bag. Dominique remained quiet as he took her satchel in his other hand. She trailed him up the old worn stairs and down the hall. Shabby carpeting, appearing as though it had once been red in a former life, showed stained and faded.

Colton found their room. As he turned the key, he heard a sound come from Dominique. She had gone from having a healthy pallor seconds ago to bearing a pale hue. "What's wrong?" he asked, alarmed by her sudden change.

Worry lines appeared on her smooth, high brow. "I'm sorry, but I can't do this."

Chapter 8

Colton ushered Dominique into the room before anyone in the rooms across the hall could hear them. As soon as he closed the door to their cramped accommodations, she launched herself towards the opposite wall like a cornered tabby cat.

"What has gotten into you?" He tossed their bags upon the bed. A bed just slightly big enough for two people, he noticed.

"I can't do it," she repeated in a voice slightly above a whisper. "Not this." She raised her arms and spread them apart. "Or that." She turned her hands out and gestured towards the bed.

"This. That. What?" Colton followed her movements, looking from the ceiling to the bed and back to her. "What can't you do?"

"We can't share a room. We will *not* share a bed." She spoke that at normal voice, and quickly covered her mouth. Her eyes looked left and right at the walls.

Colton remembered to keep his voice down, too, in case their neighbors in the next rooms were to hear. "I can't do anything about the room." He put both keys on the little end table next to the bed. He shoved the bags over to one side and plopped on the bare straw mattress to rest his feet. The wood and rope frame creaked under the sudden increase of his additional weight. "You can have the bed to yourself."

Dominique kept staring at him, tightness still in her eyes. "This ruse can only go so far."

"I always thought the French were more lax about these things."

He shouldn't have teased her. His words only made her grow

incensed.

"Well, you were wrong." Her body grew taut as a wire. "You're not my," she mouthed the word *husband*, "and this isn't funny to me. I agreed to work with you, but there are certain boundaries I do not cross. This," she took to gesturing to the room and bed again, "is one of them."

"Shh." Colton put a finger to his lips. "I think I hear someone coming."

Dominique quieted as a knock sounded upon the door. Colton opened it to the desk clerk from downstairs. He held a bundle of linens and pillows in his arms.

"Forgot your towels and bed linens."

"*Merci.*" Colton took them. "Actually, can we have another set of blankets? My wife gets cold easily."

"It costs extra."

"I'll pay for it. I want to see to her comfort."

"I'll be back with more linens, then." The clerk left.

Colton shut the door again. Dominique seemed to have calmed herself during the brief interlude in which he spoke to the clerk. Her shoulders were looser, anyway.

He moved their satchels off the bed and began to put the linens on the mattress. "Dominique, I never intended to share the bed with you, but there's nothing I can do about the room. We're in the guise of husband and wife. We'll draw attention if we get separate lodgings. And that's if they have another room to spare." He folded a sheet corner and tucked it under the mattress. "I will work at night. We won't see each other but for a few minutes early in the morning and evening."

Dominique slowly came away from the wall. "I still don't like this situation."

He placed the blanket on top of the sheet. It bothered him that she persisted in acting as though he were a wolf, intent on coming for her. But in this situation, trust wasn't going to be instant. She'd have to see that his actions would follow his words.

A few minutes later, the clerk returned with another set of linens and blankets. Once she left, he took one of the pillows from the bed. "I'll make a pallet on the floor."

He opened his bag down and removed a folded mat. He laid it out on the floor while Dominique watched.

"Thank you for doing this for me." Her voice became shy and hesitant. She folded her arms in front of her, embarrassed.

He spoke in a gentle tone in attempt to make up for his previously ill-timed banter. "I meant what I said. And as you stated, this is just a ruse. We'll act married in public, but in here, we'll keep our distance." His hand bumped the wall by accident. "You get the figure of speech."

She chuckled, finally beginning to relax.

"That's better. You don't need to be so jumpy around me."

"Who said I was jumpy?"

"You didn't see yourself a few minutes ago."

She started putting her field equipment away in her bag. Colton looked away politely when she removed her corset vest. "I have a question." He fashioned his bed pallet in the corner. "If you feel this strongly about virtues and all, how could you work in that flour mill, knowing what it was about to turn into?"

She came close so she wouldn't have to project her voice. "I didn't know. Broussard only revealed that when he came to inspect it. Before then, I was looking for evidence of violations that would shut the mill down. But you saved me the trouble."

"Glad to know you're finally looking at it differently." He yawned, realizing that he hadn't slept in over twenty-four hours. He reclined on the pallet. "I'm going to rest before work tonight. Wake me in the afternoon." He kicked off his boots.

Dominique dodged them. "But we have work to do now."

"There's little I can find out about the foundry until I go back there tonight." He fluffed his pillow. "You should rest, too, before you go searching for work."

She didn't budge from her spot. Her stance indicated that she wasn't going to take a nap with him there, even if resting would have refreshed her. "I'm going to secure a job immediately." Her stomach issued a loud groan. She folded her hands in front. "On second thought, after breakfast."

Colton yawned again. "I didn't like how those men at the foundry looked at you. Keep that knife or pistol close. Preferably both."

"Don't worry about me. I can defend myself." She removed the pistol cuff from under her sleeve and put it in her bag. "But it's kind of you to care." She took the utility knife from the pocket of the corset vest.

Colton didn't know if kindness was the right word for how he felt. He did want her to be safe, but another emotion was present behind his concern that he couldn't determine.

He closed his eyes after watching her take one of the keys from the table and slip out.

***

Dominique mused on Colton's honorable actions as she went down the lodging house stairs. Maybe it was time to change her perceptions of British men. Some of them did know how to treat a lady with decency, even if she wasn't one of their own.

While it was common thought that the men of New Britannia kept rules of strict propriety among their own women, more than a few of them acted completely different when they went abroad. She'd seen it in Le Havre, especially amongst the fishermen and the tourists. She was happy that despite Colton's joking about her country's reputation for amorousness, he knew to respect her.

The scent of toasted bread wafted from the dining hall downstairs, whetting her appetite. If sleep was not to be gained as of yet, at least she could satiate her gnawing stomach.

She continued to follow her nose until it led her to the dining hall. Rows of tables filled the space. Men occupied the benches before them, eating from trays.

She looked about. Where were the other women?

"It's your turn to wait tables. My shift is over." A tall, plump woman approached, bearing a large tray of dirty dishes in her arms. She took a good look at Dominique's face and stopped. "Oh, I thought you were an employee for the lodging house."

"I just arrived here with my husband." Would that word ever become natural to say? Dominique hoped she sounded convincing.

"Are you looking for work?" Clad in a dark dress, the woman appeared to be in her late thirties. One loose blonde braid dangled over her shoulder.

"I am, but I wanted a bite to eat, too."

"The women and children's dining hall is beyond the kitchen that way." She jutted her chin in the direction of a set of doors. "I'll be there once I finish collecting dishes."

"Let me help you." Dominique walked with her to a near empty table.

341

Three men got up. Dominique took their plates and stacked them on the round tray once the serving woman set it down.

"*Merci*, Mademoiselle...?"

"It's Madame Roland. I go by Minnie." She had to stop herself from cringing.

The serving woman stacked the coffee mugs in the corner of the tray. "My name is Lottie, short for Charlotte. I'm the head housekeeper. When did you get here?"

"My husband just acquired employment at the foundry today."

"Ah, *bon.*"

"I was told I can apply for work here. Are there any vacancies?" Dominique lifted the heavy-laden tray and transferred it to one hand.

Lottie noticed. "Where did you learn to balance a tray like that?"

"I used to work in a boulangerie."

"Our cook Gustave needs another food server. Can you wash clothes well, too?"

"My husband has yet to complain."

"Follow me. We will talk over breakfast. I'm famished."

Dominique carried the tray for Lottie into the kitchen. Gustave the cook, a man almost as wide as he was tall, stood before a large stove, slicing potatoes into a pot of boiling water.

"Gustave, my shift is over," Lottie called to him.

He raised the hand holding a half-sliced potato in acknowledgment.

"Just set the tray on that counter, Minnie." Lottie directed Dominique through the kitchen. The space was littered with table scraps, vegetable peels, and an assortment of pots and pans. "The women and children's hall is this way."

Dominique and Lottie came to a room identical to the first hall, only the rows of tables were fewer and the benches were occupied by ladies ranging from Dominique's age on up to steel-haired matrons. She counted about twelve children, from infants to maybe ten years of age. The sat quietly, eating oatmeal.

Lottie maneuvered between the tables to get to the food on the back table. "We dine separately from the men. It keeps things more orderly that way."

"Are all the women married to laborers?" Dominique took a clean bowl from the stack.

"Oh, *non*." Lottie laughed, grabbing a bowl. "Some ladies simply come here from town to work." She ladled oatmeal from a large kettle. "If you want to sit with me, you are more than welcome to."

"*Merci*."

Lottie chatted on. "I've worked at this lodging house since my brother and I came up north. He's at a factory in the south now."

"Do you think you can help me learn my way about? I'm so very new."

"It is always good to have extra help around here." Lottie took a mug of steaming coffee from the beverage table.

So far, so good. Lottie probably had knowledge of just about everyone in the lodging house. Dominique wondered what information she could provide about the nearby foundry, but that could be discovered later.

She sat down at the table, pleased that things were going smoothly so far. Colton really should have come to the dining hall. He could have talked to the men and began establishing his presence among them.

But that was his choice. She would do things her way. He would do things his. She hoped their efforts proved successful. The sooner they gathered information to catch Broussard, the sooner she could reestablish her family's boulangerie and get back to the life she once knew.

Dominique reached for her beverage. And the sooner she would not have to share a room with Colton. The thought of that continued to make her nerves flutter much more than coffee ever could.

***

True to her word, Lottie introduced Dominique to the other ladies after breakfast and secured her a job as a laundress and table server. Dominique's first task of the day was to clean the linens.

At midmorning, she left the lodging house and followed Lottie and ten of the ladies to an unmarked building. Her arms weighed down with a basket of linens, towels, and dish cloths from the kitchen. A jug of fresh water sat on top of the pile, her supply of drinking water for the afternoon. Lottie told her that she would need it.

"This is where we take all of the dirty laundry. We used to have to wash everything by hand down by the muddy riverbank," Lottie explained, as they entered the building. "Not anymore since the lodging house acquired these new machines."

Dominique stared in awe at three large steel drums that sat in the center of the room. Standing at seven feet, they resembled giant cauldrons connected by a set of hoses. The hoses' origin lay at a pipe built into the wall, approximately twenty-four inches in diameter. A scaffold was next to each cauldron, where a person could climb up and place laundry into the drum. A system of gas burners lay in a grate below each machine.

"Watch how the machines are activated," Lottie instructed. "You'll be doing this soon."

Two of the women began lighting the pilots for the burners. Three more went to a pump next to the pipe on the wall and moved it up and down. A gurgle and then a rush of water could be heard.

"Is that coming from the river?" Dominique asked.

"*Oui*. The pipe captures water from upstream. It'll travel through the hoses and fill the wash drums. As the water heats, we can add soap to it and start the washing."

After the drums filled with water and the burners below them got it to heat, Lottie taught her how to mix in the lye and soap flakes before tossing in the soiled laundry. The next three hours were spent cranking a handle on the cauldron to sift the clothes through the soapy mix, draining the cauldron, and then letting it fill with a fresh batch of water to rinse the laundry. The building's windows soon filled with steam as the confines of the space grew hot.

An additional three hours had Dominique fishing the laundered items out with a wooden pole and helping to transfer them to a steam turbine dryer at the rear of the facility. The dryer required eight women, four at each large handle, to crank the machine and turn the internal drum over and over to dry the laundry. However, to Dominique's dismay, most of it still remained damp even after being in there for a long time.

She surmised that she would have strong enough arms to hoist a telegraph pole by her mission's end. After the laundry was done, she attempted to ignore the strain of her muscles as she lugged a basket of half-damp clothes back to the lodging house. She drained her jug of water dry an hour ago.

Lottie walked next to her in the beeline of women. "We'll deliver the dry clothes to their owners' bins and then go back to the dining hall for the afternoon shift."

Dominique blew a strand of limp, damp hair that fell in her eyes. The women's work wasn't any less strenuous than that of the men in this commune of laborers. "Do you follow the same routine every day?"

"We clean the facilities in the lodging house and help in the dining hall every day. The laundry is done twice a week."

"That gives my arms time enough to build stamina."

"You will get used to it. What other work did you do at the boulangerie?"

Dominique chose not to mention the flour mill. "I prepared the cakes and pastries. The owners allowed me to create my own recipes from time to time."

Lottie's dark blue eyes lit up. "I'll speak to Gustave about letting you work in the kitchen some days. It's better than serving some of the men workers. A few of them can become very rude. But you will have to prove yourself to Gustave. He is very strict."

"I'll give it my best."

They filed into the lodging house, where Lottie showed her the cubicles for tenants to pick up and drop off their laundry. "There is one more work opportunity. Once a week, some of the women go during the interim of day and evening shifts to clean the foundry. It's dirty work, but it pays an extra five francs a week."

That was her ticket into the foundry to uncover its inner workings. It was well worth the sore muscles and stained hands. "I'll do it."

Lottie looked surprised at first. "Ambitious girl, aren't you? That is very good." She stuffed a man's shirt into a cubicle. How she knew where everything went and what belonged to who was beyond Dominique. "You'll go far here. Maybe you and your husband will be able to save enough money to buy a house in town."

"But we're so close to the foundry, staying at the lodging house."

"How long have you been married?"

"Almost eight months." Dominique made up a number.

"Ah, *ma petite*, you're still newlyweds. But wait until you have little ones. Then you'll want a house of your own."

"I don't think we'll have to worry about that." Dominique fought the urge to look away for embarrassment.

"You never know," Lottie said in a singsong voice. She looked up at the clock on the wall. "It's almost time to serve supper. Do you want to help? Wait, *non, non*, you've learned enough for one day. Take the afternoon."

Lottie left the room while Dominique finished folding the sheets. She placed them in the general bin for lodging house linens. The housekeeper soon returned with a covered tray in her hand.

"Two helpings of shepherd's pie. One for you and your husband. Be back in the dining hall tomorrow morning at five. The morning shift starts early." She wondered if he was awake yet.

Dominique accepted the warm, savory-smelling tray, grateful for the chance to sit down to a hearty meal. *"Merci*, Lottie." She carried the tray gingerly up the stairs to her and Colton's shared room. She wondered if he was awake.

Chapter 9

Dominique shifted the tray over to her left hand in order to find her key to unlock the door. Colton was already up when she came in. "How was your rest?" she asked.

"Refreshing. Did you secure employment?" He looked up from tying his bootlace. "Oh, you did."

Dominique peered down the front of her travel dress, very wrinkled and dotted with flecks of soap flakes. Her wet sleeves were rolled to her elbows. She knew without consulting a mirror that her hair was disorderly. "I'm now a laundress and a table server."

"You have been busy," he said with a hint of admiration in his voice.

"I brought supper. I hope you like shepherd's pie." She set the tray on the end table and sat upon the bed. The mattress felt like the closest thing to heaven at that moment, never mind that it was stuffed with straw. She couldn't wait to recline fully upon it, just as soon as Colton left for work.

"Did you find anything pertinent to our mission?" Colton took a fork from the tray and dug into one of the pies.

"Not quite, but you should see the machines used to wash clothes around here. They pump water from upstream and send it to big vats that heat with gas pilots. They are so newfangled."

"We've got work to do. Don't get too distracted by the shiny machinery."

"I won't." Dominique's eyelids began to grow heavy. She remembered that she hadn't had any real sleep in many long hours. "But now I'm able to speak with the head housekeeper. She might reveal something about that foundry. I'll let you know what I find soon."

"If I don't find it there tonight first." He shoved another forkful of shepherd's pie in his mouth.

"I wouldn't be too confident if I were you. It's your first time on the job. The overseer or one of the shift supervisors will trail you all night."

"I can still be observant. And right now, you look like you're about to fall over any minute. You really should get some sleep."

"I intend to."

"Don't stay awake on my account." He finished the pie and set the empty plate back on the tray. "Thanks for supper. See you in the morning, Madame Roland."

Dominique was too tired to fire off a quip at him. She didn't feel too keen on eating her shepherd's pie, either. Her muscles hurt too much to even lift a fork.

After Colton left, she made herself eat half of the pie. Too fatigued to change out of her clothes, she removed her shoes and stretched out on top of the blankets. It would be easier tomorrow, she told herself.

***

Rested and satiated, Colton strode easily to the foundry. Only several of the other workers had arrived for the evening shift. They put on their gloves and leather aprons to prepare for charging the blast furnaces with more coal. He guessed the others were still at supper.

Though the late summer temperature had cooled over the evening, it did little to the temperature inside the foundry. Colton felt no breeze drifting through the open windows.

Monsieur Louis flagged him down. "Did you get your lodgings?"

"I did."

"*Bon.* Time to get to business, then." Monsieur Louis pointed to the crucible. "See to greasing the hinges on those suspension cables. They started creaking this afternoon. There's a canister of oil and a brush on the scaffold. And see to the pulleys while you're at it. I'll be in the office." He turned and walked off without another word.

The overseer went in and out of his office during the next two hours, surveying Colton and the other laborers. At eight o'clock, he came out of the office for good, carrying a small valise. "Monsieur Totou the nightshift overseer will be coming in. Just do as you're told, Roland." He locked the office door.

Colton came down from the permanent scaffold. Not much chance of picking the lock on the office door while the other workers were there to see him. If this was the usual routine, then he needed to find a way to get into that office during the daytime when the overseer kept it open. But even then, how much time would he have to search it? Monsieur Louis may as well have kept a revolving door on the hinges, he went in and out of the office so often.

"Where is the new engineer?" came a call from the entrance.

Colton attached the voice to a dour-faced man, dressed in tan breeches and light brown shirt. His clothes were as yet unstained from sweat and coal. It was the nightshift overseer, Monsieur Totou, freshly arrived.

"I'm the new engineer." Colton got his attention.

"You have disposal duties for the next hour," the overseer announced, without pause for introduction or ceremony. He strode to a corner and took hold of a wheelbarrow, piled high with old coal dust and burnt metal castoffs used to charge the furnaces. He gave it a turn and thrust it handles first Colton's way. "Grease and coal tar keep gumming the inside walls of the cupolas. Take this slag to the river and throw it out. Then come back for the second round." He jabbed a finger in the direction of more slag that collected in a pile in front of a coal grinding machine.

The other men snickered as Colton took hold of the wheelbarrow. "Plenty more where that came from," one called out. "That pile was scraped from the machines this afternoon."

Colton wheeled the slag out, letting the door swing shut behind him as the workers continued to jest from inside. He'd come to expect such cajoling on his first night as a new hire. The men and the overseer were testing the bounds of his temperament. They wanted to know how he'd fare working alongside them, he rationalized.

Colton went around to the back of the foundry, where he stumbled on the rocky slope. The wheelbarrow flew from his hands and tumbled down the hill, clanging over rock after rock before he heard it land at the base of the river.

"Pick it up," Monsieur Totou hollered out from a side window. "Every last bit of it. Don't come back in until you do." His head retracted inside. A shovel sailed out from the window moments later, clattering at the base of the foundry.

Colton rose and scraped rocks and pebbles embedded in his elbows. Now his temperament was beginning to lose some of its rivets.

He made his way down the hill, able to see just enough of the slope in front of him to avoid stumbling again. Moonlight off the water guided his way to the bottom. He fished the wheelbarrow from the dirty shallows, grasping its handles, slick with cold, wet grease. A portion of the slag remained stuck on one side of the wheelbarrow.

Colton doubted he had been so fortunate that most it had fallen into the river. He hitched the wheelbarrow onto an area of flat land where it couldn't easily roll back into the downstream of the Gouet and set himself to scrounging for the slag among the runoff from the foundry drainage pipes.

The foul-smelling, concentrated scent of burnt coal and ash made him breathe through his mouth. The pipes above his head gurgled before releasing more of the thick sludge, gleaming black in the moonlight as it splattered on the riverbank, in the water, and on Colton's shirt.

One of the workers released the valve. On purpose, no doubt. He stepped out of the pipe's range and looked up at the full series of them.

The drainage system shouldn't have dropped waste the way it did. The pipes should be running cleaner. He suspected there was a clog.

He stepped through the rocks and grass. A series of clogs was more like it, he judged, from the oil and congealed grease sandwiching under his boots. Colton gathered what machine excess he could with the shovel and disposed of it. Then he set to the task of lugging the wheelbarrow back up the slippery slope.

"What took you so long?" asked the overseer, when he came through the door. Some of the men standing behind the overseer laughed at the new stains on Colton's shirt.

"I cleared the wheelbarrow, but I saw the drainage system in the back. I think there may be a backup in the pipes."

"Those pipes have been functioning without a hitch in the past year. Nothing's wrong. Get back to work instead of musing on the conduits."

"Monsieur, this is dangerous. I've seen before what this problem can do to engines and pipes. You really ought to—"

"Don't advise me or tell me what I ought to do. This is your first night of work. Get back to it."

Colton watched the overseer wander off to the draughtsmen's station,

350

where he devoted his attention to making charts on a new design. Colton went to find the shovel again to scrape one of the smaller blast furnaces that went unused during the night. The sooner he had a chance to uncover the goings on of the foundry, though, the better for his mission and the safety of all the workers.

And Dominique, hopefully, wouldn't have long to grieve over washing his dirty clothes.

***

A week later

"*Zut*, what a mess."

Dominique forgot to take her laundry basket downstairs with her when she started her shift at dawn. She returned to her lodgings to find an extra addition to the dirty clothes pile.

She lifted Colton's shirt from where he discarded it in the laundry basket earlier that morning after he returned from work. That was the third shirt this week that was coated in grime and soot, not counting the others that were riddled with smudges of coal.

She viewed the oil stains decorating his other shirts and pairs of pants in the basket. His first seven days at work and already he started to make their shared lodgings look like an extension of the overseer's dirty office. What had he gotten himself into at that foundry?

She dropped the stain-streaked shirt back into the basket. The greasy black substance that marked the fabric came off on her fingers. It smelled worse than it looked. She went to the ladies washroom down the hall to clean her hands before going to the dining hall to serve breakfast.

The hall was already filled with men when she arrived. The servers darted back and forth between tables. Dominique greeted Lottie before hurrying to Gustave, who waved frantically to her from the kitchen window.

"Pass these biscuits out." He lifted a large basket of the baked goods and pressed it into her arms. "They are a little crisp, but these rough laborers will not notice."

Dominique wasn't too sure about that. The tops of the biscuits were burnt brown.

"Lottie said you used to work for a baker. You can help me with some of the baking on Friday." Gustave tossed her a linen napkin to pick up the bread.

Dominique passed them out at each table. The men accepted the biscuits without complaint. She saw Colton seated at the table closest to the back wall. He and four other men sat apart from each other.

At last, a chance to speak. She hadn't run into him too often since he left on his very first night at the mill, thanks to her revolving work shifts. One day she'd chop vegetables in the kitchen at dawn. The next she would spend all afternoon and early evening in the laundry building, missing her only chance to speak to him before he left for work again.

"*Bonjour*, monsieurs." She set a biscuit on each man's plate, coming to Colton last at the far end of the table. "Hello, husband of mine."

"You baked these?" He grasped the hard biscuit between his thumb and forefinger.

"Gustave did." She took a moment to notice how handsome and fresh-scrubbed Colton looked. He had on a clean shirt, one that fit him very well, if she had to say so. His hair was damp and combed back. The brown dye seemed to be holding well, even with the frequent washings it had to endure on account of exposure to the foundry's filth.

"I thought it was Gustave." He bit into the burnt surface of the bread and chewed. "I don't think a certain Paris-trained chef would be able to ruin bread."

She tucked her hair behind her ear. "How go your shifts at the foundry?"

"Untidy."

"I know. I saw the laundry basket. Those coal stains will require a vat of lye to get them out. But that's not what I meant." She sat down on the bench beside him. Despite the peculiar little butterflies that took to flight in her stomach, she reached up and put her hand on his shoulder.

Surprise flickered in his eyes, but then his mouth shifted into a wry smile. "You're friendly this morning."

The butterflies fluttered their wings rapidly in response. "I have questions to ask you, but I can't keep talking while standing in front of everyone. *S'il vous plait*, pretend that we are, what's the word they say in New Britannia?"

"Canoodling?"

"Oh, *non*. That is such a silly-sounding word. It cannot be pleasant."

"Clearly, you don't know what it means."

She felt his arm slide around her waist as he turned his body towards her. She was wrong. Canoodling felt much more pleasant than its awkward consonants and double vowels implied.

The butterflies inside her sent themselves into a frenzy when Colton leaned in and brought his face close to hers. "What about 'tryst'?"

She shook her head, trying not to notice how, when his mouth formed the word, it was also the same motion that one did in preparation for a kiss. "I think we would have to meet in secret for that. But, I don't mean to stall on semantics. Tell me, have you found anything in the foundry that may point to Broussard's involvement?"

He tossed a glance down the table. The other men dug ravenously into their food, charred biscuits and all. They were oblivious to their conversation. He turned back to her and spoke low. "I found little so far. The foundry ships iron and crucible steel weekly to other factories in France. The production load's large, but that in itself isn't illegal."

"Does the supply go through Saint-Brieuc to be taken to the docks in the bay?"

"The freight's hauled to the river docks here before dawn for one of the carrier ships to take it out of the area."

Dominique thought of how such practices were conducted in the ports of Le Havre. Ships bearing cargo from well-known destinations usually had the goods clearly marked. "Is the freight marked? Do you know where they're being shipped?"

"No. The pallets are unmarked, save for a number, but the overseer gives the freight orders to the ship captains. I talked to some of the men who've been at the foundry for a while. They said this practice is standard for them."

"I wonder why."

"Could be that most foundries ship metals to factories or businesses, where the assembly is done there. No need for a complicated system."

Dominique gave him another biscuit from the basket, stalling for time. "I go to the foundry later today to sweep the floors between shifts. Maybe I can learn more while I'm there."

"I don't think you will. I've been in that place for more than ten hours a night, seven nights a week."

"I'll do a thorough job of sweeping every nook and cranny. And I won't get my clothes dirty in the process."

"Let's hope not. It'd be a shame for coal dust to touch any part of you."

A tingling crept up the back of Dominique's neck. It continued to spread when she noticed that his eyes traveled her frame ever so discreetly before returning to gaze at her face. Her cheeks burned.

To her chagrin, Colton saw the reaction he produced in her and winked.

"Are you—are you flirting with me?"

"You said to pretend." He took a swig of water. "It would be pitiful of your husband to not find you attractive, wouldn't it?"

He may have referenced his guise, but she was unsure if he was still pretending.

A laborer pounded his mug at the opposite end of the table. "Here, woman." He spilled coffee. "You gave him two biscuits. Give me more."

Dominique found her legs and walked around the table to deliver the famished man a biscuit.

"About time you stopped dallying about and do your job." He snatched the basket and looked for a choice biscuit. *"Femme incompetente."*

His loud outburst stole attention. Conversation in the dining hall lowered.

Colton rose from his seat and walked over to him. "Pardon me for keeping my wife. I work the late shifts and can only see her in the dining hall."

"That's not my problem, now, is it?" The man tossed one of the biscuits over his shoulder, where it hit Colton's chest before falling on the floor. He then plucked a choice biscuit from the basket and prepared to send than one down his gullet.

Colton's fingers clamped down on the laborer's shoulder. "Treat her like a lady, and *you* won't have any problems with me. Understood?"

Dominique saw the man's jaw weld shut to avoid making a noise. He lowered the biscuit onto his plate and nodded.

Colton released him. The laborer rubbed his shoulder. Colton handed Dominique her bread basket. "Do you need anything else before I go?"

She shook her head.

"If you do, then you know where to find me." He made a quiet yet confident exit from the hall.

Dominique returned the bread basket to the kitchen window. The hall slowly buzzed again with the murmur of discourse. A handful of workers got up to go to their morning shift.

Lottie joined Dominique in cleaning the first table. *"Ma petite,"* she dropped her voice in heavy implication while quirking a fair eyebrow. "With a man like that, I do not know how you make it to your shift on time."

Dominique tucked her hair behind her ears, then wished she hadn't. Her earlobes were hot. They must have been bright red. "Monsieur Roland is protective of me."

"Do not be so formal. I see how you both look at each other. Now I know the real reason why you volunteered to clean the foundry. You want to stage a rendezvous with your husband."

At least she and Colton were giving a convincing performance. Dominique thought of using Lottie's perception of things to her advantage. "You have found me out."

"Two other ladies will be with you. The floors and machines need a good scrubbing. Even with the three of you, the job may take longer than expected."

"I don't mind."

"I'm sure you don't. Time enough for you to have a visit with your husband, *non?*"

Time enough for her to find out what information Monsieur Louis kept in his office. Although, she wouldn't mind seeing Colton again to thank him for standing up for her against that rude laborer.

Dominique finished helping Lottie clear the table and went to go eat breakfast in the women and children's hall. Her mind was already thinking about the afternoon to come.

Chapter 10

The foundry managed to become filthier since the last time Dominique visited. At least two new layers of grime clung to the floor and machinery. She cast a skeptic look at the broom and tiny dust pan Lottie armed her with before she left the lodging house.

"We're unable to scrub the foundry completely clean, but we can remove some of the grit," Madame Gilles, one of the two ladies accompanying Dominique, said. While the other woman proceeded to sweep the floor near one of the grindstones, Madame Gilles took a coarse brush to the conveyor belt of a coal grinding machine. The belt moved at a slow pace, as its engine was being operated at low power. She sneezed as she disturbed the dust.

"I'll sweep here in front." Dominique proceeded to stoke a similar black cloud at her own feet near the entrance.

As Madame Gilles and the other woman worked, Dominique moved her broom along a path to Monsieur Louis' office. She turned the door handle. Unlocked.

She slipped inside. The filmy gray window cast filtered light on the grime embedded in the wooden desk and chairs. The hardwood floor was black in places where the overseer's shoeprints tracked.

At least the half-eaten sandwich was gone. But she wondered just how Monsieur Louis came to have made it disappear.

Dominique carried the broom and dustpan with her to the desk. She set the pan on the floor and had a look at the desk's surface.

Papers sat stacked in the right corner, the parchment still relatively white. The overseer's thumbprints decorated the edges. He must have brought them here only recently.

Not wanting to leave her prints behind, she leaned over the papers to read them. Letters were printed by hand in bold, black ink. *Freight Order for M. B.,*

M.B. Who could that person or company be? Not Broussard, Dominique thought. His first name began with the letter 'e'. She noticed the comma at the end. The overseer hadn't finished writing the order.

The door creaked.

Dominique backed away from the desk. Still holding the broom, she pretended to sweep the floor.

Monsieur Louis entered. "Madame Roland? Why are you in here?"

"I'm cleaning. The foundry needs sweeping, *non?*"

"My office is not to be cleaned when I'm not present. You're new, so I will not say anything this time, but remember in the future. *D'accorde?*"

"My apologies, monsieur."

He held the door open for her to exit. The door closed almost before she could get her broom out of the way.

Monsieur Louis had something to hide. That freight order may have been one of many documents that he wished to keep secret.

A high-pitched scream made her drop her broom.

"Help me," Madame Gilles called.

The hem of her skirt was caught in the conveyor belt of the coal grinder. The belt dragged the fabric through, steadily pulling her along with it into the mouth of the machine.

Dominique raced to her. She withdrew the soldier's knife from her dress. Madame Gilles tugged and stumbled, fighting against the strength of the machine. The other woman came from the back of the foundry. She gasped at what took place.

"Hold her," Dominique commanded. As the woman tried to keep Madame Gilles from being fed into the machine, Dominique got in close. Madame Gilles' double layers of dress and petticoat collected in the wheel at the top of the conveyor. Dominique slashed at the fabric. Her blade brushed against the grooves of the metal wheel, producing sparks. She cut through the layers of fabric again and again.

Suddenly freed, Madame Gilles fell back against the other woman. The two of them staggered to regain themselves.

The wheel of the conveyor snatched hold of Dominique's sleeve. The button of her cuff snapped off as the fabric immediately fed into the wheel's grooves. The knife fell upon the conveyor belt. She grabbed it with her other hand.

"What are you women doing?" she heard the overseer shout.

Panic rose in Dominique as she saw the wheel's grooves coming to close upon her bare skin. There was no fabric left to cut near her wrist. She pulled with all her might to free herself. The fabric of her sleeve ripped all the way past her elbow. She hacked at the remaining shred of fabric that connected her to the machine.

The machine let out a loud, angry thump as it swallowed half of her sleeve before releasing her. Dominique fell onto the hard stone floor.

Monsieur Louis pulled her to her feet and turned towards the other two women. "What were you all thinking?"

"You told me to clean the machine," said Madame Gilles, her face red from distress and now, anger. "You wanted to keep it running instead of shutting it down."

"I told you to secure your garments first so this wouldn't happen. Now I have to get the fabric out of the wheel. All of you, out."

Dominique inspected her forearm. Though the skin was red from having been scraped along part of the conveyor belt, she was largely unharmed. Her heart pumped hard still. "Are you alright, Madame Gilles?" she asked slightly breathless.

"I will be when I tell Lottie that I will never clean the foundry again." The matron turned to go, limping. The other woman helped her to the door.

"I said, leave, Madame Roland," Monsieur Louis said as he set to the task of stopping the coal grinding machine.

Dominique pocketed her knife and left, even though all manner of words and phrases for the overseer remained on her tongue, begging to be voiced.

She rolled up her sleeves and assisted in helping Madame Gilles walk back to the lodging house. Once she saw the woman to her room on the second floor, Dominique went around the hall and to her own dwelling in number eight.

She opened the door and found Colton behind it, preparing to go to the dining hall before work. His cap was in one hand.

"You've returned early," he said.

She closed the door. She didn't want to tell him of what just transpired at the foundry. Not just yet. She wanted her nerves to cool first. "I found a document in the overseer's office," she stated, low. "It was a freight order for a company or a person with the initials M.B., but that could be anyone."

"What else did it say?"

"There was a comma after the initials. I don't think Monsieur Louis finished writing it. He came in and drove me out of his office."

"Dominique, your hands are shaking."

Before she could hide them behind her back, Colton took them both. He caught sight of the reddened skin along her forearm, as well as the torn sleeve that began to unfurl from where she rolled it up high. His lips parted. "What happened?"

Dominique hesitated before answering. "One of the ladies got her dress caught in a machine. I ripped my sleeve when I helped to free her."

"Why would you both go near the machines?" he demanded, abruptly.

Dominique became startled by his sharp tone. "I told you that I was going to help clean the foundry today."

"You said sweep the floors, not clean the machines. Especially while they're still running. You could have been maimed or even killed."

She looked in his face and saw deep worry. "I-I am sorry. I heard Madame Gilles call for help. I had my knife to cut her dress away from the conveyor belt."

Her hair fell in her eyes. He reached to brush it back, but he didn't drop his hand afterwards. Instead, he lingered to touch her face, his hand gently cupping her cheek.

"Colton?" She stared into his gray eyes. Their color had darkened, changing with the course of his mood.

The warmth of his body traveled to hers. He was close enough where she could smell the soap that he shaved with. "Promise me that you won't go near the foundry machines again." His voice deepened with raw emotion that she never heard come from him before.

She had gotten out of the foundry. She was safely away from machinery. Why was he acting this way? "Colton, I couldn't get to the overseer's office unless I volunteered to—"

"It doesn't matter if we never find out what's in that office. I don't want you to put yourself in danger like that." His compelling eyes held hers, emphatic. "Promise me, Dominique. You won't go in that foundry again unless I'm with you."

She didn't understand. Colton didn't want her to be in any danger. That made sense, but other dangers lurked all around them. They put their lives at risk for their respective agencies by taking part in the mission. Broussard was still wandering about France. Why did the potential perils of being around machinery suddenly become the most poignant spark to ignite his caution?

"I won't go in the foundry again unless I'm with you," she voiced softly, still feeling the warmth of his touch upon her cheek.

He sighed. "Thank you."

It occurred to her that he was still holding her hand, too, but she didn't pull away. His touch was comforting, soothing. Her hands had stopped trembling.

Perhaps he felt that she could only be safe if he was present. But his behavior was too intense to be classified as simple good old-fashioned chivalry. He slid his fingers away from hers.

"Don't say anything to Monsieur Louis. He's already angry that Madame Gilles and I broke his machine."

"That's all he cares about?" Colton flattened his lips. "He's going to have more than a broken machine to be angry about, then."

"No, Colton, don't be rash. I said I wouldn't go back there without you."

She worried when he offered no direct response. He touched the doorknob. "I'm going to see if the lodging house has some balm for your arm. Then I'm going to work."

Dominique watched him leave the room. She prayed her accident wasn't about to cause them both more injury.

***

Colton saw that Dominique had liniment for her arm before he went into the foundry. Sure enough, he found Monsieur Louis at the coal grinding machine with a knife, cursing to himself as he tugged and cut away at scraps of fabric caught in the wheel and conveyor belt.

The overseer raised his small eyes and narrowed them into slits when he saw Colton. "You're late, Roland. The other men got here fifteen minutes ago."

"I had to see to my wife's care. She and another woman got their clothing caught in that machine."

"And I'm still trying to get it back operational. I told that old Madame Gilles where to stand when she's cleaning the conveyor belt. It's her fault."

"The machine shouldn't have been operating on its own. Someone should have rotated the belt manually so she could clean it."

Monsieur Louis set his knife on the floor. "I have a business to run here. I can't stop production because two addle-pated women don't know how to secure their dresses."

The heat of anger rushed through Colton's body. "Those women help keep your business running. If it weren't for them, we'd be buried in coal dust."

"Do you want to work in my foundry, Roland? If not, there is the door." The overseer picked up the knife and pointed the blade tip at the entrance. "Otherwise, keep your mouth shut if you want to keep your job."

Colton walked away from the overseer. The other foundry workers took view of the exchange. They pretended to resume their activity as Colton passed each of them to go to his work station.

He picked up a sledgehammer and started smashing pig iron to use for charging the furnaces. In all his time spent working in industry, he never understood how some overseers had little regard for the people who kept their facilities running. It made him sick to think that if Dominique had not been carrying her knife, she would not have been able to save herself or the other woman.

Their close call was a story all too familiar to him.

He set another piece of pig iron on the ground. His hammer came down too hard, sending pieces of the metal scattering. The men at nearby stations dodged the flying debris. Colton held up his hand in apology and took to breaking the pig iron with less forceful blows. He worked until his ire gradually wore off and transformed into a determination to proceed with his objective.

He thanked fate for sparing Dominique's life. Now he hoped that he could curb his temper at Monsieur Louis long enough to not cost them the mission.

Chapter 11

Forty days later

Although Dominique suspected that Colton had words with Monsieur Louis over the coal grinding machine incident, he made no mention of it to her in the days and weeks that followed. Instead, he became less talkative, growing more focused on the happenings at the lodging house and at the foundry.

She had several notions as to why. As September had turned into mid-October, their mission stalled. So far, they were unable to find any information that linked the foundry's increased productivity to Broussard. The COIC and the Bureau had to be on edge, waiting for them to send word of substantial findings.

Dominique also noticed that despite Colton's quiet turn, restlessness brewed just under the surface of his reserve. It showed in the way he hurried through his meals in the dining hall, even in the mornings when he had just finished work and had the full day to himself to rest.

Only he didn't rest.

One warm, windy late afternoon, while she was carrying laundry back to the lodging house, she saw him coming back from the main road. His steps were exact and tightly controlled, as though he was some great animal stalking prey. As he got nearer, she saw the calculating expression on his face. His mouth was set in an intimidating grim line. She almost thought twice about greeting him.

"Where did you go?" she asked, while trying to keep her linens from blowing into the Gouet.

He waited until the other laundresses passed Dominique before speaking. "I went to town to send a report to the COIC. The Secretary isn't very happy with our progress, or lack thereof."

"That man doesn't understand patience. Rome wasn't built in a day."

"Maybe not, but it does feel like we're getting nowhere fast."

Dominique had the same feelings, too, from time to time, but it didn't do any good to dwell on them. "It's still too soon to give up."

The four o' clock bell rang out from the lodging house roof, indicating that supper would start in an hour.

Colton sighed. "I'm going to rest before I eat and go to the foundry. I'll carry your basket inside the lodging house."

"I can do it." Dominique didn't want to burden him. He looked irritable and tired enough. Tired of working seven nights a week, only to return from the foundry with nothing to show but coal dust on his clothes and hands.

She glanced at her own fingers as she carried the laundry indoors. Her skin was chapped and sore from so much cleaning and scrubbing. At least it made her cover as a cook and laundress all the more believable.

She put the linens away and went upstairs. In forty-five minutes, she needed to be in the dining hall, ready to serve supper. That gave her just enough time to bathe and change in the washroom. She didn't think Colton would mind if she went to their room momentarily to grab clean clothes and a hairbrush from her satchel.

A loud bang rattled the lodging house just as Dominique reached the top stair. It sounded as though it came from outside. She flew to the window at the end of the hall and peered out.

Black smoke and steam poured from the back of the foundry. The drain pipes looked as if one of them had fallen away.

A door swung open and shut behind her. Footsteps pounded her way. Colton's reflection came up behind hers in the window.

"I told them that would happen," he remarked, shaking his head. "Pig-headed overseers." He turned and headed down the stairs.

She glanced out the window again and saw people rushing out of the lodging house to see what transpired. She ran back down the stairs as other tenants on the second floor started coming out of their rooms.

Dominique got out the door and sighted Colton's tall form racing for the foundry. She ran after him. What was he doing, venturing so close to the site of the danger?

She eventually caught up to his long strides as he slowed down upon nearing the front of the foundry. Most of the smoke came from behind the building.

Monsieur Louis emerged from the entrance. He cursed, tossing his hat in the dirt.

"We heard a blast," said Colton. "Is anyone hurt?"

"No, but something's gone bad with the runoff drain pipe and the steam pressure valve." Monsieur Louis viewed the dust cloud rising behind the foundry and cursed again.

"Who's inside?" Colton asked, already turning to go in.

"It was only me." The overseer shifted focus and yelled to the handful of workers that started making their way to the base of the foundry. "Don't go down there yet. Wait till the smoke clears."

"I'll turn the engine valves off." Colton went inside the building.

Dominique sidled in as the overseer continued to shout at the flux of incoming workers and onlookers. He was still too close to the door for her to get into his office unseen.

The interior of the foundry was bathed in warm steam and unsettled dust. Several lighter machines and workbenches had fallen over from the initial blast, but the heavier equipment went undisturbed. The damage occurred mostly outside.

Dominique navigated through the haze until she found Colton at what she presumed was the main engine station.

"Dominique, you know what I said about you being in here."

"I'm with you, though. The foundry appeared to be working fine up to the blast."

"Machines can break down with no notice." He grunted, forcing down a pressure lever on the engine. "But this is different. I told Monsieurs Louis and Totou that the pipe was in danger of clogging with coal tar. They wouldn't listen."

Dominique only heard Colton mention the nightshift overseer Monsieur Totou once or twice. But she did know Monsieur Louis, and given the man's age in regard to Colton's, she guessed he wouldn't stand to listen to someone younger than him.

"They're very lucky the pressure built on the outside, or someone could've gotten hurt. Stand back." He forced down another lever.

Dominique jumped as a great torrent of steam shot from the vent. It formed a wall between her and Colton before the pressure dissolved.

"Get out, both of you," Monsieur Louis called from the doorway. "There might be another break in the valves."

"Now he worries for our safety." Dominique heard Colton mutter as she walked out with him. The crowd of onlookers had grown since they went inside the foundry.

"I turned the pressure off," Colton told the overseer. "But there's probably buildup in the smokestack's flue. Someone should get to it before it starts trapping heat and smoke in the foundry."

Dominique noticed the effect her fellow agent's air of collectiveness had on Monsieur Louis' frenzied state. He calmed down enough to finally stop swearing.

"Scaping out the flue and pipes will put us behind production for hours."

Apparently he still wasn't worried enough for his workers.

Another man ran up to the overseer. "Monsieur Louis, half of the pipe has fallen into the base of the river."

"Can it be reattached?"

"*Oui*, but it will have to be welded to refit. And we will need hoists to lift it back up on the drain's base."

"Days, not hours, behind production," the overseer corrected himself. His gaze swung towards Dominique. "Roland, tell your wife to go. Unless she wants to bring the men water to drink, she'll just be in our way."

"I can bring water." She saw an opportunity to eventually get into the overseer's office while he was indisposed.

She went back to the lodging house to fetch clean water and containers from the kitchen. Lottie met her when she returned outside. "I'm going to take the foundry workers something to drink. It looks as though they will need it."

Lottie's head bobbed anxiously as she wrung her hands. "This is awful. Those foundry workers have a schedule to meet. If the foundry is down, no shipments will go out, either."

Dominique thought it a bit odd that Lottie would concern herself with the foundry's schedules and shipments. Then again, the lodging house depended upon the foundry workers to sustain their business. Lottie and the staff didn't make money if the workers couldn't earn any wages.

Dominique tread back down the road to the foundry, a jug of water strapped on each shoulder. The smokestack above the foundry proceeded to slow from a stormy outpour to a gray wisp. Monsieur Louis and most of the dayshift workers started down to the base of the building.

She entered the foundry and saw that Colton and only a handful of men were inside. Colton focused their attention on the flue of the smokestack. None of them looked towards the front as Dominique walked into the overseer's office.

She closed the door and set the water jugs in front of it. Avoiding being seen from the window, she skirted around the desk, walking in Monsieur Louis' footprints.

Monsieur Louis kept no paperwork on his desk today. A cup was overturned on the desk, likely from his reaction to the pipe's initial blast. Flat ale continued to drip over the desk and onto the floor. Hops and the omnipresent smell of charred coal mingled in a stale, unpleasant aroma.

Dominique used her handkerchief to open a desk drawer, so as not to leave her fingerprints. She found an open valise inside, containing a roster of foundry employees and two records marked Bills of Lading and Freight Orders.

She picked up the Bills of Lading record. All of the bills were signed by the same captain. She saw that his ship was part of a standard line of carriers who also did business in Le Havre.

Talk from the men outside at the foundry base reached the office window. Dominique heard Monsieur Louis give orders to begin hauling the broken portion of the pipe from the river. She hoped that he would be too busy salvaging the foundry equipment to come back into his office for the moment.

She hoped Colton could keep the workers inside distracted, too.

Dominique covered the tip of her finger with her handkerchief and turned through the pages of freight orders next. The first several entries looked nothing out of the ordinary. A shipment of iron slabs to a rail company in Lyon. Brass fittings to be sent to a cabinet maker in Saint-Michel. All of the orders were assigned numbers, confirming what Colton said about how the pallets were arranged to be shipped.

She skimmed the names on the orders, looking for the initials M.B., but a different set of letters caught her interest. She came upon them next to last from the bottom, listed as freight order number twelve. *Four sheets of iron slabs to E.B., factory, Nantes.*

A deliberately vague entry in lieu of the detailed orders for the foundry's other customers on the list. She wondered if the freight order she found last month with the initials M.B. had actually stood for *Monsieur* Broussard.

Dominique perused the older entries, her interest building. The same initials E.B. and M.B. appeared regularly every three to four weeks, with orders calling for sheets of iron, copper pipes, and crucible steel. If the shipments were for Emile Broussard, what was he building with so much raw supply?

She tore out three pages of older entries dated from the spring. The two sets of initials were on each. She searched the book for a facsimile of the freight order that she saw on the overseer's desk over a month ago. She was unable to find it. It could have accompanied the shipment.

Dominique folded the entries and tucked them up her sleeve and buttoned the cuff. She opened the other desk drawers, but found nothing except for spare, blank order books, pencils, and a mix of coal and sawdust that collected in the back corners.

After listening to ensure that Monsieur Louis and his workers were still busy fishing for pipe in the Gouet, she took the water jugs and departed the office.

The foundry remained humid from the steam of the hydraulic pressure valves. The men were eager for a water break. Dominique poured cool water into each of their tin cups. They took their drinks and scattered throughout the space of the foundry, leaving her and Colton to themselves at the base of the crucible.

"Did you find anything this time?"

Dominique filled his cup. "Freight orders of iron slabs shipped to Nantes, paid for by someone with the initials E.B. Do we dare guess who it is?"

Colton drained half his cup in two gulps. "Broussard could have a facility in that city. Most of France's industry is there."

"I think it is Broussard because each entry marked E.B. had no address, save for an unnamed factory in Nantes. The others listed a specific destination. Oh, but it will still be a nuisance trying to find him. Nantes has many factories."

"Our job was to report suspicious activity here. If our agencies confirm that Broussard is the one buying the metals, they'll work to trace the shipments, and they'll stop production here."

Dominique glanced at the idle machinery, dormant from a combination of the clogged pipes and the overseers' greed. "It's not as though that hasn't already been accomplished."

She faced Colton again. Her eyes flitted away from his to view his shirt. The hour she spent scrubbing it clean in the laundry had been in vain, as he had quickly dirtied it up again with coal, sweat, and smudges of soot. But even in its rumpled state, the shirt molded against his chest and flat planes of his abdomen to slip under the trim cinch of his belt.

But why was she always finding herself distracted by his work clothes?

Dominique suddenly wanted a drink of water for herself. "May I borrow your cup?"

He gave it to her. "We still have to get the information over to the agencies."

"I'll send it tomorrow when I go to town with Lottie to buy food."

"Send word to my people in the harbor, too." He referenced the COIC. "I'm guessing I'll be too busy here to leave."

Dominique listened carefully as he gave her the code name to use for the COIC in a telegram. "Really?" she asked, upon hearing it. He nodded.

The supper bell rang.

"It's five o' clock. I am late. I still have to change before I serve food." She gave the cup back to Colton.

"More workers are out here than there are in the dining hall."

"Still, Gustave will be so upset." Dominique picked up the water jugs. "I'll see you tomorrow."

"Don't forget about the errand."

"I'll remember."

"*Au revoir*, Madame Roland." One tiny spark of his former humor returned as he waved goodbye.

She shook her head good-naturedly before hurrying back to the lodging house.

Chapter 12

"Minnie, I can't tell you how grateful I am that you volunteered to assist me with the food shopping. With the men hard at work getting the foundry running again, I need all the help I can get."

Dominique carried a sack of vegetables in her arms. She brushed fennel leaves from her field of view as she trailed after Lottie in the Saint-Brieuc market square. She squeezed between two men as they haggled over the price of a crate of cider.

With only a basket of fruit on her arm, Lottie nimbly entered down another part of the square. "Saint-Brieuc has the choicest vegetables and freshest seafood. The fish stalls are this way."

Dominique hoped she could get to the post office to send a telegraph soon. At the rate Lottie was shopping, the office would be closed by the time Dominique arrived.

Lottie put a distinctively large fish in front of her face. The fish stared at Dominique with its bulbous eyes. "This cod is fresh, don't you think?"

The cod moved its mouth in two sudden gulps before it wiggled out of Lottie's hands to land in Dominique's sack of vegetables.

"Freshly caught, would be my guess." She got a grip on the slippery tail and passed the fish back to Lottie. Would you mind if I went to the post office? I wanted to mail a letter to my uncle back home."

"Go ahead. I will have one of the fishmonger's sons help me carry the food to the wagon. Sorry about the cod," Lottie added, giggling. She was in a surprisingly better mood today after she fretted all afternoon and evening yesterday when the foundry pipe busted.

Dominique gladly put the bag of food in Lottie's arms and went back up the street. She patted her coat pocket, where the freight orders rested, safely tucked away from flowery fennel and flying fish.

The post office had one operator seated behind the telegraph station. He was busy clearing materials off the counter when Dominique came up to the window. "You just made it in time. I was about to close for the day."

Dominique hunted for coins in her pocket. "I have two messages to send to Le Havre."

He slid two pieces of paper and a pencil through the window for her to write them down.

She wrote a message for the Bureau first, starting with its code name: *Uncle you were right about the apples here* **Stop** *But they are turned to cider in Nantes* **Stop** *Look for the mail* **Stop**

She smiled at the nonsensical message. Only the agency would know what she was referring to. She wrote a verse for the COIC on the second paper: *Old girl there is strong tea here* **Stop** *but a real brew in Nantes* **Stop** *Uncle has letter saying so* **Stop**

She read the messages. If the COIC and the Bureau put them together, along with the freight orders that would follow in the mail arriving by boat, they would figure it out.

The operator scanned the messages and looked at her. "You want to send these?"

"I'm a cook. I like to discuss food with family and friends."

The operator shrugged and turned to relay the messages through the telegraph. While he did that, Dominique purchased an envelope and postage and placed the folded freight orders inside. She addressed it to one of the Bureau's secret mail posts. When she first started working with the agency, Agent Joubert said it fronted as a confectionary store in Le Havre. She hoped that the news being sent to them would be just as appetizing.

"The telegrams have been sent," said the operator. "I'm closing up now. You'll have to come back tomorrow to see if the receivers replied." He pressed a button under the counter. Bars came down from the top of the station window.

Dominique's happy mood grew tentative. That wasn't so good. She had hoped that the operator would agree to keep the telegraph station open a few minutes longer. She needed to know if the COIC or Bureau had further instructions.

e dropped the envelope in the bin for outgoing mail and left to find Lottie.

Colton wasn't going to like this additional stall in progress. He'd been so eager for fruition to come of their task. She began to suspect that his behavior was due to something more than just the desire to complete the mission, but what was it?

***

Colton paced back and forth across the lodgings he shared with Dominique. She went into town that afternoon to send a report to the COIC and the Bureau. What did they say in reply?

Three steps had him to the back wall.

Dominique had cooking duty during supper today. Colton missed his opportunity to speak with her because Gustave kept her behind the kitchen window. Now it was after six, and Colton had to report to the foundry soon.

Where are you, Dominique?

Tired of pacing, he sat on the edge of the bed. Minutes later, he heard light footsteps coming down the hall. His head shot up when he heard a key turn in the door.

He opened the door for Dominique.

"Oh." She looked startled to see him. "I thought you would be on your way to the foundry by now."

"I wanted to talk to you first. What did the agencies say?"

She moved her head side to side. "We won't know until I go back to the post office. I sent the telegrams just before it closed."

"You won't have time. Your shift doesn't end until evening. My shift's been extended until noon." He sat back down on the bed. "I'll go to Saint-Brieuc afterwards, then."

"You will be so exhausted."

He threw up his hands. "It has to be done. Plain and simple."

"Colton." Dominique's eyes grew wide. "I don't understand. You've been impatient like this for the past month."

"All of this waiting and watching isn't doing us any good."

"But we've found information and sent it to the agencies. It's in their hands now."

Colton shook his head. He knew she was right, but waiting on the

COIC and the Bureau to respond was too taxing. "The longer we have to wait, the more chance of workers getting hurt in that foundry."

"You'll have to keep showing them proper safety measures. In the meantime, I could attempt to go into Monsieur Louis' office again, if you think there is more evidence to find."

"No. You're not doing that again."

He realized too late that he snapped at her.

Dominique straightened her back and regarded him with surprise. "I'm only trying to help."

Colton had never felt so ashamed of himself. He put his hand to his forehead. "I'm sorry. I shouldn't have raised my voice."

Dominique was quiet for several moments. "Both of our neighbors are still at supper. No one heard you."

"I shouldn't have done it, anyway."

"Are you still angry at me for getting my sleeve caught in the coal grinding machine?"

He raised his head. "Is that what you thought?"

Her eyes lowered. She scraped her thumbnail against her palm. "I don't know."

"I said I'd look out for you."

"You have been protective of me, but you act different when it comes to me being around machines. What is it about them…or me…that angers you?"

"I'm not angry at you." Colton pressed his hands against his legs. He didn't expect that his fear would come out like this, how it could grow out of the past and leech into the present. He thought he had concealed it so well before Dominique. "I don't talk about this much."

"What is it?" Even with the remnants of his words still making her shoulders tense, she stepped closer. The soft cotton of her skirt touched his arm.

Colton gazed upward. She had an angel's face, but her beauty wasn't a mask. "You sure you want to hear this?"

She nodded. True warmth and openness was displayed through her eyes.

Seeing that gave him courage to speak. "My mum—mother—worked as a machine sweep for the factories. She said my father left before I was born. We lived with another family in one of the tenements on London's east end."

Dominique nodded again.

Colton took a deep breath. "She'd go to work when the factories closed. Her job was to get the machines clean enough to where they could operate the next day. Well, there was a canning factory that opened up by the docks. One of the machines there cut aluminum to make lids. There was one problem with it. The rotary blade couldn't be kept stationary. It came down when she went to dust the machine's cutting surface."

Dominique brought her fingertips to her mouth.

Colton forced himself to go on. "They found her beside the machine the next day. There was even talk that she could have survived if someone had been there to call for a doctor." He felt the knots clench hard in his stomach.

"Colton, I am so sorry." Dominique touched his shoulder. "How old were you?"

"I was nine. It was fifteen years ago. The constables ruled it an accident, said it wasn't the factory's fault, and that my mum didn't look for the blade before she started cleaning."

Dominique shook her head.

"They sent me to live in an orphanage. I suppose that's better than living in a tenement. I stayed there, learned to read and write. I left when I got old enough to work at the locomotive factory. You know the rest, or most of it." He put his hand atop hers.

She spoke in a choked voice. "I can't fathom what you went through."

"I got older. Went on, you know. Mum always said to forge ahead, but a couple months back, a report landed on the COIC archives desk."

Dominique's eyebrows rose.

"It was found in one of the Scotland Yard offices, dated from 1824. The canning factory closed a year after the accident. The overseer couldn't keep up with paying his workers, so he closed down shop. The banks traced the factory's investors to see what they could do. Broussard's name was among them. He sold his share of the stock, but he held the patent for the aluminum cutting machine. Turns out, he removed the mechanism that kept the rotary blade stationary so's to cut down on cost."

There. Colton said what he had been keeping in for months. The pain was still there, but it didn't sting as it once did, now that he told the story to Dominique. "After I read that report, I wanted to confront Broussard. But even more, when I thought there was a chance that you…" Colton couldn't finish. "Sometimes it's too close for comfort."

"That's why you wanted me to be careful in the foundry," Dominique said.

"Yes."

"And why you wouldn't let me get to Delacroix's office in the flour mill."

"I knew the job I had to do when I sabotaged the bolting machine. I knew the time it would take for everyone to get out. I wasn't going to let you stay behind to look around, I don't care how good a spy you are."

"You were protecting me then, too."

"As strange as it sounds."

She had tears in her eyes.

Colton wiped one that slid down her cheek. "I didn't intend to make you cry."

"*Non*. I feel terrible for how I've challenged and bantered with you, as though our agencies were in competition. If I had known all this, I would have refrained."

"I kind of like our little joke-jostling. Makes for a less dull mission that way."

Her lips drew into a little smile.

"That's better." He traced their rosebud shape. "We can't both be down in the doldrums."

Her mouth was soft against his fingertip. "But I don't want you to be sad."

"Don't worry about me."

"How can you say that when you worry about me? We are partners."

"Fair enough, but don't get too worked up about me. I can look out for myself just fine."

"*Arrete.*"

"What?"

"Stop." Her lips caught his by surprise.

The taste of her lips was sweet, and the touch of them soft, like the rest of her when she brought her body close. Colton was unprepared as her arms slid like silk behind his neck.

"Dominique." Her name escaped his lips. She put her finger against his mouth.

"*Arrete.*" She drew it away slowly. She kissed him again, long and soft and indulgent, until he forgot what or if he was going to say anything in the first place.

He gave into the gentle demands of her mouth. She was innocent and playful, nipping delicately at his lips at first. Then she kissed him with a sophistication that soon made him moan.

"You could only have learned to kiss like that in Paris."

She gave him another one that sent heat coursing through his body. "And how would you know? Have you ever been to Paris?"

"No." His hand came to cradle the nape of her neck. "But if this was taught in Chay Oiseau, I think I would have heard of your village long before I came to France."

Her laugh was a soft little bell in his ear. Her hair fell forward against his face, the satin strands veiling his eyes from view of the room, making him see only her.

Colton became enclosed in her clean, powdery scent as they fell back onto the bed. The long hem of her dress blanketed them both. He put his hands upon her waist, slowly following the outline at its narrowest point below her ribcage on down as it gradually fanned into the roundness of her hips. His pulse quickened as his fingers rested upon the lush curves. He wanted to lose himself in the fullness of her.

Her chest rested upon his. As she shifted upward, he thought he could even hear her heartbeat.

She gave a tiny gasp of pleasure as his hand came back up, this time to travel the curve of her spine. He could continue to touch her, to kiss her. He wanted to do much more than that, but instinct told him that it was wrong.

"*Arrete.*" He moved Dominique's beguiling frame onto the bed. His whole body cursed at him when he shifted away. "We both need to stop."

Her brown eyes, languid with desire, blinked long black lashes. She rose on her elbows. "*Pourquoi?*"

"Why? Because we got carried away. Dominique, I want you, but not here. Not like this. You know it isn't right."

She tucked a strand of tousled hair behind a pink-tinged ear. Blush rose along her cheeks. "I...well, you see how I feel about you. I didn't want to say anything."

"You deserve better than to be taken unwed in a lodging house."

Colton sat up, allowing the sparseness of the room and the fact that he had to leave for work to draw him to his senses. He had found comfort in Dominique, but was too close to taking it too far. "I'm not going to dishonor you."

They kept silence for several minutes. The heat of the moment gradually faded, but Colton knew if he looked at Dominique long enough, he would be vastly tempted again.

"I have to go to the foundry. You get some rest. I'll see you sometime tomorrow afternoon."

She sat up in the bed, her flushed skin still showing signs of her ardor.

Colton could kick himself. It all started off as a harmless bit of flirtation. How could he let things get to this point?

He didn't want to leave her in the room by herself, but he knew if he didn't, he would not be able to control himself. "Forgive me, Dominique."

He reached the door in two steps and walked out.

Chapter 13

Colton thought about his time with Dominique as he worked the evening shift at the foundry. Even with the sound of hammers clanging and the stench of coal burning in the smaller furnaces, he could still hear her soft laughter in his ears and smell her powdery scent as it lingered in his nose.

His fellow workers situated themselves outside, using hoists to lift the pipe off the ground and outfit it back into place. He worked inside, scraping the clogged pipes. All the while, Monsieur Totou kept snarling at him.

"Roland." The overseer came to Colton while he was stationed under the foundry's main furnace, scraping tar from its crevices. The overseer banged the side of the iron door to get his attention. "Roland."

Colton stuck his head out.

"What are you doing?"

"Cleaning tar from outside the furnace."

"You could have used the pressure hose to clean it if you hadn't shut the pump down on the steam valve yesterday," the man went on his tirade. "What have you been doing all this time?"

"I couldn't use the rubber hose because the day workers used it to clean out the refining furnace. The dross from the iron caked onto the pump."

Colton came out from beneath the furnace and showed him the drain hose that he had to disassemble. Layers of gray and black impurities from the iron settled inside, blocking over half the space. "That has to be scraped."

"Just use a solvent to flush the dross and be done with it." The Monsieur Totou made it obvious that he had never cleaned the foundry's drain system before.

Colton again had to explain why that would only make the foundry's problems worse. "The acetone in the solvent will eat away at the rubber hose."

Monsieur Totou threw up his hands. "Then hurry up and boil some water to flush it out. Get it from somewhere. The kitchen, the laundry facility." He marched off to yell orders over the shoulders of other employees.

The process was repeated in the morning with Monsieur Louis.

"Production's completely stopped," Monsieur Louis complained to everyone in the foundry and no one in particular. "All of us are going to be in dire straits at this rate if we don't get more of that iron shipped south."

Colton paused from working. He knew exactly where in the south Monsieur Louis referred to, thanks to Dominique's foray into his office for the shipping orders.

"Back to work, Roland. We've no time for dallying," Monsieur Louis snapped.

Colton resumed his unpleasant and untidy task of cleaning the main furnace. He disappeared underneath the iron burner. He kept one ear open to the idle chatter from the workers nearby.

Amid the sounds of scraping and shoveling, the overseer's voice distinguished itself from nearby, but this time, it reached a higher pitch. He was talking timidly to someone as opposed to giving orders.

"Monsieur, I certainly did not expect you here."

"I came as soon as I received word."

Colton's chisel stopped in mid-stroke. Broussard's unmistakable smug timbre sounded in the foundry again.

"You told me that the drainage system you employed for foundry runoff was sound, Monsieur Louis."

Monsieur Louis coughed. "This has never happened before."

Colton slid partway from beneath the furnace. Broussard stood in front of the overseer's office, towering over the squat Monsieur Louis. He had his arms crossed over his pressed dark suit as he took a patient, though firm stance. The bowler on his large cranium made him seem even taller as he regarded the overseer.

"This is very bad for my schedule. You were aware of the project intended for construction in Nantes."

The overseer's head bobbed up and down. "We are doing our very best to resume normal work flow."

Monsieur Louis was sweating enough to make Colton believe that he couldn't have been the one to send word to Broussard that the foundry's production had temporarily shut down. If Monsieur Louis didn't tell him, who did? And how did he get here so quickly? Saint-Brieuc was inaccessible by rail, and both New Britannia and France had their agents patrolling the sailing routes further south.

He must live somewhere nearby. Maybe even in one of the surrounding tiny towns in the valley.

Broussard walked out to the foundry floor, confident and sure in his stride. Colton's anger flared at the sight of his approaching form, but he remained still.

"My sister's letter stated that the foundry's pipes had burst. What caused that?" Broussard asked.

His sister? Colton never read anything in the COIC dossiers about Broussard having a sister. His familial status was unknown.

Not anymore, though. Broussard's female sibling was walking about the Saint-Brieuc area, in fact. Or maybe even on the premises at the lodging house.

Monsieur Louis slinked along after Broussard, tail between his legs like a dog anticipating a beating. "Coal and tar built up along the pipes."

Broussard stopped to look at the idle steam pressure valves. "That makes me ponder."

Colton slipped back underneath the furnace again as Broussard started walking towards it. He chiseled very softly at the gummy tar while he listened.

"I had a similar destructive incident occur at my flour mill in Le Havre. I get the suspicion that my facilities and those that I do business with are victims of sabotage. What say you to that?"

Colton held his breath. If the overseer put it together that he and Dominique's arrival coincided shortly after the mill fire, then they both would have their identities exposed.

The overseer stammered. "I know nothing of sabotage here. What happened to the mill?"

"It burned down, due to a bolting machine catching fire. The overseer was jailed by the Bureau de l'Industrie for unsafe working conditions, but I think that new engineer he hired started the fire. The engineer may even have been a Bureau agent."

Colton gritted his teeth, hoping that Broussard would move along.

"I hired a new engineer over a month ago," Monsieur Louis replied.

"You did?"

"He seems to be good with engines. Although, he can be irksome. He thinks that he knows machinery better than I do, but he can't be older than twenty-five."

"Show him to me."

Colton's ears took a beating as Monsieur Louis pounded the side of the furnace. He pulled his cap down over his brow and rubbed a bit of tar across the bridge of his nose for good measure before he slid his head out.

"That's him," said Monsieur Louis, peering down. "Carl Roland's his name."

Colton matched Broussard's stare. It was apparent that Broussard was trying to determine if he had seen him somewhere before.

"Lift your cap, young man."

Colton raised the brim off his forehead.

"The engineer Delacroix hired had red hair. This one has brown hair. You may put your cap back on."

Colton did so without delay.

Broussard straightened the lapels of his coat. "We must be ever secure these days, Monsieur Louis. Bureau agents are roaming about Nantes, Le Havre, nearly everywhere in France. Since that day at the mill, I've felt compelled to travel with my own iron guards now."

"Iron guards?"

"Automatons. I've been producing them in Nantes for some time, but I've recently discovered new ways to improve upon them. Observe." Broussard called to the door of the foundry. "Come forth."

Iron clanked before a tall shadow filled the doorway. Colton twisted to see a six and a half foot automaton enter the foundry. All gray and silver, it moved past the stunned, scared workers towards Broussard. Its long arms hung at its sides, though a cannon-like device protruded from above its left elbow.

Colton immediately saw the similarities to the Aspasian automatons.

The body structure, the head shape, everything was the same except for the machine's monochromatic color scheme and its unnerving eyes. Two red orbs lit with a strange light, never blinking.

It responded to Broussard's voice, continuing towards the industrialist as he talked.

"This is one of my newest creations. It not only does what I say, but it is also armed. Show them the weapon," he instructed the automaton.

The machine raised its right arm, and a pistol emerged from a groove at the junction above its elbow. One of the men made a sound of surprise. The automaton swiveled the gun towards him.

"Weapon down," Broussard commanded. The automaton obeyed. The gun retracted into a built-in compartment as it lowered its arm.

The men in the foundry exhaled a collective sigh of relief.

Colton didn't take his eyes away from the automaton. There was the end product of the metal supplies the foundry shipped to Nantes. It made sense that Broussard had the largest of the freight orders. He was building an army.

"That is quite a sight to behold," Monsieur Louis said to Broussard while simultaneously keeping distance from the automaton.

"There is another outside." Broussard spoke of his creations as though he were a proud father. "They'll stay with me for the duration of my time here."

"You're staying here, Monsieur Broussard?"

"This foundry must resume production. With the Bureau mobilizing its agents south, I can't wait for the shipments to go to Nantes. I've brought the main component of the engine with me to assemble here. Your men will work on it."

"Monsieur?" the overseer asked, confused.

Broussard waved him off. "Clear the space on the floor. We don't need these furnaces and forges. We start the first round of assembly tonight."

***

Dominique kept the images and details of yesterday evening in her mind when she woke up the next morning. Thoughts of Colton stayed with her throughout the morning, from her trek to the dining hall to the laundry facility.

She tossed another armful of shirts in the heated vat of water. She started to add more lye when a woman came her way, calling her name.

"Minnie, Gustave wants you in the kitchen immediately." The woman, one of the table servers, huffed and puffed from running.

Dominique handed the box of soap flakes to another laundress on the scaffold and climbed down the ladder. "Did he say why?" She thought that someone may have complained that she added too much pepper to yesterday's stew.

"He did not," the table server murmured after catching her breath, "but he said to send for you at once."

"I'm on my way." Dominique wiped her damp hands on her apron before removing it and throwing it into a clothes bin. She ran after the table server who was already out the door of the laundry facility. Gustave never sent for her when she wasn't scheduled to work in the kitchen. Whatever could he want?

Outside the laundry building, she viewed the dormant smokestack of the foundry. Business continued to stall since the foundry's drainage pipe went bust. Some workers had reduced shifts while others like Colton were forced to work multiple ones. More than a few of the latter complained about having to work double shifts without the extra pay.

Dominique felt sorry for all of them. It wasn't their fault that the foundry overseers were negligent in maintaining their machinery. She hoped Colton could get the pipes and machinery operational again soon. The tension between the workers was liable to start a scuffle.

She proceeded to the lodging house. As she neared, she spotted multiple wagons interspersed along the road. They collected alongside the foundry, their large steel-axle wheels leaving great ruts in the dirt. Oilcloth covered their frames.

What was this?

Dominique squinted to see men moving along the stationary caravan. One group carried benches and smaller furnaces out of the foundry. Another retrieved large metal parts from the wagons and carried them inside.

Did the overseers order a new pipe to be outfitted to the drainage system behind the building? A new furnace, perhaps? She couldn't tell what the parts were for.

Dominique looked towards the river and saw a small carrier docked several hundred feet downstream. The late morning sunlight shone on covered objects on deck.

Colton said that carriers delivering shipments for the foundry arrived at dawn. It was nearing noon. What was going on today?

She hurried to the dining hall of the lodging house. Trotting past workers idly waiting for their shifts to commence, she went into the kitchen. Gustave stood at the far counter with his back to the door. His butcher knife rose in the air and went *twack-twack* on a particularly bloody cut of meat before rising again.

"Gustave, you wished to see me?"

Gustave whirled so fast with the butcher knife that Dominique jumped back. "*Bon*, you're here. Lottie is cleaning windows. I need you to help me prepare supper in her stead." "What is taking place? I saw wagons near the foundry and a boat on the river."

Thwack-thwack, went the knife, so loud that Gustave didn't hear her. He dropped the knife on his cutting board alongside the meat and wiped his hands on the front of his apron. "We've great work to do. Come to the vegetable table."

Dominique washed her hands at the sink and reached for a clean apron before joining him at the vegetable table. Rows of emerald-green leeks and golden potatoes lined the surface.

"Minnie, remember those braised leek and potato pies you made last week? You must do so again, and the crust must be as buttery golden as it was before. No, even better. There can be no mistakes, no charred edges." He shook his head firmly. "And then, I need you to bake a soufflé."

"You want me to bake a soufflé for all the workers?" Such a feat would take hours and with that many soufflés in and out of the oven, several were bound to be burned.

"No, I need you to bake one soufflé. One perfect soufflé. We have a distinguished guest taking supper at the lodging house tonight. Industrialist Emile Broussard is here."

Dominique dropped her knife. Gustave clucked his tongue and fussed as she bent to pick it up from the floor. "There can be no clumsiness tonight, Madame Roland. The food must be superb. The service must be *excellente*. Do you understand?"

"*Oui*, monsieur." Dominique washed the blade and returned to the vegetable table. Having no choice, she began paring the leeks while he looked over her shoulder, scrutinizing her every motion of the knife.

The mishap at the foundry must have drawn Broussard out of hiding. He had great stake in the metals produced. Naturally, he would inquire as to why production had stalled on them, but to risk making a personal appearance instead of sending a representative, this mysterious project of his had to be important.

But where was Broussard now?

"Gustave, when did this Monsieur Broussard arrive today?"

"Just this morning. He is at the foundry as we speak."

Colton was still working. What if Broussard recognized him, even with his hair dyed brown? The knife shook in Dominique's nervous hand. Unless Colton kept his head down and nose to the grindstone, there was a good chance that his cover would be found out. Both of them were at risk.

"Steady your blade, Madame Roland."

"I'm just a bundle of nerves. I'm cooking for an important man." What were she and Colton going to do about Broussard when there were so many people around?

"Focus on the task at hand. I must finish preparing the boeuf." Gustave ambled back to his station and started hacking at the cut of beef again.

Dominique's eyes began to tear as she sliced the leeks into green discs. Her vision became blurry just as several figures entered the dining hall. What was that strange clanking sound?

After she wiped her eyes with her handkerchief, she saw Broussard strolling past the tables, flanked by Lottie as she carried towels and a bottle of vinegar. Dominique immediately averted her gaze from Broussard, not wanting to risk him recognizing her. Her eyes went from him to the last entrant into the dining hall. The silver-plated automaton cut a slightly ungainly path behind Broussard, its glowing red eyes focused on him. The clanging of its feet made noise in tandem with the wooden floor as it protested the machine's weight.

The men in the room ceased their card games and stared in stunned silence as the automaton went by. Their eyes darted to the automaton's arm, and the curious cannon-like aperture built onto it.

Dominique realized that she pressed the knife so hard that part of the blade stuck into the table.

"So this is what you workers are being paid to do, sit idle while those more skilled than you are laboring at the foundry," Broussard's rumble broke the silence. "There will be plenty of work for you all, starting this evening."

The way he voiced the statement to the men gave Dominique cause for wonder. What work could be done if production had stalled?

Lottie chirped as she bustled past Broussard into the kitchen. "Minnie, *merci beaucoup* for taking my place. I'm ready to help now. *Bonjour*, Gustave."

Gustave looked from Broussard and then to Lottie. "What is he doing in here? Supper is not till five. He cannot see the preparations."

Broussard heard Gustave's fussing and turned. Dominique pretended to focus on chopping the remaining leeks as he walked to the counter. She turned, so that he could only see her profile. She lowered her head. Her hair fell forward to cover the side of her face.

"I would have a portion of cheese and cider to tide me until supper, if you would, Gustave."

How did Broussard know the chef's name? And why weren't Gustave and Lottie wary of the automatons as was nearly every other person in the room?

From her peripheral vision, Dominique saw Broussard approach the counter. She kept her head down. She took to peeling a potato.

Gustave scrimmaged for a hunk of cheese in the icebox. Lottie set a clean glass on the side of the vegetable table and poured from a bottle of the costly cider.

Dominique's eyes watered as the sulfuric fumes from the leeks began to overpower the area. She gathered them into a bowl before returning to the potatoes. Broussard sniffed and backed away from the window.

Gustave removed the leeks to another table. "*Pardonnez-nous*, Monsieur Broussard. We will be serving supper at five."

"Have a worker bring it to me outside the foundry." Broussard took his cheese and cider and left, automaton lagging behind him. No sooner did the machine clear the doorway did the dining hall fill with surprised chatter and whispers.

"Get back to work, Madame Roland," Gustave ordered. "Those pies must get in the oven. Now, hurry."

Chapter 14

Once the last of the pies were in the oven, Dominique excused herself from the kitchen and went to see if Colton was upstairs in their room. She opened the door to an empty space.

He was supposed to leave the foundry after the morning shift, but that was before Broussard arrived. Dominique grew restless as she wondered what was happening in that building. From the upstairs window at the end of the hall, she saw the wagons still in front of the foundry. The carrier vessel had left the dock.

She returned downstairs to serve supper. Colton did not make an appearance.

She placed the last slices of leek and potato pies onto plates to be served to the workers that straggled in just before six. As soon as she set Broussard's soufflé to baking, Dominique saw her chance to leave. "Gustave, may I be excused?"

The cook hemmed and hawed. "This is the second time, Madame Roland."

"I am not feeling well." She clutched her stomach for effect.

"Go." He looked disgusted as he waved her off. "But see that you are here again at five in the morning sharp."

Dominique whipped off her apron and left the dining hall. She ran up the stairs to the second floor.

Colton still wasn't in their room. By light of the wall lantern, she changed out of her dress and into one of the spare sets of clothing in her satchel, a pair of breeches and a canvas shirt. She pulled her boots over the pants. Dominique then reached under the bed and withdrew a carefully folded towel that she tucked away weeks ago. Her fingers peeled the towel back to reveal her COIC-issued firearm.

She had the cuff of the retractable pistol on her wrist when the door opened. Dominique lowered her arm and breathed a relieved sigh when she saw that it was Colton.

He entered and swiftly closed the door behind him. "Broussard's here."

"I know. I saw him in the dining hall today."

Colton stopped in his tracks. "Did he recognize you?"

"No, I was in the kitchen. He didn't pay me any attention. Where is he now?"

"At the foundry. He's brought some machine to be built. The foundry floor is being cleared for its assembly now." Colton forced a sigh. "The mill fire was one thing, but the pipe bust got him spooked. He thinks it was also sabotage. He plans on not leaving until the machine is assembled."

If those wagons and carrier were all present to transfer the parts for only one machine, Dominique shuddered to think of the size it would be upon completion. "What is he building?"

"We don't know. The parts haven't all been taken inside yet. He won't let the workers start until every piece is organized by station."

"I'm going to town to send a telegram to our agencies. We need aid."

"Not right now, you can't. The main road is blocked with wagons and it's just past sunset. You'll have to wait until dark and the lodging house shuts down for the night. You can leave when I go out again for the midnight shift."

"You're not coming with me?"

"I can't. Broussard already saw me at the foundry. If we both go missing, he'll put it together and figure out that we're agents tracking him. He'll try to run again."

Dominique rested her hands on her hips. "How did he know of the foundry's stalled production?"

"His sister sent him a letter."

"What?"

"That's what he said to Monsieur Louis."

Dominique put her hand to her mouth. "Lottie."

Colton looked at her. "The housekeeper?"

"She told me on my first day here that she had a brother who worked in industry. Now I see that she was talking about Broussard. She may be blonde, but she has a similar stature and face shape. How could I not have noticed before?"

"You can't worry over it now. You have to be ready to go to Saint-Brieuc. Take the field equipment with you."

"Let me get that vest. I took the mail out of it so that it could fold easily in my satchel." She went to her satchel for the mailed corset vest.

"You shouldn't have done that. It takes hours to get that mail back in place. Every link has to be lined up right or it's no good."

"Well, we do have a few hours to spare."

"I could think of better ways to pass the time."

She looked up. "Really, Colton. I dare not ask."

"I was thinking of a nap." He smiled. "Where is your mind, Agent Fontaine?"

She faltered at that. "How can you think of napping at a time like this? You were on pins and needles but three days ago."

"You try working rotating shifts and see if you don't fall asleep, criminals afoot or no." He unfolded the pallet and plopped down. "Wake me before twelve."

"Sleep, then, while I put this vest back together."

By the time she got the mail lined up properly in the vest, it was almost time for the midnight shift. Dominique didn't have to shake Colton awake. He came out of his doze and watched her slip the vest over her shirt.

"You can't wear that in plain view when you go out of the lodging house. People will know you're a woman. Wear one of my shirts over it and put on a cap." He opened his satchel and handed the garments to her.

A minute later, Dominique rolled the long sleeve of his shirt down to cover the cuff on her wrist. "Now do I look like an engineer?" she asked, after tucking her hair under the cap.

Colton paused from putting on his own mail-lined waistcoat. "Maybe if you had a few smudges of coal on your face and arms."

"You have some on your nose. You forgot to wipe it off." She offered her handkerchief.

He declined. "It's there on purpose to keep Broussard from recognizing me."

"By hiding your freckles?"

He found a gun in his satchel and tucked it beneath his waistcoat. "I don't have freckles."

"But you do. Itty bitty tiny ones, on the bridge of your nose. I saw them yesterday." She paused. "Am I making you bashful?"

Colton rubbed the back of his neck. "Are we ready? It'll soon be after twelve."

Dominique returned to seriousness. "Lead the way."

He switched the lantern light off before opening the door. The hallway was dimly lit with one sconce at each end. Dominique counted four men descending the stairs. She and Colton fell in line behind them.

Two of the men talked to each other.

"You saw those iron guards he brought with him. I don't know what he's up to, but I say we take our wives and leave while we can."

"We can't risk it, Jean. Once our shift's done, maybe he'll let us go."

"I don't know. Have you seen Cesar? Vouvray said he didn't work his shift in the morning, nor did Manche or Bernard in the afternoon. 'Fact, I haven't seen any of the in-town workers come from Saint-Brieuc today."

Dominique became chilled upon hearing that. Colton looked at her over his shoulder. Whatever was going on in town, she was about to find out what it was.

She pulled the cap down tight over her ears, tucking an errant strand of hair back underneath. She kept her head lowered as she passed through the empty lobby and outside.

Colton suddenly halted. She stopped herself from bumping into him. She looked around his shoulder as the four men walked on ahead. "What is it?" she whispered.

"The foundry. Look." Colton pointed to the open entrance of the building.

An automaton stood guard at each door while the workers went through. Dominique focused her gaze on one man that didn't go inside with the rest of them, but remained near the automatons. A rifle was in his hands. He stopped each worker as he passed and had him empty his pockets and roll up his sleeves. "Is that Gustave?"

"Yes, and he's checking everyone for weapons." Colton uttered something inaudible. "Dominique, take the gun from under my waistcoat."

She lifted the waistcoat in the back and found the gun tucked in his belt.

"Head to the pastoral fields on your left. Stay off the main road for a while until you reach town."

"Be careful, Colton." His gun rested heavy in her hands.

"You, too." He waited for her to cross over to the field before he continued down the main road to the foundry.

Dominique slipped into the shadows, out of view from the lanterns alongside the road. She watched Colton go up to the foundry entrance. Gustave said something to him. Colton showed his empty pockets. The cook then pointed to his waistcoat. Dominique stilled her breath, praying that Gustave wouldn't notice the mail lining.

Colton turned the waistcoat outward at the collar. He flicked it in one quick wrist motion, making the garment appear as though it were merely fashioned of leather. Gustave nodded and motioned for him to go inside.

Now it was Dominique's turn to do her part. She pulled the safety of Colton's gun and started for town.

***

Colton gazed again at the two automatons that stood guard at the foundry door, along with the cook Gustave. Inside the foundry, two other men of Broussard's hire trained their rifles on him and the laborers.

"Engineers at Section Four," one said.

He buttoned the first button that came undone on his armored waistcoat. The situation had very little room for him to manipulate. No one was going to come in or go out. And no one was going to go anywhere near Broussard.

The industrialist stood on a platform and surveyed the activity on the floor. The overseers Totou and Louis both watched alongside him, ensuring that the laborers didn't slack from the assembly work set out for them.

"Section Four," Broussard bellowed down to Colton's group from his lofty perch, "pick up the slack. I want that column to be attached to the medial core within the hour."

Colton put his head down and began tightening the bolts of a panel to the nine-foot column. It was obvious that the wires were meant to attach to another panel. He'd seen the structuring before in the Aspasian automatons. But this, whatever it was Broussard had them building, was too big to be a self-operating machine.

A few minutes later, he lifted his head and saw the workers in Section Five raise an identical iron column upright using a cable system. The column began to tilt. Men shouted. Two reached for the pistons at the top of the column and strained to hold it while the rest of their section scurried to stabilize the base.

"Broussard is going to have us all shot," the worker to Colton's right murmured. "Look at those automatons blocking the exits. We're never getting out."

"Those doors will open," Colton replied. He spoke to the five workers in his section, intent on quelling their rising panic. "Broussard has to get the machine outside the factory to fully assemble. He can't do it in here."

"What does that matter? Then he'll shoot us after we finish assembling it outside." The socket wrench shook in the laborer's hand as fear mounted upon his face. The wrench rattled upon the column.

"You can't lose hope."

"Easy for you to say, Roland. Your wife's still abed in the lodging house. Mine is in town. Who's to say if those automatons aren't outside our home?"

Knots lined in Colton's stomach. If more automatons were patrolling Saint-Brieuc, then that made every inhabitant a prisoner in the town. Dominique was headed to the main square.

His shoulders ached as anxiety came to weigh on him. He thought it would be safer for Dominique to go to town while he remained at the foundry. He may have been wrong.

Colton watched Broussard move from one side of the platform to the other.

"Engineers, to Station One," he called from on high.

Colton slipped the socket wrench back into his toolbelt. "Keep working, men. Those doors will open soon and we'll all be out of here."

"What do you think you're going to do?" A fellow worker scoffed before Gustave came from the entrance and fixed his rifle upon him from fifteen feet away.

"Back to work."

Colton narrowed his eyes. He should have known from those burned biscuits that Gustave could never have been a real chef.

The laborer put his head down and did as Gustave said. Colton was forced to cross between Gustave and the rifle. That gun looked like it could take down a team of pack horses in one shot.

At Station One, he found twice the number of men working on the assembly of a boiler engine. Hoses extended from it to disappear under a large dome-shaped object, its span and height equal to that of a four-seater couch. The object itself was concealed under a tied sheet of oilcloth.

"What is this?" Colton asked one of the foundry's dayshift engineers.

"All Broussard said was that it's to attach and sit atop those twin columns," the man said, looking back at the ongoing work of Stations Four and Five.

Broussard's voice carried down the platform. "Take the cover off that cockpit."

Cockpit? Colton untied the rope tethering the oilcloth. The heavy oil-treated fabric fell away to reveal that which he had no comparison.

Brass and steel beget the circular frame of a glass orb. The glass provided both part of the frame and the window for an enclosed space housing two leather seats.

"Is that a glass carriage?" the day engineer asked.

Colton looked closer. This was no vehicle for transporting ladies to the ball. A system of control switches and buttons lay splayed before the seats. Straps and harnesses were sewn into each seat. "It's a cockpit for an engine."

In his head, he began constructing an image. The twin columns. The smaller columns at Stations Two and Three. Colton lifted one of the hoses. "We're building a pilotable machine."

His engineer compatriot spoke again when Broussard went to survey the other stations. "Is Broussard mad? We can't put a boiler engine beneath the cockpit. It could combust."

Or building the machine could be their way out of the factory, Colton thought. And enable him to get into town. His hopes rose again. "It's our job to see that we build the best machine we can, isn't it?" He tossed the hose to the engineer. "Best get started."

Chapter 15

Dominique made it through the fields and followed the road into Saint-Brieuc. It would be dawn in a few hours, and the lodging house staff would know that she went missing if she didn't make it back before first light.

The old-fashioned oil lamps stood as silent sentries on the main road at junctures. Half of them remained dark as the small town emerged ahead.

Dominique slowed her pace and moved from view as she saw a figure in the middle of the road. Why was he simply residing there? Was the person looking for someone, or standing in wait?

Dominique gripped her gun. Her retractable pistol remained on her wrist. If she fired using either weapon, she'd risk someone hearing her. She got off the road again and crept up along a hill while keeping a watchful eye on the strange figure below. The person stood with his back to the town. His head never moved left or right.

A breeze swept through, causing one of the oil lamps to shake and cast its light on the figure at a different angle. The automaton's head gave off the faintest metallic sheen.

Dominique gasped. Broussard traveled with more than the two iron guards he appeared with in the lodging house. This one he left to guard the way into town.

She moved along the hill. She saw two more on the main road below, interspersed among the shadows between the oil lamps. They stood, waiting for the errant traveler to come traipsing along. Dominique grimaced each time she snapped a twig or disturbed a pile of dry leaves, but the sounds were too soft for the automatons to register as a threat.

She moved forward. Yet another automaton was planted below. No wonder no one had seen the in-town laborers since yesterday. They were unable to get past the automatons.

She came down from the hill when it was clear and resumed travel upon the main road. It took her to a juncture where it led past the yard of a medieval church. She stepped over the perimeter of the churchyard and moved behind the old Gothic structure.

"Mademoiselle."

Dominique held tight to her gun as she looked right. The frightened face of a young woman appeared in the open window. A faint glow of a candlelight emanated behind her.

"You shouldn't be out there. Come inside with us." The woman waved her closer.

Dominique approached the sill. Two large groups of people huddled on the floor before the altar of the sanctuary. It was too dark in the room to count how many there were. "How long have you been in there?" she whispered

"Since mass this morning. Come inside, please. The metal soldiers will get you."

"I'm going to telegraph for help."

"You can't. The soldiers are on the main road."

Dominique looked left and right, in case one of the automatons she saw before had somehow discovered her presence and come clanking across the churchyard looking for her. "Is there a way to reach the post office from here without taking the main road?"

"There's a side street that leads to the square. The churchyard extends down to it."

Dominique nodded. "Go back to the others. Take this." She gave the woman Colton's gun. "Keep silent and don't go near the windows again."

She cut through the tree-lined yard and behind the church, moving fast in case one of the automatons detected her movements. She removed her soldier's knife from her corset vest pocket before darting into the narrow side street. Her feet followed the winding and uneven path of the ancient cobblestones as it took her behind residences and shops. She came to an opening that led to the main road.

Dominique peeked out between two buildings. The town square lay empty, with surrounding shops locked down, probably having never opened that morning.

No automatons were in proximity. Knife in hand, she emerged from the side street and kept close to the storefronts until she reached the post office.

The street lamp cast light on the building and the lock on the door. She hastened to use the lock pick on the utility knife to get inside.

She left the door open wide enough for the streetlight to cast a dim glow into the post office. Dominique walked through the space. The flickering light from outside caused shadows to move about the walls and slink behind the counter. The old floorboards groaned with even the tiniest step she made.

Dominique winced when she pushed the small door to get behind the counter at the telegraph station. The iron hinges voiced their complaint in a series of creaks.

The telegraph machine sat before a glass window. Dominique laid the knife on the table in front of the machine before getting to work. She soon got the needles working and the circuits ready to send a message to the Le Havre station. She put in Broussard's code name.

Oil slick is in Saint-Brieuc **Stop** *Heavily armed with*— Her fingers stopped inputting Morse code. Did a code for automaton even exist? *iron soldiers* **Stop** *Need help now.*

The machine let out a series of beeps as the message was transmitted. She counted the minutes, drumming her fingers on her knees in nervousness.

She was wringing her hands by the time a message came back in what seemed to be very much later. The beeping made her jump.

She tore the paper from the ream as soon as it had finished transmitting. *Acknowledged* **Stop** *Agent outpost alerted* **Stop** *Stand by for further instructions.*

Stand by. How much longer did the Bureau think she could do this?

Dominique rifled through the box of telegrams in case coded agency correspondence was sent in lieu of Broussard's arrival yesterday.

"Someone is very anxious to hear from her uncle."

Dominique went to press the switch to release the pocket pistol at her wrist.

"I wouldn't do that, *ma petite*. I have a revolver pointed at that hard head of yours." She heard the chamber of a revolver click shut. "Turn around slowly. Hands in the air."

She followed instructions until she stood facing Lottie. The blonde woman smiled at her through the service window, half her mouth obscured by a steel and brass firearm. The black silencer extended through the bars of the window's opening.

"I find it odd that you would come out this late at night to send a telegram. Does your husband know that you have trouble sleeping?"

"Does insomnia run in the Broussard family?"

Lottie giggled. "Industry never sleeps. Anyone who wants to profit from it shouldn't do much sleeping, either."

Dominique slowly began to see the physical resemblance now that Lottie's hair was pulled back. Her moon-shaped face, the large nostrils, and the lips that curved easily into a mocking smile of self-satisfaction all pointed to the Broussard familial traits. "How did you know I left the lodging house?"

"I didn't. I went back to Saint-Brieuc after supper to guard the town square. I walked up this street just now and saw the door to the post office was ajar."

"Have you posted the automatons along the road?"

"Emile has me making sure the townspeople stay in their homes. He has a project to complete, and he doesn't need interruption. Bring me those telegrams." Lottie nodded at the table where Dominique perused the box of messages. "I would see who you are truly relaying messages to."

A whirring sound came from the doorway. Dominique took her eyes off Lottie to see an automaton fill the space. It maneuvered one ball-socket joint limb after another to get into the telegraph office. Her skin grew clammy as the automaton's red eyes turned on her.

"I don't know how you got past the iron guards along the main road, but there will be no getting around that one." Lottie put her left hand under the gun handle to support it. "The telegrams, s'il vous plaît."

Dominique turned sideways.

"Slowly. Keep one hand in the air where I can see it."

She touched the messages on the table and slipped them into her grasp.

"That's it. Now slide them between the bars."

Dominique took two steps forward to the window. She lowered one hand, putting the telegrams halfway through. Lottie took a hand off the gun. She looked down.

Dominique hit the bar release button on the counter and ducked out of Lottie's trajectory as the spring-release window bars came flying up. Lottie shrieked as the bars retracted into their slots, trapping her wrist between the window pane and the base of the bars. The gun fell from her grip, clattering off the counter and onto the floor.

Dominique dove for the weapon.

"Get her," Lottie shouted to the automaton.

Dominique came up, Lottie's gun in hand. The automaton was at the half-door of the telegraph station. The hinges of the door peeled back like paper as the automaton barreled its way through. She aimed the gun at it and fired. The bullet gave a muted whistle as it shot forth.

A hole appeared in the automaton's shirt where the bullet lodged in its chest. The machine kept moving forward.

Dominique aimed the gun for the automaton's head. A side of its metal cranium fell away, exposing its gears. They whirred and spun. The automaton jerked, twisting its neck at a ghastly angle. One of its legs ceased to move. Dominique sent a bullet through its right eye.

The gears stopped making noise. She backed against the wall as the automaton crashed face down on the floor. Its limbs twitched one last time before they remained still.

Dominique's heart pounded in her ears. Her palms coated the gun barrel with sweat. "What is Broussard building in Nantes?"

Lottie's eyes widened as she took in the fallen form of the automaton.

"Answer me, Charlotte."

"Some-something to dissuade his competitors and the Bureau from coming after him."

Dominique turned the gun on Lottie. "What does that mean?"

Broussard's sister swayed, then slumped against the window frame, supported from collapsing onto the floor only by her trapped wrist.

Zut, but now she wanted to faint?

The telegraph machine beeped. Dominique pulled a sheet from the paper ream and took note of Agent Joubert's instructions. *Aid en route from outpost* **Stop** *Coic by sea* **Stop** *wait at bay*

The door to the post office crashed in. Dominique dropped the message and lifted the gun to three automatons, all clambering to get through the entrance at once. They must have come at the sound of Lottie's scream.

She had to shoot the first automaton multiple times. There weren't enough bullets left in the gun for all of these three. And Dominique wasn't about to get within close range to use the tiny pistol affixed to her wrist.

She turned Lottie's gun towards the window behind the telegraph machine and shot out the glass.

The gunfire made the automatons move faster into the office. Lottie moaned. One stopped at her side. The other two went for the entrance to the telegraph station. They reached for Dominique even as they had yet to step over the fallen automaton.

Dominique climbed out the window and ran through the back alleys again. She headed north, away from town and to the port. She gripped the revolver tight, ready to fire upon the next automaton that would get in her way.

No going back to the lodging house now that her cover was revealed. She had to wait for reinforcements. She hoped Colton was faring better at the foundry than she was in town.

***

The glass dome of the machine was open. Colton peered into the cockpit from his position of fifteen feet in the air. A pilotable, walking engine.

He balanced on a rickety portable scaffold as he worked furiously with the other engineers outside the doors of the foundry. With the dawning sun overhead and Broussard barking orders from the ground, they attached the last two appendages onto the machine.

The hoist carrying the machine's right "arm", a seven-foot long column of pistons and wire, was wheeled closer. Colton caught the front and guided the metal limb into a paneled slot on the side of the steel frame supporting the control pit. His scaffold swayed beneath him. The wooden structure should have been relegated to kindling years ago.

Someone climbed the scaffold beside him and handed him a rivet gun. He proceeded to seal the arm in place.

The hoist operator released the machine's arm once he completed the task. The appendage lowered at the machine's side, its crab-like pincers ready to grasp whatever was placed in front of them.

"Good work, but remain up there," Broussard commented to Colton before yelling at the engineers on the ground. "Ready the boilers."

Colton edged away from the smokestack located on the frame of the control pit. He understood an invention needing economy of space, but the idea of allowing steam and hot coal gases to release so close to the engine controls was chancy.

The engineers began heating and charging the machine's small, efficient furnace. Within minutes, the engine began to gurgle as steam pressure build.

"Put in coal, then seal the engine panel," Broussard ordered.

"But Monsieur Broussard," a dayshift engineer said, "shouldn't we wait to see if the boilers hold before we seal them?"

"I designed that boiler engine myself. It's cast with steel and aluminum. It will hold."

The engineer ceased to voice his concern as a rifle-carrying guard released a casing from his firearm for show.

Colton saw movement out of the corner of his eye. A woman came running from the main road. Two automatons trailed her, but she didn't appear to be fleeing them. She clutched one of her hands to her side.

"Emile!"

Her cry reached the factory. Even the voice-responsive automatons looked to the voice's origin.

On her second shout, Colton recognized her as the table server Lottie. The men cleared a path for her and the flanking automatons as she came close to barreling into them. She stopped before Broussard, her blonde hair flying in every direction.

"Charlotte, what's wrong with you?" Broussard was curt. "Why did you leave Saint-Brieuc's square?"

Lottie held up her right hand, supported by her left. Colton grimaced at the sight of the appendage, the wrist swollen and tilted at an unnatural angle as it extended from the crumpled cuff of her sleeve.

"Madame Roland did this. Minnie, that new girl I hired a month ago, the one whose soufflé you loved so much."

Dominique made it into town. She defended herself against Lottie, but where was she now? Colton's worry over her only grew.

Broussard gave a passing glance at Lottie's injury as though she were showing him a hangnail. "You weren't supposed to leave your post. How did she get by you and the iron guards?"

"She is a trained spy, that's how. I found her in the post office, sending a telegram to the Bureau in Le Havre." Lottie produced two crumpled messages from her skirt pocket. "Agents are on their way here. They're going to come to the bay."

A murmur went up from the laborers. One of Broussard's men shot a bullet in the air for warning.

"Get that man on the scaffold. He is Minnie's partner."

Colton suddenly found Lottie's finger pointed at him. Broussard's face turned up at him. The industrialist made a move to approach.

Colton rose on the scaffold. The wobbly structure leaned forward. He shifted his weight and it went backwards, pitching sharply to the left. He leaped into the cockpit of the pilotable engine just as the scaffold fell against the machine's arm and crashed, splintering onto the ground.

Colton landed sideways into the arm of one of the leather seats in the cockpit. He grunted as the wind knocked out of his lungs. Pushing himself into a righted position in the chair, he heard the engine boiling steadily stronger to life beneath him. It muffled the sounds of disruption outside.

"Get him out of there." Colton heard Broussard command his hires. The engineers climbed over the fallen scaffolding to get out of the way.

Colton's hand moved towards the first lever within reach and pushed it all the way forward. The machine gave a sudden lurch. He grabbed the arms of his chair to keep from pitching out the window. Men scurried to clear out from beneath him. Lottie made a beeline to the lodging house.

He pushed the left lever forward. The machine's left leg responded accordingly, moving the entire structure from its original position. He heard what remained of the scaffolding snap and splinter beneath the apparatus' iron feet.

Rifle fire cracked in the air. Colton heard the bullet strike the lower side of the engine, glancing off the steel rivets. Broussard's hoarse, furious shout followed.

"Don't fire near the furnace, Gustave."

Colton's eyes darted left and right as he tried to make sense of the control panel. Brass knobs, switches great and small, levers, and buttons made a roadmap to nowhere. He had to try something, though, else he'd be a sardine waiting for Broussard and his men to pluck him out of a can.

He tried another lever, just above the first one that he pushed forward.

A creak ensued outside on the right of him before he saw the machine's arm swing forward. Gustave caught the brunt of it. His rifle went one way, he went the other, screaming in mid-air before he landed in a bush of thorny thistles.

A laborer that Colton recognized from Station Four picked up the fallen weapon. Two more rifle-bearers came into view on the left, aiming at the man's head. Colton reached to the far left of the cockpit. He maneuvered the corresponding arm lever and made the machine sweep it across their path. Like toy soldiers, Broussard's men fell. Foundry workers closed in on them and their guns.

The laborer gave Colton a nod of thanks as he lifted the rifle. He shouted for the other workers to rally with him.

The field between the lodging house and foundry soon populated with men. Broussard's workers became lost in the shuffle. Broussard himself was nowhere to be seen. Did he run into the lodging house after Lottie to take shelter?

Colton rotated a dial in the center of the control board. Air rushed through the cockpit as the frame turned one hundred and eighty degrees. Two pairs of red eyes gave vague stares as Colton came to view Lottie's two iron guards.

He pulled the machine's right arm lever. The seven-foot column swept to backhand the automatons with its pincers. They fell onto their backs and moved their arms up and down in a metallic rendition of toppled turtles, unable to turn themselves over. Colton rotated the dial again, returning the cockpit to its prior position. He experimented with the leg levers until he had the machine turn its full structure around. He now could move forward on the main road to Saint-Brieuc.

The ghoulish red light of the automatons' eyes dimmed as the machine stepped on both of them. Colton heard and felt the impact of their iron bodies crushing beneath the greater weight of the pilotable engine.

The sound of the laborers revolt still reached his ears. He trusted that their larger numbers could handle the other two automatons that remained operational. As for the overseers and lodging house management staff, he hoped they had the sense to surrender peacefully.

Colton powered the machine to move forward, getting the knack for the levers. Oddly, the machine dragged on the left, taking more effort to pilot. The engine's size made it slow, but it was much better for him to remain inside than it was for him to attempt a trip into town on foot. No telling how many automatons Broussard had roaming the area.

He ducked as the machine moved under a set of trees. Leaves and brush fell into the cockpit. Where was the button to close the window panel?

A thump sounded from the back of the cockpit's frame. Colton turned, but the steel frame and steam billowing from the smokestack blocked his view. Must have been a heavy branch that fell. He resumed his path.

It soon became obvious why two people were needed to efficiently pilot the machine. The levers and switches that corresponded to its left set of limbs resided near the copilot seat. Colton struggled to maneuver the leg levers in tandem, having to stretch his arms across the expansive control panel to reach them. As a result, the machine clanked and lurched along as the dirt road gave way to cobblestones.

Up ahead, he saw several men. With rifles in hand, taken from Broussard's hires, they raced headlong towards town. Colton glanced in the side mirrors. Other laborers followed, sprinting to see about their families being held captive within the square.

Colton caught up with the men in front. They stopped before an automaton that stood guarding the way into town. It registered the sound of their approach and moved forward to attack.

Rifles fired, seeding the air with smoke and gunpowder.

The automaton didn't stand a chance. The light in its red eyes faded as it fell forward on the ground in a rush of sparks.

The laborers parted for Colton to go through. Why not clear the rest of the way for them, he thought. He was operating a big machine after all.

The engine churned as he drove the machine faster. The noise drowned out the men behind him. The view from the side mirror showed them as they started to shout and point his way. What was wrong with them? They had the upper hand now.

Four automatons waited on the next stretch of the road. Was that what the men were warning him about?

Colton lowered in his seat as the automatons fired their weapons at him. The bullets glanced off the machine's frame. The machine continued to pummel through, ramming the automatons in the process.

Colton braced himself on impact as their metal frames crushed against and under the machine's leg columns and solid iron feet. Clearing the hurdle, he drove the machine onward through the town, passing the cathedral and houses on his way.

He'd lost Broussard again, but the industrialist's hold on the foundry and its workers was diminished. But Colton put Broussard from his mind for the moment. Dominique's safety was more important to him than chasing after the criminal. He had to get to the bay fast.

The engine chugged along as the town square appeared ahead.

Chapter 16

The dawning sun was an eerie red as Dominique kept on the move. She saw no one on the road outside Saint-Brieuc. She kept Lottie's gun in one hand and the retractable pistol on the other as she hastened along the winding path to the bay.

A sinking feeling came over her each time she thought of the automatons patrolling the foundry and the town behind her. What was Broussard building that he felt he needed to have the entire area cowering within doors?

The sun climbed higher, appearing over the trees as the minutes passed. Dominique neared the sea. Dirt paths gave way to sandy soil. Salt carried on the brisk wind, along with the cries of gulls and curlews calling to each other.

The road began a downward path to the shore. Dominique slowed to make her descent among the jutting rocks on the slope. She cast her vision out in the distance, expecting to view the wide bay waters.

A great ship overshadowed her view. The size of a galleon, its two steel-riveted masts towered high over the quay to which the vessel was anchored.

Dominique halted her descent. A line of automatons were mounted before the ship. They stood arm to arm along the quay, maintaining a barrier.

Their red eyes were turned towards the road back to Saint-Brieuc, and upon Dominique.

She climbed back up to the road. She retreated from view of the automatons, taking cover behind prickly brush. The automatons' faces remained turned in the general direction inland. Perhaps she was too far for them to register her presence. As long as she didn't approach the quay, they wouldn't come after her. She hoped not, at least.

She peeked over the brush thorns. That ship looked like no British or French vessel from the northern ports. The ship's twin flags flapped in the air. Their red silks bore no insignia.

Broussard hired pirates and stationed them along the Mediterranean. If this ship was a pirate vessel, then it was a long way from its post. How did it get to northern France without being stopped by authorities patrolling the southern coastal waters?

She looked beyond the ship at the surrounding bay. Morning mist hovered over the piers and fishing docks of smaller towns in the distance. She remembered the first time she traveled to Saint-Brieuc with her family, going into the bay and seeing the inlets and islands that peppered it. Even a vessel as large as the one that sat at the wharf before her could nestle within a hidden cove just off the coast.

Dominique wrinkled her brow. What if Broussard had taken up residence on one of those islands? Some were out of view from the mainland, and lay largely unoccupied. When he wanted to sail for Nantes, he could venture out to the sea before drifting back in, dodging most of the patrol along the western coast.

She shook her head. All this time, he could have been coming and going from the Saint-Brieuc area as he pleased.

A man caught her attention as he walked on the deck of the ship. From her vantage point, she saw that he was dressed in the regional attire of seafarers. His cap and thick corded sweater shown faded in the sunlight. He carried a rifle over his shoulder.

He called out, and the automaton at the end of the quay, closest to Dominique, raised its arm. She knew then that she had been spotted.

Sunlight glinted off a metal panel that slid back from its forearm. Smoke issued from a round object that it launched in the air. It sailed towards the brush.

Dominique jumped from her cover as the object landed short of the brush. She got four yards away before the incendiary went off, taking her cap and raining dirt and rocks around her.

The man called out another command. She looked back through the clearing smoke and gunpowder as the automaton prepared to issue a second mortar round her way. Dominique removed the silencer from Lottie's gun to increase its firing range. She aimed at the automaton and fired.

Her bullet caught its shoulder, lodging harmlessly within its plates, but the impact was enough for the automaton to drop the second grenade. The man on the ship's deck raced to the other end as the grenade exploded on the quay.

The automaton and the one beside it fell victims to the detonation. Their chest plates split apart, exposing the engines inside. One combusted in a fit of steam and flame, catching fire to the wood beneath it. A loud groan issued from the quay before a portion of it collapsed into the bay, taking three more of the automatons.

The man reappeared with his rifle, positioning himself on the ship's stern to get a good shot at her. Another crewman emerged from below deck, followed by a third.

Dominique fired a distracting shot before taking off on the road again. She couldn't stay at the bay and wait for agent reinforcements to arrive now that Broussard's pirates knew she was there.

Dominique kept close to the trees, darting around their meager vegetation for shelter. Her mail-lined corset vest weighed her down, slowing her run, but she didn't dare take it off. A bullet zinged past her.

She hoped the agents due to arrive in the bay would be prepared for an exchange of fire with the pirates. There was little she could do to ensure their safe passage into the docks.

She thought of the people still trapped in and around Saint-Brieuc. There was little she could do to see them all to safety, too.

And Colton. He was left to face Broussard by himself. She hoped he could hold out a little longer.

**

Colton heard another noise come from the back of the cockpit's frame as he piloted the engine through the square of Saint-Brieuc. Something had indeed fallen upon the machine and remained lodged there.

He sidestepped citizens as they began to emerge from their homes and shops, fighting back against the few automatons that remained in town. One automaton stood beside the fountain in an empty section of the square and shot at Colton. Bullets pinged off the machine's legs.

Colton still couldn't figure out which button closed the window. Was it the quarter-sized brass button on the lift, or the dime-sized silver button on his right?

The pilotable engine shook as a spring-loaded projectile shot from the right shoulder. The projectile landed on the statue of a water-spouting cupid within the fountain before detonating, sending up broken marble, water, and automaton parts to rain down on the cobblestones.

It wasn't the silver button, but he had no complaints.

Colton heard a grunt before a second thump resounded on the frame. This time, the sound traveled to the side. Broussard's head came into view in the side mirror.

Colton yanked the left arm lever all the way back. The appendage creaked as it rose in the air. Too slow. Broussard slipped from view in the mirror before the machine's arm reached its top vertical point.

Colton shoved the arm lever forward, attempting to fling Broussard off the frame. Broussard hauled his large stature behind the cockpit again, the hobnails on his shoes making screeching noises against the steel.

The machine's arm remained stuck in the air. Colton moved the lever back and forth. The machine's gears grinded against each other.

"Shall I show you how to pilot the machine?"

Colton raised his head. He saw the flash of a gun in Broussard's hand just before the industrialist pulled the trigger.

***

Dominique escaped the range of the pirates' gunfire. Their shots finally faded behind her. She stopped on the road and caught her breath.

No bullets remained in the gun she had taken from Lottie. She stored it in the leather pouch at her waist.

A group of men approached from up ahead. Dominique touched the cuff on her wrist as she got off the road. No trees were there to provide shelter. She'd have to face the men head on.

They were dressed in the regional Breton shirts, pants, and outer vests, but the brass and bronze-studded weapons they carried were a stark contrast to their traditional attire. Were they local citizens or Broussard's men dressed as such? She counted eight of them. Nausea filled her stomach as she did the math. She had five bullets in the retractable pistol.

The leader raised his hand for the men to stop behind him. They all stood twenty feet from her. "Agent Fontaine?" the leader called. His accent had none of the Breton inflection.

Dominique kept her gun ready. "Who are you?"

"Agent Trevelyan of the Bureau northwest outpost. We received urgent message to come to Saint-Brieuc."

Relieved, she lowered her weapon. "Broussard is here. He's sealed off the bay."

"We saw the ship from a distance. How did you get out of Saint-Brieuc?"

"The way was clear once I got out of the town square, but Broussard has automatons still patrolling the streets. To go back, we'll have to get past the docks first." Dominique pointed back to the pier. The red flags of the pirate vessel could be seen from the smoke still rising from the pier. "Tell me you have metal-piercing bullets. And plenty of them."

Agent Trevelyan looked past her at the ship. "We have nothing that will take down that vessel from land."

"We don't need to take it down. Just the automatons guarding it. They're armed with incendiaries." Dominique dusted brush leaves from her hair. "We must hurry. People are being held prisoner in the town and the foundry. My partner, COIC Agent Smythe, is there, too."

Agent Trevelyan removed a cartridge of bullets one of the large pockets in his vest and gave them to her. "This is for your protection, nothing else. I will be taking over from here. Now let's go."

Chapter 17

Colton hadn't awakened with aches and pains this bad since he fought bullies at the orphanage. His lungs strained to breathe. His chest felt as though a blast furnace collapsed upon it. Groggily, he opened his eyes to find himself still within the cockpit of the pilotable engine.

He was in the copilot's seat this time. His hands were bound to the seat's arms with its restraining harnesses. Outside the window, a pastoral scene drifted by. The distant outline of Saint-Brieuc receded in the side mirror.

"I left that town to its peasant revolt for now."

Broussard was in the driver's seat, piloting the machine. He moved the levers with a calm precision. The machine treaded along.

"There are Bureau agents coming into the bay that I have to take care of, thanks to that *femme* of yours." Broussard then switched to English. "I should have known you weren't French."

Colton's ribs hurt when he drew breath to speak. "What gave you that idea?"

"The tailoring of your waistcoat. Only the COIC has that bullet-resistant design. Chainmail went out of fashion in France a very long time ago."

Colton saw where the bullet still caught in the lining of his vest, the links exposed through the torn outer layer of leather. He shifted. The bullet dislodged and rolled on the cockpit floorboard. "And I thought you were going to say it was my accent that gave me away."

He tested his bonds. The harness was weaker where it held his left wrist. He tried to loosen it.

"You're the engineer from the flour mill." As Broussard registered that fact, his profile gave way to a direct, challenging stare. "Did you start that fire?"

"That I did."

"And did you damage the foundry drain pipe?"

"That was your own overseers' folly."

"Two *grande* accidents have happened in short succession. I don't believe you."

"Makes no difference to me."

Broussard moved a switch on the board, and the engine responded with a roar. "Young man, do you have any idea why I didn't simply shoot you again, after I discovered you were with the COIC?"

"I have other things I'd rather ask you." Colton's anger mounted as he studied how controlled and placid Broussard continued to remain.

"And I've questions for you as well, which is the only reason why you're still alive. Why is your agency haranguing me?"

"You really don't know the answer to that? You tried to turn a mill into a brothel, you created a spy ring in London, had your men attack COIC agents on British and foreign soil, and you stole a supply of Aspasian metal meant for New Britannia."

"I haven't been to New Britannia in years since my London investments went under."

Colton wondered just what investment that could be. He thought of the coal grinding machine that took his mother's life.

Broussard tilted his head. "You're a simple engineer. You may not have heard of something called industrial rivalry. New Britannia participates in it often. I think your COIC just doesn't want to have any competition."

Colton found the knot of the harness near the first knuckle of his left hand. "You're trying to do more than compete. You don't care what you have to do to get rich. "

"And why does a young engineer think himself to be so astute?"

"I've been acquainted with your work from an early age."

"Tell me. I need to pass the time until we reach the bay. Your partner will be waiting there for the Bureau reinforcements. I'm afraid I will have to dash her hopes." Broussard moved the machine's arm up and then down.

A cold sensation washed over Colton at the hinted intention. He wasn't going to let Broussard harm Dominique. He started loosening the rope knot with his thumb.

***

Dominique took shelter on the ground with the other agents as another grenade launched from the automatons. The projectile landed just short of the road, bouncing off the embankment. It rolled back down the slope, sending up pebbles and sand.

"We cannot keep doing this." Agent Trevelyan brushed debris from his neck. "Those pirates are letting the automatons fight for them. They know we will run out of ammunition first."

Dominique checked the remaining bullets in her gun, wishing that she had one of the larger rifles that Agent Trevelyan and his team carried. "It's hard to get a target on the automatons from this position."

"If we move closer, we will make it much easier for them to launch explosives at us. I already told you, Agent Fontaine, this is no longer your fight." His head turned as rifle fire sounded from the deck of the ship.

"The pirates seem to think it is just as much my fight as it is yours."

"Look out," another agent shouted.

Dominique ducked as she saw an automaton raise its arm. She heard Agent Trevelyan open fire with his rifle. The shot sounded just before the grenade exploded.

The grenade must have landed no more than ten feet away. Dirt rained down. Dominique's ears rang from the sound of the explosion, drowning out the sound of the world around her, except for the hard, frantic beating of her heart.

She never thought being an industrial spy would take this violent and dangerous turn. The self-defense tactics of grapples and throws, besting her opponent with fast reflexes, the codes she had to memorize to communicate with her agency in secret, she imagined that would be the extent of her risks in working with the Bureau.

But she couldn't let her comrades down because she had been faced with such a daunting challenge. She couldn't let Colton down.

The dust cleared. She rose up on her elbows. None of the other agents had been harmed. She looked to the pier. An automaton was now missing an arm. "You hit one of them, Agent Trevelyan."

He reloaded. "These potshots we are taking have little effect."

"It can't fire upon us again, at least." Dominique shot twice at the four automatons that remained. Her bullets landed in the wood portion of the ship's hull.

"Enough, Agent Fontaine." Agent Trevelyan stayed her hand. "I've allowed you to fire from a distance, but I won't let you to take part in this type of combat. I am in charge."

She wished he'd stop asserting his authority as leader of a squadron. "How do you think I even made it to the bay in the first place?" She went back to viewing the ship. Its anchor was retracting. "The pirates are leaving."

"Get a shot at them, men," Agent Trevelyan commanded, pulling back on the trigger of his firearm.

The combat team followed his lead, but they missed their mark. The air filled with the *ting-ping* of their bullets glancing off the automatons metal plates. The automatons continued to form an iron wall for the pirates scrambled to prepare the ship to cast off.

Agent Trevelyan growled as the ship began to turn away from the quay. "If they get that ship out far enough, we'll have no chance of reaching them. They can fire cannons on us at will."

He was right, Dominique thought. With a clear line of fire, the pirates would have no trouble unleashing the cannons on the road. "We have a chance to go past the automatons and run inland."

"No. We'll be outnumbered by the automatons in Saint-Brieuc."

"Agent Trevelyan, we can't just leave people trapped in their homes at the mercy of Broussard. Colton is still back there, too." Dominique caught her slip in address too late. Agent Trevelyan regarded her, his frown carving in deep disapproval.

"Your partner," the combat team leader spat the word with distaste, "that COIC agent, will have to deal with Broussard on his own for now. There's nothing we can do but wait here for the rest of our reinforcements."

"Surely you don't—"

"I mean every word I say, Agent Fontaine. I'm not about to place my men in reckless danger in attempt to rescue your lover."

Dominique didn't know what to be more stunned about, his decision to doggedly continue dodging mortar rounds in the open or what he referred to Colton as. Time was running out for Colton and the inhabitants

THE CURIOSITY CHRONICLES: BOOKS 1-3

of Saint-Brieuc if no one went back to help them.

"Agent Trevelyan," a combat team member interrupted.

The leader took his scowl away from Dominique. "What is it, Agent Leroux?"

"We can't go inland. See behind you."

Dominique turned with the others to view the portion of road behind them. Her stomach sank as she beheld the finished product of Broussard's creation.

The large, metal monstrosity overtook the way back to Saint-Brieuc. White smoke billowed in the air around it. Its arm pincers clenched and unclenched as it walked an ungainly path on two metal columns towards them. The sound it made caused Dominique's blood to curdle.

***

Colton couldn't imagine there was ever a good time when he saw a cannon-spewing sailing vessel in the distance. This time was no different.

"It looks like my men have run into some opposition," Broussard remarked. "I told them to stay near shore." He sped the engine to advance into the fray.

Where was Dominique? Colton hoped she wasn't among the handful of individuals that were situated on the road, fighting back.

As the pilotable engine got closer, the quay came into view. He saw the automatons lined up along the walkway. A portion of it had splintered off into the water. The automatons fired incendiaries at the people on the road.

"You have yet to tell me how you knew of me when you were younger." Broussard interrupted his thoughts.

Colton still worked on the knot to free his hand. He paused when Broussard looked at him.

"You couldn't have been an engineer when I was in London fifteen years ago. You would have been a boy."

"My mother worked in one of your factories. She kept the machines clean."

Broussard wrinkled his already jowly face. "I didn't sire you."

Bile bubbled up in Colton's throat. The criminal industrialist was so smug that he assumed that was where the exchange was leading. "You patented a machine that ground coal. The design didn't have a stationary rotary blade. My mother suffered an accident and died."

"And?"

Colton realized he had made his right hand into a fist. It strained beneath his bonds. "Had you put in a mechanism to stay the blade, she would still be alive today."

"Is that what this is? You've decided to infiltrate my facilities and break my machines to avenge your mother?" Broussard closed his eyes just slightly. Colton couldn't determine whether he was narrowing them in anger or simply crinkling them with humor. "Tell me you are not so simplistic."

The knot loosened on his left wrist. Colton could almost untie it. "I worked undercover in the mill and the foundry to shut you down. I won't let you go on exploiting people."

"Machines, their inventors, and the factory owners aren't responsible when a laborer agrees to work. Your mother knew that. If not, then she was a fool more so than the son she bore."

Colton battled the rage building within. "You're deranged. You've no regard for another's life. I'll see you put in prison."

But Broussard's attentions had already turned. His eyes were fixed to the window. Two cannonry explosions sounded in the bay.

Colton looked out. One of the pirate ship's masts was broken in half, the top of it dangling by wood splinters. Advancing upon the ship, *The Enlightened* left a froth of sea foam in its wake.

"The COIC needs to learn to not interfere on foreign soil." Broussard positioned the machine's right arm in the direction out to sea. He lined it up to *The Enlightened* and prepared to press the silver incendiary launch button.

Colton lifted his leg and kicked Broussard's hand while it was still on the lever. The lever lowered the machine's arm towards the pier just as the mortar round shot forth, detonating on impact. The automatons were engulfed in flames, bursting apart in fragments of charred metal upon the burning quay.

Broussard reached for his gun. Something hit the window, shattering the glass.

Colton delivered another kick to Broussard's hand. The gun dislodged from his fingers and plummeted out the broken window.

"Idiot." Broussard backhanded Colton across the face. Colton took the hit while he freed the knot and began unraveling the harness about his hand.

A second shot rang against the cockpit's frame. Broussard returned to manning the controls.

Colton heard shouts from outside the pilotable engine. The men that were on the road had come to do battle with the machine. Broussard swept the machine's arm overhead in one swift motion. The men hit the ground for cover. The machine's pincers caught someone on the end.

Colton watched in horror as Dominique was plucked off the ground. Her legs thrashed in mid-air as the machine's arm arced back. "Let her go."

"I don't believe you meant that as you say." Broussard moved the arm's control lever until the arm crossed in front of the machine and rose high. He brought Dominique's dangling form into view.

Colton knew he couldn't make any more rash moves for the controls. Dominique hung from the machine, one of her arms free of the pincer. Colton grimaced as though he were in the machine's grasp himself as he saw her struggle. One slip and she would fall to her injury or worse. "Put her down gently."

She looked to Broussard and then to Colton. Her eyes, already filled with fear, enlarged when she stared into his.

"My, how she looks to you." Broussard made the observation as though he were viewing it from the box seat of an opera house. "There's something to be said for how yet another woman you care for has gotten herself caught in a machine."

"Colton," Dominique called his name in a plea for help.

Colton freed his left hand of the harness. He kept it on the arm of the seat. "Broussard, I'm the one who destroyed your flour mill. She's done nothing to sabotage you."

"Except go undercover and infiltrate my operations." Broussard toyed with the lever, widening the pincers.

Dominique lifted her free arm. A hint of gunmetal showed on her sleeve.

No, Dominique, don't...

The pistol unfurled from its spring-loaded base at her wrist, landing in her palm. Her fingers closed around the handle and she squeezed the trigger.

Broussard grunted as the bullet struck his arm. He slumped to the right, letting go of the controls.

Colton freed his other hand and reached across Broussard for the lever. He used it to begin lowering Dominique to the ground.

Broussard rose and hit a button. The pincers released, dropping Dominique the rest of the way down. Colton swung his fist into Broussard's face. He recoiled.

Colton peered at the ground for Dominique. She rolled out of the way of the machine. Thank God the drop wasn't so high that she was unable to break her fall.

He moved fast to push and pull the levers. The engine chugged as it plodded down to shore, past the smoldering remains of the quay and away from where it could harm Dominique and the other agents. Colton hit the silver launch button to discharge rounds at the pirate ship.

A heavy fist slammed into his back. Colton fell onto the controls, nearly flying out the broken window headfirst. He rolled over as Broussard delivered a downward punch. Instead of Colton's face, Broussard's fist slammed into the control panel.

The engine gave a great cough. Hot steam kicked and sputtered from the smokestack, blowing over the cockpit and out to sea. The machine wobbled on its legs into the shallows.

Broussard fought to regain control of the engine as it piloted itself farther and farther away from shore. Water lapped the base of the casing that housed the engine boilers. He hit buttons and threw switches to no avail.

"Give up, Broussard." Colton caught his balance as the machine started to sink in the sand underwater. "The engine's about to combust."

"I will not be taken in by the COIC." He pounded another set of buttons.

Colton pried him away from the control panel. Broussard swung at him again. Colton dodged the hit and grabbed his arm, forcing it behind his back. "We have to get out of this thing before it sinks."

Water seeped in the cockpit, rapidly flooding the floor and rising. Steam from the smokestack scolded Colton's face. Broussard tried to pull his arm away even as the water rose higher, past their knees. "I'd sooner drown than be on that British vessel headed to prison."

"You don't get a choice."

Chapter 18

Dominique witnessed the machine shift in the shallows, beginning its sliding descent into the deep. Fright overtook her as she knew that Colton was still inside.

She pushed to her feet, ignoring the ache in her limbs. She had to get to him. The hard ground gave way to sandy shoreline beneath her boots as she broke into a run for the beach.

"Agent Fontaine, *non*," Agent Trevelyan's cry reached her ears.

She didn't look back as she treaded into the shallows. Ahead, the machine was up to its neck in water, half the cockpit frame already submerged. She saw movement inside, Colton and Broussard locked in a struggle.

The dying engine gave a death roar, drowning out all other noise, including the cannons being exchanged between the pirate ship and *The Enlightened*. Smoke blew from the smokestack and covered the frame from view. Dominique panicked as she could no longer see where Colton was.

Suddenly the engine below the cockpit burst in a hissing fit of steam and flying parts. The cockpit frame snapped and fell into the sea. Dominique ducked underwater as broken gears and relay coils rained overhead.

She opened her eyes while still submerged. The explosion was muffled by the water rushing around the explosion site, but she saw the growing mushroom of debris the explosion left in its wake.

Flames glowed orange before they were quickly doused by the sea. Steel bent and groaned as the machine continued to break apart, a mass of mangled metal. She couldn't make head or tail of the machine's limbs as they crumbled and fell over each other. She couldn't see the cockpit anymore. It must have tumbled into the deep.

Dominique was forced to come up for air. Her head broke the surface as coal lumps from the engine and wood fragments from the quay burned on top of the water. She saw Trevelyan's squadron running to another area of the beach, clambering to get to a tall figure washed up to shore.

Her hopes rose, only to fall when they turned the man over and proceeded to bind his wrists. Broussard coughed up water as he was dragged off the beach.

Dominique ducked her head under again in search of Colton. The water had clouded to the point of no visibility as debris churned and disturbed the seabed. Bits of machinery brushed and scraped against her clothing. She couldn't remain near the wake of the engine blast for much longer. The seabed was getting beyond her feet as she allowed the water to carry her further out into the deep. The chainmail within her corset vest threatened to pull her even further under. Dominique fought against the current and used all of the strength in her arms and legs to propel herself upward.

Her lungs burned for air as she swam back towards the shallows. The muscles in her limbs strained to tug her to shore, her heart as heavily weighed as the armor and clothing that covered her body.

She was unable to find Colton. He was still down below in the cold water, possibly still inside what remained of the cockpit as it continued to sink ever downward. He drowned, and she failed to get to him.

She attempted to touch bottom in the shallow. A spongy bed of kelp gave way to firmer rock and silt. She came up for air only when she couldn't stand it any longer. Her tears mingled with the saltwater of the sea. She wiped them on her wet sleeve.

Agent Trevelyan still called to her from the beach. His words were lost on the rush of the wind and the rolling of the tide. She had swam a greater distance from her original entry point than she realized.

Other agents began yelling at her alongside Trevelyan. They motioned with their hands, pointing. Dominique looked over her shoulder and saw another person emerge from the deep.

Colton swam, making long strokes to shore. He left the rest of the machine's twisted frame behind him as it disappeared below the water's surface.

Dominique felt the joy bubble up inside her and overflow as she made her way towards him. She called out, splashing in the shallows as she moved against the water's inertia.

Colton came to a place where he was able to stand, chest-deep. Dominique didn't allow him to get any closer to shore before she reached him and threw her arms about his neck.

The strength of his frame grounded her against the shifting flow of water and harsh wind that whipped about them. He wrapped his arms around her. Some of the chill left her body as she allowed herself to meld against him, accepting with certainty the fact that he was alive, safe and sound.

"I don't think you've ever been this happy to see me." Despite his humorous tone, his voice was tinged with an emotion.

"When the machine went under, I thought the worst."

"I had no intention of drowning today. But it's a good thing you shot out the window. Things may have been different if you hadn't."

She didn't want to think of the battle anymore. It was over. "What are partners for?" She stopped, noticed a change in him. "Your hair is red again."

The wet strands on his forehead showed dark russet. Colton ran his hand through his hair and looked at his palm. "The dye came out. Must have been the brine of the water."

"Good. I always liked your hair's true color."

A ship's foghorn blasted through the bay.

"That would be *The Enlightened* headed into port." Colton frowned at the mangled quay. "Or what's left of it. Let's get out of the water."

His arms lingered around her waist before he let go. Dominique became aware again of the chilly water soaking through her clothes. She waded back to shore with him.

The Enlightened and its crew had made short work of the pirates. Dominique shielded her eyes from glare as she remarked upon the sight of several men boarding Broussard's ship. They commandeered the vessel. The ship slowly turned and followed *The Enlightened* closer to shore.

"We caught Broussard," Colton nodded towards the industrialist, "and the people of Saint-Brieuc have regained their town. We have to get Lottie and Broussard's men in custody and then we can go back to Le Havre."

Dominique watched Agent Trevelyan as he ordered his squadron to take Broussard back up to the road. "I'll ask Agent Trevelyan to take his squadron to the foundry while I watch Broussard."

"I think the COIC has things under control from here on out."

She caught the hint of a smile on Colton's face. "Are we back to being rivals again so soon?"

"No. I thought we would at least wait until we finished paperwork, especially the French portion." He gave her a mischievous side glance. "But I've learned a thing about teamwork. I can think of no other agent that I'd want by my side."

Dominique felt a warm flutter in her chest. "Why, *merci*. I feel the same way about you." She patted his shoulder. "But you're going to have to start doing your own laundry again. There are only so many coal smudges an agent can take."

***

Le Havre, November 1838

Colton tossed his satchel down from the ship onto the loading dock. Footsteps rapped on the deck as Captain Rhys walked up beside him.

"Are you sure about this, Smythe? You've finished your engineer apprenticeship, and can take a position anywhere the COIC needs you. It's not a decision to be made lightly."

"I've thought about it for a while now, Captain," Colton said, tossing another satchel with his belongings down. "The Secretary's already confirmed my new agent status and given his approval. There's no going back."

"If this is what you want to do, you'll have the crew's backing. And mine."

Colton took a view of *The Enlightened's* deck and its crewmembers as the rest of the men came forward to wish him well. He learned much from being in their company and he would take that knowledge with him to his new position. "I'd better say goodbye to the crew."

"Aye," the bosun Malcolm hailed, as he lifted a mysterious wrapped parcel. "And I have a parting gift for you, lad. I insist that you not leave without our cherished galley fare." Malcolm pushed the parcel into his arms.

Colton balanced the gift. It seemed to be a container beneath the wrapping. He heard its contents slash inside. "What is it?"

"A full three days' supply of salmagundi. It'll keep you full for a little while until your belly gets used to the wee victuals the French call food."

"You know me well. My thanks, but not all French fare is as you think. I know someone who could change your mind."

Colton hoped she would still be where he first found her.

He made his rounds, imparting to each man a fond fare-ye-well. He faced Captain Rhys last. "My sincerest thanks for allowing me to work as part of your crew, sir. It was a privilege to be in company with some of the bravest sailors and stalwart agents of the COIC."

"We couldn't have asked for a more hard-working engineer," Captain Rhys said. "And I know McNamara would say the same. I suspect why he's not coming out of the engine room. He'll miss you the most. You were like a son to him."

Colton nodded. Saying goodbye to McNamara had been difficult. In a year, he had gained a teacher, a mentor and a friend. "I said goodbye to him earlier. He joked and said he'll have to get used to working double shifts again."

Captain Rhys laughed. "That sounds like McNamara. I'll let him borrow my wife's automaton assistant. She's visiting her family in Aspasia and won't need it for a while." He shook Colton's hand. "The COIC will stay in communication with you. Fare you well, Agent Smythe."

"Thank you, sir." Colton saluted the crew of *The Enlightened* one last time before departing the ship.

***

Village of Chay Oiseau

Agent Joubert ate the last bite of his éclair. "*C'est magnifique.*" He praised Dominique's culinary skills.

"*Merci.* It's made with ingredients I ordered from Paris." She took his empty plate and put it on a tray to be washed later.

Agent Joubert sipped his cup of coffee at the table. "I cannot believe how swiftly your family started the boulangerie again. The courts only recently returned the villagers' money from Broussard's holdings."

Dominique listened to her brothers clang dishes in the kitchen. Ever since she returned home from her mission, she loved to hear the sound of life returning to normal in the Fontaine household. Her siblings and parents were happy once more. "Most people in Chay Oiseau were eager to rebuild after Broussard was put in the Bastille. Is there any word on his factory holdings and investments?"

"Most have folded since his capture. His sister, the lodging house staff, and the foundry overseers were jailed. The foundry where Agent Smythe worked just reopened under new, legitimate management."

"*Bon.*" She felt a tug inside at the mention of Colton. She missed his easy smile and irreverent humor. "Most of the foundry workers were simply doing their jobs. They didn't know that what they crafted was meant for Broussard's automatons and weapons."

"Those were also seized after he confessed to the location of his other properties. He had an island hideaway near Saint-Brieuc and two homes in the Riviera."

"Is that everything?" Dominique wiped crumbs from the bread shelf in preparation for the next batch to come from the oven.

Agent Joubert set aside his coffee cup and shook his head. "There is still more work for the agency. Broussard's pirates have scattered since his money is no longer there to bind their loyalty. They've taken to attacking resorts along our southern coasts and Mediterranean trade routes. It's a regional problem now."

Dominique thought of *The Enlightened*'s frequent forays into that area, both as a merchant ship and one of espionage. Was Colton still in the ship's engine room, keeping the vessel and crew afloat? Her heart warmed when she considered him.

The last time she saw him was when he appeared at Broussard's trial in late October, shortly after they both escorted the criminal to Le Havre. The COIC Secretary was there with Colton. Both men were present to ensure that New Britannia would have the opportunity to try Broussard in their own courts after his sentence in France was served.

But they would have a long wait. The judge sentenced Broussard to forty years within the walls of the Bastille.

When the trial was over, Colton and the COIC Secretary went back to London to complete more paperwork. Now that the mission was complete, she surmised that her days of partnering with the ginger-haired engineer were over. She told herself not to be sad, that this was what it meant to be an agent.

Still, a wistful and bittersweet ache arose every time she thought of him.

"I should return to the agency." Agent Joubert stood. "There are still mountains of reports and paperwork that I must complete."

"What will the COIC do about the pirate problem?" Dominique wondered aloud. "It affects them, too."

"New Britannia will work to eradicate the pirates. And, it will also do what it always does: Progress, compete, run headlong into frays. *C'est la vie.*" Agent Joubert shrugged a shoulder. "That is nothing for you to worry about. Your assignment with the Bureau is completed. You can return to life as you know it."

Dominique took stock of her surroundings, the newly revived boulangerie, being at home again with her family. Although she was beyond grateful to have some semblance of her former life restored, it would never be as she once knew it.

Before she met Colton, she had been solely focused on restoring her family's business and bringing prosperity back to Chay Oiseau. But now, after the time she spent with him, risking life and limb with him to bring Broussard to justice, she felt a deep bond to her former partner.

Yet the bond went beyond their shared mission. Dominique felt a longing for Colton's companionship in ways that she could not share with anyone else.

She did wish she could have told him when she had the chance. Still, given her and Colton's separate lives—*allegiances*—would it have mattered?

Agent Joubert donned his outercoat and hat to brace the first snow of the season outside. "Best wishes to you and your family, Mademoiselle Fontaine." He showed himself out the door.

Dominique took his empty cup and carried it along with the tray into the kitchen in the back. The scent of fresh crepes and warm bread offered a comforting aroma. Contentment ran through her at the sight of her mother and father cooking over the large stove, and her two boisterous brothers washing and drying the dishes.

She handed the tray to Fabian at the sink. "Here you are, *mon frère.*"

"What did Agent Joubert say?" he asked, putting the dishes in the soapy water.

"He wishes us all the best."

"I know he spent more time talking about your past missions than he did well wishes."

"How would you know? Were you listening?"

"*Non.*"

"*Oui.*" Antoine put in while he wiped a baking pan dry. "He tried to from the door, anyway."

"But Fabian was not given the chance," Dominique's father said, looking up after flipping a crepe over on the stove. "Your mother and I told him that those dishes needed to be clean for lunchtime customers."

Dominique laughed before turning to her brother again. "Fabian, I'm sorry to disappoint you, but Agent Joubert only came to tell me that my work for the Bureau is over."

Fabian's sleeves got wet at the elbows from where he accidentally splashed water. "You're no longer an agent?"

"*Non.* I'm back to just being your bossy, older sister again." She smiled sweetly.

"Well, I am glad to see you home for good." Her mother spoke up as she folded the crepes. "Good riddance to those dangerous mills and their criminal owner. Oh, Dominique, you should know that I'm still very upset with you for leaving the village this summer with no notice at all."

"I know, *maman.* I'm sorry."

"Mission or no mission, if your father and I were home to see you take off, we would have put a stop it."

Her brothers told her parents the truth after all. She looked to Fabian and Antoine. They returned her sweet smile from several moments ago.

"Oh, goodness, the bread," her mother exclaimed. Madame Fontaine opened the oven beneath the stove. Black smoke spilled from the door, smothering the pleasantly-scented kitchen with the stench of charred bread.

Dominique reached over the sink to open the window. She joined her father and brothers in fanning the smoke out.

Once the smoked was reduced to a light haze, Madame Fontaine withdrew a blackened lump from the over. "That was the baguette." She set the pan on the counter before removing her oven mitts.

Monsieur Fontaine tilted his head to look into the oven. "We've always had trouble with this oven. I cleaned it thoroughly before we started using it again."

"Maybe someone forgot to close the door to the coal burners and it overheated," Dominique said.

"Which one of you stoked the burner with coal this morning?" Monsieur Fontaine asked his sons. Neither Antoine or Fabian volunteered an answer, but Fabian's expression betrayed him.

Dominique sighed. "I'll go outside."

"Be careful," said her mother.

Dominique took a shawl and the pair of thick, padded gloves from beside the counter before going outside. The winter's first dusting of snow blanketed the ground in a fine sheet of white. She went around the boulangerie to the back, where the oven and stove's valves connected to a four-foot long box that housed the furnace.

Fabian did forget to shut the door. Smoke and steam fizzled out from the box. The steam froze in tiny crystals as it drifted in the air. Dominique could almost appreciate the unexpected source of beauty, that is, if the boulangerie wasn't about to stand to lose a full day's business.

She turned the burner valve off. She proceeded to pull out the coal feed.

"I wouldn't recommend you opening that, mademoiselle. The coals are still hot."

Dominique raised her head at the sound of Colton's voice. He appeared from around the boulangerie, in the direction she had come. He wore a coat and wool engineer's cap over his pants and boots.

Delight bloomed within her. She left the coal feed alone. "I have to determine if the oven overheated or if someone broke it."

"Is there a vandalism problem in this village?"

"We deal with saboteurs from time to time." She removed the padded gloves.

"Who would do such a thing?" he posed the question innocently.

"I have my suspicions." Dominique smiled, no longer able to contain it. "I used to know a man who specialized in it."

"And what did this saboteur look like?"

"He is tall. He has a good, strong build. *Beau*, if one finds men with ginger hair to be attractive."

He crossed the space between them and took her in his arms. Dominique gave into his kiss with pleasure.

"Do you find him attractive?" he asked.

"I do. But my opinion may change if I find out that he broke my oven."

"I just arrived in the village square. You can ask the innkeeper."

"I know one of my brothers left the door open. I was just teasing you." She stepped back and wrapped her shawl closer about her shoulders. "What brings you back to France, another mission?"

Colton motioned no with his head. "I don't have a mission for the moment, but I've been given status as a sleeper agent. I keep watch in case someone like Broussard appears. Then I notify the COIC and get my assignment."

Dominique was surprised. "What about being an engineer on *The Enlightened?*"

"That was an apprenticeship. Once I completed it, I could go where the COIC wanted me."

"But being a sleeper agent. That means long stretches of watching and waiting."

"I can use the rest after what we've been through."

"I hope the COIC Secretary didn't change your status out of spite. I remember how irritable he could be."

"Dominique, I requested the status change."

She stared at him. "You did? Why?"

"Let's just say I wanted a slower pace."

"But where will you be stationed as a sleeper agent? The industrial districts of Lyon? Nantes?"

Colton raised his head and looked around the village. "I did say once that I could get used to provincial life. From the looks of things, Chay Oiseau and the flour mill are rebuilding. Plenty of machinery here in need of repair or maintenance."

Dominique felt the butterflies stirring to life in her stomach again. "In that case, you can start with the oven."

The oven's boiler coughed a cloud of steam as soon as she said the words.

She winced at the ill sound it made. "I'm afraid it might take most of your time and very careful attention."

"Believe it or not, I can be patient." He reached out and tucked her hair behind her ears. "But right now, I can think of someone that I'd rather give my time and careful attention to first." He leaned down for another kiss.

Broussard may be imprisoned in the Bastille, but the agents of the COIC still have their hands full with his renegade pirates and a new mysterious element that's taking New Britannia by storm...

A sneak peek at *The Aether Alchemist*
Curiosity Chronicles, Book Four

COIC Headquarters, London, New Britannia
April, 1839

Armand stared at the set of handwritten numbers and old Arabic displayed on ancient parchment set in front of him on the desk. He picked it up and then looked at the beautiful raven-haired woman seated across from him. What claims she made, saying this old slip of paper had the power to change history. "I don't understand this writing."

"It is half of the lost formula for an aether fuel solution," she replied, in accented English.

Armand couldn't pinpoint the origin of her speech, but like his own, it was different from other citizens of New Britannia. Her elegant voice carried notes hinting of a land continents away.

She leaned forward in her chair. Her long, tightly spiraled strands spilled over the shoulder of her claret dress. "It's been in my family for generations. My great-great grandfather brought many other formulas with him when he came to New Britannia from Ethiopia over a hundred years ago."

He put the parchment down and took a long look at her. Her dark eyes, ringed in black fringe, made large, compelling windows in her dusky brown oval face. Her full lips bore no artifice, but they tinted a dark rose when she pressed them together in bottled frustration.

Her companion, a large fellow who shared her hair and skin coloring, stood waiting by the office door. Armand corrected himself. *Guarding it* seemed to be the better way to describe the man's carefully positioned stance. Though dressed fashionably, with a black frock coat, paisley waistcoat, necktie, and two-tone spatterdashes, his demeanor was anything but whimsical and carefree.

His legs were planted apart. He had uncrossed his arms. They now hung loose at his sides and slightly upraised, as though preparing to ensnare Armand should he make any sudden movements towards the lady. The man's large hands looked strong enough to do damage. He curled and uncurled his fingers as his firm, stoic face surveyed the two of them.

Armand turned back to the visitor at his desk. The lace at the woman's slender throat moved as she made a sigh of impatience. "Will you help me find the other half of the formula?" she asked.

"When you say part of the formula is lost, do you mean stolen?"

"I believe it went missing from my family's vaults years ago in our old country. We thought a relative may have misplaced it, but this half was sent to me in an unmarked box yesterday evening."

"Do you have the box with you?"

The woman spared a glance at her companion. He reached behind the lapel of his jacket and withdrew a slender wooden box, no bigger than half the size of an envelope. He crossed the office in three loping steps to hand it to her. She, in turn, placed it before Armand. The wood emitted a strong smell of freshly cut cedar.

"I found the box on the doorstep of my home, exactly as you see it."

Armand lifted the box lid. The inside was lined in silk. "Was there a message?"

"None. Just the formula. I looked for the initials of the woodcarver. There are a number of them where we live in Scarborough, but none I know of who use this type of cedar."

"It comes from Lebanon." Armand traced the grain of the light gold wood.

"I'm impressed. How did you know?"

"I collect wood carvings. There is a store in Piccadilly Circus that imports them from the region."

"Perhaps you can start by making an inquiry there. I wish to know who sent this box."

Armand closed the lid. "What was your name again?"

"Miriam Brehane." Her long fingers curled upon the arms of the chair.

Miriam. A pretty and lilting moniker. "Miss Brehane, you must realize what you're asking of me. I'm in charge of the investigations division here, but the Cabinet of Intellectual Curiosities is a scientific agency. You would do better to hire a private detective to aid you in your search for the mysterious sender."

Her face fell. "Oh, I was truly hoping you wouldn't say so, for I am afraid a private detective would be of no use to me. I'm not as concerned about the origin of this box as I am of how the sender came by this formula. It's my belief he or she is not from New Britannia."

"Couldn't one of your distant relatives have traveled here or sent the box ahead of them?"

"No one in my family lives in Ethiopia anymore. Most are in Europe. My grandfather was the last to go to Ethiopia before he died last year. He went in search of the lost formula, but had no luck finding it."

"But now you have one half, while the remainder is still missing."

She nodded. "If the person who sent this has the other half, then I must know. This particular aether formula may have the ability to power machines without the use of other fuels."

Armand's interest piqued at such an idea of machines not using coal or steam for power, but he had grave doubts about the aether formula's capabilities. For one, aether was an unseen, gaseous element that existed between the space of air and solid objects. Though it could be harnessed through a long method involving condensation, most of its properties still remained undiscovered.

Second, such grand promises of powerful elixirs and secret potions were touted in the back pages of newspapers and penny dreadfuls every day. In fact, he knew of several amateur inventors who advertised their wares in those sections as a last resort after being rejected by the COIC. "Again, Miss Brehane, you'll need to consult a private detective. The COIC doesn't deal in alchemy."

She sat up high in her chair. "I didn't come to you with hokum and magician's tricks, Mr. Torres. I, and everyone who works at our Scarborough facility, have studied extensively in chemistry and science. Despite popular myth, we are not alchemists."

Clearly, he had struck a nerve. He wasn't trying to offend her, but if she only knew of the sensationalized and embellished cases that came across his desk every week. He'd been in the office since six o' clock in the morning combing through eight of them. Most couldn't be given serious contemplation.

Nevertheless, he attempted a gentler approach in denying her. "I understand why finding this formula is very important to you and your family's legacy. Still, the fact remains you want me to look for something appearing to be steeped in arcane lore." Armand picked up the parchment again and viewed the writing. "Do you know what it says?"

Her shoulders fell slightly, an indication she did not know what was written on the parchment. "I'm in the process of translating it. The language uses letters from the Amharic alphabet and Ge'ez, Ethiopian script. The formula may be old, but I have strong reason to believe once the ingredients are combined, the result will be as real as any other chemical element."

"The discovery may be of interest in some…circles." He stopped himself from saying *esoteric*, after witnessing her prior reaction to him referring to her work as alchemy.

She tilted her head and observed him from an angle, as though she were delving deep into his mind. "Wouldn't the COIC wish to know once and for all if machines can run on something other than dirty coals and costly oil?"

Her eyes compelled him to garner the same enthusiasm, but Armand held his words as he searched for a careful answer. The COIC would like to know about many of the inventions and formulas being created around the world, but it didn't mean all of them should be pursued.

Some were legitimate claims. Others were just flukes. Last week, Armand had to reprimand a COIC agent for bringing in a street peddler who claimed his boxes of matches could be lit underwater. Then there was the Oxford physics student who claimed to have invented a machine to make bread rise in half the time. The janitors were still scraping dried dough from the walls of the testing laboratories.

Still, the question of the aether formula's capabilities begged to be answered. What if there was the smallest possible chance what she said could be true?

As an investigator, Armand could no longer suppress his growing interest in Miss Brehane's intriguing dilemma. "Even if I wanted to investigate this case for you, I'd have to get approval from the COIC Secretary," he said, informing her of the process. "That may be difficult. There are numerous projects the agency has been researching or commissioning as of late. The financial means may not be given to pursue this."

Miriam shook her head. "I will personally see to any business expenses you and the agency incur."

She didn't give up her pursuit despite a potential lack of funding. Perhaps her case did have merit. Armand placed the paper into the cedar box. "We still have a basic problem. The agency needs proof of whether the formula can be replicated first. The latter half of this is missing. We can't test what we don't have."

"What if I were to provide something else? Chemists and doctors regularly send for supplies from our facility. I can show you another use of aether, such as its solvent properties."

"It might be helpful, but I still can't make any promises." Armand pushed his chair back and stood. "Come back with one of your other formulas, and we'll see about replicating it on the premises."

Miriam took the box and rose from her seat in one flowing motion. "I can do so now."

"So you did bring additional formulas and supplies with you?" He glimpsed at her companion. The man squinted back at him.

"No, but we can go to the facility and test one there. If you don't believe me, bring your agency's laboratory supplies so you can be certain our testing uses standard methods."

"You said you came from Scarborough. The town is a day's train ride away. Wait a moment." Armand stopped. Her explanations didn't line up properly. "You said you received the formula yesterday evening. How did you get here so fast?"

Miriam smiled mysteriously. "I'm surprised at you. I thought COIC agents, of all people, kept abreast of the latest modes in transportation."

Armand went to get her coat from the rack by the wall. "I'm afraid I don't follow." An object fell from one of the coat pockets when he took it off the rack.

She bent to pick up the object, a pair of goggles with coated lenses and a leather strap. She dangled the strap on one long, graceful finger. "Surely, Mr. Torres, you have heard of the dirigible?"

From the Author:

I hope you enjoyed reading this boxed set of *Curiosity Chronicles, Books 1-3*. If you could take a few minutes to leave an honest review on the site where you purchased this collection, I would really appreciate it. Also be sure to follow me on Twitter at https://twitter.com/AvaMorganAuthor and Facebook at https://www.facebook.com/pages/Ava-Morgan-Author/164868403723785 for the latest news and updates.

About the Author

Ava Morgan loves romance, retro style, and reading everything she can get her hands on, especially steampunk, fantasy, and old pulp fiction. The Curiosity Chronicles series came from her love of history as well as its quirky anachronisms. When Ava isn't planted in her writing chair, she can be found bicycling with her husband or running up a tab at the local coffeehouse.

Made in the USA
Monee, IL
17 September 2020